Lainey and Jed

Book 2

FROM THE SERIES
FIFTEEN THOUSAND TIMES FOR FIFTY YEARS

Lainey and Ted

Book 2

TRILOGY BY
CLARE CINNAMON

MILL CITY PRESS

Mill City Press, Inc.
2301 Lucien Way #415
Maitland, FL 32751
407.339.4217
www.millcitypress.net

© 2020 by Clare Cinnamon

All rights reserved. No part of this publication may be reproduced, stored in a retrieval system, or transmitted, in any form or by any means, electronic, mechanical, photocopying, recording, or otherwise, without the prior written permission of the author.

Printed in the United States of America

Library of Congress Control Number: 2020902008

ISBN-13: 978-1-6305-0698-8

From the series
Fifteen Thousand Times for Fifty Years

Lainey Cash, Book 1- Available now
Lainey and Jed, Book 2 – Available now
Delaina, Book 3–Coming soon!

Others coming up in the series:

Asunder
An Atlanta construction company empire, a marriage under fire

A Town Called Lake
Military life and a woman dreaming of a Nashville career
who finds herself in a messy hometown love triangle

Ayla From Atlanta
City girl, country boy with a few twists, of course

Sunshine and Lev
A struggling artist and successful architect fall in love,
amid a major lawsuit, on the South Carolina coast- JUNE 2020

From the series
Islands of Legend and Love

Return
A Halloween time travel love story – OCTOBER 2020

Tin City
The prominent Cramer brothers use their parents' inheritance
to buy an island on the Florida Panhandle – Coming later

For Clyde Cinnamon and KK Cinnamon –
Stay true to whatever matters to you, then don't hesitate. –CC

Table of Contents

One: Night 1

Two: Morning 9

Three: Afternoon 19

Four: Webs 32

Five: Revelations 48

Six: Despair 59

Seven: Cabot vs. Jed 70

Eight: Fleeing 76

Nine: Finding 70

Ten: Now 104

Eleven: You 118

Twelve: Me 126

Thirteen: Us 140

Fourteen: Pain 143

Fifteen: On the Road 154

Sixteen: On the Road Again 169

Seventeen: Hometown 179

Eighteen: Happy Birthday 189

Nineteen: My Boyfriend's Back 202

Twenty: Wild, Wild West 215

Twenty-one: Hotel California 229

Twenty-two: Awake 243

Twenty-three: Welcome 257

Twenty-four: Summer Romance 279

Twenty-five: Cash Way 291

Twenty-six: Independence Day 300

~ ~ ~

If I believe in magic
magic I will find

in twilight
in wide open spaces
in sunlight
in rushing waters
in moonlight
in green pastures
in streetlight
in blue skies

you are gone
only, life is so magically arranged
that I can never see anything beautiful
without feeling you

oh, that you would see me
two times in a day
or once in a month
my life would be complete

If you believe in magic
magic you will find

you will never look at a sunrise and a sunset
or the full moon
without feeling me

~ ~ ~

ONE

Night

Stars twinkled. Beings slept. Life went on.

Jed's attorney poured himself another cup of coffee. Accustomed to closing real estate deals in daylight, he needed more than an overdose of caffeine to properly assess his client's predicament in the middle of the night.

Soap operas didn't have a thing on little ole Mallard.

Jed McCrae and Delaina Cash were certainly framed by the man with whom Delaina currently flew home to Mississippi. Their land was under siege. Jed's first cousin was being paid to spy on him by his own stepfather. Authorities were crooked. The unlikely duo had fallen in love. "Jed, three words sum up what you've told me the past hour."

Jed rubbed his hands over his face. "I'm not guilty?"

"You've been screwed."

"That's for sure." Jed scrubbed his fingers through wayward black hair. After he left Delaina at Calla Hotel, all he knew to do was keep moving. Her choice to get on an airplane with Cabot Hartley tore him up inside.

Cabot might kill her.

Jed should've tied her hands behind her back and hauled her home kicking and screaming. He should've made his presence known in her hotel room, prompted a showdown with Cabot, anything to keep her safe. Hindsight.

...Overriding that, he had stayed level, slipping out of Calla undetected. If he had made his presence known, he might've been arrested. Still might be. Little good he could do her behind bars.

LAINEY AND JED, BOOK TWO

Jed held on to hope that Cabot wouldn't kill her since he also seemed determined to take her *home* from the hotel. "That leads me to the reason I was in Delaina's room. I assume you've figured it out. I'll spare the details. You probably need to know she's twenty, and it was..." He had to clear his throat to finish. "Our first night together." Little good he could do her if he turned into a blubbering sap.

The attorney sipped, contemplated, slightly awed. His eyebrows scrunched together. "This isn't my specialty, you know."

"Of course not, why would I need a criminal attorney?"

"You're certain Delaina Cash isn't in on the scheme?"

"Positive."

"You wouldn't favor a strategy to shift attention to her?"

"Hell no."

"I'm calling a friend in New Orleans as soon as it's daylight. His name is Stuart Lowry. This approach you favor isn't looking good for you."

Jed walked the room. "I know."

"You haven't had any sleep. Last thing you need to do is fly yourself home."

"Runnin' on adrenaline. Got a personal issue to handle in Jackson." Delaina didn't have her phone on her, thanks to Jed's original plan for her to be untraceable during their weekend in Houston. He had to talk to her, implications settling in, outside Mallard.

His attorney didn't have to check the determination in Jed's eyes twice to know he had unfinished business with the Cash lady. "Go discreetly and be done with her until we know more, or I don't know how to help you."

"I need to meet Jeffrey at the hangar in..." Jed looked down at his wrist, brushed his hand over his arm, and swore. He left his watch in her room. "Thanks, I gotta go. Send me a bill." He disappeared out the door, going to Calla. His father's watch. He had to have it at any price.

~ ~ ~

Standing in a discreet corner of the atrium of Calla Hotel in Houston, Texas, Cabot answered his phone in a hushed tone. "You should not bother me for any reason! I don't have time for you."

"But..." "But nothing. I was in the middle of telling Lainey about Cash Way, and my phone vibrated constantly. She can't know about you, Red. It'll screw up everything."

2

"You need to know, Eli Smith is near 'bout dead," Dacey Boyd stated across the line.

"What? *Eli?*"

"He was drunk as a polecat and hit a deer on Cash-McCrae Road. Near 'bout killed him."

"For God's sake, Dacey. Please keep quiet."

"You know I will. Be careful. Bye."

Cabot sat. ...Everything felt incomplete and complicated. Lainey hadn't signed Cash Way's farm management papers like he planned, and she knew where Jed McCrae was for some reason. Eli Smith, fighting for his life.

His head went to a place it often did, a nagging memory. Crouched in the corner of the conference room at the bank, fresh out of college, his father's ruthless finger jammed in his temple. His ruthless words jammed in Cabot's heart. *'You know your problem, boy? You're like that block-dumb mother of yours. Too worried about who's at the party instead of why they came. I should've gone with my instinct and brought your sister home for this job.'*

Years later, Cabot was buckling under pressure. His father knew he would. He wasn't made for the intricacies of dirty work. Light sweat dampened his brow.

"Excuse me, mister?" He looked up to the pleasant face of a young desk receptionist. "May I help you?"

"Yeah, uh, could you ring room 600? Delaina Cash."

"Of course. What's your message?"

"Tell her I'm ready. To get down here this minute."

"Does I'm-ready have a name?" she asked, a please-the-patron smile pasted to her face. "It's Calla Hotel policy."

"Cabot. C-A-B-O-T." He glared. "Hurry up."

She looked from side to side, no one watching. "You are the rudest man." She rang Delaina's room. "Hi, Miss Cash. Someone at the desk is demanding for you to come down. His name is Cabot. He wants you ASAP."

~ ~ ~

The silence lasted endlessly after Holland Sommers Smith's untimely pregnancy announcement. Maydell's gentle sobs, Moll's glare, Rhett's stare.

Rhett disappeared from the hospital waiting room first. Moll followed. Holland sat beside Maydell, who dabbed her eyes with a tissue and blew her nose. "I didn't know you had been seein' my boy long enough to get pregnant. How far along are you?"

"I'm two weeks late, positive home test."

"Eli's a good man. He's gonna pull through." She paused. "Go on home and rest."

"No." Holland shook her head. "I belong here."

"Do you love my son?"

"I didn't realize I loved him until I lost him and..." She couldn't finish.

Maydell patted her leg. "There's room for you in this family, seein' that you treat my Eli good."

"I will if he'll let me."

"Did y'all have a fallin' out?"

"He left me because of the trouble at Cash Way. We have...some explaining to do to each other. I know the farm means a lot to your family, having worked there all your lives. Truthfully, I'm unclear on what Eli could be involved in regarding this marijuana bust."

"*Oh Lord.*" Tears spilled from Maydell's eyes. "My Eli will do right by you. His brother Rhett will do all he can, too. My sons are close."

Their heads turned when Moll appeared.

~ ~ ~

Dread chilled Delaina's body like ice water running through her veins. She had stalled for over an hour. Pulling her suitcase toward the door, she scanned her once blissful Calla Hotel hideaway.

Jed's watch glimmered on the nightstand!

She hurried to it and clutched it in her fingers. How could she have been so wrong about him? Their fantastic day. Baseball and laughter. Their dinner date. Deliciousness and desire. Their night... everything she could've wished for and more, until Cabot showed up. Glorious Jed. *Gone.*

To leave with Cabot, nothing felt right about it. Nothing in the world felt good or safe. She couldn't postpone it, didn't look back at the room or bed. She dragged herself forward to the elevator, those doors where Jed had said, '*I love everything about you. Everything. And don't you ever forget it.*'

She reached the lobby, red-eyed and out of time.

Then she saw him, and her knees felt unusually weak; she grabbed hold of a beige balustrade. Bent over the water fountain, he gulped.

NIGHT

He flashed his dimpled grin. Water drained through the fountain tray. "I should ram your head under that fountain." Cabot draped his arm over her. "You came here alone; I had to chase you down; you took an hour to get your things packed."

They left for the airport without a word in reply from Delaina.

~ ~ ~

"Wanna know what my son and I were fightin' about when he took off in that drunk rage?" Holland trembled under Moll Smith's stare. "You and that baby he ain't sure is his. Don't try to butter us up while he can't speak for hisself. I'd greatly appreciate it if you'd remove yourself from this hospital until Eli can say if he wants you here." Moll sat in a chair beside his wife.

Holland stood. "I'm not leaving. Yes, Eli and I have problems. We'll never work them out if I abandon him like he abandoned me. You don't have to accept me. You do have to tolerate me unless Eli asks me to leave." She walked away to find another place to wait.

For the first time in her life, Maydell felt the urge to tell her husband off good. Never mind the Bible instructed a woman to submit. "Moll Smith, don't take your frustrations out on that poor girl." She pointed her finger in his face. "It's your fault. You upset my son to the point he couldn't think straight, and he drove off in a fit. If there's a grandbaby and Eli don't pull through this, I'll never forgive you for taking that baby's daddy from it." She took a breath. "Lord, I hope Lainey is okay. I'm worried sick about her and what's going on at Cash Way. Leave me alone. A woman prefers to mope by herself."

Moll left the hospital on a mission. He would take care of another matter, telling someone about seeing Jed and Lainey dancing at the river together weeks ago, since he wasn't welcome in the waiting room or at home for now.

~ ~ ~

Delaina rested her head against the airplane seat. She wanted to sleep, knowing she needed it to face the day's events. Too many worries needled her brain.

Cabot had informed her of Eli Smith's tragic accident. She must get home to Maydell and Moll, the closest thing she had to a family, as fast as she could. She wasn't too upset about her land because she knew she was innocent. Truth be admitted, she worried more about Jed and what he might be involved in. Cabot seemed jumpy. Sitting close to him caused Delaina to think about Jed's claims of his hardcore partying and womanizing, but one question danced with the force of tap shoes. "Cabot, how did you know where I was?"

Cabot hadn't thought about how to answer since his paid informant Boone Barlow tracked her. "I have my sources. Good business, you know?"

"You had me followed."

"I had you *protected*. You didn't let anyone know where you were."

Cabot's hiring someone to follow her infuriated her; however, she was smart enough to get off the subject of Houston. "When we get to Mallard, do you think that authorities will question me?"

From the beginning, Cabot had figured they'd fake a routine questioning since the marijuana plants were primarily on Lainey's land. He and Chief Raybon Hall had discussed it. He never realized she'd be walking such a thin line. Her weekend diversion threw an unexpected bend in their smooth plans. "Serves you right as irresponsible as you've been."

"Oh, but you can take off to Biloxi doing only the devil knows what for a bachelor party?"

"I didn't take off, Lainey. You knew how to reach me. Shut up. I'm tired unless you have any fresh ideas about how we're going to get out of the narrow crack you jammed us in."

"I'm the one in a crack, not you."

Cabot jabbed his finger in her chest. "I'm marrying you next week."

"Our marriage and my land are two separate things, Cabot. When are you going to get that through your head?" "You're so damn stubborn," he mumbled.

If there had been anywhere on the plane to move to, she would've. He hadn't seen stubborn yet. She'd show him. She didn't need anyone to get out of this mess! Men were necessary for weak women. No more.

~ ~ ~

District Attorney Warren Gage hadn't slept all night. He didn't have a good feeling about the drug bust scenario. Everyone placed blame too quickly on Jed McCrae though the bulk of marijuana was on Cash land. He had become particularly suspicious of a comment that Boone Barlow, one of Jed's farm workers and his first cousin, made during his interview. *'Jed has me working on a few of the farms. None where plants were found...'* How did Boone Barlow know where plants were found? Authorities hadn't told anyone

NIGHT

where plants were found because they hadn't been successful contacting Jed or Lainey yet.

Gage wouldn't nail an innocent man. While a fast conviction would be nice for his coming campaign, to uncover a big conspiracy would be better. He called a colleague involved in state criminal investigation work. "Hi, Cardin. Attorney Warren Gage in Mallard County. Sleeping, huh? Well, rise and shine. You're about to make a Sunday morning drive to our little pinhead on the map. I'll explain."

~ ~ ~

His watch was gone, which didn't bother Jed much, considering Delaina had it.

Surely, she wouldn't destroy it or throw it away or lose it. Calla Hotel employees had been most helpful when he returned to look for it. The front desk receptionist commented she liked him better than the other man who came to get Delaina. Jed explained that Cabot got angry because Delaina slipped off to Houston. The receptionist laughed and told Jed that she didn't blame him for sneaking around with Delaina. She called Delaina a real-life Barbie and he made the perfect Ken.

He flew his private plane to Jackson to, maybe, see a real-life Barbie. Hopefully, he could catch her without Cabot. She had her own car there.

While Jed flew, he allowed himself to think about her. Every moment of their weekend had been like no other. Delaina Cash held his heart in her hands. He felt vulnerable on the throes of such a discovery. He had worn a suit of armor his whole life, made of tangible things like nice trucks, getaway baseball games, weekend camping trips on Big Sunflower River, casualness with interested, elegant women. Things to satisfy a man for a long time but not a lifetime. That kind of armor held up flimsily, like trying to cage lions in tissue paper. Inside him were real feelings, the intangible things, that now unleashed would not be satisfied with captivity. He watched stars fade as he landed on the runway.

Making love to Delaina had not been a mistake.

Doing it without protection was, for two reasons. One, he never got to reassure himself about the Pill; thus, she might be pregnant. He scratched the greedy glimmer of hope that came with that awful possibility. Two, he felt her in the most intimate way, as close to heaven as he'd get. Once would not suffice.

7

~ ~ ~

Cabot slept. Delaina dug Jed's watch out of her purse. It smelled like his skin.

Try as she might, she couldn't believe the truth. Inconceivable that Jed would put his land in jeopardy in a risky plot.

She read the watch inscription. *J, 3 hearts now. Cassie 5/22*

The significance slapped her. Jed's deceased father's watch, given to James Ed by Jed's mother on the day Jed was born. Jed must be worried what happened to it. Delaina would take the best care of it, regardless of what he did to her. His gracious mother Cass Kendall deserved that show of respect.

How love hurt. One more try. She had been mistaken. Jed was better than Cabot claimed.

Her mind and heart sparred again.

The truth was, love and hate couldn't be flipped willfully like a coin, first one way, then the other.

Only time, agonizing time, would determine their fate.

Two

Jackson, Mississippi's airport appeared quiet and uncrowded early on Sunday.

Jed squeezed in a nook as passengers filed by. Young parents with two sleeping kids, an older man, two middle-aged women, then Cabot. Alone with a disagreeable face.

Where was Delaina?

Four more passengers filed out. Cabot walked toward the parking lot, no intention of waiting. Jed's concern ceased as a coconut breeze danced by. He'd recognize that smell anywhere; he washed her body with the gel hours ago. Head down, Delaina disappeared into a restroom. No one else had entered the area since he'd been there. He stepped in as she flushed the toilet, crept beside her stall, and cleared his throat.

Delaina froze. A masculine throat-clearing. She gripped the lock on the door.

"Delaina."

She almost fainted.

Jed? She looked at the floor. Those were his shoes though she preferred his bare feet skimming up and down her bare legs. Those were his jeans though she preferred no clothes at all.

"Delaina, are you comin' out or am I comin' in?"

"I'm not comin' out until you leave."

Jed braced his shoe on the stall leg and pushed himself up the side. Delaina plowed her fist down on his fingers. "Leave me alone." She scurried into the open to wash her hands then dashed for the exit. His massive frame pinned her petite body to the door. Each felt the huffing of the other's ribs. "You're not going anywhere."

"Don't."

"Don't what? You have no idea what I'm about to do." His arm wrapped around her waist as he whispered against the nape of her neck. "Although you told me what you'd like to do in this position."

"Stop it, Jed. Please!" Delaina twisted and struggled to escape. "I'll scream rape."

"Go ahead. What a story on the heels of the other."

"Shut up!"

"Then you talk." They stared until Delaina turned away. Her heart pounded. Jed's heart pounded. "Why did Cabot leave you?"

"I have my car here, remember. Your neat little weekend plan for us."

Jed twirled her around. Her pretty blonde hair, yanked in a careless ponytail. Her pretty green eyes, threaded red. She had been crying. A lot. "You're still wearin' the ring."

"I asked Cabot to leave me alone this morning while I get my head straight. I...don't think he knows you and I were in Houston together."

Jed shrugged. "Fine with me if Cabot knows what happened in Houston. I have nothing to hide." He touched her cheek. "You've been crying." She flinched. That galled him. Seconds ticked. "Do you have a strategy for Cash Way?"

"I wouldn't tell you if I did."

"So, you don't."

She wouldn't look at him. "I have your watch. Your father's watch."

"Keep it." Jed scanned her. "We'll give it to our firstborn son. He might make his grand appearance in about nine months." Delaina stepped out of his reach. "Answer me. Is there a chance you're pregnant?"

She turned on her heels. "I...don't think so."

He winced. "You're not on the Pill."

"No."

"Damn."

"Don't worry. I mean, it was my first..."

"Doesn't matter. What was I thinking? You're so...young." *A decade* younger than him. Jed swallowed. "Majoring in obstetrics when I quit med school."

Delaina rolled her eyes. "Not surprising."

He walked the floor. "What time of the month for you?"

"Uh...oh gosh. Today is the fourteenth day after..."

"Aw hell." Jed propped his hands against the lavatory edge and studied wavy lines in the marble. "Combine that with eager sperm and the precedent my father set, and you get yourself a..."

"Maybe not. What precedent did your father set?"

He looked directly at her. "My mother got pregnant after her second night out with my father."

Delaina raised her eyebrows. "Prim and proper Ms. Cass Kendall?"

"You mean, nineteen-year-old, sassy, rich, naïve, blonde Cassie Jane Darrah." Jed had a slight grin. "With big, tall, thirty-two-year old confirmed bachelor-farmer James Ed McCrae." Delaina's expression slipped into suspicious panic. "Now that I know you could be pregnant, I'll tell you my strategy. Then I'll leave." Jed took her hand. "I'm going to cooperate at every level, and I'll tell the truth except when it would endanger you."

She dropped his hand. "I know I'm innocent. I'll do whatever it takes to save Cash Way, and I don't care if I lie or who I incriminate in the process. How's that?"

"Spoken like Tory Cash raised you." He closed in, scraped her cheek with his hand. "So much I didn't get to say to you last night, Delaina." He stopped when he saw tears. "I don't suppose you have any parting words for me."

"I do."

"Go ahead."

"I believe in abortion."

Jed blinked. "You love me too much to kill our child. I'm glad you believe in it, considering you don't seem to believe in any birth control. I hope you hack up every one of Cabot Hartley's kids."

"Hush! That's awful." Delaina's hands covered her face. "We have to stop this. I'm *sorry,* Jed, about last night. Doubting you so quickly. I'm confused. I allowed myself to trust and love someone, you, for less than a day and, my God, how could you?"

"How could you believe Cabot instead of me? He's a liar, he uses women, and he's a criminal."

Delaina looked at the floor. A baby? Oh God. Oh. God. "What about that morning-after pill?" The words felt ugly coming across her lips, compared to their extraordinary night.

LAINEY AND JED, BOOK TWO

Jed looked at her hard and seriously. "What I remember from school, it works best immediately. Not as effective during ovulation. Whatever you want." He seemed entirely exposed. She put her arms around his neck and pulled his head to hers. She stood on tiptoes and kissed his lips. "I don't know what I want." She *thought* she believed in abortion in general *before she* had sex. That pill wasn't a big deal, right? But if she made a child with Jed from so much passion last night, that pill would be kind of like abortion *if* their child was already forming. Or how soon was a baby alive? Her mind, absolute junk. She stepped away. "What I know is, I can't get you out of my head or my heart."

"I'll drive your car to Mallard. You have too much on your mind."

"And risk arriving together? No. Besides, I don't know...if I trust you."

"What have I done to make you not trust me?"

"Made love to me knowing whatever it is you claim you know that will destroy me, unrelated to these drug charges."

Jed shook his head no. "Don't start. I warned you ahead of time."

"I said I didn't need promises or more from you, but maybe I do. I don't *know*."

"What would help, Delaina?" His blue eyes fell soft on her.

She focused on the floor. "For me to know the whole truth on every issue and still have the heart to love you when it's all out."

"I can give you that."

"No. Only I can give myself that, when I'm ready. I'll return your watch one day, Jed. I hope for love's sake."

"Regardless of what else happens, I want to be the first to know and I want to be included in whatever decisions are made about a baby, in complete confidence."

Having lived with her mother's abandonment, Delaina appreciated that. "I should go to the doctor anyway because of what happened between us. Time to grow up."

Jed embraced her. "Delaina, I love you."

"I don't know what you've done behind my back or why, but I won't waste our time denying it." She gripped his arm. "I love you. Unfortunately, I'm finding out my love for you controls me more than I control it."

"It will bring you back to me when the time is right."

MORNING

"Or I'll come to my senses." Delaina pushed past him and apologized to an impatient woman for the blockade at the door.

~ ~ ~

Cabot wasted no time making calls when he got to his car. First to Boone Barlow, who bragged he executed his part perfectly.

Next, he called Sheriff Boyd, not as optimistic. "Do you want me to tell you what you've got us into? A hell of a mess! Attorney Gage is as suspicious as a skirt on a street corner. He got this idea for us to bring Lainey and Jed together to talk it out, which ain't altogether bad, maybe we'll get her cleared quick that way. I doubt Jed'll agree to it. But, uh, he called in someone from state."

"What?"

"Yeah, an investigator. They're sayin' this is big enough to justify help."

"Jesus Christ! You turned it down, didn't you?" Cabot sensed his plan raveling.

"That would be too fishy. God, I hope there's nothing incriminatin' any of us. Get Lainey to Mallard in a hurry. She and Jed are set to meet with this guy at one o'clock. A lot of pressure on them to agree. We need to tell Gage the truth before then."

"No." Cabot gnawed on his cheek. "Warren Gage is too strait-laced. We'll go with what we have." Cabot jerked his car onto a side road, got out, and faced the highway. He had to talk to Lainey. She didn't have her phone. They had to discuss what she could and couldn't say. In minutes, he saw her. She stopped and got out.

"I talked to Sheriff Boyd. They have you scheduled at one o'clock."

Delaina sipped coffee. "Oh God. For questioning?"

"They're considering it more of a good ole boys' meeting with you." Cabot pressed his fist to his lips. "And Jed." Delaina's eyebrows shot up. "Sorry about things I said on the plane. Look, I can help. Do you have anything to hide, Lainey?"

"I don't." Telling the truth, not an option.

"I want you to act horrified if they make mention of a collaboration. That hatred for Jed you displayed in the hotel room, conjure that up. Very convincing."

Delaina looked at the sky. Dawn, a blobby orange stain on dingy gray flannel. She should be waking in Jed's arms in Calla bliss. They were robbed of their first morning together. "It's turned to bitterness now, Cabot."

13

LAINEY AND JED. BOOK TWO

"Bitterness is good. Go home. Rest. You have a production to pull off in a few hours."

"I'm a good actress." Delaina gave him her best smile.

~ ~ ~

Holland knelt by the bed and took Eli's hand. She stroked his fingers, long and lanky like the rest of him. He wasn't wearing his wedding band. His condition had worsened. "Cowboy," she said timidly, talking to him like nurses told her to do. "Show me what you're made of." She missed his bright eyes, smooth voice, frequent laughter. Unable to bear the contrast, she walked out. "Maydell, go in."

Maydell nodded, tears running out of her eyes. "I can't stand to see my Elijah like this."

"Is Elijah a family name?"

"Elijah was my father's name. Eli is Mollfred Elijah Smith."

"I like Elijah." Holland patted her tummy. "If it's a boy, I'll name him Elijah Garrick Smith. Garrick is my father's name."

"Eli's got to wake up for that." Maydell went in to see her son.

Holland walked around the corner. "Mr. Smith?"

"Ma'am?"

"I'll go to the doctor to have a pregnancy test confirmed. Maybe that'll help how you feel."

"Eli told me that even if there is a baby, he ain't for sure it's his."

"Answer me this, Mr. Smith. Why did I marry him if he's not my baby's father?"

"You tell me."

"Please give me a break. I care about Eli."

"I'll let Eli speak for hisself. In the meantime, how 'bout stayin' with Maydell? We live in the guest house at Cash Way. Plenty of space in the big house for ya. I'm gonna stay with Rhett over at the rental house where he and Eli were livin'. Maydell's not real happy with me, and Rhett might be in some trouble."

"I don't mind staying, but won't Delaina be there with her?"

"Who knows where she'll be after what's happened? I pray to God, not in the slammer. Excuse me, I'm headed for a cup of coffee."

Holland thought about Cash Way for the first time in hours. She bowed her head and prayed for two miracles: That Eli would recover and he wasn't involved with Cabot. A hefty prayer for a woman who never prayed much.

14

"Holland?" Jed McCrae stood at her heels. "Let's talk." She turned unsteadily. He angled them to an empty waiting room. "Why didn't you have Eli transported to a bigger facility?"

"Doctor didn't know if he'd survive. They're discussing a med-helicopter now."

"At any rate, congratulations on the wedding. You and Cabot are slick."

"I didn't marry Eli because of Cabot's plans. I'm done with Cabot Hartley."

"Come on, Holland. I'm no fool."

"I'm pregnant with Eli's baby."

Jed's eyes turned dark. "That's what I call sealing the deal."

"I know you think I'm not capable of the feelings most women have, but I do care about Eli. I married him because he's the first man with no motives. Not to mention how cute and sweet he is. He tells these nasty country jokes, has a great sense of humor." She stared at Jed with genuine eyes.

Jed put up his hand in surrender. "I believe you. If you know anything that will help me out..."

"I have to protect Eli foremost. He and I never talked about what he may be involved in. I'm sorry I stayed true to Cabot this past month instead of swinging back to your side. Eli's paying the ultimate price." She squeezed her eyes shut and began to sob.

"Hey, you're tough." Jed hugged her. "We go back a long way, you know? I know what you're made of."

She nodded, comforted. "I swear to you, if there's any way I can help you without hurting Eli, I will."

Delaina gasped when she saw them in such an intimate embrace. "Excuse me."

Jed let go. "*Delaina.*"

For a minuscule span, it was there. Perhaps no one else would have detected it. Holland had uncanny intuition. In both faces, she saw extreme emotion. Longing and confusion. In a word, love.

Delaina went first. "Hello." She squeezed Holland's hand. She gave Jed a glance. "Jed."

"Hang in there and keep me posted, Holland." He looked at Delaina. "My understanding, I'll be seeing you soon."

She shuffled her weight. "Briefly. I plan to get myself out of there quickly."

"Yes, that's the plan." He walked out.

Holland's mouth hung open. Jed and Delaina, positively in love.

Delaina ignored her stunned expression. "Tell me about Eli."

~ ~ ~

Jed drove to his farm workshop, due to meet with his criminal attorney in minutes, and found him waiting. Medium height and build, early forties with salted brown hair, he looked honest and intelligent. Jed stepped out. "Good mornin', I'm Jed McCrae."

"Hello. I'm Stuart Lowry." They shook hands.

"My attorney says you're good at what you do."

"I am, but you're in a major predicament."

Jed shoved his hands in his pockets. "I'm innocent, and I know who framed me. How can we prove it?"

"Let's go over your story again. Every detail."

~ ~ ~

District Attorney Warren Gage finished up his explanation to Police Chief Raybon Hall on why he requested a state investigator. "We need a stickler for rules. We don't get many complicated cases around here. I'm suspicious of what Boone Barlow said about the location of the plants. Not to mention we're dealing with the biggest names in this town. I know you hold a grudge against Jed McCrae's mother and father. I'm Delaina's lawyer in the settling of her father's will. Too many factors involved. Your men need a third party, someone who's willing to sit on the fence, so to speak."

"You could've checked with me first." Raybon sucked on his cigar.

"There wasn't time. Wanted him here ASAP. He'll be at the interview. Cardin Morris."

"Carden Morris...I don't like nothin' I've heard about him. He's young and cocky. I resent the fact that you don't think we can do our jobs. If he don't work with us, and Lainey ends up in trouble, you can blame yourself. That would've made Tory Cash real happy. Not to mention Cabot."

~ ~ ~

Stuart Lowry, Jed's criminal attorney, pondered, "We don't want to overthink this meeting. They act like they simply want to talk to you both. Gather information about who owns what, who works where, et cetera. Even if someone in authority is part of this scheme, you are still protected by your rights and the laws regarding an arrest."

Jed shrugged. "I'm giving them the benefit of the doubt, that they're trying to work with us instead of hauling us in with handcuffs on. To refuse the meeting would suggest guilt, wouldn't it?"

"Probably." Stuart Lowry frowned.

"Besides, if I refuse to attend the meeting, couldn't they skip the small talk and arrest me? Plants are on my land."

"Landowners are liable for any misuse of their land. We could explore possible statutes that limit your liability because others enter and use your property. Bottom line, though, you are the owners and ignorance of illegal activity is not a defense. They could arrest you at any point now."

"Or her. I'll go to the interview."

"It's difficult to represent someone who is more concerned about another potential suspect than himself. Considering everything you've told me, you'll take it one question at a time in there."

Officials requested no lawyers present. The meeting qualified as a meeting. Stuart Lowry didn't like it but understood small town ways, albeit often misguided or crooked, of handling things. He and Jed could learn a lot about officials' intentions by playing along. "If things get heated, you have the option of leaving because you're not under arrest."

Jed dug in the dirt with his shoe. What foolishness. He told Delaina to trust him. He wouldn't forgive himself if he trapped her into pregnancy. Everything else paled in comparison.

"It's supposed to be casual. No accusations or arrests made onsite, they told me."

"Right." Jed shook his head.

"Don't look at Delaina when you speak. They look for clues in people's expressions."

"Okay."

"Don't say anything you can't provide proof of. You don't have to answer their questions or, better yet, try to answer their questions with questions, so they do most of the talking. Speak ahead of Delaina when you can."

"Got it."

"And Jed?" He stopped moving his foot and looked up at his lawyer. "Try not to make *that face* every time you hear her name."

~ ~ ~

Given the closeness of the hug, Jed and Holland were doing more than business. Sitting on her bed, Delaina wiped stupid tears. Jed must think of her as the most gullible female in world history. She poured out her heart in an airport restroom, discussing the possibility of carrying his child, and he couldn't get home to Holland fast enough. Poor Eli, were they using him too?

She tried to think of another explanation for why Jed would go straight to the hospital and hug Holland. None. She had to let it go, let him go, and accept the nasty truth.

Jed McCrae didn't owe her anything. Besides, after making love to him, she'd been the one to toss him aside like worn-out boots.

To end up in Tory's study was probably, subconsciously, planned. His presence, like the scent of a pipe, drifted and caught hold. Her father would have been disappointed in her. No one disappointed Tory Cash.

Delaina sat in his desk chair and searched conception and birth control facts on the web. She leaned back and closed her eyes. She had lived here her whole life, primarily a life of bewilderment.

When her eyes opened, she saw floorboards that carried her from crawling to walking to dancing. Walls that kept her deepest secrets, knew her laughter and her fears. The small closet where she hid to play with dolls or to spy on Tory's tantrums or to cry. Her eyes swept outward to the foyer, where Kemp Rainwater, her first boyfriend, greeted her on Homecoming night. Perhaps her father, her grandmother Victorine Kelly Cash, whose wedding portrait hung above, and her great-grandparents had experienced their first kiss there, too. They all learned to walk, dance, play, and hide in these rooms. A legend of Cashes made the spirit of her home, entrusted to Delaina to see that life continued here. For future Cashes.

Tory had expectations. She had failed him by running to Jed, like a foolish female. Cash Way dominated her first twenty years and still should. She'd save it, make it better. The courthouse interview would be the next step.

THREE

Afternoon

M allard County Courthouse, a two-story historic building in desperate need of remodeling, stood behind the town park on Main Street.

Delaina arrived with Cabot at his insistence. He led her to a conference area on the second floor. Sunlight blasted long windows. Dust floated. District Attorney Warren Gage greeted her and assured her that the meeting served the purpose of informing her and helping her. He excused himself. Investigator Cardin Morris along with Sheriff Dan Boyd and Chief Raybon Hall were spread over chairs banking one side of the conference table.

"Good afternoon." Cabot pulled out a chair for Delaina then shook each man's hand, introducing himself to Cardin Morris. Sheriff Boyd spoke up, "Cabot, I don't know if you…"

"Save your breath. I'll wait in the hall." He gave a slick smile. "I doubt she'll need help. She's pretty convincing." He bent and kissed her cheek. Delaina resented his interference.

Cardin Morris requested, "Miss Cash, please move to that chair across from us." Chief Hall fired off, "Stay where you are, Lainey."

She looked from one man to the other. "I'll move." She stood up, male eyes upon her. With a goal of unpretentious sexiness, she wore a sleeveless blouse, short black skirt, and black pumps combined with her gold cross earrings, flyaway hair, and soft makeup. She read somewhere that male law officials had trouble implicating attractive women.

The sound of footsteps caused everyone to watch the door.

LAINEY AND JED, BOOK TWO

Delaina clenched fists. *Tory Cash and Holland*, she repeated mentally. Her fingernails dug into her palms. She heard Jed's voice before she saw his face. The huskiness crept over her spine as he spoke and shook hands with men. From her downward gaze, she saw his hand outstretched, the honest grip. God knows, it was there in his touch last night. Impossible to believe he could fake that feeling. He had reached for her hands and held on, watching her experience sheer pleasure for the first time. She stepped forward.

"Miss Cash. Delaina." He cupped her hand. Warm skin swiped hers. Hopes of fighting him, of burying him, of incriminating him, submerged in the dimmest corner of her brain. Dark hair smoothed, cool blue eyes, expensive shirt with collar loose and rolled at the sleeves, perfect-fitting pants. Ooh, heavens. She could *not* think about his pants right now, especially the contents. She dropped her hand. "It's cool in here." *Liar, liar. Pants on fire.* "I should've worn a sweater. Is the air conditioner on?" Local officials moved toward the thermostat. Only Investigator Cardin Morris stood watching Jed and Delaina.

"I'll check." Raybon Hall went into the corridor and called back, "The air isn't on. Rather warm in there to me."

Jed's eyes streaked over her. "One of these men could offer you his sports coat." He didn't wear one.

I am Tory Cash's daughter. I must do this. Delaina ran her hands through her rumpled hair and smoothed her tight skirt. "Sharing a coat won't be necessary, thanks. Things will warm up in here."

Investigator Cardin Morris directed, "Miss Cash, Mr. McCrae, would you sit over on that side?"

Jed eased onto his chair, sliding it from the table so he could lounge. He steepled his fingers in front of his face and spoke casually. "How 'bout first names? This formality is stuffy. Here in Mallard we're known for hospitality, aren't we, y'all? Is there a state law against being friendly, Cardin?" Delaina sat beside Jed as she'd been asked. He smelled too good.

"First names suit me fine," Cardin answered.

"Good. Get started." Jed clucked his tongue and gave a sideways grin. "Astros are playin'. Possibility they'll sweep." He paused. "I'd like to listen to part of the game."

Cardin Morris jotted on a pad for all to see, *Houston Astros*.

20

Delaina's mind went to her afternoon in the stadium with Jed. Beer, popcorn, cotton candy. High-fives, laughter, kissing. Bliss.

"Do you ever see them play in person, Jed?" Cardin asked.

"Yesterday, matter of fact. Heck of a game."

Delaina tried to conceal her surprise. Why would Jed admit they were both in Houston? Was he trapping her?

"Were you aware that Miss Cash was there?"

"At the Astros game?" Jed answered with a question. "That's not what I meant," Cardin said. Raybon Hall interrupted, "This is my investigation, Cardin. I'll holler if I need ya. Lainey, you know what we found on your land."

"Yes, sir. Cabot told me. Marijuana."

Jed watched from the corner of his eye. He faked interest in tapping his fingers.

Raybon nodded. "We found a small stash on your place, Jed."

"That's what I hear."

Delaina watched him from the corner of her eye. She faked interest in the table.

"Lainey, did you know about any of this?" Raybon inquired.

She directed her answer to each man. To everyone but Jed. "I knew nothing until Cabot came to tell me. Exactly where is it?"

"Spread around," Sheriff Dan Boyd answered vaguely. Investigator Cardin Morris intervened. "Do you have a theory about how the plants got on your land?" The sheriff countered, "You don't have to speculate, Lainey."

She shrugged. "I have no idea." Cardin Morris continued, "One theory is that you two are in a collaborative effort." Chief Hall and Sheriff Boyd anticipated Lainey's adamant denial. Neither Jed nor Delaina flinched. The only sound in the room, silence. Jed commented as slick as buttered leather, "I guess that's supposed to be a question."

Raybon Hall shot Cardin Morris a go-to-hell look. "She already answered. She knew nothing about it." Cardin ignored with, "Jed, would you like to speak on the collaboration theory?"

Jed pushed off the back of the chair and leaned across the table. "For it to be collaborative, I'd have to know I was in on it, wouldn't I? I knew nothing about this marijuana beforehand either. Besides, what would be our motive?"

"It was found mere footsteps from your cabin," Sheriff Boyd stated.

LAINEY AND JED, BOOK TWO

"Sheriff, what was found on my land is *two hundred yards* from my cabin through a jungle of trees and underbrush uncut for years. Took two hours for *me* to find it this mornin', and I know the whole place better than my own name. Know what else is walking distance from my cabin?" Jed held up his fingers to count as he named, "Dale Barlow's house, my farm shelter where *several* men work, Fain Kendall's hunting stand, a Cash storage shelter, Boone Barlow's mobile home, and Big Sunflower River."

"How convenient," Sheriff Boyd replied.

"Jed has a point. People have access to his land. It is a jungle out there." Cardin turned, "Jed, we were told you had a spat with Miss Cash at your office about a month ago. The plants appear to be planted around that time. What were you arguing about?"

Jed cocked his head to her. She allowed their eyes to meet. Every inch of her body knew the significance of that smoke-over-ocean color. Pure desire. "Delaina and I were the only ones present, so unless she told someone we had a... spat, did you call it, anyone else would be gossiping. Our business does get serious sometimes because it's stressful in nature."

From the Sheriff, "Lainey, you agree?"

"I..." She studied an unsharpened pencil on the table.

Heeding his attorney's advice with considerable effort, Jed looked away. All his life, he practiced self-control and self-reliance. Both disintegrated in her presence. He linked his fingers to keep from touching her and tightened his lips to stop him from telling the men to leave her the hell alone. Delaina spoke tentatively, "We didn't... have a spat. I left in a hurry because it took longer than expected to get business accomplished."

Cardin Morris broke in, "What business would that be?"

"We...were caught up. I mean, we were...entangled in deep... discussion because we share...an irrigation system on the big field known as Farm 130."

She hadn't lied as effectively as Tory Cash would. Jed nodded. "That's right. A necessary meeting, but it came, unfortunately, on the same day as the settling of her father's will. She was understandably upset."

Cardin summarized, "All I've heard is how you two despise one another, how it's impossible to theorize you might be in an illegal drug operation together. Sitting with you now, you seem to get along well enough."

Neither Jed nor Delaina made a motion. So many pairs of eyes focused on their movements and reactions. Locals embedded in Cabot's conspiracy had hoped Lainey Cash would act appalled when forced to be near Jed McCrae. She had not.

Earlier, Moll Smith had been to see the state official and confessed what he saw: Jed and Delaina dancing at the river a month ago. Cardin Morris pursued possibilities. "Lainey, classify your relationship with Jed."

Delaina slipped into a hole of contemplation. Reality hurt as much as it consoled. Jed's whispers in darkness, *'Without any effort, you're everything I need, everything I want.' 'I'd make love to you every night.' 'I'd be faithful to you until death.'* Deep inside, she knew Jed meant every word. She might be paying a king's price for a peasant's pants. She went on instinct. Jed McCrae loved her. Tory Cash never really did. "Classify our relationship? Can you give me an example?"

Jed could give her a crotch-throbbing example. He pressed his fingers on the table edge which caused him to see, for the hundredth time today, her bite marks on his hand. Visions of her teary eyed, lying beneath him, whispering, *'I don't want to be a virgin.'*

Raybon Hall stood up. "Dang, this is going nowhere. She didn't know about the plants."

The investigator chimed in. "This *is* going somewhere. Somebody knows something." Jed and Delaina were guilty of, at least, passionate interest in one another.

"I want my name and land cleared of this today," Delaina inserted.

"Let's try this. Classify the nature of your relationship with her, Jed," Cardin Morris said.

"You mean categorically?"

Cardin sprang to his feet and banged his fist on the table. "Women and men can work together, be business associates, acquaintances, exes, enemies, strictly friends, romantically involved, sexually active, married, and/or parents together. Now, answer."

Delaina spoke before Jed could. "Business associates." Cardin to Jed, "Do you agree your relationship is neatly packaged into that category?"

"Your method is too harsh. This is a meeting," Raybon Hall intervened. "Last time I checked my law books, it wasn't a crime for men and women to be involved in a relationship."

Jed massaged his neck. He had a feeling he did not need to lie. Cardin Morris knew *something*. Delaina jiggled her foot nervously under the table. Cardin queried, "Should I define romantically involved, Delaina?"

Delaina rolled her eyes. "I'm marrying Cabot Hartley on May first. That defines it." She held up her ring finger. "Doesn't my engagement count for anything?"

"I don't know, does it?" he retaliated.

Raybon Hall slapped his hands across the table. "I swear. Somebody has a tremendous drug operation going on Cash-McCrae Road. I don't really care if these two are screwing their brains out. There are more pertinent questions related to Jed McCrae's character or *lack* of character."

"Excuse us." Cardin Morris motioned for the men to follow him into the hall.

Jed and Delaina were alone.

Jed jammed his fist into his splayed hand.

Delaina's eyes went huge. *Oh my God, his hand.* She had mauled the top with her teeth. She got up from her chair, bare legs close to Jed's face, and dug peppermint out of her purse. Instinctively, his eyes moved up her short skirt, to her waist, the indentations of her breasts, to her face. When their eyes met, she blinked. "What were you doing with Holland?" "You asked for space. Why do you care?" "You know why I care." "We've known each other my whole life. I brought her here on business months ago."

Delaina's eyes widened then narrowed suspiciously. "That was a tight hug."

"I've never been with her."

She spun around and walked to a paneled glass window. She peered at the park below. "How are we supposed to answer?"

"First, they hid behind the guise of casual discussion. It's an interrogation. Of me. Locals want you cleared. They know something, though...about us...being together." Jed had risen and walked to her. He wanted to touch her but refrained. "Nobody wants you cleared more quickly than I do." She turned. "Delaina, I met with a criminal attorney, to be smart. I'll explain the best approach, but what we feel for each other might as well be painted on the wall in here."

~ ~ ~

"Glad I caught you." A young man walked up to Cardin Morris, in the middle of heated discussion with the men. "Two new developments."

"Who the hell is he?" Chief Raybon Hall asked, spitting tobacco juice into a foam coffee cup.

"My assistant." Cardin Morris eyed the disgusting habit.

"We don't need no damn assistants."

"Perhaps you'd like to hear what I have to say," the chipper young man added.

Raybon Hall dreaded it. He made eyes with Sheriff Dan Boyd, who smoked a cigarette. Cardin Morris's assistant continued, "First, a helicopter pilot claims radar detected marijuana near an old farmhouse. He led me to it. A Cash rental house. Moll Smith's rented it for years. His sons live there now."

No one seemed surprised, Cardin Morris noted.

"Second, local florist, her name is, let's see..." He reached for a notepad. "Nance Mathis. Says Jed McCrae sent Lainey Cash a floral arrangement costing hundreds of dollars when her father died. Miss Cash sent an equally expensive arrangement when his mother died three months before that. Mr. McCrae ordered in person, signed the card privately, and asked for it to be delivered specifically to her. According to Ms. Mathis, Miss Cash knew the flowers were from Jed before she read the card."

"Hundreds of dollars?" Sheriff Boyd.

"Yes sir, that's what she said."

The sheriff whistled. "He's a smooth bastard, ain't he? I tell ya, rich folks don't live like us. It's a-whole-other world out there that we ain't got no clue about." He smashed his cigarette in an ashtray. "The cocksucker."

Cardin Morris cleared his throat. "We need to send someone from state here to give Mallard law officials an instructional seminar on professional conduct."

Raybon Hall defended, "We don't get much excitement other than drunks breaking beer bottles over each other's heads and rednecks shooting deer out of season. Besides, personal grudges run deep in small towns."

LAINEY AND JED. BOOK TWO

Morris decided, "Which is precisely why I will ask questions from now on. I'm almost certain I know what happened. Watch Miss Cash. If this Jed McCrae is a, hmm, smooth bastard, isn't it possible he sucked her in romantically then once he had a hold on her, he talked her into letting him use her land for the marijuana?"

Sheriff Boyd answered, "Not possible. Don't you get it? Their families hate each other." He shrugged. "Anyhow, the questioning is inappropriate. This isn't an interrogation."

"I need to know, and based on our suspicions, the questions are absolutely appropriate. They have the option of walking out."

Sheriff Boyd sighed. Lord, this thing flew out of control. Cabot Hartley would be furious if the interview didn't come out right. "She's gettin' hitched to Cabot Hartley. They're having a weddin' that'll cost a hundred thousand dollars accordin' to my wife. Jed McCrae and Lainey Cash have been taught to hate one another. I believe our theory that Jed attempted to frame her is more accurate."

Cardin Morris interrupted, "There's something between Jed and Lainey. We had an interview with Moll Smith, who told me that this morning. If Jed's using her to hide marijuana, we need to know. We also need to question Rhett Smith about what the radar found at the rental house. What if it's neither Jed nor her? A lot of men work around there. Acreage is tremendous. Looks like this circus may have more than two rings."

Raybon Hall muttered a curse and swung open the door to the conference room.

~ ~ ~

Jed and Delaina sat with an empty seat between them. Delaina held her head high. Jed had an intimidating look across his face.

"Which of you wants to tell us about the flowers you sent Miss Cash?" Cardin Morris barely concealed his smug satisfaction.

Jed characterized him with a glance. For sure, he had been raised on a blacktop street, never knew the feel of dirt between his toes. He looked disgusted dealing with backwoods hicks. Jed had dealings with city slickers. Cardin Morris's superiority ran no deeper than Carr's Creek. "I'll answer since I sent the damned thing when her father died in March. Delaina sent the same arrangement when my mother died last December. I'm no good at that stuff, knowing what's proper at a time like that. Best to send what she sent."

26

"Why did you go to the shop in person and specify it go to Miss Cash?"

Jed smirked a you're-a-genius smirk at Cardin. "I called several times, no answer. Figured the place was swamped, so I drove there. As for the request that it go to Delaina, she is Tory Cash's only immediate family."

"Why did you sign the card privately?"

"Ask around, I'm private." Local men nodded, agreeing.

Cardin turned questioning to Delaina. "Why did you send an elaborate arrangement to Mr. McCrae's mother's funeral in December?"

She gave Cardin Morris a bored once-over. "I'm rich, I'm compassionate, and I'm generous. Ms. Cass Kendall was the classiest lady who ever lived in Mallard. Nothing less would do."

Jed's heart clenched. No one could disagree.

Cardin found the nearest seat and commented, "Romantically involved means two people find each other sexually attractive and have made gestures to steer the relationship in that direction. Now, Mr. McCrae, classify your relationship with Miss Cash."

"Look at her. If you were cooped up in a stuffy office with her for two hours, wouldn't you make gestures to move the relationship in that direction?"

"I'm a married man, and she's engaged."

Jed shrugged obnoxiously. "I'm neither."

"So, you're saying you have been romantically involved with Miss Cash?"

Jed winked at Delaina in bachelor fashion. "Tell me, Cardin, was that a gesture?"

Cardin loosened his tie impatiently. "We could arrest you, both of you. Outside this building, as soon as you leave. Property owners are responsible for anything found on their land. I suggest cooperation. What is said in this room stays in this room. Do I make myself clear?" Everyone shook their heads. He scribbled on the notepad, *Cass Kendall, classy, per Delaina Cash.* "When was the last time you were alone with Miss Cash?"

Jed cleared his throat. "I saw her this morning."

"This morning?"

"I ran into her at the Jackson Airport. It was uncrowded."

"I see." Cardin paused. "You've touched her. Intimately?" Jed's facial expression didn't change. Inside, mad as hell. Cardin Morris meant to rattle Delaina, to make her so uncomfortable she would admit something important and incriminating. "Should I interpret your silence as a yes?"

"Yes, that was a yes," Delaina interrupted.

"How recently?" Cardin watched Jed's increasing annoyance.

"He came to see me when my father died and gave me a kiss, a, uh, peck on the cheek, an affectionate, sympathetic..." Delaina stopped. She lied and said that Jed kissed her the one day he didn't.

Cardin Morris continued, "You are romantically involved, and I know it. Let's make progress, if you're so concerned about your land." No one had the courage to breathe, and neither Jed nor Delaina saw it necessary to deny the accusation. "How current is your relationship?"

"We are here because someone else planted marijuana on our land, which we deserve to be investigated fairly," Jed stated. "We maintain *twelve thousand acres*, requiring our undivided attention on such a clear afternoon, instead of sitting around in here playing cat and mouse for your entertainment. Legal crops planted for this season can be verified. Our yields are impressive statewide. Frankly, I'm addicted to hard work, gambling on the damn weather and markets, and tight financing. Goes against the grain of a good farmer to toy with a sketchy side business."

Delaina felt the sun come out, the world right itself. Praise God! *Finally*. She *did* know Jed McCrae for all his worth. A tear of gladness rolled.

Heaviness lifted from the room, erased by glistening truth. "I apologize." Cardin shrugged his shoulders. "Delaina is sweet and young. She's also rather uncomfortable in your presence. Neither of you defined your relationship. Easy to think you take advantage of her, the proverbial 'putting stars in her eyes,' so you can grow marijuana on her land. She'd get blamed if it were ever found."

Jed frowned. "Delaina is feisty, smart, and independent. What she's more than likely *uncomfortable with* is this line of questioning. It'd take more than a romp in the sack to convince her to let me plant..."

"I explained the relevance. How current is your relationship?"

"This is crap," Raybon Hall yelled. "A bad idea in the first place." He, as much as anyone in the room, wanted to hear more out of human curiosity. Cabot Hartley would serve their heads on a dinner platter due to the dangerous path the interview had taken. "You're using the oldest trick in the book, Cardin."

"No tricks here, Investigator. I go after the truth."

Delaina did her best to appear unaffected, staring at a wall poster dated 1978 advertising Mallard's cotton gin.

Sheriff Boyd rose to his feet and cussed. "Look at her, she's near to cryin'." Everyone looked except Jed. Raybon Hall shouted, "Shame on you, Cardin Morris, you've embarrassed her to tears."

Delaina took advantage of the loophole. "This is a mortifying conversation considering I'm engaged to be married in days."

Raybon Hall concluded, "We'll have no more of it. Leave, Lainey. We've got others to question." Delaina stood and pushed her chair aside. Cardin Morris put up his hand. "Wait. I'm not sure how I interpret her tears."

"Son of a bitch," Raybon muttered.

"What emotion do you feel for Mr. McCrae?"

Delaina moved behind Jed's chair, glad she could not see his face. Her answer came easily. "I do not appreciate what has been insinuated. What an insult to my professional integrity, and to Jed's, because what you refuse to understand is that we would not jeopardize our land by involving it in anything illegal regardless of potential financial gain. Besides, we're rich as west hell without marijuana. I hope your future meetings with Mallard citizens will be conducted with more dignity." She did look at Jed, with courage. "I, too, firmly believe this drug bust is a scheme, and there are people in this town who have opportunity and motive. Jed McCrae has neither. He works grueling hours and treats me with respect. There you have it, I respect him. Perhaps y'all should take lessons in dealing with one another. Good afternoon."

It'd take a lot of lessons to groom Sheriff Daniel Boyd. He commented as soon as the door shut. "That's a doggone smart prissy gal."

Cardin Morris spoke. "Jed, for now, you can leave but stay close. We may call you again considering you've got that Mill's Pond marijuana incident under your belt."

"Under my belt is an appropriate phrase. I went to Mill's Pond because Sheriff Boyd's daughter Dacey and I were friends, and she called me, seriously inebriated, and asked me to pick her up and take her home, to my house, to my bed." Jed cleared his throat. "Days before she was supposed to marry someone else. I planned

LAINEY AND JED, BOOK TWO

to take her *to the Sheriff's house* as sloppy drunk as she was. Cops came right after I got to the party. Someone may have been trying to make a quick escape and dumped the bags in my truck, but I believe it was planned and deliberate. How convenient. I have that incident in my history." Jed passed an accusing look to Sheriff Boyd. "Since the sheriff and I came to a little agreement that night, I suppose no one's heard that particular version of the story."

The sheriff threw up his hands. "I've never asked my daughter Dacey about it; I let her mama deal with it. She and the Pollock boy broke their engagement. I reckon Jed's tellin' the truth."

~ ~ ~

Cabot had been sitting on a hard chair for over an hour, smoking cigars. He had anticipated, at most, a ten-minute meeting. Delaina seemed bothered to see him. "Slow down. What in hell took so long?"

"I got raked over the coals, but I came out on top."

Cabot grabbed her arm. "Tell me about it."

"No! I've talked enough about this for today." She squinted as she stepped into sunlight.

"Tell me about it, damn you!" He skipped down steps, on her heels.

"Where has your polished respectfulness gone lately?"

The answer came from another mouth, the sweetest, sexiest mouth she ever touched. That touched her in places no other mouth had. "My guess would be on a boat full of women and drugs headed south. Want me to drive you home?" Jed cupped Delaina's arm.

Delaina turned to face Cabot. "Serves you right."

"Lainey, wait!"

"No, Cabot, you can wait and worry and..." She rolled her eyes. "...smoke."

She followed Jed to his truck with Attorney Stuart Lowry, who had also waited in the hallway. Jed gave a rundown while he drove. His attorney responded, "You two pulled it off today, but watch your step. You're the landowners, and though the culprit is someone else, you're liable."

Jed used his rearview mirror to make eye contact with Delaina in the back seat. "You're comin' with me?"

"What?" She looked into the mirror, eye to eye. "No. I can't. Like you said, there's work to be done and..." She looked away, out the window, to tiny plants and sunshine. "I told you, I need space."

The interior became uncomfortable to the trio. A mile rolled by. "Let me be more clear," Jed said into the mirror with a hardened face. "You're comin' with me."

Delaina sighed. Attorney Lowry cleared his throat. Jed drove. Eventually, the attorney advised, "You should probably stay away from each other to lessen talk of collusion. Delaina needs professional security."

"Professional security?" she screeched, and their eyes met in the mirror again. Jed nodded. "Heck no, Jed."

Jed looked over at Stuart Lowry. "Got anybody I can talk to about that?" Delaina rolled her eyes at him in the mirror.

Two men, all business, as if she weren't present. "Yes. I'll have someone call you ASAP. Both of you, don't speak to anyone again without a lawyer present. No exceptions."

They arrived at Cash Way gates. Jed dropped off Delaina at the entrance.

FOUR

Webs

A crack had been widening for more than thirty years, threatening with rumbles on occasion.

Chief Raybon Hall's wrath usually hid beneath his law-man facade. He had waited for the perfect moment to obliterate everything that mattered to the only son of James Ed McCrae. Like any earthquake, the time came for him to split wide open with his unprincipled, unforgiving rage. Jed McCrae had slipped out of the room, slipped out of the investigation, with the ease of a greased dime through a horse's ass.

"I could kill him!" he roared, slamming his fist into a pencil. It broke in two pieces with a low thud. The eyes of every man remained on one of the pencil pieces until rolling ceased. From Sheriff Boyd, "Raybon, buddy, this isn't the time."

"Thirty years is long enough, and you can bet your last breath, Tory Cash would've pumped him full of lead if he heard what we heard!" He slammed his fist into the table again.

Cardin Morris cleared his throat. "I don't think he's guilty of trafficking marijuana. Regardless, your behavior is inappropriate. You should never make threats, and in front of officials."

Raybon stalked up to the man. "Let me tell you what's inappropriate. Your scrawny, city-brained self waltzin' in here like you own this place. This is my town, these are my people, this is my room. Go back to the state office, better yet, go to hell." He stormed out.

Cabot stood on the courthouse steps. Raybon Hall boomed out the front entrance. His barbaric form hovered. Cabot flinched in the killer's face. "We're gonna have to kill 'em."

WEBS

"Settle down and let's talk, Ray. Death would be too easy for Jed. We want to make him suffer first, don't we?"

Raybon Hall took several breaths. "Tell me what to do, anything, and by God, I'll do it."

~ ~ ~

Awful steamy for an April afternoon. Not a whisper of breeze. Sunshine glared hot yellow in the hazy white sky. Rhett Smith hung his head out his truck window as he soared along the highway toward town.

Only one way for him to look at it. He stood barefoot on a mountain of cow manure surrounded by a ring of fire. He had made up his mind to do the easiest thing. Confess. He parked in front of the courthouse, sucked in a paralyzed breath, and stepped out. He rubbed sweat off his forehead with the back of his hand. "Chief Hall, how ya been?" he mumbled as he walked in. Raybon Hall, chewing on a cigar, didn't answer.

Inside the conference room, Rhett shook each man's hand with sweaty palms. He hardly let the last greeting fall before he spoke. "I ain't gonna waste nobody's time. I've been dragged through burnin' hell these last twenty-four hours, and I don't have no idea what my brother Eli might be involved in 'cause he can't talk for hisself. Right now, he's fightin' for his life over at the hospital." He paused. "I'm admittin' I do grow some weed. I'm tellin' you as honest as a Sunday is long, what I grow don't amount to nothin'. No more than containers at the time. Hell, I could piss on it to keep it alive. Far as I know, Eli ain't growin' nothin'."

"To whom do you sell it?" Cardin Morris asked calmly. "To answer will lessen the severity of your punishment."

"Depends. Mostly them boys over yonder at the college."

"How long?"

"The last couple years, uh, since Tory Cash has been out of commission, I thought I could get away with it."

"Have you sold it to Jed McCrae or grown it with him or for him?"

"Uh. Yeah, matter of fact, I have."

Sheriff Boyd relaxed. Finally, maybe they'd catch an unexpected break.

~ ~ ~

LAINEY AND JED, BOOK TWO

Jed attempted to get some shut-eye, lying across the quilt on his bed. After a shower, he landed there facedown and dead tired. Lucy slept downstairs on a rug near the sofa.

He wanted Delaina under his wing. She was too stubborn and shaken to agree. Professional security, his next best option, would require a conversation with her before six p.m., when the first officer was scheduled to be stationed at Cash Way, no argument. Jed's next stop would've been a head-to-head with his cousin Boone Barlow whom he hadn't been able to locate yet. He would get to that after a quick refresher nap. His ringing phone startled him. "Yeah?"

"Hey." Her voice registered at the same time as the name on his phone. *Delaina Cash.* "Were you taking a nap?"

"Uh, huh."

"I tried to nap poolside. I can't rest or keep my mind on what needs to be done on the farm. I'm anxious to hear the truth."

"What?" Jed scratched his head and blinked. "Now? That didn't take long. You asked for space."

"I need you more. In fact, I want the whole world to know how I feel about you. I told people in Houston before I told you."

"I didn't know you have friends in Houston."

"I don't. I told strangers. I realized it in Houston, you know. That I love you. After you left me to get ready for dinner, I went absolutely crazy in a boutique and proceeded to tell people how I feel about you."

"You stayed crazy a little longer." Jed smiled at the memory of Delaina in her gold dress.

"When did you realize it?"

"That I love you?"

"Yeah." Delaina made the word bubbly and suspenseful.

"That night at the river. Somewhere between playin' with your hair while you talked about lickin' Boone's Popsicle and, uh, the beginning of the second dance."

She giggled. "That night?"

"Uh, huh. Why are we talkin' on the phone? If you want the truth, come over."

"I can't. What if someone sees me?" Delaina asked dramatically. "Kidding! I'm on your front porch."

Jed tossed the phone, slipped on jeans and a T-shirt, and rushed to the door. She stood there, innocent as a girl scout selling cookies,

34

twirling her hair around her finger. "Will you forgive me for doubting you?" She looked at handsome him, at his good jeans and Bleu Cotton shirt with words *Size of the stalk counts*. She giggled again. "Jed, I think I loved you from the first day, when you stomped around on this porch in your BC jeans and said you were glad you got your seed in the ground. Took me some time to..."

"Come to terms with it." He pulled her body close. She, dressed in a triangle-cut bikini top and short shorts. His mouth tipped into a lopsided grin. "You're forgiven. I think I loved you when you halfway nodded at me that night at MacHenry's months ago." He shrugged, perplexed.

Delaina shook her head reflectively. "I remember. Let's see, you were with..."

"Doesn't matter. Too caught up in watching you with..."

"Cabot, our first public appearance. By the way, you were with Dirty #11, Samantha Hensley."

Jed snickered. "AKA wham-bam-thank-you Sam." Delaina jabbed his ribs. "Really, I'm thinking maybe I've loved you since that night I caught you and two other girls..."

"Mary Beth Bell and Waverly Wallace?"

"Skinny-dippin' in Carr's Creek," Jed finished, eyes glittering.

"I was, like, fourteen."

"I know, but I liked it that you were the only one wearing underwear."

She rolled her eyes. "And my very sexy training bra." She had run like a kicked rooster when she saw him way back then.

"Even then, you had running from me mastered."

Delaina was floored that he remembered. Their hands joined; she rocked back and forth.

"Hell, I'm not sure. Maybe I've loved you since my tenth birthday. I had more blue balloons than you did pink ones."

"What? The day I was born?"

Jed rubbed his chin. "My mom put balloons out so everyone would know which driveway was ours for my Star Wars party. I remember, she said, 'You'll have more balloons than they have over at that gaudy mansion. The Cash baby arrived, a little girl named Delaina. There must be twenty pink balloons tied to the gate.'" He chuckled.

"Why did that make you love me?"

LAINEY AND JED, BOOK TWO

"To hate you would've been the other option. Never quite sure why I was supposed to hate you, then you came home from college and took over the farm like a pro."

"You never hated me?"

"If I did, I can't remember it now." Jed looked at her hands, held in his. "Delaina, we have to talk about what I know. It's..."

"Shh. Soon. I wanna kiss you." She grinned, licked her lips, pulled his head to hers, kissed him thoroughly. "Hundreds of people expect me to marry Cabot Hartley in millionaire style. I have to take care of that." She inhaled. "Based on the courthouse interview, you and I shouldn't be together right now."

"It's obvious to authorities that we're romantically involved. We may have a better shot if we head off this drug bust together, rather than apart."

"Your lawyer didn't think so."

Part serious, part playful, Jed looked at her. "Well, if you're not willin' to stay right up under me, you're under full security starting today."

She replied, part serious, part playful, "Staying under you is quite the offer." She made a face. "I don't wanna live under constant security."

"Well then, I guess you're sayin' you're willing to stay right under my nose."

Hands held, they stared into each other's eyes. "You and I have a lot of bridges to cross, Jed."

"We have to build them first, sweetheart." Jed pulled her along behind him. "Come to my bedroom. You're the only woman who's been up there, besides my mama when I first built the cabin and not counting Ms. Gertrude, my weekly maid."

"You're kidding. Gertrude doesn't sound like one of your..."

"She's gray-haired and married."

"No trespassing in your bedroom, huh?"

"I told you I'm selfish." He ducked and kissed her. "Good to see that ring isn't on your finger. Come on, I have something to give you." They started climbing the magnificent staircase. He admitted, "I didn't know whether to laugh or cry when you buried those jerks at the courthouse this afternoon." They neared the top.

"It didn't take me long to realize you'd never jeopardize your land in a sketchy plot."

Standing on his amazing perch above the rest of their world, Jed locked eyes with hers. "Or my feelings for you. I'm no authority, but I'm beginning to understand being in love is about acceptance and forgiveness. Remember that in an hour."

Delaina looked around. Good Lord, what a perch. "Dark the last time I came up here, and I was on a mission." Jed opened a drawer. "Outside your cabin is *very* misleading. This is…"

An exaggerated ceiling height, tented in an open grid of bark-covered logs. Walls of the same logs mixed with gray-painted sheetrock and not much décor. The opening to solid rooms below and clear windows to the woods impacted, instead of decorative accessories. Being raised on that land, on that river, sent Delaina's steps toward the balcony. She opened glass doors in the middle of the glass wall. "Like you live and sleep in the woods. Like you walk on water. What a dream."

Jed closed in, when she leaned on the outside rails and stared through treetops. "I think," he said, "this was supposed to be for you." He motioned to the house, the bedroom, the view. "Ours," she commented. "It's all ours, and *how dare* anyone take that from us." They started kissing against the rail. Their arms and bodies wrapped. Jed stopped, plagued by the confession to come.

Delaina watched him, in love with him. She picked up his marred hand, looked at the bruise and scabs. "I'm sorry."

"I'm not." His middle bumped against hers. "Are you okay? Since last night. I don't want you to regret it."

She softly smiled. "I like the way it feels today that I can't deny… I've been with you."

"Delaina, that's…just don't ever hold back with me." Another facet of *Jed and Delaina* had taken root, last night and now. Nothing off-limits.

Jed led them to sit in exterior rockers facing Big Sunflower River. He took her hand. "You… are what I want." Nature sounds complimented his voice. "But I've had years to live for myself and be free and all that. Even if you still want me when we finish this conversation, I'm not pushin' you into anything."

"Our night felt honest." She looked at their joined hands. "I wanna let it be whatever it's meant to be *if* there happens to be a baby." She let go of his hand. "At least I think I do."

Jed admired her bravery. He also felt guilty. "We'll figure something out *if*..." He ran his hand through his hair. "I said a lot at Calla, and I meant it." He shrugged his shoulders. "When I put you on that bed, I told myself once was what you wanted, and once would have to be enough. Truth is, it'll never be enough." He took a jewelry box from his jeans pocket and removed a simple gold ring, a wedding band. Circled it in his fingers and looked at it. "Damn it, Delaina. For a few hours in Houston, we were invisible. We've already hurt each other so much."

Delaina tried to pay attention to what he said. *What was he doing?*

"These days you've been engaged to Cabot were pure hell." Eyes met. Regret played favorites with Jed's; remorse won hers. "I'd relive that hell again to have one minute alone with you." His look became helpless. "However long you need..." He bent before her.

Her voice and smile trembled. "What's this?" She took the ring.

Jed's voice and smile trembled. "It's, uh..." He swallowed. "Mama's wedding ring. They, uh, Mama and my dad..." He took a breath. Delaina had tears in her eyes. "Eloped. She wore this the first year. He, uh...gave her a bigger, nicer ring when he took her to New York for their first anniversary. I want you to have this, Delaina." He looked at her right hand. "I think it should go here." He slid it on the middle finger. It fit perfectly. A tear rolled down her cheek. A tear rolled down his cheek. "What I've decided to tell you is devastating. I want you to know I care. I cared *before* I knew. I already loved you, and I'll love you regardless."

Scared to death and happy, she stared at the ring on her hand.

"Accept it on these terms: No matter what you decide, for the rest of your life, you remember someone did care about you. You mean more than any of this." His hand swept everything around them. "Not easy to give you that." He looked at the ring. "That's how much I care. How much I *already* loved you."

What in God's name did he know? She touched the ring. "I accept. I'll always remember you cared first, before you knew, and that I mean more to you than all this. Is that what you want me to say?"

"Yeah." Jed stood. "We have a lot of bridges to build, sweetheart."

Her left hand clasped her right finger, rubbing the ring. Jed went inside. Delaina followed. He cut his eyes at her as he opened a drawer in the bedside table and pulled out two marijuana joints.

~ ~ ~

Jed's stepfather was almost dead. Fain Kendall's wife cried and held his motionless hand, twirling the wedding band on his finger. Monitors beeped intermittently, marching closer to his final breath.

This woman hadn't had much of anything in her life. She had loved Fain Kendall fiercely, and if she never did another thing right, she would live knowing she made his last days happy.

Watching her husband die, she found comfort in sitting by his bed, recollecting their lives decades ago. She retold their love story to his lingering body. "Fain, remember when we first saw each other, that freezing Christmas morn..." After that initial introduction, she had desired Fain from a distance for a couple years, and he knew it and wanted her as much. They sometimes met; they talked or touched, but they hadn't acted on it. Both were married to someone else.

When they could fight it no more, they saw each other often and became physical and agreed to share a night away, a sticky-warm August night beneath a gigantic full moon in New Orleans. He was there for a convention; she followed him in private hope of getting pregnant. Her husband couldn't father children, didn't want anyone to know, and needed an heir desperately. He had demanded she find someone anonymous to do the deed.

Outside the hotel, she stood waiting for Fain's conference to adjourn, watching a fountain reflect on silvery sculptures. Her honey hair whipped in the breeze. He slipped up behind her and held out his hand to reveal a shiny penny. "Make a wish," he whispered, his golden eyes shining like stars against a big round moon. She wished and tossed the penny. Within seconds, her wish came true. He put her down on a bench submerged in fern fronds with the trickling of the fountain as their love song. He made love to her passionately while they sucked in steamy air, her eyes fixed on the sky, on God.

She prayed for conception.

So long ago, far away, and utterly surreal, this woman beside Fain now should've doubted it happened. She had living proof. They conceived a baby that August night, a child they didn't raise together. Della Cash gave herself a constant, secret solace. Her daughter carried a first name made from a subtle combination of hers and Fain's. Delaina.

~ ~ ~

LAINEY AND JED, BOOK TWO

"That poor Smith boy couldn't catch tadpoles in a 5-gallon bucket, much less organize an operation the size of the one we've busted up," Sheriff Boyd claimed.

"More likely, he's an accomplice to the larger organization. Spending tonight in jail should make him talk," Cardin Morris answered. "I want to question Miss Cash again, this time without McCrae."

"Why?" Sheriff Boyd threw up his hands. "I'm tellin' you, it ain't her."

"She's the key. Get her here tomorrow. I've done enough law work for Sunday. Let's start again in the morning. Send Chief Hall my message that he can cooperate or replace him altogether."

~ ~ ~

"I got here quick as I could. What's so dang pressin'?" Dacey Boyd burst through the door at the Hartley camp house.

Cabot mumbled, "I need someone. I'm losing it."

"I didn't have no idea the extent of your plans till yesterday, Butterscotch. I figured it out, though." She looked at him judgmentally with her gypsy-like turquoise eyes. "You got me to call Jed McCrae that night from Mill's Pond and pretend I was drunk so you could have somebody put weed in his truck, didn't ya? Now Jed looks guilty." Cabot didn't answer. "Everybody thinks I broke my engagement 'cause of a silly last-minute crush I had for Jed. My mama has give me some kinda grief."

Cabot used his sweetest look. "I'm sorry, Red. I thought you'd enjoy it. You love to put on a show."

"Well, yeah, I do." Cabot kissed her. "Ah, well, Butterscotch. I didn't wanna marry Coby Pollock no way."

They sat on a sofa in the den. "I don't want to marry Lainey Cash."

"Ain't nothin' but business."

"Red, I can trust you more than anyone. I swear I believe Lainey is seeing Jed McCrae."

Dacey's mouth flew open. "Never! Butterscotch, what in hell has you thinkin' such a fool thing?" He proceeded to tell his reasons. By the time he finished, she was convinced. "That scrawny slut."

"Sometimes I wanna forget it. Skip town, you know? Make a new life."

"Honey, with you I'd go anywhere."

"New Orleans. We could be there by five. Our family house, you haven't seen it. They're not doing more investigating until tomorrow."

40

"You're pullin' my leg."

"Let's do it. We'll eat at a nice restaurant, drink wine, smoke joints, and spend the night."

"Ooh wee, yes! That Jezebel Lainey deserves it, and I've earned some fun."

~ ~ ~

Things weren't going great for Cabot Hartley. Boone Barlow didn't give a rat's ass. He already got his payment for playing his role. If everyone involved undercover kept their mouths shut, they wouldn't have any real worries.

Headed to his destination, Boone drove his truck onto the row between the two sides of Farm 130. Many days, he worked until his skin blistered and the moon glowed in a black sky while Jed was at college, only to have Jed show up and take over like he never left. He felt a twinge of guilt, here and there, because Jed was kin. Really though, Lainey Cash was the perfect choice for Jed McCrae. Spoiled and arrogant with more money than they had earned.

~ ~ ~

"My lighter's downstairs. Stay here." Jed patted Delaina. "Hey, baby, it's okay." She had clenched her fingers and jaw. Jed hurried down. He found a lighter and held one joint. The crunch of gravel and pounding of footsteps barred his movement. His front door flew open. Boone barged in. Jed rolled the joint around in his fingers, nowhere to hide it.

"Well, well, what have we here? A little Sunday afternoon smoke fest?"

"Boone," Jed said loudly for Delaina's benefit, hoping she stayed put. "Why don't you step outside and knock this time? See if I let you in, you double-crossin' son of a bitch."

"You know they've questioned me, Jed. They wanna talk to me again in the morning. What I'm seeing now is pretty dang incriminating."

"More importantly, why do you want me incriminated? I plan to tell them myself why I have in my possession two measly joints I got from Rhett Smith this morning. Investigation of my own."

From Rhett Smith? Delaina cringed as she listened. Jed's joints had suspended her somewhere between fear and skepticism, and they hadn't even started talking yet.

LAINEY AND JED, BOOK TWO

"You beat me to it, Boone. Headed your way in an hour or two. We have a lot to discuss." Jed dropped to his sofa, reclined, and propped his feet on the coffee table. "Why are you here?"

"I'm here to congratulate you about Lainey." He snarled. "From the look on her face when she first met you in Calla Hotel, she *does* like her some ole Jed McCrae, and I have the pictures to prove it." He sneered. "Although she did kick your ass out of there the first night." He snickered. Truth was, Boone didn't leave immediately after spying on Lainey and Jed's fight inside the hotel. On second thought, he followed an emotional Lainey to Calla Contemporary 600 to know for sure where she spent the weekend. Darting among shadows and plants, thanking the Lord above that he had experience in following them and sketchy night work, Boone had escaped Calla security by the skin of his teeth. He watched her, pretty, tearful Lainey, until she went into her suite. Then he left. "If Lainey finally gave it up to you Saturday night, it's only slightly more than I can say for myself...or Cabot. Congrats."

Jed forced himself to continue lounging and found a temperate voice. "What do you want?"

"I want money. A lot of it. Right now. Or I'll call authorities and..."

Boone never had the satisfaction of finishing, interrupted by a syrupy voice. "What was that you admitted to me one morning at Carr's Creek? We were fishin'. Let's see, you told me the numerous ways you've cheated your way to first place in various tournaments. You know, I heard you on a podcast weeks ago, boastin' about using homegrown worms and plain old fishin' line from a dime store." Delaina paraded by Boone and plopped beside Jed. Lucy followed, making a cozy scene. Delaina rubbed one hand over Lucy's coat. Her face focused on Jed. "It's lonely up there, sweetie." She clucked her tongue at Boone. "I sure would hate to tell Larry what's-his-face, the interviewer on what's it called, Friday Nite Fishin'. Yeah, I could schedule an interview and tell him that his most frequent, popular guest is a fraud. They probably wouldn't let you fish in tournaments anymore, would they? How much does he pay you to come on the show and how much do you win at one of those thingies, anyway?" Delaina shook her head in pity.

Jed put his arm around her. Boone looked at both. He couldn't confess that Delaina was in Houston *with Jed* to get extra payment from Cabot now. Cabot would be too furious at him for withholding valuable information. "Okay, let's deal."

"That's more like it." Jed stood; Delaina rose with him. He slammed Boone against the wall. Lucy barked. "Here's the deal, you coward. Tell us what you know, and there'll be a nice bonus in your next paycheck from the farm, granted I'm gonna work you to death in the dirt and heat this week."

Boone struggled to escape Jed's grip. "You already know I'm the one who's been paid by Fain Kendall to keep tabs on you two, from the text I sent you in Houston." Boone didn't dare mention his deal with Cabot.

"Why?" Delaina asked in a shrill voice.

Jed raised his palm. "I know why. I'll tell you later."

"Like I said in the text, I saw you two at the fancy hotel." Boone looked back and forth. "I swear I haven't told. I have pictures. I figured you'd pay more to keep it a secret, especially because of this drug bust. I bet her crotch is worth thousands to you now."

Jed reached out with the flippancy of a maid using a feather duster and repinned Boone against the wall with a flick. "Apologize to her." "

"I'm sorry, Lainey," Boone said tritely.

"Try again. Look her in the eye, and tell her you're sorry for what you've said, past and present. Damn it, *you know* she doesn't deserve to be talked about like that, Boone." Jed released him. Boone squared his shoulders and looked her in the eye, said how sorry he was for anything he ever said about her.

"Leave before I hurt you." Jed stalked Boone out the door and shut it behind him. He jammed Boone against a porch post. "Don't you blame Delaina. We're not in any scheme. I'm warnin' you. Keep her name out of it. She's too good for this."

Boone smirked. "Not *too* good. She's low enough to dirty down with you."

Jed let him go and turned to view the river on the far end of the porch. He spoke in a voice as malicious as a sharpened knife. "Breathe a word, and you'll float down the river on your face all the way to hell as sure as I take my next breath. There's only one thing that would give me more pleasure."

"Eliminating Cabot Hartley."

Jed shifted his weight to one foot and crossed his arms over his chest in a stance of masculine intimidation. "What do you know about this drug bust?" Boone made a strange face and shrugged. "Nothin'." Jed watched his shifty brown eyes. Boone and Cabot had been card-playing buddies at the Hartley camp house for years. "You're the one who told Cabot where Delaina was." It *had* to be Boone.

"Hell no. You know Cabot's got all kinds of connections and sources."

"Well, you know she hasn't had sex with Cabot, for some damned reason." Jed stared him down.

Boone blinked. He shrugged. "We, uh, play cards with guys at the camp house a couple times a month. You know that."

Not the time for this conversation with Delaina just behind the door, Jed would sequester him, and drill him about Cabot again, when she wasn't around. "When have you last talked to Fain, and what did you tell him?"

Boone looked surprised that Jed didn't know. "I never got a chance to tell Fain about Houston. He's 'bout dead."

Delaina wanted to follow the men outside. She knew Jed wouldn't like it. Inside, his phone rang, an unknown number. She shouldn't answer. She couldn't resist the urge to live in truth. "Hello?"

"Hi. This is Fain Kendall's wife. I'm calling to speak to Fain's stepson. Isn't this Jed McCrae's number?"

"Yes, it is. I didn't know Mr. Fain had remarried."

"About a month ago. I live in New Orleans. May I ask who you are?"

Jed had slipped in the house and followed Delaina's voice. "I'm, uh, Jed's neighbor. He stepped out. What can I do for you, Mrs. Kendall?" Silence on the other end lasted, from Delaina's perspective, too long. "Hello?"

In a choppy whisper, she answered. "Tell him to call me. I'm at the hospital." She hung up. Delaina stared at the phone in her hand.

"Delaina, angel, we've gotta go. I'll drive you home so you can change clothes and pack your things. You need to call Moll or Maydell; tell them you'll be gone overnight. Make up something; tell them the truth, but we're leavin'." His face, expressionless. Hers, questioning.

"That was Mr. Fain's wife on the phone." Jed nodded. She went on, "We're supposed to stay in town, and I need to stay close for Moll and Maydell. Eli's like a brother to me."

Jed's severe features, tense movements, and solemn demeanor scared her. "We're going to New Orleans, Delaina, to see Fain Kendall. I'm makin' this choice for you." He stroked her hair out of her face. "I'll explain on the way."

~ ~ ~

Maydell and Holland Smith napped on opposite ends of a vinyl sofa in the critical care waiting room at Mallard's hospital. Moll slipped in and tapped his wife on the arm. "Maydell, honey?"

She rubbed her eyes. "What is it?"

"Sit up." She did and Holland stirred. Moll sat in a chair and blew out his breath. "Well...Rhett's spendin' the night in jail. Turns out he's been growin' marijuana at the rental house. He claims it ain't much, but..."

Maydell's shriek interrupted him. "How much does the Lord think one family can take?" Holland sighed. "Eli ain't in on this too, is he, Holland?"

"I sincerely hope not."

Maydell looked at her husband. "You ain't kept much of a hold on our Rhett. I've warned you that he won't do right."

"For Pete's sake, Maydell, Rhett is thirty-three. Whatcha want me to do? Chain him in a pen?"

"Get out! Don't come back here 'less I call you or you've got news on Rhett."

"Now, Maydell, we could deal with this heaps better if we stick together."

"I'll come to you when, or if, I'm ready."

~ ~ ~

Naked, Dacey climbed onto the sherbet orange coverlet on the bed inside the Hartley NOLA home and spread her legs. Cabot came at her like a snake. Without asking, he yanked her arms behind her back and bound her hands with his necktie. Her shimmery turquoise eyes tried to reach his. No dice. Her head banged against the headboard as he entered her body in a swift strike. "This is a mighty nice place you got here, Butterscotch." She tried to smooth his edges.

"A nice place for a bad girl."

Dacey became the receptacle for Cabot's worries and frustrations, an outlet for unconventionality. His roughness shocked. He left bite marks on her neck; he jerked her curly locks; he clawed her skin. He slung her from one pose to another, driving into the wall

LAINEY AND JED, BOOK TWO

of her femininity over and over. She cried out, and cried, from pleasure and pain.

Finished, they lay subdued. Sun baked glass windows. The air
conditioner hadn't had time to cool the house. He mumbled, "Let's
rest, then we'll get dressed and go sightseeing."

Dacey felt used and abused. She cut her eyes at him. "You ain't
thinkin' straight, are ya?" He didn't respond. "There's liable to be
vacationers from Mallard. Sunday afternoon in New Orleans."

"We'll wear hats and sunglasses and stay away from popular
spots. I have to get out, to...escape for a day."

~ ~ ~

"It'll take more than two hours." Jed put on sunglasses. Delaina
concentrated on Cash and McCrae land sliding by while he contemplated a route to New Orleans on her GPS.

"Cabot took fifty-five south."

"I'm sure he knows the fastest way. Wouldn't wanna miss one
of his gals."

Delaina laid her head against the headrest and sighed. "There's
still a lot I don't know."

"Start askin'."

"Start tellin'."

Jed shrugged. "I know I've flung a lot on you. If you're not gonna
nap, I might as well talk."

"Jed, *why* did you pull out the joints in your bedroom?"

"Two reasons. First, I got it from Rhett Smith this mornin' after
much finagling. I talked him into admitting to authorities that he's
growin' and sellin' right off the back porch at the Cash rental house."
He glanced at her appalled face. "You needed to know that. I figured
I'd need the proof to convince you. The other reason is last night at
Calla you told me that Cabot smelled oddly sweet when you spent
the night in New Orleans." Jed scanned her profile. She watched
road signs pass by. "I think you smelled a freshly smoked joint."

"I've never seen Cabot smoke a joint, but I almost saw you
light a joint."

"I was gonna let it burn."

Her body shivered. "My God, how risky."

"It's time to get risky, Delaina. These folks are playin' mighty dirty.
Do you know what it smells like?" She shook her head no. He gripped

46

her thigh and cocked his head. "Cabot likes marijuana. He always has, and he's been buyin' from your Smiths for a long time."

"What would it prove if Cabot had smoked a joint that night?"

"Based on the age of the plants, it's the same week they were planted. He had marijuana on his breath and the Cash Way plot on his mind." Jed chose not to say more. He'd let her think about that.

~ ~ ~

The nurse finished her exam and pulled a sheet over Fain Kendall's chest. "Mrs. Kendall, my sympathy. You should get your personal items and go home. The morgue will contact you."

Della Kendall smoothed Fain's hair away from his forehead and kissed his cheek. "I have no regrets," she whispered, gathered her things, and left.

FIVE

Revelations

Delaina looked untouchable, propelling Jed's need to do just that. She dozed, head tilted against the seat, hands folded in her lap, lips pressed together, gold ring on. She had dressed in the same outfit she wore to the courthouse. His eyes fell to her short skirt, her smooth thighs. The skirt fit her hips like she fit him, like a bandage. He shifted his body in the seat and his pants against his body, clearing his throat louder than intended. Her eyes blinked open. She lowered her eyelashes.

They had been riding for over an hour. He had made a phone call, while she slept, to postpone security till she got back. Soaring at eighty-plus, he swung onto a side road and drove until he saw an unmarked dirt path. He parked in a sunken clearing in the woods. Delaina could see the green-brown waters of a pond. Rich amber shadows, the first hint of a sunset, reflected on it. They were hidden in a divine place for a late afternoon detour. A golden, dusk-on-Sunday shrine blessed for lovemaking.

"Jed, this isn't New Orleans."

"No, it's not," he commented. She raised one eyebrow. "I'm going to tell you what I know before we get back on the main road."

She took his hand. "I'm not sure I want to know."

...Previous days, since Jed had known Fain and Della's secret, he wondered what it would be like to be Delaina. To have nobody. He didn't grow up with much family. He had his mama. Devoted, stable, loving. To have no mother. He could not imagine. What would it be like to have only Tory Cash? What would it be like to have Tory as your nobody and to learn that even *he* wasn't yours? God bless her. God help him, for what he had to do.

The windows were down. Humid breeze blew, dusting Delaina's hair across her shoulders. It shone like branded butter in auburn sun. Jed perused her face, his eyes a tight blue-on-black. "God," he mumbled before he kissed her. He gripped her shoulders. "Delaina..." He put his head against her forehead. He longed to hold on. To live in this mutual love beyond comprehension, one step from perfection. Yet no denying one lethal step, a demon smiling in his face. "I can't put it off. We'll go sit on the pond bank."

They sat in the grass and watched the swirling mirror of water. She twisted the gold band on her right middle finger. Jed wanted to back out, to make up something, to run, to die, anything not to hurt her. He turned her face to his with his hand. With his voice stretched with emotion, he said, "You know I love you, Delaina. I realized it that night we were at the river. I stayed up all night contemplating my actions and decided to go to Cash Way the next mornin' to tell you. I had a scheduled meeting with Fain first, early. He told me things that were...unbelievable." Jed twisted toward the water. "Your daddy, Tory, years ago he had an illness. After it, he..." Jed swiped his hands over his face.

"Please go on."

"Doctors said he likely wouldn't have children." Jed scrambled to get the rest out. "When Tory and your mother tried to conceive, it became evident he was sterile. Your mother and Fain became lovers. They... Fain Kendall, my stepfather, is your father."

"What? Oh my God! No!" She jumped up. "You liar! Why? What's your plan now, Jed?" She stepped backward into smutty darkness. "Do you think I'll fall for this? You will not get my land from a lie this ridiculous!" She ran.

Jed ran behind her. "Stop, Delaina. You'll get lost."

"I am lost!" He caught her. She shook in terror, no tears, only lonely childlike eyes. "I am lost, Jed. I had a prostitute for a mother, and she left me with a drunk for a father. Now my daddy isn't who I thought he was? I own a huge farm in need of a qualified manager and under scrutiny for *drugs*. I quit college! I'm very smart, and I quit Ole Miss, Jed. I quit Mallard Community, for God's sake! Days from now, thousands of people expect me to marry a man you claim is a criminal with a town full of willing women. I had sex with the only man in the world who knew my life was a lie, the only man who knew the truth, I may be pregnant, and I... I'm twenty. *Twenty, Jed!*" She banged her fists into his chest, shoving his unbending body. "I hate you. I *am* lost. I have nothing." She slumped to the ground. Then came the sobs.

"There's more."

"Can't you see? I can't hh...handle...mm...more. I don't want... your pity, but I...don't deserve this!" Without Jed adding fuel to the fire, truth continued to burn her brain, flames stacked upon flames. "You! You knew. Oh my...God, that day at the...ff...funeral home when I cried over mmm... my...ddd...daddy's body. You knew the answers to my helpless questions. Oh God."

Jed knelt in the grass beside her. "Please let me finish."

"Today, your cabin, the...phone call. Mrs. Kendall, tell me... it wasn't."

"Your mother."

"My god, you've known where my mother is, all these days that I've known *you*."

Dragging her along, he made his way to her car before dark dissolved them. He reached out to hold her.

"I'll never forgive you."

"Let me finish, then you can do whatever you want. I wanna tell you about Fain's will. He saw us at the river that night. It was him in the boat that caused us to break apart, do you remember?" Stupefied, she halfway nodded. "The timing is incredible. You gotta believe me. The same night I admitted to myself that I was in love with you, he made stipulations in his will, Delaina, based on what he saw, based on his belief that we love each other. The stipulations are tough. He wants your mother to have a relationship with you. Tory almost killed her when he found out you were Fain's daughter. He threatened to kill her if she tried to take you or if anyone found out. They had a prenup. You belonged to Tory. He asked your mother to find someone anonymous; that's why he married a...prostitute. He wouldn't consider infertility methods because he didn't want anyone to know he couldn't father an heir for Cash Way. She hated your father from livin' with his rage and drunkenness, the height of betrayal to make a baby with Fain, and she knew Fain wasn't going to have a child of his own otherwise. My mother was determined I would be her only child. You see, in her eyes..."

50

Delaina comprehended. "You were the only child Cass *McCrae* Kendall wanted. Her beloved son with James Ed. Ultimately, Jed, you're the reason my father is Fain Kendall. My life until this minute has been a lie. Do you know what that's like?"

"I don't." He held out his hands despairingly. "My mother and I lived a lie, too, though. Fain cheated on her for years. He had a child with someone else. She died not knowing. We never knew."

"But you had a mother, one who valued your life above any other." Delaina was a shell. No joy, no passion, no spirit. Everything Jed loved about her sucked out from the force of truth. "If you love me, why haven't you told me?"

"Fain threatened me not to. What he had for ammunition was bad." Jed reminded, "I was in the process of telling you, regardless of consequences, last night in Houston when Cabot showed up."

"Yeah, after you had sex with me."

"Delaina, last night, the whole night, felt incredible between us, you know it, and it was your choice." Jed would not back down on that. "I came close to telling you the truth many times! Fain didn't want us together until he died, to be certain you wouldn't find out while he was alive. He promised he had eyes in the back of his head and threatened to tell you that I already knew what would be revealed in his will, if I broke his stipulations." He dropped his head and sighed. "He would've cut me out and sold my land, probably to Cabot. Fain wasn't going to live long. I thought, hoped, you and I could overcome it."

"I see." Delaina nodded. The land held more importance. Always. "You thought wrong." She touched the ring, heard in her mind, *You mean more than any of this.* Jed had made a gesture toward the land. *Not easy to give you that.* The ring. *That's how much I care. How much I already loved you.* "This ring is a trap."

"That ring is the truth. Keep it on your hand. You always run, Delaina. Keep it on and accept the truth. I'm riskin' everything taking you to New Orleans, don't you see? That's not what Fain wanted. I'm breakin' a stipulation by giving you a chance to see your father before he's gone."

"I don't wanna see him."

"There's more. You could wait for the will. I'd rather tell you now."

"It's not up to you, Jed. You determined my very conception and thus the course of my life for twenty years too many. Heaven forbid, you tell me anything that might jeopardize your precious McCrae land. I don't wanna go to New Orleans. I don't wanna be with Fain Kendall, alive or dead, or my mother or you. I wanna go..."

"Home? Where is that, Delaina? We're exhausted. We haven't really slept in days. We're minutes from Hammond, Louisiana. You'll think more clearly when you've rested, and you need to think before you decide you don't wanna see Fain. We'll be close enough to take you quickly. Neither of us is in the right frame of mind to face the problems in Mallard tonight." He paused. "It's not safe there anyway. We'll get a room."

"You have a lot of nerve. I'll get myself a room, you'll get yourself a room, and I won't say another word to you."

~ ~ ~

"That was one good meal, honey, and it cost you over two hundred dollars! I swear, Butterscotch, I do believe you love me. That was the finest tastin' shrimp I've ever had."

Cabot chuckled. "That's because it was lobster, Red. You want another smoke?"

"No, let's get in that hot tub." Dacey clutched a bottle of chardonnay and walked through the bedroom. "I'll drink every last drop!"

"Can't drink too much. Have to wake up early. I'll take you to this place in Hammond, Patty's Porch, in the morning. The best pancakes. Then I have to get back to Mallard."

"Honey, I do love me some pancakes and grits."

"I know, Red. Patty's is your kind of place."

~ ~ ~

"Eli's not responding as well as we hoped. I've requested air transport to Jackson." The doctor looked grimly at Holland and Maydell. "You two can have a minute each with him, then you should go home and rest. You're going to need strength for tomorrow. We won't let you see him again tonight."

Rubbing her tummy, Holland watched out the hospital window. A chalky moon hung low in the charcoal sky. She had abandoned prayer hours ago. She spotted a bright star, a hunk of glitter pasted to black construction paper. She would hold her sweet, funny Eli again. He would live. He had to. They had a life to build together and a child to love.

Maydell rubbed Holland's back. "I sure hate to stay by myself. Lord only knows why Lainey's gone again."

Holland had a feeling Lainey was with Jed. "I'll stay with you."

"Let's say our goodbyes and go home. You look worn out, and I know I must look a fright."

~ ~ ~

The peroxide-blonde, a-little-on-the-trashy-side desk receptionist at the Slumberful Inn in Hammond shook her head. "Nope, ain't no other vacancies. A pure slew of them motorcycle men stayin' in town tonight on a road trip to San Diego. We got one left. Well, there might be a room at Pink Palmetto, that motel there 'cross the street, but it's a rat's..."

"We saw it." Jed shook his head no. He faced Delaina, his eyes sunken. "I'll drive us home." Delaina said to the receptionist, "We'll take the one room."

She typed on a keyboard. "It's sure nice. We don't reserve it much. There really ain't no need for a honeymoon suite when folks can drive on and be in New Orleans."

"Honeymoon suite?" Delaina blurted.

"Yes'm. King bed, heart tub, chocolate mints on ya pillas, them shiny sheets, nice red satin. Here a month or so ago, me and my boyfriend stayed in there. Them sheets feels good."

Jed sighed. Damn their luck. He handed her his credit card, turned to Delaina. "You sure?"

She sighed. What luck. "I'm too tired to care." She handed her card to the receptionist. "We'll split the cost."

The woman cackled. "Lovers' quarrel, huh?" Neither answered as they signed slips. "Y'all come back when you've patched your differences 'cause I'm tellin' ya, them sheets..."

Jed held up his hand. "Thank you. Could I have the key card?"

"Well." Delaina looked around. "Goodbye, Calla." Jed set their overnight bags on the floor and walked to the obnoxious red heart tub surrounded by tall mirrors in the corner of the room. He got a towel from the edge, went in the bathroom, and shut the door.

In a minute, Delaina went to the tub, turned on hot water, undressed except for the ring, and slid in. She closed her eyes and soaked. She asked God to *please* relieve the burden of a possible baby and drifted into sleep.

Jed walked out in boxer shorts and a T-shirt, feeling a tad refreshed. Welcome refreshment coiled into unwelcome recognition.

LAINEY AND JED, BOOK TWO

Delaina lounged asleep in the tub, nude body visible. He allowed himself the indecent privilege of looking at her. He might never again have the opportunity. "Delaina." Armed for her wrath, he held a towel. "Delaina." He pulled her hair gently. She sat up; they stared... She got a dose of damp-hot Jed. Her pulse quickened. Her mind remembered. Just last night. Calla, their shower, crawling into bed, damp and naked. Pillow talk. Their sweet and open and funny conversation. She wanted him still, loved him still. Why, oh why, didn't he tell her from the start about Fain? She ripped the towel from his hands, wrapped in it, went in the bathroom, and slammed the door.

Jed sat on the bed, not certain where he would be told to sleep. He picked up the remote control and turned on the television. Delaina stepped out wearing her towel as a woman cried from the television set, "Oh, sugar-honey-stud-man, spank me!" Delaina's mouth flew open. "I cannot believe you! Don't you have any respect, any sensitivity, any manners, my God!" A man, not Jed, panted in response, "Oh, honey. You're wetter than water." Delaina stomped to her overnight bag. Jed pressed the power button off, stunned. She bent over. He could have enjoyed her exposed bottom peeking from the tiny towel. He didn't look. She tossed clothes around. "I'd rather sleep with those motorcycle men in the next room than stay with you. You're dishonest and insensitive!"

He attempted, "I turned on the TV and..."

"No excuses! You took advantage of a view of me naked in the hot tub then turned on porn."

"Enough, Delaina!" He stood up and scanned her impatiently. "What do you think I am? I've done everything in my power to keep from hurting you! Can't you give me credit?" He paced. "For weeks I've been miserable, wondering how you'd handle this. Today's the worst thing I've ever had to do! I'm too miserable to touch *you*, much less..." He motioned to the television. "I won't tolerate the way you doubt me every five minutes. What will it take to convince you?" He looked into her eyes. "I'm the only thing in your world that's real."

~ ~ ~

Della Kendall had taken the afternoon and evening to compose herself at home. She assumed Jed would return her call from earlier. She hadn't heard from him. Sinking into the nearest recliner, she sipped coffee then dialed.

Jed's phone ringing interrupted his angry stare. Delaina turned away. "Hello?"

"Jed. This is Della Kendall." He stepped into the bathroom and closed the door. "Hello, Della."

"Fain passed away this afternoon. He'll be cremated with a private memorial for me and his family next week. His sisters, the nieces, and such are flying in. I want you to come. Fain thought more of you than you realized. I'll text you details for the service. New Orleans Lifeway Chapel. We can settle the will later in the day to save you another trip. Your and Delaina's presence is requested for that."

"I'll be there for all of it."

"Jed, today at your home...that was...I talked to..."

"Delaina."

"How is she? Does she know?"

"She's with me. We stopped in Hammond. I took it upon myself to disregard Fain's orders and give her the choice to see her father while he was still alive. When she found out the truth, she didn't wanna come. I'll talk to her about being at the reading of the will."

"I'm worried about her." Della, void of tears until that moment, paused. "That's part of why Fain stayed in Mallard, once he found out that she was his. Who'll watch over her now?"

"Your daughter puts up one hell of a fight. No need to worry. What she can't do, I will."

~ ~ ~

Holland Sommers Smith tossed and turned on her bed in a guest room at Cash Way. If she had followed Eli when he sped down the road. If she had told him the truth from the beginning. If she had kept her deal with Jed. Oh, if she had only known dishonesty would lead to this, she would have sacrificed anything.

Suddenly, she couldn't remember Eli's voice, his touch, his eyes.

She felt odd and longed for their night in Meridian. They sat on the back of his truck and laughed. She could hear the laughter. She couldn't picture anything except the marvelous breeze.

She got out of bed and pushed open the balcony door.

~ ~ ~

Cabot Hartley was too patient. He preferred that wait-and-see approach. Chief Raybon Hall had waited thirty years too long. Past time for Jed McCrae to feel real fear. Raybon was no fool. He saw the way the bastard looked at Lainey Cash at the courthouse.

LAINEY AND JED, BOOK TWO

Therein was the answer to revenge.

He held her wedding invitation as he walked quietly and quickly through the woods.

There were no lights on at Jed's. He crept up to the front porch and tacked the invitation to the door. He stood back and surveyed his work. It was subtle. Not quite enough. Raybon strolled off the porch and headed for the pen where a dog barked fiercely.

~ ~ ~

Jed came out of the bathroom to Delaina sitting in a hard chair, rubbing lotion on her legs. He felt like a chastised husband avoiding his mad wife. He picked up a pillow and stood before her. "I'm ready for bed, and I assume you're sitting on mine."

She stood. "You can sleep with me. I found extra pillows. We'll put them between us. Sorry I accused you of watching trash on TV. I turned it on myself. Every channel has porn on it."

"This *is* the honeymoon suite."

She clucked her tongue. "I would think anybody on their honeymoon wouldn't need extra persuasion to get them in the mood."

"On the contrary," he said.

Delaina cocked her head. "I won't argue with you, Mr. Dirty Dozen."

He let the insult go. "A lot of couples get off watching that stuff together. Me, I'd rather..." He cleared his throat.

She viewed him suspiciously. "Say it."

Jed lowered his blue-going-steel eyes to meet hers. "I'd rather spend our wedding night exploring ways we can satisfy each other. Watch it play out in the form of private jokes and perfected moves all our lives."

Her heartbeat doubled. "I'll get the pillows."

~ ~ ~

"Cabot!" Boone Barlow yelled. "Answer your phone."

"I took the day off after that scene at the courthouse."

"Bad idea. Jed knows it's you. He questioned me."

"He can't prove it, especially now that Eli Smith is shut up."

Boone chuckled. "True enough. God's on our side, isn't he?"

"Looks that way. Hey, don't worry about Jed. If we don't get him, I swear Raybon Hall's gonna kill him."

"That man looks like he's capable of murder."

Cabot answered, "Relax and take the night off. We have it under control."

56

"You seem awfully confident. I'm not sure you've got Lainey right where you want her."

"That's because right now I'm working on another woman. Call me later. Smoke a joint in the meantime. It puts the mind at ease."

~ ~ ~

Jed pulled back the bedcovers. Delaina placed the pillows in the middle, stacked. She paused, removed the top pillow, and placed it in front of the other to make a narrow barricade. She climbed in and covered up to her chest. Jed turned off the room's only lamp and felt his way to bed. He said, "Goodnight," though neither fell asleep instantly. Several hours later, they sprang up, scared breathless from a siren-like wailing. "What the hell is that?" Jed called out.

"The alarm clock," Delaina groaned. "On that table over there."

He stumbled out of bed and snagged his foot on something. "God a'mighty damn." He staggered to the mattress. Delaina couldn't see. "Are you okay?" She reached into darkness. The wailing pierced on.

"I cut my foot."

"I can't see." Delaina found the remote control and pressed buttons until the television came on, giving them light. *"Oooh, sugar baby, suck me."* She switched on the lamp. "Ugh," they groaned in unison as they squinted. She rushed to the alarm, fumbled with it, couldn't make it quit. "It's four a.m. Why did you set it so early?" she shouted. She picked up the clock and hurled it at the floor. It splintered into pieces. The shrill sound ceased.

Jed stared. "Why didn't you unplug it?"

"Shut up." Delaina saw blood drips coming from his foot.

On television, a man hollered out, *"Uhh, I'm coming."*

"I didn't set that alarm," Jed said, applying pressure to the cut. "Do something with the TV, please." Her image jolted into his groggy brain. Delaina wore a skimpy BC gown, words *Cotton Soft Everywhere* swept across her chest. Jed already knew she felt cotton soft everywhere and it was his job to take care of cotton. He forgot about his foot. *"Baby, let's come together,"* floated through the room. Sounded like a good idea to Jed. He counted his pulse beating a steady path downward.

"Oh goodness, Jed, you're bleeding a little." Delaina bent and touched his foot, treating him to a nice view of softness everywhere.

"Am I?" Erotic groans and moans filled the room.

LAINEY AND JED, BOOK TWO

"It's stopped." Delaina crouched between his legs. "There's a sliver of glass in the carpet. You stepped on it."

"Did I?"

She stroked his leg. His hairs stood obediently. *"Ooh honey, you hit the right places."* Delaina glanced at the screen. Her eyebrows went up, chin down, impressed by the pornographic couple's current acrobatic position.

Jed checked what she saw. Aw, hell, they were gonna do that anyway; he moved it higher up on his mental 15,000 times-with-her list. She switched off the TV. She turned; Jed reached out. She allowed him to pull her with him as he backed across the bed, knocking the gate of pillows away. He pointed to the shattered remains of the clock. "You've got a mean pitching arm." Delaina smiled. "I miss that smile," he whispered and expected the words. For him to stop. His hands caressed the back of her legs and moved up to bare buttocks. "Hmm..." His eyes narrowed. "No cotton here."

"Your foot's okay?"

"In better shape than the rest of me." Their eyes met.

Silence lingered, stretched, stretched. Popped. "When I look at you, a nasty voice chants in my head that all this time you knew about Daddy."

Void of the right words, Jed sighed heavily. Delaina crawled over to her side and crept under the covers. Jed shut off the lamp and turned to face her back. "These sheets are a joke. If I come closer, we'll go sliding over the edge."

"Try and see," she said through sniffles.

He moved in and spooned her, brushing a kiss on her neck. "Don't cry."

"I don't know what tomorrow will bring. I'm so lost."

Again, void of words, Jed settled for holding her while they fell asleep.

Six

Despair

The sun raised its chipper head much too early for Dacey Boyd's drunk one.

"Come on, sleepy. We're going to get pancakes."

"In a minute."

"Get up. In a minute, it'll be too late." Cabot's impatience brewed.

She stumbled toward the shower. "I can be ready in fifteen flat."

"Good, we'll be in Hammond on time."

~ ~ ~

Jed woke the way he fell asleep, spooned into Delaina. Their first night of falling asleep and waking up together. He didn't want to let go.

She stirred and asked, "How's your foot?" without pulling away.

Who, besides her, woke up with minty-good morning breath? No one. Not a woman he had known. "Foot's fine. You smell good." If he didn't let go, he would embarrass himself. He reclined on his back. She turned over, watched him, and stated, "I need a favor. I want you to manage my farm."

He couldn't think about anything but her, without panties in red satin sheets. "Can this wait till we're dressed?"

"I thought about it for hours. Sorry, I need to know now." She sat up. One strap drooped. He looked at her shoulder, her collarbone, knew what she looked like beneath her cotton-soft gown. What wonderful agony to be so close. "Regardless of how much this ordeal with Fain has hurt me, I know you wouldn't jeopardize Cash Way, and honestly, I need someone who knows what it takes."

"You can trust me."

Underneath the covers, their legs touched. Had been touching. Delaina caressed the gold ring on her finger. Half a minute passed. "Is he dead?"

How it hurt to hurt her. "Yes."

She cringed, looked more hurt, and more beautiful. Her shiny green eyes watered. "My mother called last night on your phone?"

What had he done to deserve this torture? "Yes, Delaina."

"Do you know if..." She bit her lip. "Fain and Della continued their affair?" She held her heart. "If she came to Mallard often? To meet Fain."

Knives. Jed stared at her. "They continued. Through the years, your biological father knew where your mother was. He didn't know you belonged to him until after she left, and I think...they mainly met in New Orleans, not Mallard."

She nodded, hand gripping her gown over her heart. It would've been easier to go on believing Tory had been too mean for her mother to stay or come back to see her. Her biological parents didn't want her. Delaina got out of bed and closed herself in the bathroom.

~ ~ ~

Sheriff Daniel Boyd, Police Chief Raybon Hall and Investigator Cardin Morris gathered for breakfast at MacHenry's to discuss the day's itinerary. Cardin told the group that he and his assistant had uncovered nothing else unusual so far. Dan and Raybon exchanged confident looks. They had been instructed by Cabot Hartley to continue going after Jed McCrae, and if that didn't work, to blame indefensible Eli Smith.

~ ~ ~

Eli struggled to live, confined to a hospital bed. In his unconsciousness, there were dreams. Hours of white light, blackness, angels, demons, then for mere seconds, Holland alone. She stood in morning light, a yellow gown as sheer and sweet as candy draped on her body. Tears streamed down her face as she held out her arms.

Eli sensed that she cared about him. Her image faded, replaced by a boy with a freckled face and light hair. He ran with his beautiful mother in green pastures. "Wait for me, Elijah," she called out as they ran, her chocolate eyes shining. Eli called for them to wait for him, too. They ran until they were gone. Left him alone. Loneliness changed into bleakness. Bleakness ran into nothingness. Nothingness gave itself up to death.

~ ~ ~

In the glint of morning sun, Holland felt a breeze, its swishing sound stirring memories. Lazy smiles, soft touches, and passion. Jokes, the voice low and dirty, mixed with her laughter. The same voice whispering, "It wasn't me, Holland. Save me." Serenity crashed into comprehension.

Eli died.

She dashed from the balcony into her room. She pulled on her clothes then scrambled for her phone. It rang before she could dial the number to the hospital. "No!" she screamed and dropped it. She scurried to the balcony, flung her head over the ledge, willing a breeze to blow. A still world mocked her. A diminishing mouth of moon frowned.

Maydell Smith climbed stairs to Holland's bedroom and found her sitting on the balcony, leaned against the rungs. "Come on, honey. If you've got the strength, I sure could use help tellin' Moll. He ain't never gonna forgive hisself for this."

"I'll help him, Maydell. It's not Moll's fault. It's mine. Our innocent child will bear the pain for my mistakes."

Maydell sat and sobbed. Holland offered soothing words until she could stand.

They went to the rental house. Moll sat in a rocking chair in the corner of the den, smoking a pipe and holding his Bible. Before they could say anything, he spoke. "I knew when I heard your car engine. My son, he was a fine man. The Lord promises peace that passes all understanding."

He dropped his head. His body began to shake. He flung his Bible across the room. He reached out. "Maydell." She went to him. Holland watched the scene, her own tears pouring.

~ ~ ~

Jed pulled out of the hotel parking lot. Delaina's eyes were shaded by sunglasses. News of Eli's death had been delivered to her by phone call from Moll. Everything happening came down on her hard.

Jed mumbled, "Your low fuel light came on. I'll stop at that convenience store over there."

"I need a restroom."

LAINEY AND JED, BOOK TWO

"It'll be cleaner at the cafe." He motioned to a restaurant beside the gas station. He parked. Delaina got out, crossed the sidewalk, and entered.

"We're low on fuel, Red. I'll pull in at this convenience store. You go over to Patty's and get a table. We don't have an extra minute to spare," Cabot said, patting her thigh.

"I need caffeine. My head's killin' me, and my eyeballs are floatin'." Cabot parked at a self-service island. Dacey got out, crossed the sidewalk, and entered the restaurant.

Jed had been paying attention to the gas pump until he heard a car pull up behind Delaina's. Cabot Hartley stared him down. "Cabot."

"Jed."

Jed disengaged the pump. "Need something?"

"An explanation."

"You'll get one when I get a confession."

"Okay, I confess. I don't like you at all and I don't care what happens to your silly land." Cabot closed in. "What the hell are you doing with Lainey's SUV?"

"Can't think of a reason to explain why to you."

Cabot never took his eyes off Jed. "You fuck with me, you'll both go down."

Jed never took his eyes off Cabot. "I've never wasted my time fuckin' with you. From what I hear, neither does Delaina." Jed got into her vehicle and cranked, considering why Cabot was in Hammond, Louisiana, on a Monday morning. Driving away, he watched in the rearview mirror as Cabot filled a blue Ford loaner with fuel.

Delaina came out, head bent, shoulders slumped. Once inside, she whispered, "Please let's go."

Facing the mirror to wash her hands in the restroom, she had come apart, due to Moll and Maydell's loss, Tory's absence, Fain's secret. Then she saw Dacey Boyd in the cafe and Dacey tried to slip by without speaking.

Jed decided they'd ride for a time before he mentioned Cabot. Delaina seemed wholly overwhelmed.

~ ~ ~

Holland tiptoed into Eli's former bedroom at the rental house. She climbed in his bed and pulled sheets around her. She smelled faint cologne on his pillowcase. Over and over, she rubbed it. Things would get better because they could not get worse. She repeated that like a counting-sheep hypnosis until her drooping eyelids were heavier than her heart.

~ ~ ~

In his second interview, Boone Barlow claimed he knew where the marijuana was planted because he'd been standing near the deputies who were discussing it on the day it was discovered. Unaffected by the questions, he concluded with a claim that he walked in on Jed McCrae about to smoke a joint at his cabin yesterday. Boone kept his deal with Jed and didn't say anything about Delaina. Jed McCrae might kill him if he did.

"That McCrae is one cocky lowlife," Chief Raybon Hall said when Boone left. He pointed his finger at Cardin Morris. "You're half my age and experience. Maybe next time you'll listen. The joke's on the Mallard County law office one more time, folks. McCrae strutted outta here yesterday *with the Cash girl* and couldn't get home fast enough for a joint to celebrate." He shook his head and chuckled. "I'm glad we consulted someone from state."

Cardin Morris intervened, "Like it or not, I'm in charge, and I want Delaina Cash by herself."

~ ~ ~

Jed took it upon himself to rub salt in a different wound, while he still had Delaina in his possession. Miles outside of Hammond, he attempted a hint. "I guess we have an appointment to make."

Delaina looked at him like he had gone crazy. He sighed and gave up subtlety. "You had sex for the first time, night before last. With me, remember. A possible pregnancy, a checkup, maybe birth control..." He showed her his hand in case she tried to deny it. The marks looked like he stuck the side of his hand in a paper shredder. His voice was kind. "My friend Meggie is ob/gyn in Houston if that helps."

Delaina's hair hung limp. Her lips were dry. She scrolled on her phone. She did not trust handing over the pregnancy scenario, or her post-sex gyno appointment, to his sexy connection in Houston. "I won't need birth control." She sounded like a bitch, even to herself. She slid her finger back and forth on the pad. "I went to a gynecologist once in Vicksburg for a minor issue. Miss Maydell sent me."

"How about get us an appointment there? If you think it's confidential enough."

Her fingers shook as she typed. "Hi. This is Delaina Cash. Yes, patient of Doctor Welch. Years. No female problems. I, uh, need to see if I might be...yes. A couple days ago unprotected, and I had never, I, uh, right. Probably ovulating too. Uh, pregnancy, not really birth control...*STDs*? Oh gosh, okay, yes. Got it. Okay, no earlier than that, then? Thank you." No attempt to inform Jed, she resumed her stare out the window.

He had not given her a godforsaken STD. Aggravated with everything dumped on them, that made Jed mad. And she did need to talk to someone about birth control because...age twenty, and technically sexually active, she seemed smart enough to know she *should* have that talk with her doctor. "Well, when do we..."

"Appointment two weeks from today, late or not, if you *must* know." She sighed like Jed was her biggest problem. He was not her biggest problem. "I don't need you to go and hold my hand. Home tests are accurate at 8-12 days after conception, so I wanna do that, too." She reached in her purse and pulled out an envelope. "Right now, please say you're going to manage my farm."

"I will if Gage will agree."

"Here are the papers. He may not like my choice, but I don't think he has to formally approve it. Assuming you're not implicated on marijuana charges."

"Or that I didn't give you an STD," he remarked, took the papers, and put them on the console.

"I know you didn't," she gritted out. "It's routine." Jed had given her undivided attention since day one, capable of tenderness like no men she had in her life. He deserved something. "I'll cherish that night together always." Her hand fluttered over her stomach. "But this is the reality of living like that."

~ ~ ~

Summer Lynn Moss curled her hair and applied glossy lipstick, dressing for her job at Mallard First Financial Bank. She couldn't keep her mind off Jed McCrae, disappointed the drug scandal came when he finally paid her attention. She still got tingly thinking about his waltzing into the bank like a male god wearing a shirt as blue as his eyes. They had an enjoyable lunch, and he kissed like Prince Charming. He had said he would call her. He hadn't yet.

Summer Lynn decided she would call him when she got home from work today. If nothing else, she could offer to take his mind off his problems for passionate minutes.

Pleased with her appearance when she finished dressing, she decided to give him a surprise morning visit before work. She drove along the dirt road, guessing where to go, taking the most worn path. It led to his cabin. His truck was there. She got out and walked onto the porch. Tacked to the front door was an invitation to Delaina Cash and Cabot Hartley's wedding. With a red marker, someone had written, *I'll kill the bitch.*

Frantic, Summer Lynn ran to her car, then a scary thought occurred. What if someone had seen her driving there? Everyone knew she'd been infatuated with Jed for years. She couldn't leave that invitation. She might be blamed.

She tiptoed to the porch and knocked on the door. She knocked harder, waited. She called Jed's phone. He didn't answer. She got the invitation, got in her car, and texted him, *Need to see you ASAP.*

~ ~ ~

"Mama, Daddy..." Rhett Smith pulled off his cap as he stepped into the parlor at the funeral home.

"Rhett." Maydell sobbed into her son's shoulder. He held her and swayed, squeezing his eyes. "Mama, there's nothing we could've done to change this. It was his time."

Moll Smith stepped forward. "Son." Eli's threat haunted, *'Don't ever call me your son again.'* He shook his living son's hand.

Behind Rhett, Holland came in, dressed in old jeans, tennis shoes, her hair unbrushed, no makeup. Her eyes fixed on him. He started to hug her but halted, undone by her fascination. She walked into his arms. "Miss Holland." She breathed in the same smell as Eli. She relished the thought and let him hold her. Moll and Maydell Smith watched, perplexed. Rhett pushed her away. "They're wantin' us to make arrangements?" Maydell nodded with her eyes on Holland, who continued to watch Rhett.

~ ~ ~

Jed read the farm management papers while he waited on Delaina at a convenience store. She held two drinks and candy bars when she slid in. It was a bad sign that he considered such a small gesture a huge step forward for them.

LAINEY AND JED, BOOK TWO

She put his drink in the cup holder and unscrewed the cap on hers. "I don't know if you like caffeine or caramel, but I do." She gave him the candy bar and started chewing on hers.

"I read the papers. I accept the role. We'll have to sign at Gage's office, I think." His peace offering to go with hers. She nodded, said "Good," started to set her bottle in the cup holder, and her pleasantness disappeared at the same time he cranked.

Jed had not yet told her that he saw Cabot Hartley in Hammond. Until this slight change of momentum, she seemed too bewildered. What an awful frown. What now? Jed pulled out of the lot.

"You missed a call," she said in her *I-won't-need-birth-control* tone.

They had synced Jed's phone to her Bluetooth on the way to New Orleans yesterday. Now, cranking the engine alerted them on the dash screen to a missed call on his phone from...Summer Lynn Moss? Jed looked at the screen like he had no idea.

He 100% forgot she existed. He nearly ran a red light.

Delaina, looking out her window, jumped when the screen started speaking, "Text message from... Summer...Lynn...Moss." Jed exited the screen before the voice read the text aloud.

Delaina slid on her $$$ sunglasses and finished her candy bar. Cabot's bank girls were apparently Jed's bank girls. Liar! Summer Lynn Moss. Older, busty, stylish. She twisted Cassie Jane McCrae's lovely wedding ring on her finger.

"You take it off, and I'm done," Jed said. "I'm *so* done," she bit back.

"Dang it, Lainey, we had lunch last week to..."

"I didn't ask, and don't call me Lainey." He met her for lunch last week? Delaina had known her father was not Tory Cash for less than a day, and somehow Jed's tiny confession stabbed as deeply. "Four bank girls. Cabot would be impressed."

"Four?" Jed drove too fast.

"Jenna Lee, Dacey, Holland, Sum..."

"Aw, screw that." He passed a car like it stood still.

"I'm sure you did." Delaina wanted to fight with anybody about something. She didn't want to fight with him about this. She believed him about Holland and Dacey never being his lovers, only said their names to lash out. She reached into her purse. "Here." She put his phone on the console. She had packed their phones and chargers in her purse when they gathered things at the hotel. "Probably

66

important since Summer Lynn called *and* texted." She drank from her bottle.

Jed watched trees and yellow lines blur by. "Read it. I'm not gonna text and drive." He shrugged.

"Oh God, don't you shrug about her!"

Jed laughed laughter of disbelief. "Come on, Delaina."

He drove for miles. She got his phone and scrolled. "Needs you to call her ASAP." Summer Lynn's one text to him, the only text between them. "Why lunch with her last week? More importantly, then why invite *me* to Houston?"

"I thought she might know something that could help me." Jed looked at the woman he loved, hurt beyond hurt for a number of reasons. "To keep you safe from Cabot." He sniffed. "So, I...dressed up, went to the bank, and, uh, employed proven tactics to make females talk."

Budding adultness held Delaina level. "She knew something." She believed Jed. The day she took cookies to him at his cabin. His blue shirt, great pants. His lunch date.

"Yeah. She overheard something serious might go down that Saturday, which I plan to tell investigators today."

"So you invited me to Houston." They passed road signs welcoming them into Mallard County. "I have Summer Lynn to thank for my weekend with you?"

"If you wanna look at it that way."

"Exactly what proven tactics, besides lookin' hot as hell in an outfit way too good for her, did you employ?" She shriveled him from head to toe with her scan.

"Compliments, flirting, lunch invite." He sniffed. "A boring kiss."

"A kiss. Ugh. Stop that annoying sniffing." She took a breath. "All to save my life?"

"It got you to Houston." He went for broke and smiled.

"I like Summer Lynn." She pushed her sunglasses onto her head.

"Hmm, okay. " He doubted it, and it showed. "I've never lied to you." Jed turned onto Cash-McCrae Road. Both knew that wasn't totally true. If he lied about Fain/Tory, he had to, she supposed. That thought brought Delaina back to the future. They had no future. Tears watered her eyes for the umpteenth time this morning, for the umpteenth different reason.

"*Delaina.*" His hand touched her arm.

"I miss us, Jed." She watched their land, their heritage, their everything, passing by. *"We...were...crazy."* Her laugh hurt. *"Funny, hot, sexy, sweet. Now..."* She shook her head no, folded her hands in her lap, sniffed, and sniffed again. *"I..."* She pulled her shoulders straight and pulled herself together. *"...look forward to workin' with you while you manage my farm. Look forward to learning."* But I can't forgive you about Tory and Fain, she didn't say aloud.

Everything in Jed wanted something more substantial. They had been thrown into a ferocious sea of troubles, pushed overboard by choices other people made, most before they were born. He turned off the main road. Tiny plants swayed in fields. Sunlight glowed across their land. "Stop a minute," she said.

She stepped outside. So did Jed. She reached for his hand, urging him toward the woods. They came out on the other side, the far end of Farm 130. The ground sloped upward, a bridge into clouds. Delaina turned to him, bent, and scooped dirt. "This is the only thing that sustained me. From the moment we met, you've been confirmation it's okay to feel strong selfishness about this place. You understood like no one has. I would've preferred to believe I was Tory Cash's daughter regardless of consequences." She looked across the field. "Now, this isn't really mine."

Coolly, Jed spoke. "I understand." He pointed. "Mine isn't mine either. You could own McCrae Farms, depending on how you and your mother handle Fain's will. But, hey, looks like I'm the right one to control Cash Way for now." His midnight blue eyes revealed a blend of defeat and satisfaction. He began to walk away.

Weeks ago, Delaina sought Jed against her better judgment and shared all of her farm, and then herself, with him. His damning words, from the first night they talked, came to her with undeniable accuracy.

'We want the same thing, Delaina. This land, free and clear and without needless worries.'

Nothing would change that.

~ ~ ~

Cabot Hartley stood talking to Boone Barlow on a deserted road ten miles outside Mallard. "I told them to forget it. Blame Eli Smith. A dead man can't defend himself. This marijuana scheme isn't enough to bring down Jed. Raybon Hall has told me that he'll kill Jed. I believe that maniac would kill Jed *and* Lainey. God knows, it's not hard to get them together at the same time. They're staying under each other."

Boone inhaled on a cigar. "Cabot, you realize they're actually stayin' under each other."

"I know. That cheating slut."

"I don't wanna be in on a murder plot. Can't you make money some other way? This has gone nuts."

"No one said there's a murder plot. Truth is, Boone, I received a colossal offer. A casino on the riverbank. Only their land will do, in Mallard County, and I'm gonna get it. It'll save the town. You don't have a choice. You've done a lot of bad things."

Boone shifted his weight from foot to foot. "I need more money."

"Soon. We gotta let things rock on. Suspicions will die down and then bam! We'll find a way for it to be over with the blink of an eye."

SEVEN

Cabot vs. Jed

"Oh, Miss Maydell, oh goodness. Moll..." Delaina hugged them and cried. "I'm so sorry."

"There ain't nothin' to say," Maydell sobbed.

"We'll have everyone visit you here. Inside the big house."

"No." Maydell shook her head. "You got that wedding to pull off. We ain't gonna clutter up this house and yard."

Delaina took a sharp breath. "I insist." The front door crack opened and Holland walked in. "I'm sorry," Delaina said.

"Me too."

Maydell patted Holland's back. "She's been right here with us, Lainey."

"I'm glad she was here for you. I'll call the funeral home to direct visitors here. I absolutely insist."

Maydell conceded, "That's so sweet."

"You're my family. All I've got." The hollow inside Delaina widened.

Looking at her, Holland requested, "Let's go sit and talk. I need to take my mind off Eli."

Delaina nodded and motioned to the den. Holland sank into the nearest chair. The grandfather clock ticked. Delaina broke the awkward silence. "I can't imagine how you feel."

"I don't want to think about it. You spent the night in New Orleans?"

Delaina chewed on her lip. "Jed and I had unavoidable business. Have you been there?" To Cabot's house, she held back from asking.

"No." Delaina watched her. Pretty, in wrinkled clothes with flat hair and no makeup. Holland rolled her eyes. "I look terrible." "You look beautiful. Always." "You too, Delaina." "Thank you, but right now I look like a witch. Almost no sleep the last three days." "Me either."

Holland started hesitantly, "I caught on to you and Jed at the hospital." Delaina twisted toward her. "It's none of my business, but I can't recall a time I've seen Jed quite so..." She searched. "I've noticed changes. I think you have something to do with that."

"We've developed a working relationship since my father's death." Delaina walked to a window. "I wouldn't flatter myself into believing I'm responsible for noticeable changes in Jed McCrae. He lives for himself and to please himself."

"Sounds like you know him well."

"I guess, for what it's worth." Delaina couldn't resist prying. "Until I saw you at *Salon Doreen's* that day and you mentioned Eli, I thought you were Jed's girlfriend."

Holland smiled. "I was never brave or stupid enough to try very hard. I've known Jed for years."

"Do you think Jed is ruthless?" Delaina watched Holland's blinking eyes focus on an object over her shoulder.

"Ruthless as Hitler, and that's on a good day," from a voice Delaina was certain would haunt her to the grave and into eternal damnation. She twirled around. Jed stood in the archway. His stance so obnoxiously masculine, Delaina would have been intimidated, had he not heard her. The fact *that he had* rendered her mute.

Holland stood. "Jed." He moved past Delaina with the indifference of a jungle animal cutting a trail through underbrush. Unfortunately, she wasn't spared a whiff of the animalistic scent that went with the move. He hugged Holland. "I'm sorry."

Delaina didn't bother excusing herself. They were oblivious to her presence. She retired to her bedroom and sat on the chaise lounge by the window showcasing both farms. No boundaries, Cash ran into McCrae, McCrae into Cash, on and on. So much history. More to forgive now.

"Lainey?" Masculine arms reached out. "Thank you for coming," she said blankly when he hugged her. "I don't wanna be alone." Cabot let go. "Please tell me you aren't in any way responsible for this marijuana problem."

He raised his eyebrows. "What would give you such an idea?"

"I have my reasons for questioning everyone, everything."

Cabot clucked his tongue. "Sad."

LAINEY AND JED, BOOK TWO

"What?"

"Eli. There's evidence. Multiple sprout boxes purchased by him weeks ago. This will be difficult for the Smith family." Delaina's mouth fell open. "Eli?" "It seems he dabbled with marijuana for college kids and decided to go bigger this spring. I hate to be the bearer of more bad news."

Delaina turned to the window. "Today seems to be a gracious host to bad news. What about plants on Jed's place?"

"Investigators are theorizing that Eli put some there purposely in case he got caught or got property lines mixed up, which is easy to do out here." Cabot laid his hand on her shoulder, surprised how she received him. He tested his renewed luck. "I don't suppose there will be a wedding this week under the circumstances."

~ ~ ~

Jed and Holland rose from the sofa where they'd been talking when Rhett Smith entered the room. They hadn't acknowledged Cabot Hartley's arrival. He paraded up the winding staircase. To Delaina's bedroom, Jed assumed. Jed came to pay condolences to Holland; he also came to tell Delaina about Cabot in Hammond, which he never got around to with so much happening during the car ride.

"Rhett." Holland hugged him.

A terrible thing for a man to think, considering his brother wasn't in the ground yet. Rhett thought about how good Holland's voluptuous curves felt against his body while Holland breathed in as much of Rhett's cologne as she could.

Jed observed the scene. Rhett looked a lot like Eli, often mistaken for twins. People did strange things in grief and mourning. A mantle clock struck twelve times. "Jed," Rhett said as they shook hands.

Then he started, "Well...Sheriff Boyd's claimin' the marijuana operation was Eli's. They found where he bought sprout boxes. I don't know how the hell I'm gonna tell my folks."

Holland gasped. "I refuse to believe it." She looked at Jed. "What do you think?"

"I think Cabot Hartley is a smart bastard."

"Yes I am." Cabot walked in and shook Rhett's hand. "Sorry about your brother." Holland studied him curiously. Cabot turned to Jed. "Jed, would you like to tell us why you think I'm so smart? Or should

I tell *you*?" Delaina appeared in the doorway. "Lainey, your business buddy here called me a smart bastard not knowing I heard him."

The atmosphere in the room exploded. Cabot moved beside Delaina and smiled. "My beautiful fiancé put up a respectable fight, saying we should postpone our wedding based on this dreadful turn of events. I talked her into getting married as planned. No one expects us to wait. The details were tedious and expensive. Holland and Rhett, please understand." Cabot looked to Rhett apologetically. Rhett watched Holland. Holland watched Delaina. Delaina watched Jed. Jed watched no one.

"Of course," Rhett finally said. "Eli, if he was here, he'd want you to go ahead." Holland's lips trembled. She went to the nearest arms, Jed's, and sobbed into his shoulder.

"Hey, it's gonna be okay."

"How will I take care of the baby?" She looked at everyone. "All of you know I'm pregnant, right?" She abandoned composure and cried, "I want his baby, but I'm scared to do it alone." She clung to Jed. "I'll miss that man."

"We're sorry, Holland." Delaina touched her arm, aware of her proximity to Jed. If he breathed, she'd feel it on her face. "You'll be a good mother, and you have Eli's family to share the baby. Babies need...families who...live together...and love each other. If anyone knows that, I do. You'll have that."

Jed spoke to Rhett. "Take care of her." He meant Holland. "Cabot, Delaina, let's step outside." He understood Delaina's words; her possible pregnancy would end in abortion or his baby would end up as Cabot Hartley's.

When hell froze. Delaina hadn't seen a war.

"Rhett, tell your parents they have my sympathy." He brushed his hand across Holland's back. "Call me." Cabot and Delaina followed him out because Holland and Rhett didn't deserve another scene. The trio stood, uncomfortably, on the stately white front porch.

Jed, assuming the duty of a good farm manager, recognized that the following dialogue was required, to act appropriately and responsibly on any matter related to Tory's legal heir entering contracts. Delaina marrying Cabot qualified as a legal contract.

He would've done it anyway.

"Cabot, she's asked me to be her farm manager and I've read the papers. Also, you should explain what you were doing in Hammond this morning in a loaner car to your fiancé if she still chooses you, when I'm done speaking." He allowed himself to look at Delaina. "Delaina, baby, you're gonna marry him?" His eyes honest and blue, soft on her face. "You're in love with me."

Delaina's mouth opened. "Oh my God, Jed." He stabbed her in the back with what he knew about Tory, and now he pushed her flat on her face, revealing this.

"Cabot, she's not in the frame of mind to make a good decision today. Not in the frame of mind to know who she wants or trusts. She's been through a private hell you know nothing about." Delaina felt unbelievably betrayed. She kept looking at Jed, anguished. He forged on, picking up her hands. Eyeing both rings. "You can't wear both, little girl."

Cabot had an odd expression. He laughed.

"Kind of funny, isn't it?" Jed looked only at her. "That shocking diamond and my mother's simple wedding band. Time to choose, sweetheart." Cabot still laughed, anxiously. Jed decided to smile, looking in her eyes, clutching her wrists. "You should also know, if she failed to tell you upstairs, she stayed in Calla Hotel on my dime. Willingly. Best weekend of our lives until you showed up. Did you tell him, angel?"

Delaina stared into blue eyes and blue skies back and forth. How could he?

"Lainey, you cheating bitch. Your sorry ass is gonna marry me! We will talk about this privately. Get rid of him. *Now*."

Jed dropped her hands, gazed at their land. "Sounds like a blast, *Lainey*, to be married to him."

"I'm about to kill you." Cabot pulled his fist up and lunged at Jed. Jed grabbed his arm.

"Stop!" Delaina inserted. The men struggled, banging around the porch, about to fight. "Stop it now! Jed, *please*."

Jed held his arms. "This isn't the place and she asked me to stop." He looked like a predator. Cabot looked like his captured prey. "You'll get what's coming. You can bet your pathetic breath on it."

"Enough, Jed!" Delaina glared at both men. "I can handle myself."

They broke apart, huffing. Jed circled Cabot like a rabid animal. "What do you want, Delaina? Tell us." She handed Cabot the engagement ring. "It's over."

Cabot peered at Jed then laughed again, arrogantly. "No way."

"Leave my yard or… I'm gonna inform authorities that…I'm fearful of you." Suddenly, she was. "Don't come back. I won't be here. I'm going away," she lied. She didn't know where she would be. She knew Cabot might harm her if he thought she stayed at Cash Way. "I'm overwhelmed and angry and resentful, so I caved in upstairs. But, Jed's right. You and I don't love each other. Leave." A harder statement to make, "You too, Jed. Leave."

Cabot backed down steps. "Lainey, I'll give you space. Call me when things calm down." Jed went down the steps. "You heard her. Leave." Cabot ignored him and begged, "Come on, Lainey. He's not for real. He wants this land and used a weekend in that fancy hotel to get it." He looked beyond Jed to her. "Call me soon. I warned you about this asshole!"

Jed stalked him to his uppity foreign car. "Get. Off. Her. Land."

Cabot stood staring at the porch then left. Jed turned. Delaina had vacated the premises. Jed stood staring at the porch then left.

EIGHT

Fleeing

Time ran together for Holland Sommers Smith in a haze of food she didn't want, people she didn't know, tears she didn't fight, and unexpected support from Delaina.

Personally, Holland assumed Delaina concentrated on her to take her mind off canceled wedding plans. Holland's own wedding day had been a week ago. She stood on the porch of Cash Way and watched thunderclouds form. Tomorrow she would bury her husband.

"Miss Holland." Rhett tipped his cap. "You ain't ate in three days. You need to eat ya somethin'."

"Not right now." She sat in a rocker. "Have a seat, Rhett...I know you think I'm crazy, the way I've clung to you since Eli died." She batted thick eyelashes. Rhett got lost in rich brown eyes. "You and Eli are so much alike. I miss him."

"Hey, it's okay. I feel close to Eli when I'm with you. We'll get through this. I don't know about mama." His head went down. "There ain't no hope for Daddy. Eli was the apple of his eye."

"We'll stick together and help them."

"I sure do hope you're plannin' on stayin' around."

Holland had closed her eyes to let his voice soothe her. "I'm here indefinitely."

~ ~ ~

Chief Raybon Hall couldn't relax, disgusted with the investigation. He put his good name on the line in hopes of Jed McCrae's demise, and now they had nothing. He wasn't happy about blaming a basically innocent dead man, either. Moll and Maydell Smith were good people; they didn't deserve a kick in the gut when they were down.

The invitation tacked to Jed's door and the dead dog had not satisfied his need to make Jed suffer. Raybon Hall rubbed his hands together. James Ed had taken Raybon's sweet Cassie Jane Darrah. Raybon would take Jed's sweet Lainey Cash. He looked through the blinds shading the windows of his office. No one was coming. He slipped a liquor bottle from a drawer and sucked on it. Time to act.

~ ~ ~

Jed drained his glass.

Over the years, he had experienced the mellow feeling that came from drinking. He'd had a hangover or headache before. He'd never finished off vodka, beer, and started on Tuscan wine by late afternoon, bent on drinking until he drank everything he had. He'd been sitting, and sipping, by the river all day. Daylight near gone, a rain-threatening breeze blew.

He didn't have a clue about the actual time, considering his watch was held hostage by a sea-scented nymph with angel eyes and satin thighs.

He had moved out of the wait-worry-smoke stage. That was one-sided and for lovesick fools. He resided in the rant-rave-kill stage. It came when you knew that the person you had waited, worried, and smoked over loved you as much as you loved her but chose to be unforgiving and gone. He belched, an ode to masculine drunkenness.

After three cigarettes and the vodka, he decided if he could castrate himself, he'd survive. By the time he opened the wine, he accepted that what he felt for Delaina occupied his mind and his heart. Those parts couldn't be cut off.

He had been to see Cardin Morris and told him all his suspicions. He would get serious and do more investigating of his own soon. It would require Rhett and Holland's cooperation. Neither had been in the mental state for it and wouldn't be until after the funeral. Jed had until tomorrow to drown himself.

Since he returned from the overnight trip to Hammond with Delaina, his dog had been missing; no way she got out of her pen and no sign of her anywhere. That pained him, bothered him, stumped him. Cabot Hartley was capable of a lot, but dognapping or dog killing?

Delaina was not safe.

He gave her space to simmer down after their face-off with Cabot. It scared him beyond all sensibility, if he were honest, to leave her

LAINEY AND JED, BOOK TWO

alone. He hoped the funeral activity around the Smiths at Cash Way would protect her from harm.

Reaching his limit, at dawn today, he sent one text, *Stay with me for your own good.* No answer. He didn't want her out roaming around the farms, he didn't want her out in public, he didn't want her...out of his sight. He made a phone call to the potential security team, seriously considering sending a uniformed guy to the door of Cash Way. Her protests be damned. They required her consent before assigning shifts, yet another snag. The drinking started, to stop him from stealing her against her will.

Last time he looked, three Sunflower Rivers traveled east, west, and north toward the sky. This time, one river flowed as big as the Amazon and traveled backwards. Head swirling, he reclined in the grass. His eyes met with a nice pair of smooth legs running under a short skirt.

"Hi, Jed."

"Summer Lynn." He made no effort to sit up. His stomach had a vodka-pissing bull stomping around in it. Besides, he couldn't complain about the view. He stroked her ankle.

"Cool place you have here. I texted you a couple of days ago. It's important."

He heard it before. Different women, all the same. "Uh, huh." He burped and didn't apologize.

She walked over and picked up the wine. "Nice." She curled her lips to the bottle and flung her head back. Jed propped on his elbows. He didn't think Summer Lynn really danced, but she did sway. He flashed to guitar music and river water. He saw a baby-faced naked blonde swaying and singing. His gut curled tight as a fist. His cock refused to be outdone. "Drink, Summer Lynn."

She pointed her finger like a teacher correcting a first grader who said *damn* for the first time. "I've heard about you." She raked her indigo eyes over his body. "You are dirty, Jed McCrae."

"Says who?"

She tucked her hair behind her ear with a graceful finger. "Girls at the bank. I'd prefer to contribute something about you to a gossip session."

"I'm actually pretty particular." He chuckled at his notion and gave Summer Lynn the once-over. Nothing reminded him of Delaina.

78

Summer Lynn swallowed a sip, knelt, and ran a painted finger-nail over his chest. "About my text message... Are you too drunk?"

He blinked his eyes. Not too bad yet. "Big Sunflower is flowing through that tree over there but go ahead."

Summer Lynn pulled off her blazer. Underneath, she wore a silk blouse. Despite the amount of liquor Jed consumed, some of man's best handiwork was not subject to distortion. Firm breasts the size of mountain apples, albeit fake fruit, waved at him through the thin material. He might have waved in return. She sat beside him and made a face when blades tickled her legs. Women like Summer Lynn Moss didn't dirty themselves in vibrant green grass. Oh, but Delaina. There went that fist in his gut, the competing lead pipe in his pants.

She pulled the invitation out of her purse. "I came by Monday morning to see if you were up for a, uh, surprise visit, and I found this tacked to your front door." Jed glanced at it. He vaguely recognized the ivory vellum paper. "Cabot and Lainey's wedding invitation," she said. *I'll kill the bitch,* with Delaina's name underlined, jumped out at Jed. He jerked it from Summer Lynn's hand and came to his feet.

"What time did you stop by?"

"Around eight-thirty." She stood.

"You didn't see anyone?"

"No."

"Do you remember if you heard a dog bark or saw one?" He pointed toward Lucy's pen. "A red mutt." Summer Lynn's forehead wrinkled in concentration. "No. Eerily quiet."

Jed rubbed his temples and cursed his drunkenness. First things first. He had to get rid of Summer Lynn. "Honey, I need to check into this immediately. There's a lot of stuff going on, okay? I know you've probably heard." He touched her hair, tried to take time to smile. "You've gotta trust me, and keep this to yourself, please, I mean it. I'll make it up to you...in spades, later." "Jed, let me help you..."

~ ~ ~

Chief of Police Raybon Hall paid his respects to the Smith family at Cash Way and overheard Maydell say that Lainey just left for a walk. There could be innumerable places to take a walk around there. Raybon Hall figured her shoes had automatic pilot to Jed McCrae's cabin. His plan came together easily. He parked his truck on a deserted path, pulled on a camouflage jacket and mask, and crouched in darkening woods to wait.

~ ~ ~

Thunder rolled in a black sky. Delaina neared the trail leading to Jed's. She moved briskly, anxious to outrun the potential storm. As she made it onto the worn path, soft rain began to fall. Her movements froze. The shadow of a man sat on the edge of the woods. She patted her back pockets. Her phone, no gun.

"Jed?" No answer. "Jed?" she called louder. She looked left and right and saw no one anywhere, surrounded by tall trees and darkness. Rain poured. The man's form crept toward her like a stuffed monster. She grabbed for her phone. He clamped her hands. She opened her mouth to scream. Nothing came out as barbaric appendages shoved her into a tangling of underbrush.

~ ~ ~

Thunder shook the walls. From the sound of it, Jed assumed a substantial rain fell on the crops.

Summer Lynn had put up a fight about leaving, made him promise to call her ASAP, and finally left.

He needed a clear head to successfully kidnap Delaina. He got a cold shower, aspirin, and a handful of crackers. Except for a dull headache, he felt ready to approach another battle. Big as hell, he predicted. This time he flat refused to leave without her. He pulled a cap over his hair and left.

~ ~ ~

The hostile form smothered Delaina.

Panic choked breath from her lungs, her mouth covered by a grimy-tasting glove. After seconds of trapped silence, the man pressing her into the wet ground threatened, "You made a dumb move when you broke it off with Cabot Hartley. If I were you..." He tightened his grip on her arm and ground his gloved fingers into her mouth. She wheezed, he chuckled, and she smelled liquor. "I'd stay away from Jed McCrae."

He slipped a shiny knife from his pocket. "Do you understand?" Rain washed over her body, dripped into her eyes. Cool mud seeped into her clothes. He ran the knife down her shirt, slicing the blade in the hollow between her breasts to her stomach, splitting the knit fabric into two parts. "I hope I don't have to reinforce..." A rumbling engine hushed him.

With all her strength, Delaina pushed upward. The man above her turned to the sound. She seized the opportunity to free one hand, grabbed the skin of his neck then twisted hard. He yelped and fell, keeping a firm grip on Delaina's wrist. She jammed one knee into his stomach and hollered, "Jed!" His truck crept along the path, no way he could hear her. She wrenched her slippery wrist free and took off running through muddy underbrush. Jed's truck traveled toward Farm 130, a significant distance from them. "I'm warning you," came the voice behind her. She ran until she reached the edge of the woods.

Jed drove slowly, trying to see the path through the increasing storm. He cursed the amount of liquor he drank earlier. Now he was seeing Delaina running and screaming in silver rain. He slammed on the brakes. His truck slid sideways through the muck. A quicksilver vision of her appeared and disappeared. For real! He grabbed his pistol from the glove compartment and rushed out.

Delaina sensed the man inching behind her and heard Jed's truck door slam. "Delaina?" he called. "Help me!" she yelled as the giant dragged her into darkness, slammed her against a tree, and whispered, "Shut up. I'll kill you." She began to sob. "Start walking." The slant of the knife against Delaina's throat effectively shut her mouth and made her move. The man pushed against her back as they crept along.

Jed's heart hammered his chest. Whatever she ran from had her now. He dashed into the woods, feeling his way in silence.

Raybon Hall assumed Jed McCrae trailed close behind, likely armed with a gun, and knew the map of the woods, essentially his front yard, better than anyone. He went about his work, pulling rope from his jacket pocket. He pinned Delaina to a tree and tied her up. He yanked on her sopping wet hair, slapped her, and whispered, "Tell him it's over. Your life's in danger. He's not worth it." He disappeared.

Jed ran his hands along trees until his hand left tree bark and brushed across her wet skin, before he realized he was upon her. He jumped. "Jesus Christ!"

Strapped to a tree and shirtless, precious Delaina, covered in mud and wringing wet. He slumped against her. "Are you hurt?" She tried to shake her head no. Cutting through ropes with his pocket knife, Jed made careful movements and worked to free her.

She cried out, "Someone's going to kkk...kuh...kill me!"

"*Shh.*" She struggled to breathe. "Take breaths, Delaina. Don't try to talk." Jed frayed the last of the ropes and pulled her to him.

Drenched and shaking, she fell into his arms. "Hey, it's okay." He held her, this terrified heap of mud and wetness, while his ire raged. He took off his T-shirt and pulled it over her head. She worked it over her chest.

"Damn, Delaina, I've told you." He felt like screaming at her. Their situation presented far too much danger to lose his cool. He scanned the surroundings.

She continued to sob, her teeth chattering. "He...had a...nnn... nuh...knife."

"Let's get out of here." Jed pulled her through the woods. Delaina clutched him for support, aware of the cautious way he handled her and his pistol. When they reached the truck, he checked everything, no sign of anyone. He wrapped his arms around her. "You're okay?"

Delaina's face scrunched up. Tears of terror began to fall. She made sounds she couldn't help or control.

"Shh, I've got you." He caressed her as she sobbed. "You won't be in danger anymore." He situated her in the passenger seat and got in the truck.

Through chattering teeth, she said, "I was comin' to talk to you about my safety."

"I was comin' to get you." Jed handed her the invitation. "A message left tacked to my door. And, sweetheart...Lucy's missing. She's a smart dog, but she can't unlock her pen and let herself out."

"*Lucy?*" she sobbed. "*No.*" Delaina read the invitation. "Call the police!"

Jed removed his cap and plowed his hands through his hair. "I don't trust a soul in Mallard County. Think about that comical interview. You're with me, a matter of life and death." He tossed her his cell phone. "When I saw this invitation, I scrambled to come get you. Text Holland. Tell her you're with me."

"Holland?"

"Yeah, Holland. You gotta trust me. Tell her that it's not safe for you in Mallard, not to tell anyone, to cover for us with the Smiths, to delete the text, and I'll contact her when we get settled. She and I've been in communication. She'll do what we ask now. Hers was a mighty hard lesson learned."

"I'm so..." Delaina could hardly get the words out. "...scared. I don't know what to do. He threatened to kill me if I stay with you. *How* can we trust Holland? Or anyone!"

82

He stopped the truck. "Delaina, this is the best plan I've got."

Truth be known, Jed's head throbbed too much for driving. She was too shaken up to do it, either.

"I'm freezing, and I need a shower and clothes."

"I know, baby. I'm taking you someplace safe and warm." He had driven to the far edge of McCrae property, away from the incident and houses. He pulled off the road. Corn grew in glistening, shoulder-high rows.

"Where?" Delaina breathed in and out, struggling to calm down.

He watched her intently. "You're going to Houston to stay with Meggie Henderson. No one will look there. I thought about my apartment, but...you shouldn't be alone." Delaina didn't protest. "I talked to Meggie." Delaina's hair a scraggly mess, her cheeks red with fear, her eyes wild as any storm. He almost lost her. Jed wanted to tear up hell or take her to bed. "You're in hiding until we have answers." He tossed a towel on her lap. "Use this. It's not that clean. I had it at work." While she scrubbed her hair, he reached in the back. "Why don't you undress and wrap in this until we can stop? It's dry, at least."

For a second Delaina stared then pulled off her wet clothes. The sheet. Her sheet. She huddled it around her body. She shook with chattering teeth and purple lips.

Jed crumbled to sand. "Let me hold you a minute." He cradled her head on his shoulder.

They started kissing. Slid into it like a love song. Gently, quietly, all heart.

Jed eased away. He attempted a smile. "I have a slight hangover, drank a foolish combination of alcohol, trying to drink you away, this afternoon. Are you sore? Did he push you around?"

"I'm...starting to throb from bumps and bruises." Chills swept across Delaina's arms. "I don't wanna talk about it yet." She watched stalks sway, darkened arcs and pathways over rich soil. She tried to smile, too. "I've never been afraid out here. I stole away to a corn field, many a night, as a little girl. This is home."

His hand patted her, naked down to her teeth under the thin sheet. "We'll talk about the attack later." He also throbbed. To make love to her. "Under all these circumstances..." Jed took her chilly hand in his. "It's a disgrace how much I want you."

LAINEY AND JED, BOOK TWO

Delaina, too, could envision them under the umbrella rows, kissing urgently, grabbing on to one another, tumbling to the ground. "We survived. That's *always* when they do it in the movies." It felt good to smile and to hear Jed chuckle under his breath.

Jed exercised restraint. Delaina, banged up, wet, cold, scared, lacking family or safety, no birth control on hand, and barely once removed from virginity. More importantly, she had not forgiven him about Fain.

Bleak night stretched between them. They looked at drippy corn through the windshield. "Somebody's gotta wake up and farm tomorrow, sweetheart." Jed read her mind. "Check rain gauges. Assess what needs to be done next and where, stick to the drill, you know."

"Yes, what needs to be done is on my mind every minute." Farming didn't wait for funerals or the reading of wills, didn't care about assaults or disputes, disregarded family and safety. Delaina knew what should come next. Jed saved her life. Opening herself up to trust him, to trust anyone, felt scary. Dare she dream that *One Day*, when she got her life figured out, Jed McCrae could be truly hers? She had to start with three words. "I forgive you."

Jed soaked it in. The long-awaited relief.

"About Fain, I'm sure you've done what you had to do this past month." She felt vulnerable. Close to defeated. She wasn't even a Cash.

His knuckles tapped her arm. "We're gonna fight. On the farm, I mean. I'm tough."

He said the right words. The challenge rebirthed something inside her. "I'm tougher."

"Everything's gonna work out, baby." *How?* "Somehow." Jed kissed Delaina's trembly lips. Their foreheads touched. "Thank you," he said, "for forgiveness."

His smell, familiar now. Farmer, fresh air, faithful, forging on. She reached for him. The sheet slipped beneath her breasts. His fingers cupped her shoulders. He felt her tension. She could be sore or bruised anywhere. So many concerns. So new to trust. "Not tonight," he whispered. "Too much, too soon." She nodded to agree. "Delaina?"

She looked at him, eyelashes fluttering tears. "Hmm?"

"Someday, we're comin' to a corn field and..." "I know the rest."

He swallowed hard. "There's so much I wanna do with you, little girl. Go everywhere. Talk about everything. Show you my life. Compare the way we farm. Kiss you good mornin' and goodnight. How does that make you feel?"

She touched his mama's gold ring on her middle finger. "Loved."

NINE

Finding

Who could forget that face and body, even from snapshots? Meggie closed the gap to greet Delaina with a gait like a runway model. Wide eyes framed by thick lashes. The color startled Delaina. They reminded her of Tory's bourbon. Winter nights, he stood by the fireplace, watching embers reflect in his glass. Delaina would crouch in the doorway. The glass crashed into the fire some nights. Meggie Henderson's eyes were the color of that liquid splashed upon fire. "Hello." Meggie extended her hand. "I regret meeting you under tragic circumstances, but I've heard a lot about you."

Delaina had applied makeup and slicked her hair into a harsh bun that morning. "Yes, nice to put a face with a name." Visible through Houston airport glass, soft rain fell among sunshine. "I didn't bring an umbrella. I'm not prepared for anything."

Meggie patted her folded umbrella in the pocket of her raincoat. "That's okay. We'll share."

Delaina immediately thought that an umbrella wasn't all they had shared. "Hope I'm not imposin' on you. Jed didn't give me choices."

Sobered up, Jed had driven her to Jackson, bought clean clothes and cosmetics for her, gotten a hotel, talked at length about her attack, then they slept a few hours before he woke her with breakfast and coffee. He gave Delaina his credit card (he didn't trust anyone knowing her purchase history and location, if she used hers), and drove her to the airport. They agreed to meet in New Orleans next Thursday for the settling of Fain's will and go from there.

Meggie popped open her umbrella. "My fiancé Lewis is on a mission trip to Brazil. I need to stay busy." She paused to clarify. "Not many babies due now. Jed and I met in med school. I don't know how much you know about me."

Delaina bit her lip. "Not much. I saw your pictures in his apartment."

"Uh-oh." Meggie laughed. "From our younger days." She stopped at a sports car. Delaina loaded her new duffel bag and got in. On the main highway, Delaina said, "I don't know what you know about me, either."

"Jed and I talked in depth after you boarded." Delaina observed that Meggie didn't seem uncomfortable discussing him. "He's a man, so I'm sure his view is somewhat skewed."

Both laughed. "Jed's perception of me is disturbingly accurate."

"I've gathered you two have a special relationship."

Delaina looked out the window. "When's the wedding?"

"September." Meggie smiled and held up her hand. "See my ring. Love, love, love the man who gave it to me."

Delaina's awkwardness waned. "Beautiful." Meggie Henderson seemed easy to be around.

"I thought you might want to get settled. Later, I'll take you shopping. Jed has someone bringing his jeep, too." Meggie drove through a neighborhood of winding paved lanes and towering trees to a brick ranch-style house centered on grass. "Nice," Delaina complimented. "A big house for one person."

"I'm comfortable here. My childhood home. My brothers and their families visit."

Inside, a sizable kitchen with oak cabinets, granite countertops, and an island opened to a formal dining room. "Make yourself at home." "That's easy to do," Delaina said. "Your house feels like a, uh, home." This was what she wanted. Cathedral ceilings. Fieldstone fireplace. Unadorned windows with outdoor views. Leather-bound books, family pictures, oil paintings, and handsome fabrics on the furniture. "I may never leave."

Meggie laughed. "It'll be fun having a girlfriend." Females typically envied her beauty, especially when they discovered her intelligence and kindness surpassed it. She had no sisters, her parents were deceased, and her brothers lived on the West Coast. That's why she and Jed had been close. They understood each other, filling a void until Lewis and Delaina. "How about a cup of tea?" she offered.

"Sounds good. Yes."

Meggie heated water in a kettle. Her phone buzzed on the counter. They stood so close at the stove that Delaina saw Jed's name on the screen. Meggie picked up her phone, read, grinned, and typed something. She twisted around and smiled. "Jed, checking on you."

Delaina's phone, stuffed in her pocket, never went off. Her attention turned to the kettle as it whistled.

~ ~ ~

Eli's funeral came and went without fanfare. Fifty or so people gathered in the side chapel of the First Baptist Church. Maydell cried through the service. Moll stared into space. Rhett huddled his head in his hands. Holland sat beside him. Rain poured to the ground and washed through the streets while thunder boomed.

The graveside portion got canceled. Eli would be buried in a separate plot at the Cash family cemetery, offered by Delaina. His family went home to an empty Cash Way estate.

Days passed in a cloud of grief for the Smiths, a log of exhausting work for Jed, and new experiences for Delaina.

~ ~ ~

Tuesday, 10:17 p.m.

Hey, J. Sorry for the long text. A few things, since we haven't communicated while I've been in Houston: 1. I'd like to go to Fain's memorial service. I'm trying to make sense of everything. Maybe that'll help. Will it be okay with Della? 2. Gage approved you as farm manager, under verbal agreement until we can make arrangements to sign. I need to talk to you about the bank, as it relates to my farm and my relationship with the Hartleys. I handled it. I should've checked with you first since you're my farm manager...this will take getting used to ☺ 3. If you think I need to return to Texas after NOLA for my safety (hope not), could I use your apartment or go to Calla? Meggie is awesome, but Lewis is coming home. It would be good for me to be on my own. Hope we can set aside time to talk before Thursday. I know it must be crazy for you right now. I feel like I'm overburdening you. I can't thank you enough for your help. D

She pressed Send and a minute later received: *Hey, D. You're staying in Tx, sorry. You aren't overburdening me. Call you tomorrow to talk. Goodnight, J*

PS, I like the D and J.

~ ~ ~

"You're right. Better with banana slices and chocolate syrup!" Delaina spooned a hunk of ice cream. She and Meggie had returned from prolonged shopping. A den littered with junk food, sappy songs in the background, they accommodated girl talk and slumber party. They were friends now.

Meggie sat beside her on the sofa, eating. "I've got the ring. He has to marry me, fat or not."

They giggled. "From what you've told me, I don't think that matters to Lewis."

"We've been blessed to find each other."

"Meggie, I'm sorry I assumed you were one of Jed's women."

"No problem. We're close. You're not the first to accuse us. If it makes you feel better, I assumed you were his current fling when he told me he brought you to the ballgame. We met at a restaurant to catch up that Friday night."

Delaina probed, "How do you know that isn't why I came to Houston with him?"

"Because he told me at dinner, in the process of telling me he loved you, that he hadn't been with you *yet*..." Meggie licked her spoon.

Delaina dug through a shopping bag for skimpy black lace. "I can't believe you talked me into this. We were supposed to be shopping for your honeymoon."

"Take it from me." Meggie shook her hair airily. "It makes you feel better to dress sexy."

"It did happen with me and Jed in Houston, a special weekend for me." She looked at her empty ice cream bowl. "But I might be pregnant."

Meggie knew those facts from Jed because of the dire situation. "Jed cares so much about you. I hope I'm not overstepping." She smiled genuinely. "He asked me to remind you: pregnancy is my specialty. I'm here if you need me."

"Thank you, Meggie. Thank you for everything so far." Her middle felt odd. "May I see what you chose for your wedding night? You know *a lot* about me now. That little red fur suit you're gonna seduce Lewis with later in the honeymoon is darling."

"Glad you think so! I could use your opinion. I'll actually try them on if you'll try on that!"

LAINEY AND JED, BOOK TWO

Delaina hugged her body. "I don't have your shape. My future *husband* will be lucky to get me into this. Or out of it."

"That's the deal. I'll try on mine if you'll try on yours."

"So, I'm thinking this one for our wedding night."

"Beautiful," Delaina exclaimed as Meggie descended the staircase. "Lewis is gonna die."

Meggie twirled around in the gown. "I hope not. I have big plans for him. Men, aren't they great?"

One in particular, for sure. Delaina observed, "What I like about the gown is that it covers everything, but it's sheer."

"Yes, great combination of saint and slut." Meggie's figure looked like something out of a centuries-old painting.

"Okay, I'm not putting on the black thing after seein' your body in that classy nightgown."

"You are! I can't wait to tell Jed what you bought with his credit card."

"No, you can't tell Jed!" Delaina's eyes rounded. "I'll pay him for everything."

"Sure, you will." Meggie winked. Delaina walked into that one and rolled her eyes. Meggie gladdened to see Delaina open up each day. "Why can't I tease him?"

"We're not exactly together now."

"I think that's up to you."

Delaina wished Jed would tell *her* that. "I don't think Jed likes lingerie. He likes me, you know, naked."

Meggie laughed unplanned. "I'm sorry; it's like my brother I'm talking about."

"Oh, *I'm* sorry." Delaina put her hand over her mouth. "I've never talked to anybody about stuff like this."

"No, it's fine. But it's funny because Jed has never acted like this. Neverrr."

Delaina's stomach flipped and kicked her in the heart.

"Mrs. Lewis Alden Abner. Suits me, doesn't it?" Meggie swirled in her gown. "Then why'd you buy the black lace? If you don't mind my asking..."

"Yes, it suits you," Delaina agreed in the face of such boundless love. "I like lingerie, I decided, in the boutique. It does make you feel capable." She and Meggie exchanged a womanly glance. "I don't

90

want you to tell Jed because…" Meggie sat and draped a furry throw over her shoulders to cover the sheer. She looked like a nightgown queen. "…it's sweet that you and Lewis are waiting until after you're married. You caused me to rethink that."

Oops, sorry, Jed. "Believe me, dear, there's nothing sweet about it. Neither of us is inexperienced."

It *would* be difficult to wait, after what she and Jed shared. Uh, impossible. "I relate to you and Lewis, kind of. I went on dates with my pastor's son in high school. Josiah was…in love with me, he claimed. He gave me these. I wear them all the time." She pulled her hair back to display gold cross earrings. "For my seventeenth birthday. Then he went to seminary. He left me with a vow that I remember First Corinthians Six, Nineteen." Delaina recalled the scripture from heart, "Do you not know that your bodies are temples of the Holy Spirit, who is in you? You are not your own."

Meggie nodded. "I know the verse well now. Twenty is: You were bought with a price. Therefore, honor God with your bodies."

"I rarely skip church, but he had me on too high a pedestal. Still, it's…" Delaina looked for a word. "Neat. To be respected like that is…"

"Inspiring and intoxicating."

"Yes. Kudos to you and Lewis."

"You don't regret being with Jed, do you?" Meggie pried.

"Oh gosh, no." She fanned herself. "It was perfect, Meggie. Your best friend is…" Delaina lacked the word.

"Aw, *that Jed*. Hard to go back now, sweet Delaina. I think God… makes exceptions."

God makes exceptions. Hmm. Delaina felt unsure about that, yet she lacked regret.

Meggie shrugged. "Lewis wouldn't agree, but I'm in the baby delivery biz. I have to be, uhm, more open-minded." She leaned in and whispered, "I'm dying to do it." They laughed. "Four months to go." Meggie smiled at her love story. "Go get your skinny butt in that racy costume with your little cross earrings. I'm in a daring mood! I'll model the red and silver fur nightie. I plan to drive Lewis delirious with it." Prissily, Meggie climbed the stairs to her bedroom, leaving Delaina holding her recent purchase.

The buttons and hooks proved to be a tedious exercise in Delaina's patience. The black lace creation gracing her body had twenty satin buttons running down the front. Only her breasts were covered in material that wasn't transparent. She slid on matching underwear and thigh-high stockings, hooking them to the costume after unsuccessful tries. She bent over and shook her hair. Traces of glossy Kotton Kandy pink remained on her lips. Delaina saw herself in a mirror.

She and Meggie would laugh until they cried. She looked like a very experienced, very expensive, woman hell bent on her next seduction.

She slinked through the hall. "Okay, Meg, I'm comin' out and I know my seduction line." She swung around the corner and tossed her hair. "It's now or never."

Jed sat on the sofa, arms spread over the cushions, legs stretched on the floor. He wore a button-down dress shirt, sleeves unbuttoned. His fine black hair went in twenty directions, topping a haggard face. He held a water bottle by the neck between two fingers. She stood stunned.

Jed had imagined scenarios awaiting him in Houston. This had not been one of them. Delaina propped in the doorway in lingerie that left nothing but bad behavior to the imagination, at two o'clock on a Wednesday afternoon. "I texted Meggie when I landed. Let myself in."

The way his blue eyes took her in; she might as well. Delaina batted her eyelashes and engaged in a turn. "You could always call or text me."

"Maybe I wanted to surprise you."

"We've been caught up in girl stuff, payin' no attention to phones. Jed, she's so much fun. We..." It hit her what he said. He flew to Texas a day early to surprise her, instead of meeting in New Orleans tomorrow. Gulp. "I helped Meggie shop for honeymoon lingerie today. She talked me into this."

"Meggie's a smart gal."

He wanted to spend the night with her. Delaina's skin burned hot. She leaned forward. "You're a smart guy. What does Jed think?" Her breasts pouted over the flimsy cups.

"Your come-on line wasn't necessary, cupcake." He shifted on the cushion and crossed one leg at the knee. "The Pope would have you sprawled on the carpet by now."

A door closed. Meggie's body became discernible at the top of the stairs. She looked like a stripped-to-threads snow bunny. "I called Lewis! I described in detail what I'm wearing. He's considering a new career. Oh, and Jed's on the way."

Delaina warned, "Jed's here!" She climbed the stairs. "Wait! I wanna see."

Dressed in clothes, Meggie walked in the kitchen to Jed eating an apple and straddled over a stool at the center island. "Season's greetings, Mrs. Claus. Who's your partner-in-seduction imperson- ating? Wife of Satan?"

She grabbed his arms. "Jed, she's precious. Presh and hilarious!" Secretively, "She discovered she likes lingerie, although she thinks you don't, because, you know, you like her naked." One Jed eye- brow shot up. Meggie giggled. "Anyway, she *kind of* wants to wait till she's married now." She covered her mouth. "Isn't that cute? Delaina's perfect." She clasped her hands together, pleased. "I love her to death."

She bought dirty lingerie with his credit card but might wait for marriage now. Yep, that was his girl. Jed plunked the water bottle on the granite counter. "She's my definition of perfect, Meg. I wanna rip off the black lace with my teeth tonight." He grinned at his best friend's funny face. "I'll marry her, you can bet your life, *one day*." He frowned. "We have a ton of chaos facin' us. Mallard is...a mess."

Meggie's face dropped. "Jed, she loves you." Delaina appeared in jeans and untidy ponytail. "You two, I help with an after-school program on Wednesdays. Gotta leave shortly."

"We can't thank you enough, Meggie doll, but if Delaina says okay, I thought we might get her stuff moved to my apartment since she'll be staying there after the memorial."

"Of course." Delaina tried to look at him without looking. He seemed cool as a cucumber. "Love you, Meg. This has been awe- some." She hugged her and walked down the hall to pack. A night alone with Jed. Maybe God did make exceptions.

~ ~ ~

Cabot Hartley fisted the marble counter of his bar. "I don't know how it happened. I mean, we lost that drug-prison scenario in a matter of hours."

Lainey and Jed, Book Two

Boone Barlow sucked on a joint. "In less than a day, it went to hell in a garbage truck. Don't beat yourself up."

"I'll tell you what happened, something I never predicted. Lainey got tangled up with McCrae. The asshole acts like he knows something big about her. How long do you think those two have been hooking up?"

"Not long." Boone looked around. "Nice place you got here."

"Yeah. Another smoke?"

"Believe I will. I think Jed cares about her."

Cabot snickered. "I've never known him to care about much of anything other than that stupid land. You think Fain willed the land to him?"

"Actually, I know some of what the will says. Been paid to keep quiet."

"Are you bluffing me?"

Boone shook his head. "Nope." "Money says you'll talk," Cabot bargained.

"Fain hired me to keep tabs on Jed and Lainey after he got sick. He paid me to keep my mouth shut until the truth comes out, which ought to be any day."

Cabot sipped on his drink. "Do tell now."

"Lainey is Fain Kendall's daughter. There's a chance she *could* own everything on Cash-McCrae Road one day. Fain wants her to have a portion of McCrae Farms, at least."

For a minute, Cabot went speechless. "You should've told me this sooner." He shrugged. "It explains Jed McCrae's recent interest in her."

"Maybe, maybe not. Without an acre of land or a dime to her name, she's the lady to have."

"I think she's as boring as that wall right there. On what are you basing your opinion?"

Boone shrugged. "She and I had a thing."

"No way." Cabot found the combination incredibly interesting. "When?"

"Right before Tory's stroke. She knew how to have a good time, you know? She could make a guy laugh. Innocent, but she flirted. She liked fishin', playin' cards, swimmin' in the creek." Boone drifted into his days spent with Lainey. Exacting revenge had not been effective. He had seen Cabot and Raybon earlier in the afternoon, embroiled in a discussion, perhaps the ideal murder plot. Boone

94

would probably never touch Lainey again, so why wouldn't he want her dead? He didn't.

"Wow, I've missed out on the good parts of her. She's nothing but quiet, frigid, or drunk with me. I suppose you loved her."

"No doubt. Still do."

"Man, I never knew. I've noticed you have opinions about her, but who doesn't? Lainey Cash is the beauty mark of Mallard County."

"The mark she leaves is just as permanent." Boone took a drag.

Cabot grinned his president's grin. "I hope she brands Jed McCrae to the core. Thanks, partner. You made my next decision easier."

~ ~ ~

Jed and Delaina tidied Meggie's den and kitchen. He caught her by the hand. "Wanna grab a bite and try to relax before we go to my apartment and discuss things?" It wouldn't be an enjoyable talk.

She felt like flirting. "Are you askin' me out, Jed McCrae?"

He moved closer; she inched backward against the counter. "Yes, ma'am, I am." He leaned into her. Then they were kissing in Meggie's kitchen. Sloppy, needy, artless smacking. Delaina scooted away and went to her room. She primped and came out with her duffel, wearing a flirty cardigan over her T-shirt and sassy-casual heels on her feet. Jed incinerated her with, "Nice."

She looked fresh and exhilarated. She may never feel that way again in Mallard. Jed felt a sting becoming familiar. Tory Cash entrusted Delaina's farm agent to make decisions in her best interest, no matter what that meant.

~ ~ ~

The late afternoon defined true Houston. Warm, dry, clear. They stopped at a Tex-Mex joint with a cozy outdoor patio. Most folks weren't off work yet. They had the area to themselves. Colored pepper-shaped lights wrapped metal fencing. Spanish ballads from a Hispanic male soloist playing a guitar in the corner tempted dancing. They shared a bowl-size margarita with two straws and a basket of chips and salsa.

While Delaina leaned in for another sip, Jed perused her face with searing blue eyes. "So, now that you've had time to think about it, our night at Calla sparked a decision not to have premarital sex?"

Eyes like quarters, she held icy lime liquid in her mouth and didn't know what to say...Meggie told him something.

LAINEY AND JED, BOOK TWO

"I know we have a lot hangin' over us, but..." He sipped after her and shrugged, like they discussed the weather or sports scores. "Did it make you feel guilty? You chased me like wildfire for a month first."

Maturity tapped Delaina's shoulder. Jed wanted to talk about this. "I absolutely don't regret Calla. *You know that.* Uh, did Meggie say something?" She tried to be Jed-casual. Words "Te amo" repeated in a melody from the corner stage.

"While explaining how great you are, Meggie said it's cute that you bought dirty lingerie although you might wanna wait until you're married now."

Delaina felt herself blush. Jed acted uncomplicated. "Uh, and you need an answer this minute, why?"

His sideways grin romanced. "Because I was hoping to engage in premarital sex with you in the near future, maybe in that black thing. It might be a long time before you accept my marriage proposal."

Delaina felt dizzy-good. Ok, how 'bout tonight then? He liked the black thing. Fine, she'd let him be the one to fool with the buttons and hooks. She sucked hard on the straw, emptying the drink. "Meggie and Lewis are waiting. It's sweet. Nothing to do with you or our night." Jed looked unconvinced. "If you knew about Josiah, you might understand."

"Joe who?"

Uh-oh. "Never mind." She sucked the empty glass idiotically. Jed grabbed a passing server's arm. "Jack and Coke please. Another margarita?" "No. Lime and club soda, thanks."

"Joe who, Delaina?"

"Never mind. No biggie."

Jed looked unconvinced again.

"Josiah Ward, Pastor Ward's son. We, uh, sort of dated in high school. He positively fell in love with me." She looked out at Houston rush hour traffic beginning to thicken beyond the fence. "Still is."

"You mean PK." Short for preacher's kid. Everybody knew PK, nicest guy who lived in Mallard from the nicest family. "He's at seminary now, right?" Lainey Cash, a preacher's wife. Well, hell. Jed smiled.

"That I have a past, however miniscule, is funny to you?" She rolled her eyes. "Yeah, in Kentucky." She ate the last chip in the basket. "Comes to see me when he's home. It's been since Christmas that I saw him. I think he drops by to make sure I'm still pure." She

96

smiled warmly. "He called me after I got engaged to Cabot, crushed, to talk me out of it."

Jed gave one point to PK. "There's nothing miniscule about a future preacher from your home church being in love with you, tryin' to talk you out of marriage to somebody else." Texas breeze took long bangs off Jed's forehead, sloppy shirt blowing too. He had news for PK positively-in-love-with-her Ward. *Jed and Delaina* had a past, twenty years running.

"I mean, he is..." She flicked her hand. "Married to the Lord." A couple settled at a table close by. She lowered her voice. "I slipped out and went campin' with him on my seventeenth birthday. He was about to leave for school. I thought he might try to *you know*. He just wanted to eat s'mores and sleep on a blanket, kiss and talk." Jed had that chin-on-his-chest action going. "It was sweet." It didn't seem *that* sweet when she said it to thirty-year-old, competent, caring Jed McCrae, with all he had done for her. "He gave me these." Jed watched the crosses in her ears flip around. At some point, he had taken her hand and now touched his mama's ring. "Quoted scripture about my body being a temple to remember." Delaina looked at Jed's fingers. "The truth is, after I met you in March, I... Till Meggie and I started talking today, I..." What else to say? His hand on her hand, alone, electrified.

Jed accepted his Jack and Coke. Held it out. "To s'mores and sleeping under the stars with Lainey." He drank.

Ooh, Lainey. That usually meant he might be a tad angry. "You okay, Jed?"

"Yep." He swallowed more whiskey.

That meant nope. More people came to eat. Joy, ease, and sultry Spanish music all around. Fish tacos arrived to share. He didn't quite look at her or act quite right. She reached for his drink and sipped. "Talk to me."

He offered her a taco. Watched her chew and swallow. "I might be jealous of PK." He smiled. "Our night at the river, I wanted to sleep with you under the stars, was about to ask you when the boat... Fain...broke us apart." They'd been robbed of a lot since and would be again. He ate a taco, drank. "I knew we belonged together."

That was sweet. Delaina felt starstruck. Jed grimaced. "Tomorrow is gonna be rough, Delaina, for us. We have Fain's will to get through and meeting your mother and the pregnancy test." He halted. "I

LAINEY AND JED, BOOK TWO

mean, if you wanna do a pharmacy test." He lowered his voice. "I flew here because, yeah, we have things to talk about, but I also wanna make love to you tonight." He undressed her unashamed with perfect blue eyes. "Before hell breaks loose."

Earth moved. *He* inspired. *He* intoxicated. Delaina's mind flashed to Calla Hotel. Things they said, his mouth everywhere. Earth slid out from under the table, out from under her feet. She wanted no boundaries. They had been through hell and had a lot of hell left. "I love you, Jed."

He checked her face. Stunned and seduced. He stroked the ring on her hand. "If you wanna wait, if the preacher's kid got it right with you, tell me. Baby, you're so high up in my estimation, Josiah Ward would have to *be* married to the Lord to reach you." Jed drank the last of his whiskey.

Earth traded places with heaven. Delaina watched the sun sink in golden swaths behind him. Tomorrow would be awful. She could tell from Jed's expressions. "Yes, I chased you like wildfire, James Evan Darrah McCrae, because I wanted you. I still do; you saw the black lace. You paid for it." She laughed quietly. "Take me home to your apartment, big guy." Their hearts braided with knowing faces. "We'll talk and then..." She pulled his hand to her mouth and kissed.

He had a full grin. Gorgeous. "Something we gotta do first." He tucked a Benjamin into the tab folder and pulled her by the hand onto brick pavers in front of the singer. He bent into the breeze, into her. "Dance with me again." Earth slid unhurriedly beneath her black heels. Her body moved with his naturally, her soft curves and his hard planes. Ten or so people ate on the patio. Conversing, cocktailing. Individuals smiled, watched, someone whistled while Jed and Delaina swayed, and generally no one cared on a random Wednesday eve. "You smell good," he said into her hair. "You smell like Jed," she murmured against his shoulder.

"Hmm, what does Jed smell like?"

Delaina sank altogether. "Outdoors, things beyond my control. Breezes and river and rain, mmm, like Cash-McCrae road. Like need, Jed." Her voice oozed her own need. "What does Delaina smell like?"

"Which place?"

Her head shot up, eyes pure green. He winked, sniffed her hair and her breath. "Mint and coconuts, and tonight, lime." She put her head on his shoulder. He kissed her ear and whispered, "Farther

98

down..." His breath hissed; his crotch bumped hers. "Like fate. Dancin' and kissin' and dates and soft sheets, like everything you control. Like..." He bit her earlobe. "Desire, Delaina."

It was her breath that hissed. "You gotta stop."

He twirled her under his arm. "Why?"

"Because when you're bad, I'm worse." She backed into him, slid her bottom down his body like a senorita. The singer, entirely pleased, sang words like mi vida, princesa, amor, siempre. Turning to Jed's front, she gazed upward. Her eyes glowed golden in the happy-hued lights.

Jed kissed her solidly. "Mexican dude's been croonin' his chica into el sacko for about an hour."

Delaina laughed. "No entiendes, mi alma. El canta de siempre amora con su chica."

"Lainey Cash speaks Spanish quite well." His shirt had come untucked. He wheeled them around. "And, baby, I do comprehend that he will love his princess always. That'll croon her right into his bed." His crooked smile sinned. "So, I'm your soul?"

"Si, mi alma, you are, and si, yo hablo Espanol. Gracias, Mallard County High School." They stepped together and apart. She sounded turned on to Jed's ears. "Y tu?"

Yeah, to answer her, he spoke Spanish about as well as she did. Hers scorched him. The way she smiled, spoke a different language, and turned smoothly, if he kissed her again, he wouldn't be able to walk out the door with integrity. "Si, yo hablo Espanol. Gracias, Texas." Jed plucked a red carnation from the nearest vase. He tucked it in her ponytail. "Te amo, mi chiquita bella."

Delaina melted. I love you, my beautiful little girl, he said. She whispered breathily, "Vamos a tu casa ahora."

"Likewise, I can't wait to take you home now." He put a Benjamin in the musician's tip jar and led her off the patio.

~ ~ ~

The early evening defined true Houston. Cool, dry, clear.

They sat on his balcony, a tiny strip with two metal chairs and a round table, which opened from the bedroom of Jed's second-floor apartment. Skinny rails and a skirt of tall landscaping served as a shield from the glitzy pool area below. City lights glowed like a heap of metallic confetti tipped off the back of a dump truck.

She noticed Jed's cleaning service had been today. Turned down his bed and left each bedside lamp burning low, visible through open sliding doors. Pictures of Sophie and Meggie on the desk in the den had disappeared. Replaced by teen Jed and his mama in Paris and Baby Jed and his daddy in front of his father's plane.

Jed brought them bottled waters, sat, and pulled out his phone.

"You've got a view," she murmured. So, this is what it felt like. To know, in a little while, she would get naked with someone she loved on a bed in plain view. Delaina shivered. "That pool area is something else...like Maui or Miami."

He'd been scrolling his phone and looked up. "It's closed after dark."

"And?"

He grinned. "I do love it when Lainey Cash shows up. For now, we gotta discuss the 1. 2. 3. text you sent me." She nodded. "Fain's memorial service. I'm sure it's fine to go. Della knows you're coming for the will." He typed on his phone. "I'm sending you her number if you want to text her that you're coming to the memorial beforehand." *Besides, he already knew she'd be using the number eventually.* Jed felt a nagging burn in his stomach.

Her mother. Her mother's number. Delaina answered in a shiver of new emotions, "Okay."

"We'll leave at six in the morn, fly in my plane, okay? I'll fly you back here."

The way Jed treated her. Patiently, kindly, importantly. He had shown her what he thought she needed to know about his apartment. Told her that his best friend Pate, owner of Bonnou where they ate sushi last time in Houston, knew everything going on in Mallard and would check on her, and when he didn't, Meggie would.

"Number two is about the situation in Mallard and the bank, et cetera. You handled it, and it'll take some getting used to, checking with me as farm manager. With a smiley face emoji." He also smiled. "Gonna take getting used to for us both, cupcake. I've read paperwork and Tory's letter and crunched your farm numbers. I'm ready." His smile vaporized. "No matter what happens in the future, we must meet, discuss, attempt to agree, and take care of the bottom line. It's in the contract, and it's who I am."

Delaina, too, turned serious and confident. "I made a lot of phone calls. Attorney Gage is, uhm, fine with you as manager. He said we're under verbal agreement, since I'm out of town for my own safety. We can sign when we're both in Mallard or he can make arrangements with a lawyer here. Moll and I had a good talk, too. He saw us at the river that night. He knows we care about each other." Delaina shrugged. "You and I can only imagine what it must've been like for him and Maydell, when they first fell in love." Jed couldn't imagine what a ruckus those two caused, way back. Everyone simply accepted Moll and Maydell as part of Cash Way, nowadays.

"So, Moll and Warren support your choice?"

"They know how farm-smart you are, and I, uh...told them that I'd marry you if they didn't agree. You'd be the manager anyway, and no one can stop that." Jed's eyes were large. She giggled and sounded like...Delaina. "We've been under stress and through extraordinary circumstances. I've acted crazy at times. I'm sorry."

"No apologies. I haven't called or texted you because you needed space from all of it. From me." Jed leaned forward and pushed hair away from her neck.

Save her soul. A clear Houston sky made his hair blacker and his eyes bluer. "Jed, I talked to Cabot's father, Joe Cabot Hartley. We're in the middle of a farm season, loan papers signed, you know. That bank's been part of my family a long time. I told him that you and I are interacting, due to both wills. You're financially prepared to bail me out or lead me to sources, if necessary. I told him that Jenna Lee Lester has a previous personal vendetta." She glared. "She doesn't wanna mess with me after everything you've done." Jed smirked. "I also told him that if you call or show up, it's as if it came from me." She glanced. Jed had the neatest look. Shocked and proud. She plunged on. "I talked to Jenna Lee; she handles my accounts." She rolled her eyes. "I said, in my sweetest, most classy way, that she might be working with you, and I expect utter professionalism." She felt a bit shy when she looked over. "Uhm, okay, for now?"

"More than okay. You should sit on my lap." She went readily. "I'm not sure you *need* a farm manager." He chuckled. "To clarify, I couldn't bail you out. Well, I could, but it would wipe out my available cash. I'll inherit everything of my grandmother's, but I like makin' my own way. I favor a strategy where we begin to spread your debt around and put freed-up assets in investments. It's okay to let them think I'd bail you out, though. I'm on board." He kissed

LAINEY AND JED, BOOK TWO

her. Delaina interrupted, "If I'm not safe in Mallard, you're not, and I put you at greater risk."

"What you told them made it clear there are two people to take down. We're powerful together." He shrugged against her. "I may be in danger, but I'm, and don't get mad, the better choice to stay there and run things right now."

"Well, I might be better with a gun." She arched one eyebrow. "You're better with a bow." She jiggled on his leg. "Are you gonna help me with my bow and arrow, Jed McCrae?"

"I'll put my front to your back any day." They started their sloppy, needy, artless smacking again. Either found it difficult to quit. He pulled her hair out of her ponytail, watched it fall.

"So, I'm guessin' I'm tied to McCrae Farms, someway, after the will tomorrow," she wondered.

"Yep."

"I don't want details. I wanna hear Fain's will the way he wrote it as my biological father, without preconceived notions."

"Awfully mature of you." He kissed her hairline. "A few items left to discuss, baby."

"Then we can move on to the most interesting area of our collaboration." Her eyes glittered.

"Hmm." His hmm sounded deep. "If you want to collaborate..." His eyes became slits of intent. "I'm all the way in." She laughed. He patted her head. "Number three is can you come home, yet? Obviously, no." He told her updates from Mallard. "I hope it won't be much longer." Talk of Mallard dampened her good mood. Jed recognized the emotion. Chaos for a head with uncertainty for a heart.

"Jed, I'm tired of everything, truthfully."

"Holding that farm together and living there may not be what you want. Life's full of trades. I wanted to be on my father's land, but it's hard at times. Being away like this might help you appreciate where you come from, or the opposite. We live in a fishbowl."

"Which explains your private nature and getaways to Houston."

He nodded. "One more thing. Pregnancy. A home test could answer it now."

Delaina looked out at pretty pool lights and shiny Houston. "Not tonight. I wanna be twenty and free."

Jed didn't like the sound of that. She might be a mother tomorrow. He might be a father tomorrow. If they were a mother and father tomorrow, they were tonight. No need to point it out; she would run for the hills.

"Oh my gosh, Jed! I drank half of a big margarita and sips of your whiskey." Her hand swished over her belly. "Oh no." He felt so relieved that she cared, he slumped. "Hell, I forgot, too. Shit, would we suck at the parent thing?" Maybe they would, because she had no time to be an adult, and they had no time to be together first.

"You *cannot* cuss like that." She sounded like a mom, outdone with Baby Daddy. Delaina massaged her temples. "I can't think about it yet."

"If you are…" He stumbled on 'if' because he knew she was. "You won't drink again." She would turn twenty-one while pregnant. Wow. "*We* won't drink again. I won't do anything you can't do." Which meant no cigarettes, no alcohol, apparently no cussing, forcing her into a shotgun wedding he knew wasn't best for her, but the mother of his child would be his wife. Probably rare sex, and all that with his ten-years-younger Baby Mama…who got pregnant her first time (Her cross earrings pointed an it's-your-fault finger at him). She would be possibly vomiting, getting rounder (which would be reverent to him but what about her?), maybe embarrassed, partially educated, and they had to efficiently manage 12,000 acres through an entire growing season. Holy Lord. They would fight all the time, and he might lose his mind. This was Delaina. Jed's heart hurt. His mind bled. He couldn't show it. "We're gonna be fine." Jed, too, absolutely needed a mighty good night with her, then they needed to know results. "Delaina, I don't know what you'll feel like after New Orleans tomorrow, but when we fly back here, we could, you know…"

"Do the test?" Mood music from the apartment next door floated over.

"I think we should." The inclination for immediate lovemaking hid. The music held promise.

TEN

Now

Who would've thought JJ, nickname for Jed's wild-and-easy neighbors, might save the night?

"Gotta get something." Jed disappeared inside, returned with a blanket, a deck of cards, and a smile. He placed the blanket on her lap, cards on the table. His thumb hitched over his shoulder. He talked down low. "That's Jessie and Joey. Get ready. One of 'em is bound to pop a head over here and say any-dang-thing." He sat, leaned back, legs stretched. "I call 'em JJ. Can never remember which one's Joey, which is Jessie. They're in that phase, early twenties, two can live cheaper than one, flat broke, Ramen noodle suppers, wingin' it. She's putting herself through college and works two jobs. He sleeps past noon, sings at a club. They smoke weed, screw, fight, screw, you know."

Delaina leveled him. "I have no idea."

"You got the chopsticks, bulldog?" from the other balcony.

Jed chuckled. "You can hear *everything* out here if you use a normal voice." He shuffled cards. "Oh, and they call each other bulldog and poodle." He eased in enough that Delaina smelled his Jed smell. "Nicknames for their..." He pointed at his fly; he pointed at her crotch. "But sometimes, they call each other that."

Delaina's eyebrows raised. "You know an awful lot about Bulldog and...Poodle."

Still leaned in, still easygoing, was her Jed. "They make up nightly, which you can also hear, heads up, if you moan and bang around." He white-teeth grinned. "Lucky for us, Delaina, they're not fightin' tonight 'cause they're playing their, and I quote, 'fuckin' music'." He laughed at the face she made.

Jed, shirt unbuttoned, feet bare, BC jeans, mussed hair, trouble-free grin, shuffling cards. Delaina wanted to play along. "I love it when you do this."

His grin broadened. "Do what? I haven't done anything yet."

She used the same low voice he used. "Tell me stuff. Share yourself. You have an interesting life I know nothing about."

"Back at ya, Miss Cross Earrings."

She bubbled a laugh then looked very intentionally at his crotch. "I want names for our..."

"We lost the mother-freakin' chopsticks, Poodle! It'll be a goddang month before we can afford to wok again."

"Aw, heck no." Jed slid cards from palm to palm. "You wanna play strip poker?"

"Why not, Jed? I wanna call that..." She pointed to his fly. "Big Guy. You know you like my cupcake."

"Why're you gonna do that to me? That's foolish."

She did a cute scrunched up thing with her nose and face. "Girls like to be foolish."

"Whatever, cupcake. You win 'cause I'm crazy about ya. Strip poker?"

"Jed Rich-Ass McCrae!" Delaina watched, uh...Boy JJ's head pop around the corner. Dark spiky hair, big brown eyes, shirtless, good muscles, large Poodle tattoo on his arm. "Who is this?" He sized up Delaina and disappeared. "Hey Poodle, get out here. You're right. Jed ain't single!"

They laughed at JJ, and Delaina focused on their subject at hand. "Yeah, I wanna play. I'll kick your tail at strip *blackjack* if you know how to play." She felt fully relaxed now. Fully into it. The single-couple-sinful-city life. Utterly magical music helped. "Rules?"

"I know blackjack, darlin', and I'll undress you down to your cupcake. Make up rules. I've never strip-played cards."

Delaina rubbed her hands together. "Ooh, I get a first from the big guy."

"Baby, nicknames don't work when I don't know which big guy you're talkin' to."

"Right now, I'm talkin' to both. A first for both big guys." Then like a ball hit her between the eyes, a fact knocked fun away. She glanced

LAINEY AND JED, BOOK TWO

into the softly lit bedroom. She wasn't the first to climb willingly into that bed. Teetering between girl and grown, she wanted badly not to care. She diverted with the first thing that came to mind, "Gosh, that *is* good music. *Who* is that?" Jed had watched Delaina glance into his bedroom, then she said what she said, and he could not help himself; he started kissing her.

"Oh. My. God," from Girl JJ, broke them apart. Delaina faced JJ's balcony; Jed turned abruptly in his chair. Girl JJ was not what Delaina expected. Striking jet-black hair in messy bun perfection with pur-plish-red streaks framing her face, copper skin, lacy lavender bralette, sculpted yoga arms and shoulders. "Hi, nice to meet you," Delaina said, rubbing her kissed lips. She stood and extended her hand, manners taking over. Jed put an arm around her, same roots kicking in. "This is Delaina. She's from my hometown in Mississippi "Oh my gosh, y'all are so freakin' cute. Dang, is she your...girlfriend?" With Boy JJ's head atop hers, Girl JJ looked at Delaina. "Gal, he's been at this apartment since October and nothing, zip, zero, never a female."

"Really?" God did make exceptions! If Delaina lit up too much, she forgave herself for being way out of her league.

Girl JJ slid away. "Here. Wine." She shoved a glass at Delaina. "Tastes crappy, but we ain't loaded like Jed. How long y'all been hookin' up?"Delaina made a face. Jed cleared his throat; this might've been a bad idea. She clanged Delaina's glass and gulped. "To Dana and Jed! Bulldog, whatcha think?"

"It's Delaina," Jed enunciated.

"I think Deh-laina is fine as homemade wine, man." Boy JJ extended his arm and pumped Jed's hand. "Dude, we lost our mother-freakin' chopsticks. I hate to ask again, but..." Jed glanced at Delaina and communicated I-hate-to-leave-you-here. She answered with a got-ta-love-them smile. "Hold on, I'll get them, JJ."

"Girl!" Girl JJ reached as far as she could and gripped Delaina's arm. "That is one good-lookin' farmer." She rolled her eyes toward her own apartment where Boy JJ had gone. "I told him over and over, ain't no way Jed's single, built like a tank. What's y'all's backstory? I'm Joey, by the way. The lazy broke jerk huntin' soy sauce is my live-in thing Jessie. We met in Junior High, but that's a lot of baseball boys and backseats ago, know what I mean?" She drained her wine.

"Oh, I know a thing or two about baseball boys and backseats!" Delaina enjoyed herself. She took an itty-bitty taste of wine, not to seem rude. "The backstory: My family farm is beside Jed's. I'm, uh, a lot younger than him, so…"

"He snitched that puss on the dirt roads till you got legal!"

What? My goodness.

Joey howled and poured herself more wine. It sloshed onto her hand, same color as her hair streaks. "I'm gettin' my Tarot cards out for you two!" She hollered into her side, "Hey, doofus, make yourself useful and get my cards." She sighed. "Men."

Delaina could do this. She *wanted* to do this. To know Jed's grownup life. To be part of it. "Right, men. Definitely predict our future! We need all the help we can get." She didn't realize Jed stood beside her. Boy JJ reappeared. Jed handed him the chopsticks. Delaina set down the wine. "Joey, I love your bralette. I've been wanting one. Where'd you get it?"

Just being nice, Jed figured. Surely, she wouldn't believe Tarot cards or wear flimsy lace over her boobs in public.

"F-Mart. The sex toy, lingerie place two blocks over," Joey called out as she vanished. "By that Cigar Mania, you know, Jed."

No, he didn't, but if Delaina wanted to shop at F-Mart, he would certainly offer to go with her. Jessie, around the corner, prepared their wok meal. Joey appeared with a monstrous grape candle burning. "Y'all need a candle on the table. Jed probably doesn't have candles since women don't spend the night here." She cackled at Jed's thunderstruck face.

Delaina laughed. "Joey, you're great, thanks! Jed, is that true?" Probably so. If he leased the place since October, Delaina knew who he basically had *not* been with.

Jed knew his girl by now; Lucky Number Thirteen expected an answer. "Joey's right. Just you, if I'm extra good." He kissed her. They clasped hands. Joey watched.

Jessie poked his head over hers. "Crap, I'm in trouble. I won't hear the end of you two."

"Because you need to clean up your act and treat me right, bulldog. I tell you that every day."

"Y'all stir-fry *on* the balcony? That *is* romantic, Joey." Delaina maintained her graces.

Boy JJ answered, "First Wednesday of the month is wok-n-fok, while she's still got a paycheck." He had a sleazy look for Girl JJ. "We gonna wok and we gonna fok, just so ya know." Delaina had big eyes,

LAINEY AND JED, BOOK TWO

but everybody laughed. Swaying on her feet, she announced, "Well, I love y'all's sex music! Who is that?"

Jed cleared his throat, knowing what Boy JJ would say.

"LaMontagne for that thingy-thang." Boy JJ rubbed his hands together.

Delaina slapped her leg. "Oh gosh, y'all are funny."

Okay, then. Jed slid a pack of cigarettes from his shirt pocket. "So, JJ, need you to keep it happy this evenin', keep it on LaMontagne." He winked at Delaina. "My girl and I are 'bout to strip it down with blackjack." He gave the cigs to Boy JJ, notoriously out and bumming. "If I play my cards right, I *might* need you to turn up the volume in about an hour."

Delaina felt desired, deviant, delightful. "Yeah, turn it up later. Who knows? Jed *might* get lucky with that thingy-thang."

"Jed's already very, very lucky." His voice had gone very, very low.

Joey announced, "Your cards, Delaina! I'll be there in a minute." She turned into her balcony.

Delaina did a jig. "Ooh, can't wait." She peeked to JJ's balcony. "*Jed,* have you seen this?" Beaded curtains, bamboo placemats, Zen-like plants, drum seating, Moroccan lanterns. He stretched his head over hers, arms around her.

Joey showed up, cards in hand. She had an exemplary body, on display in her hip-riding spandex pants, plus stylish black glasses on her head. "No combined energy. Let her go." She pointed her finger.

Delaina cut her eyes. "Right, Jed. No combined energy."

"That's too bad. I like combining our...energy." He winked.

Joey shooed Jed. "Back off and sit down." Sliding her glasses on, she morphed into a scientist. "Are you interested in tapping into your higher self or capturing lover vibes?"

"Hmm." Delaina took it seriously across the table. Jed almost laughed but figured he'd get slapped. Twice. "My life's a disaster, JJ. But I wanna have fun with it." She did her scrunchy face. "Capture our lover vibes?"

Jed didn't need funky cards and a part-time yoga instructor to ascertain their status. He was going all the way again, in a little while, with candlelit Lainey Cash. He sniffed inadvertently.

"Stop that!" Delaina crossed her arms and pouted. "Anything these cards can do for his arrogance? He sniffs and..." She flicked her hand. "...shrugs and winks about his lovers."

108

Now

"That's not good." Joey spread her arms. "We must clear the past and come into the moment."

"Hey Jolene, it's time to wok-n-fok, baby!" from next door.

"Quiet, dopehead! Turn off the music. I'll be there in five."

Jed, developing a sudden desire not to get chastised or slapped, spoke seriously. "My past hasn't been brought into this space. I was thinking about her..." He glanced at Delaina. "When I sniffed." Delaina rolled her eyes.

Joey answered, "The future is not ours to choose. Open your hearts and minds to whatever the universe has in store, patterned for your most fulfilling life."

"Okay, me first." Delaina had an impulse to take Jed's hands. He might not be in her future? The odds were not in their favor. "I'm ready for whatever the universe designs." Eyes open to Jed, shirt wide, hair flopping, staring at her. She couldn't prevent her smile. It felt like hippy wedding vows. "I respect our individual fulfill-ment and how we together...might or might not intertwine for the greater good."

How was Jed supposed to let go of her? He wanted to intertwine with her for the greater good. Right now. "Same. I..." He what? *He wanted her.* In his life always. She's *twenty,* the universe whispered. "I love you, Delaina, but I let go of what I want in order to receive information that the universe has for you, for me, for us."

"Oh God, you're adorable!" To Joey, "I wanna kiss him; I don't think my energy cleared!"

Everyone laughed. Jed snatched a kiss. "Okay." Joey clapped twice. "We'll do both. Two cards. For Delaina and for your relation-ship. Delaina, close your eyes, take a breath, select." Her fingers slid out a card. She saw a lady in a crown and robe, holding a scepter. Vulnerably, she looked to Joey. "The Empress is the mother of Tarot cards, fertile and receptive. She indicates mothering and pregnancy. She is passionate, seeking unconditional love."

Delaina watched her wide-open future vanish into the Milky Way. Awful tomorrow coming at her. "I'm meeting my mother soon, and I'm exploring my relationship with Jed. My life is changing." She took a breath. "I'm starting to understand the... responsibility of allowing others in. I want to take charge as a woman, to be sensual and sen-sible, wherever that takes me."

109

LAINEY AND JED, BOOK TWO

Jed decided he would read Tarot cards with her any night.
Have mercy.

"Okay, Jed, choose y'all's relationship card. Close your eyes, take a breath."

He figured for Delaina, this proved, he'd do anything. A jolt of supernatural swished. Jed flipped and saw *Adam and Eve?*

"Oh!" Joey had a broad smile. "The prized Lovers card. The nude man and woman, hinting of Eden, are opposing forces seeking a sublime and cosmic union, balanced by the fruitful garden through harmony and trust. The serpent is a reminder of obstacles. The angel encourages openness while respecting morality and togetherness."

Jed saw his future as bright as the Texas stars. He grinned at Delaina, slightly conceited, hand dashing through his hair. "I hear the universe loud and clear."

Joey looked back and forth. "Hold hands and share the potency." Jed reached for Delaina's hands. Delaina's eyes danced. "Thank you, Jed." "Thank you, Delaina."

"Good. Great!" Joey declared.

"JJ, that was actually pretty extraordinary." Jed pulled out his wallet. "Y'all go out to dinner tomorrow night." He withdrew another Benjamin. "I insist." Joey snatched the bill and gathered cards.

He called out, "Hey JJ, your girl's headed over with cash. Give me LaMontagne, buddy." He got their playing cards, slid them from hand to hand. "No poppin' your heads over here. We're not exhibitionists like y'all."

Jed had seen them naked? Lord help.

~ ~ ~

Holland would've slept indefinitely if Maydell hadn't come in. "Holland, honey? Me and Moll's about to watch a movie downstairs. You wanna come?"

She opened her eyes. What time was it? What *day* was it? She looked around. Night, again. "I guess I should get up and move around." Yes, and work and interact, her conscience told her.

"We'll wait to start till you're downstairs." Maydell walked out.

Holland stood, swayed, weakened from doing nothing. She hadn't showered, wore the frumpy pajamas she slept in last night. Her glossy chestnut hair, matted. Her teeth needed brushing. She walked downstairs.

Moll and Maydell sat on a sofa in the great room at Cash Way, staring at the flat-screen TV on the wall. They looked lost and terrible, but God bless them, they were getting up and putting one foot in front of another every day, unlike her. "What are we watching?" She tried to smile.

A door opened and shut in the next room. The front door of the foyer. Rhett hollered, "Hey, Daddy?" Holland's head turned. He halted at the opening.

Her breath caught. He looked tired and distracted. She had come to realize from being around Jed, Eli, and now Rhett, the overworked farmer look appealed to a woman. Rumpled hair, shadowed eyes, tight jeans. A relief to feel something stir inside her besides loss.

Rhett worked all the time. Holland wondered if he'd always been like that or if it was how he dealt with the aftereffects of his brother's death. "I need you to follow me in the truck," he said to his father. "Then drop me off at my house. I'm movin' the tractor to the next field, so it'll be ready to go in the morning." A common farming practice, Holland had learned. "I'll go, Rhett. Let your parents try to enjoy their movie." She stood, swayed. "Are you sure?" Maydell asked. "Are you able?"

"Of course." She walked toward Rhett, who had become a plastic version of himself.

"Like that?" he finally got out.

She looked down. Pink ice cream printed PJs. "Sure, why not? Tractors and pajamas. It should be a thing." She reached when she got close to him, to pull on his cap, and caught herself. "You work half the night." She looked at Moll and Maydell. "Hope it's a good movie. Bye."

Rhett followed her out. "I need this, Rhett...because I'm...alive." She turned to him, humble and teary. "I'm about to drive a truck for the first time. Across this beautiful farmland, under a blanket of stars, in fuzzy slipper socks, following a good-looking, hardworking farmer in a technological, gigantic machine that scares the bejesus out of me."

That made him smile. She made herself smile. "I'm warning you, I'm stinky."

"So am I." You smell just right, she thought. "Go drive a truck, miss." He tossed her the keys

~ ~ ~

LAINEY AND JED, BOOK TWO

"Where'd you learn, D?" From Jed.

D. How sweet. Delaina smiled inside. "Rhett and Eli. Played cards with them on slow days sometimes."

Wow, she'd be formidable then. From Jed, "The basics. Aim is 21 without going over. First card is dealt facedown, second and any others show. Numeric cards are face value. Royal cards are ten. Ace equals one or eleven."

"Correct." Their look, steaming. "Now our rules about stripping. We declare our wishes before each round. We're wearin' three articles of clothing to be fair."

"Is that so?" Nice. It meant she wore no panties. Jed made a bridge of the cards in his hands. "You're losin' your jeans, Miss Cash, this round."

"Wrong. Your shirt. I'll feast my eyes on your black-haired arrow as much as I want."

He snickered and dealt cards. "You're so damn competitive."

"I'm taking Big Guy to that bed in a few. First time in his apartment. Sad. Clearly hasn't been getting any."

Jed's look seared her. "He clearly hasn't." A ten to Delaina and Jack of Diamonds to himself on top. Tied. "Hit me," she whispered. He did. She showed nineteen. Crap. He stayed. They turned over facedown cards. D, 23 J, 18. "Stand up, unzip, step out."

"Enjoy," she enticed. "It's all I'm losing." She dropped her jeans.

"Hellllo, cupcake. Shirt, this round?"

"Yeah, yours, Jed McCrae." Two could play his way. Delaina wrapped the blanket around her shoulders like a cape. "I'll take the cards." She shuffled as competently as Jed. Inches from her cupcake.

Sweet Jesus. As good as shuckin' oysters in her jeans. "Don't bite off more than you can chew, baby doll."

"I think I've proven I can chew a large bite."

Jed showed six; she showed nine. Both took a hit. Before they could flip, "Twenty-two? Twenty-freakin'-two?" from Boy JJ.

"I know this story," Jed whispered as they flipped. D 20, J 18. He shrugged out of his shirt. "She thinks he's been with six, so she says five for her. When they start drinkin', they argue how many she's actually been with."

Delaina looked at his awesome arms, taut chest, snake of black hair. "God, I love you bare-chested. *Twenty-two, really?*"

112

Now

"Back at ya, peaches." Jed sniffed. "Boy JJ's been with thirty. He does the ole guy thing and divides by 5, talkin' to her. You're losin' your T-shirt this time." He took the cards. "I'll take it off for you, then you can sit on my lap and bake a cupcake." He started dealing.

"Your jeans, obviously, and you may not get a chance to bake my cupcake, Mister 60. Sixty, Jed? Hit me."

Delaina showed 14. Jed showed 12. He took a hit. They flipped. A clanging of dishes resonated above lustful music next door. "Hey JJ," Jed called out. "Delaina's lost her pants and now her shirt. Simmer down; it's wok-n-fok night."

"Fok you," Delaina said, stepping toward him.

"Raise your arms, pretty woman." ...Down to her nude satin bra. What allure. He kissed her lips. She pulled away. "Sixty lovers, Jed?"

"You can be so female." He put her butt on his lap and draped the blanket over her shoulders. "You think I'd lie about that to you? You know I love you, Delaina thirteen. This time, my jeans if I lose, I guess. And if I win..."

Delaina thirteen. Delaina dismayed herself with how much she liked it.

"Get decent, you two!" From Boy JJ. They were decent enough, backs turned in Jed's chair, blanket over her. "We're going to bed." Their heads turned to Jessie. "I wanna say thanks. Joey's so excited about y'all, she's gone to the butt drawer! Thanks to y'all and *Fifty*."

"Ha! I know what you mean; a lot of us have *Fifty* to thank! Night."

`Lights went out. Music went up.

"What the heck do you have *Fifty* to thank for?"

"My sex education, of course. Let's play." She rubbed her hands. "*Fifty*, Miss Maydell, and church."

"I bet the book's beside your Bible in your nightstand drawer." His finger slid her strap over her shoulder.

She giggled. "Guilty." She pulled her strap up. "I haven't lost this yet."

He kissed her. "That's misleading education, darlin'. Real life's not gonna be a storybook."

"I know."

Jed sat back. That could only be directed at him. He flat refused to be jealous of a book character. She took the cards, shuffled, winked at his aggravated face. "Better," she clarified. "Real life with you is much better, and I haven't scratched the surface." She started to deal.

113

LAINEY AND JED, BOOK TWO

His hand went to her thigh, gripped the inside. "I haven't stated my intention."

Delaina gestured to her bra. "Isn't it obvious?"

His mouth whispered on her ear, "You lose, and..." Something about dipping fingers in a cupcake.

Her heart scampered on her ribs. "I have no motivation to win."

"Use that competitive spirit, Lainey Cash. Think hard." He stroked her tummy. "What happens if I lose?"

Her hips twisted. His jeans scrubbed against the back of her leg. "If you lose..." She kissed him, needing something, anything. "Game is over. I want you to take me to your bed."

His shoulders straightened. "Deal the cards, ma'am. This is a good round."

Her fingers shook when she placed two cards down then two up. Jed, the King of Diamonds. She, the Queen of Hearts. "You've got to be kidding me."

"The universe is on board," Jed muttered. "Stayin'," he said to his dealer.

"Stayin'," said Delaina. Cards flipped; breath held. Jed, Ace of Spades. Delaina, Ace of Diamonds. D 21, J 21. She dropped the deck. Cards slid everywhere. She reached around his shoulders and kissed Jed desperately. "Only fair we do both," she suggested. He pulled her back against his chest, shifted her bottom onto his lap centered, placed each leg on top of his legs, let his hands slide upward over her chest. "You cold, Delaina?"

"Mmm." Her eyes closed. "Yes and no."

"Cover up with the blanket if you want to." He pushed her shoulders forward. Her bra landed on his shirt. His legs moved out, moving hers open. She tilted into his hand. "Been eleven days. God, I've missed you, Delaina." He delivered the most wonderful satisfaction. Her arms reached backward around his neck. Delaina writhed sensually against him, her sensuality culminating gracefully.

Lips apart but close, their eyes open, the force inside burned beautifully. She pulled on his head with her hands, wanting his lips on hers to camouflage her response. He pulled his head away, watched the snaking of her hips. Whispering his name she could not prevent, without his mouth on hers to cover.

They remained heads close, holding each other tight, well beyond her finish.

Now

~ ~ ~

To be, for a minute. If possible, Delaina backed more into Jed's body. The chair cut into his shoulders. He didn't care. They absorbed the feeling until he whispered, "You have the black lace?"

"Isn't it a little late to undress me?"

A kiss on her cheek, her ear, into her hair. "I thought I might… dress you."

Holding her blanket, she stood. Jed blew out the candle. They walked into his bedroom. She sat on the end of his bed, content and wrapped.

"In your bag?"

"Hid on bottom."

He dug around. Produced a garter belt, put it back, produced an excuse for panties. Kept them. Felt around. Produced the glamorous corset. He flipped off the closer lamp; light in the room halved perfectly.

At some point, she had unbuttoned his jeans, Delaina observed. Jed personified masculinity, shirtless, pants undone, holding black lace. She dropped her blanket and stood. "I'm yours, big guy."

He drank in her nude body by faint lamp. "You okay with doors open for the music and breeze?" "I'm good." He bent down. "Step in." The seductiveness of it surprised Delaina. He took his time getting her underwear on evenly. She opened her arms out. He put the corset around her. Fastened three or four middle buttons. "You're way too adept with those buttons, Jed McCrae."

"I plead the fifth." He stood back. "Killer on you, but I wanna know…" Appraisal until Delaina felt almost shy. "…what you thought about when you bought it."

"I think you like me naked."

That Jed grin, the logo of arrogant. "You think right."

"We were in the lingerie boutique." She flicked her wrist. "Meggie sifted through all that…lacy pastel gift wrap. I saw this and thought, *me and Jed*." She executed a turn. He gripped her butt. She laughed.

He held on. His head bent down. "Why?"

"No pretending. We belong like this. Is that a good explanation?" She faced him.

"Do you know what a privilege you are?" He sounded respectful and secure. "Everything about you, I want it to unfold your way." Fifteen thousand times for fifty years, he thought but didn't say.

LAINEY AND JED, BOOK TWO

He picked her up. She wrapped her legs around his waist. Urgency took them to bed. He sat her down, his knees on the floor.

"We're gonna use a condom, Jed?" They had to. No more of tomorrow. ...His face couldn't lie. "You forgot. Tell me you didn't."

"I, uh..." Yes, he forgot. He'd been overseeing 12,000 acres and a criminal investigation for a week with her stashed away, two states over, both in danger. To fly a day early was on a whim and inconvenient and filled with wondering what would happen after New Orleans. Appropriate that he knelt because he felt an inch high. "I'm sorry. I forgot."

"Your black suit, our night at Calla. You said you had three in your pants pocket. Is the suit here?"

It made Jed ache, how much she wanted to. His finger traced the top of her corset. "Good thinking but at the dry cleaners in Mallard." Forgetting threw Jed off course. Everything about Delaina threw him off course. "You won't get pregnant, Delaina. Trust me."

Resentment manifested and said it all. "Yeah." She crossed her arms "It's hard to get pregnant when you're pregnant."

Right or wrong, that maddened Jed. "It takes two."

"Or, one to say no. So, no." She became a woman, black lace and responsible.

Jed supposed that's what he wanted her to be. He supposed for the rest of their lives she would be capable of making him this defenseless, in one way or another. Wrong of him to do what he was about to do. "I guess that's all, then." He went to shut the doors, to shut out the sexy music, colder than he meant to be.

Before he closed them, Delaina tried, "I don't wanna fight with you." She kissed his shoulder.

She was irresistible. He turned. "I forgot. Not an excuse, but the past eleven days have been..." She knew how these eleven days had been. It's why they needed tonight. "We can go buy condoms or not do anything or you can trust me." He slid his hands up through her hair. The way she looked at him. Wanting *and* unsure. He caused that in her because of last time. Because of everything since. "Lainey baby, I'm gonna pull out." She stared at his open pants, from his vulgarity or because she wanted him or because she had to decide.

"Come here." He pulled her close. "I'm so sorry," he whispered. "I feel like I let you down a lot." The shuffling-touching-needing thing

Now

they were doing was not dancing. Nor was that dancing music. "You throw me off because I care too much."

"I'm not sorry, if that's what I do to you."

He picked her up, took her to the end of the bed, held on to her too tightly, waiting.

"I trust you." His lips pursed. "Jed, I do."

He put her on the bed more forcefully than Delaina expected, stripped his jeans, and crawled on top of her. He tore through her corset buttons with his teeth and kissed her body exquisitely. With music like that and Jed naked on top of her, Delaina no longer cared about consequences. Again.

ELEVEN

You

R hett. He was, and wasn't, Eli.

After Holland followed his tractor to the field, Rhett had climbed in the truck, smelling like Eli...or Rhett...and she had driven him to the rental house. It hurt to arrive there with the wrong brother. Eli's absence wanted to grab hold.

Till she realized, maybe Rhett was the right brother. The biggest difference between the two could not be denied. Eli, dead. Rhett, alive.

They had talked in the cab, truck running- not about anything personal; she asked questions about farming and he answered. She did not go inside. He did not invite her inside. Would she have gone? She didn't know. An industrious woman until Eli's death, her pajama-farm outing did turn things around.

She had to start living again.

Now she drove down a dark Cash-McCrae Road toward Lainey's estate. Her temporary home. Holland trembled. It might've been from happiness or relief, that she got out for an hour. Mostly, she trembled from exhaustion. Tomorrow, she would rise early, dress well, get stronger, and make a plan.

Atlanta, the obvious choice. Her father would give her a job and her family could help with the baby. Moll and Maydell lived for the baby's arrival, and not much else.

She wanted to stay.

She turned into the drive, lit up in Cash Way glory. She glanced at the clock. 10 PM. Driving a truck proved fun. Windows down, stars shining, pink pajamas.

She punched the brake. The sight before her punched her lungs. Cabot's foreign SUV, parked front and center. He sat in the swing on the front porch.

Holland swayed when she stepped out. He met her on the driveway in darkness."They said I was welcome to wait."

She couldn't see his features. "Why are you here?" Her knees knocked.

"To check on you. You don't answer your phone. You've been a faithful employee. Did everything I asked of you." She caught a glimpse of his presidential grin. "Right? Everything I asked."

"Right." She made balls of her hands, to somehow hold her up.

"The least I could do is drop by to make sure you and the baby are okay."

Her legs didn't hold. She clutched Cabot's arm for support. "I'm sorry. I need to sit."

Cabot pulled her to the porch swing. "Sit." He sat by her. He pushed the swing into motion with his feet. "So, how is our baby?"

What a ridiculous sound she made. "I...married Eli."

"Which proves nothing but your bad judgment. You'll need to use better judgment tonight." The swaying stopped. "Let's revisit a different evening. When you came to offer your condolences to Lainey here at Cash Way after Tory Cash died."

No, no, no.

"You followed me into town when you left, so we could catch up on work."

Cabot had come at her like a wild animal in her apartment that night. When Eli showed up, minutes later, she couldn't believe it.

The very night before that, the night that Cabot stayed in New Orleans with Lainey, the night Tory died, she and Eli saw each other at MacHenry's, left together, and had a one-night stand in her apartment. She had hoped he'd be there when she got out of the shower. She had hoped he'd call her the next day. He did neither.

The next evening, she went to Cash Way to offer her condolences. Eli acknowledged her with nothing more than a smile. Cabot followed her home. They had sex. Eli showed up. She wanted a chance with him. A chance she would've lost, if she told him the truth.

Thus, she was intimate with both men that night. Never again with Cabot, but...

"How sad for the Smiths if your child doesn't belong to Eli, Holland."

LAINEY AND JED, BOOK TWO

The baby she carried *could be* Cabot's. Everything with Eli after that night, rushed, an effort to forget. Her extreme dramatics since his death, a result of the guilt.

Cabot whispered, "Let's not tell them that you had sex with me and Eli on the same night." The swinging began. The brown in his eyes met the brown in hers. "Let's not tell anybody that the baby could be mine. Agree?" The swing braced her back. Holland's upper body couldn't hold her. She nodded. "Want to hear what I think we should do?" Her head twisted *no* rapidly. "That's bad judgment, Holland. I'll ask you again. Do you want to hear my good idea?"

"Holland? Cabot? Everything okay?" Moll had come out the door.

Cabot stood. "I'm leaving." He clicked his mouth. "You and Maydell were right. Holland is certainly not well enough to return to work. She would need to start by getting dressed." He offered a caring smile. "She's been such a fine employee." He looked the good-natured part, standing under the porch light in his dark suit with his sandy hair. "She and I have just agreed to paid leave until further notice. She loved her job and I...have discovered that I can't do mine without her. Glad she is here with all of you. At Cash Way. Right where she needs to be." He made a face. "Sorry about me and Lainey and any problems it caused during your time of loss."

Moll frowned. "Lainey told me she was fearful of you after the episode here on the porch with Jed."

"Of course I lost my cool when they admitted she was cheating on me throughout our engagement." Cabot's face, the epitome of humility. "I apologize. I won't cause any problems."

Moll, a shell of himself, had no further objection. "Well, it's a generous offer. I'm sure Holland is grateful."

Cabot shook Moll's hand. "I know your grandchild will be the bright spot. You all take care." He stepped toward Holland. "Any questions?"

"None."

"Get a good night's sleep. Soon, I'll call you." Cabot felt like somersaulting off the porch, screaming Hallelujah.

~ ~ ~

Trust. Jed had to have Delaina's.

"Where do you least expect me to kiss you?" he asked, while kissing her everywhere.

"I don't know." Her eyes lit his. "My butt?"

"Your butt." His chuckle, aroused and surprised. "Okay, turn over." She turned into his cool sheets. She felt uncovered. He kissed her lower back then each cheek. Licking and nipping unrushed. The unexpectedness and compliance felt amazing. He crawled up her back. "Where have you never thought of kissing me?"

"Jed, I've kissed you everywhere. While you slept at Calla. Every inconspicuous place." She elaborated, "I wanted to kiss you somewhere no woman had or would."

His breath jumped. He eased onto his back. "Choose your favorite then." "Okay, but what's this we're doing?" Quietly, he said, "Revealing ourselves, D."

"Oh." She warmed to it. What girl wouldn't? To be that personal. She considered his fabulous body. "My favorite." Easy. Her face disappeared below his waist. His hand gripped her hair. "Get up here. That'll put an end to this." She crawled over him face-to-face. "Ask me something bold."

Delaina felt cherished. "Okay, who was your best lover, and why?"

"Aw, damn, Delaina." Her breasts brushed against his chest; her lace panties scratched his middle. "You're the one that I think about this way now."

"This was your idea, big guy. I'm talkin' about skills. Spill it."

He shrugged. "Mallory. Atlanta, med school."

Mallory. She never heard her name before. Delaina tensed. *Grow up. You asked.* Delaina's fingers stroked his stubble. "What was it about Mallory?"

"Both of us, older. Cool dates. We did weekends. She was relaxed. No big deal, in or out of bed."

A lot for Delaina to swallow. Mallory was the antithesis of her. *Stay unruffled and trust him.* "You loved her? What number was she?" She wanted a number to gauge how far removed he was *from Mallory.*

"We didn't talk about love or the future." Jed checked her face. Calm, listening. Wow. "I liked her." He kissed his soulmate. "Sometimes, like is enough. Love is…" He grinned and aimed. "Complicated."

Delaina shrugged. "Sorry." She wasn't sorry. They would have a life like that, and sex like that, one day. Better, because of love and patience.

"She was, uhm…" One blue eye closed. "Eight or nine, I guess. Eight."

Far enough removed. "Ended why?"

He tipped her chin. "Enough about her. I moved home."

"Okay, ask me whatever you want and kiss my booty." Each laughed.

"Turn over." His teeth nipped her spine from neck to waist. "Why don't you wanna cook for me? You weren't nice about it."

Delaina had to think hard...his jeep, on the way to the stadium. She had screamed at him that she'd never cook for her man. Or marry Jed. This man who licked the backs of her thighs. "I didn't mean it. *Jed*, that feels great. Uh, I needed to get at you somehow. For your competency, experience, and for what you did to my emotions." His mouth reversed up to her neck. He covered her atop her back.

"Delaina, these nights we've spent apart, I've thought about having you over. You in my kitchen with me. A meal at the table. A date." Delaina surged inside. Dampness from his kissing felt cool on her skin from shoulders to thighs in the breeze. "I don't know if that sounds fun to you, but..."

"Sounds like bliss, Jed."

His arms pushed under her and wrapped her. He smothered her from behind. held her like she was a treasure. She could do nothing but allow. How marvelous. "Which scares you the most about tomorrow, D? Your mother, Fain's will, or the pregnancy test?"

Marvelous disappeared. "The test, no doubt. Permanent."

Jed's weight doubled on her. He slid off, onto his back, staring upward. Delaina turned into him. She didn't want the night to end badly or sadly. She wanted to be the sensual, passionate woman of her Tarot card. Music carried on as if making love trumped all. She propped her head on her hand, watched his eyes. "What's something you really like about me?"

His finger traced her lips. "You're funny. You lack a filter. You make me laugh. We laugh."

Her finger traced his lips. "It's our night. You want me to be funny?" She could be. She could be anything, not to see Jed shut down. She caused that in him because of last time. Because of everything since.

"If you can think of something funny, that'd be great." His authenticity was heartrending.

"JJ. They're funny, Jed."

His mouth hitched. "You like 'em?"

She reached around his waist, scooted closer. "They're so real." Streamers of sharing softened their bed. "When Jessie said, 'We gonna wok and we gonna fok...'" Their laughter interweaved. "If we can ever hold it together long enough, we'll be like them. But with tact and respect. We're fun, too. Whatcha think *they're* doing now?"

Jed watched Delaina's eyes flashing. Her secret tone, their bodies close, he grinned privately at her. "Lord, I don't know. Something neither of us has done or thought about doing." He kidded, "Well, maybe you've read about it."

Delaina ran her hand between them, palm on his abs. "You gonna want a butt drawer, Jed?"

And there it was, her no-filter. "Uh."

She laughed. "Gotcha." She kissed him provocatively.

"You're the one with guilty pleasures in your nightstand, cupcake." She covered her face, peeked at him. He took her hands away. "Sweetheart, if we can ever hold it together long enough, like you said, then what I'm sure I'll want is every inch of me to satisfy every inch of you and vice versa. In time." He popped the side elastic of her panties. "Beyond that, I have no...requirements or demands." Blue eyes narrowed. "On the other hand, if you make a trip to F-Mart, you go with me."

All of it together made her laugh. She exuded confidence. "I liked it when you called me Delaina thirteen." Their noses almost touching, their bodies touched everywhere. "It's, I don't know, classified. Like between us."

He popped the side elastic harder. "I'll keep it in mind, Delaina thirteen."

Delaina wanted to give him what he gave to her. Expressiveness and seduction. She wanted to be...like Mallory. His partner. "Do whatever you wanna do to me now, Jed. I've missed you."

Jed's eyebrows raised. "Yes, ma'am." He took pleasure in winning over her body through ideal attention.

She wanted to participate. She wished for lotion or oil. She improvised. "Jed?" She licked the palm of her hand to cover it in slobber. She knew more about this than he realized. She reached down and wrapped her fingers around him. He swished breath. She knew what to do. Kind of. She loved the way it felt to hold him. "Like this?"

Jed, ready to be inside her, obvious in the hardness of his muscles bunched against her skin, obvious in the hardness where she stroked him. "Almost...perfect."

"What would make it more perfect?"

LAINEY AND JED, BOOK TWO

He patted between her legs. "This."

What bait. Her heart fluttered. She eased onto her back. Her head twisted. "Make love to me." Jed wanted to pause, rewind, replay. That would go down as the sexiest request he had in recall. He climbed over her.

The song seemed chosen by gods. Every feeling became kissing. She had no idea they could be like this, this good, this consuming, before they started. Nothing she'd read or heard did justice to their longing.

"We've got this, Delaina. Believe it." He meant *everything* here forward. Her heart hoped beyond hope. She wanted to be uniformly meaningful. So her legs parted ways. His hand came down over her mouth. "Bite."

Oh God, they were about to again. She felt heaven open. They got a second chance. She whispered, "*No.*" Eyes wide, body tense. She kissed his hand reverently, where she last mutilated. "It's almost healed."

"Leave a scar." He never stopped crashing into her, exponentially more persistent than their first time. It was nature; it was beauty. It wasn't great. Tears leaked out of her eyes.

He squinted. "You're crying."

She smiled. "Because it's good. I'm sorry that's sappy."

He touched her cheek. "Forgiven. You're never sappy. But *I'm* sorry because you're lying." How did he know? "Your eyes are bold and green. I know you."

"Keep going." Their lips found each other. She thought above the burn, thought only of him. They moved together until a vague premonition from last time condensed. Jed was almost done. Delaina felt full and empty.

"Do anything with me," she blurted.

Suddenly he seemed heavy on her. "I know you want more. Give me a sec."

Heaven opened wider. She *had* to stop crying. She swiped her cheeks. *More.* Joy, no room for tears. "Stay with me, D. It's gonna be really good, next time we're together."

She got it. This was practice. His indelicate possession, again and again. Not so good, this time. But it was. It was...something. He breathed on her ear. "I want you, baby girl, night after night." His chest expanded, overcome by the prospect.

"There'll be a next time, Jed, I swear. Tomorrow, I hope."

"Give me your feet." She bent her legs up, he held her feet, put one then the other on his shoulders. She resided from hip to hip, fireworks bursting inside. "You move, sweetheart." He grinned. "I can't. I'm sorry. You do this to me." Delaina felt indecent, beyond recognition in her display. He reached over and flipped off the lamp. Houston, Texas visited incandescently. "Now, do what you want."

She did.

The music ended. "I'm too loud," she admitted.

"I owe JJ for many nights." He chuckled. She laughed. He clasped her hips, never stopped crashing into her. It was nature; it was beauty. It was wonderful. "Let go, Delaina." It sounded like hurry, if you can. "Then give me your hands." Mouth onto hers, blistering, tasting of desperation.

She shattered into a thousand beautiful pieces.

She remembered her hands when he bolted. He pushed one onto himself and cupped the other underneath urgently.

~ ~ ~

Quietness engulfed them.

Jed had tucked Delaina beside him, his body facing her, she on her back, depleted. His hand rested on her tummy. "Delaina, soon. I'll be better at this."

What? *Better?* Goodness, she couldn't imagine better.

He cleared his throat with a smile. "When I get used to the fact that you really are gonna do this with me."

"Mmm, get used to it." Peace and prospects glowed on her face. "A lot." They grew sleepy, not wanting to sleep.

Dawn spelled *The* tomorrow.

"Jed, promise me something." He frowned. They couldn't do promises, hanging on by a thread until tomorrow and after tomorrow. "I might run."

Yes, she probably would.

She touched his mama's ring. "Show up. Remind me." Her eyes, heavy-lidded, beseeched his. "I want this and us." She fell asleep before he replied.

Twelve

Me

Jed was sipping coffee in his apartment kitchen when Delaina appeared.

He got up, got dressed, and got away from her before he took advantage of a wakeup session. He looked at home there in the partial light, his eyes skimming his phone. "Mornin'."

"Good morning." Her voice hitched. He glanced, concerned. "You okay?"

Tomorrow had arrived before morning light. "Fine," she lied, popping a grape in her mouth. Delaina never contacted her own mother about going to the memorial service. It was too hard.

"You look beautiful."

With her hair down and minimal makeup, she wore a polished black dress and her kitten heels. Jed wore the navy suit and blue shirt, no tie, she remembered he wore to church on Easter with his mama last year. "Well, thank you, to the finest man alive."

The ride consisted of driving by homes and stables until they got to a dusty road with expansive patches of grass on either side shown by headlights and earliest dawn. A blacktop landing strip ran neatly through pasture. Jed parked his jeep. Delaina followed him to a hangar. He introduced her to the airport overseer and went through a preflight check. Delaina had never flown in a private plane. Jed slid next to her and grumbled, "Seatbelt." He smelled like coffee and shaving cream, no stubble on his smooth face. Delaina stayed soundless as they taxied. She didn't know if Jed liked having passengers in the plane or if he could talk and fly at the same time. The land beneath, one and a thousand colors, swirled into an interesting picture as they climbed. What a nice feeling, to look on without having to take part. "You've never flown in a private plane?" he asked when his plane took to the sky.

She shook her head no. "I like it."

"Neat, up here. For a while, you're removed from problems and twelve thousand acres of land that need our attention, down there." He patted her leg. She watched the ground. Removing herself, for dwindling minutes. "About today, I think you're doing the right thing, D. Takes courage." She nodded.

Nothing else said, other than comments about piloting or scenery, until Jed's effortless landing.

~ ~ ~

A cab took them to a chapel. The chapel had a vestibule. Three ladies stood talking. Delaina's high heels met with the floor. A hush fell. One woman stepped forward. "Hello, Delaina." She extended her hand. "I'm Francie, Fain's sister. These are my daughters." Before Delaina could respond to *her aunt*, Francie smiled at Jed. "Hi, Jed."

"Francie, LeAnna, Lynn Rose, it's been a few months," Jed's voice resonated through the room.

"Yes, since your mother's funeral."

Jed gave the older woman a light hug. "Where's Kent?"

"Convention in Dallas he couldn't skip."

Dumbfounded Delaina stared at Jed. He knew her family by name, by face, from memories. He knew how many first cousins she had, if she had paternal grandparents, their addresses, their ages. He probably spent Christmases, Easters, birthdays and summer vacations with *her* family. They were technically *his* family. "Excuse me," she whispered and slipped out the door. She propped against a column outside. Precarious footsteps got her attention. The woman standing before her had blunt-cut, frosted hair and eyes as green as jade. She clutched a macramé bag and wore a broomstick silk skirt of earthy colors with a baggy sweater. Average in height, slim for her age. She licked her lips and mouthed Hello.

Delaina fixed her eyes on the city street. No tears came. She said, in a voice that didn't sound like hers, "I'm Delaina."

"Do you know who I am?"

Potential responses came. None fit. Delaina leaned harder against the column. Her mother took steps toward her. She gazed at a beautiful, broken, girlish woman. Her daughter. Della Kendall said the first thing she thought. "You cut your hair."

Delaina turned around to go in, trembling with emotion. "So did you."

~ ~ ~

There were thirty oak pews in the chapel.

Delaina counted to neutralize the reminiscent tale of Fain David Kendall's life. Her father came from poverty, put himself through law school, dabbled in photography, played the saxophone, owned a sailboat. He loved his new wife dearly, no mention of the daughter they shared or his first wife. Elegant Ms. Cass, avoided. His stepson referred to vaguely once, "Fain spent the bulk of his adult life in Mallard, Mississippi. He assisted in the continued success of McCrae Farms, known throughout the Southeast for its contributions to agriculture. He passes from this life knowing it will thrive under the competent leadership of Jed McCrae." When the priest sat, Delaina's first cousins LeAnna and Lynn Rose stood and began a duet without instruments. Their gentle voices glided.

Oh, how absence kills fleeting love in flashes.
How it fans the towering flames of lasting desire.
Welcome the breeze that scatters the ashes.
The strong wind that snuffs candles and kindles fires.
Far from you, the body may stray
But your love, if true, will stay.

Delaina always wished for a real father, and she wished, maybe, her father had known his only daughter. Fain's family clung to memories of a man they knew and loved. For her, reality had never been more plain. Tory Cash was her daddy.

The priest finished with a prayer. Family hugged and murmured comforting phrases, huddled in a group. Delaina stood beside Jed. Della Kendall approached them after everyone left.

Delaina's mother had an earthiness about her. Turquoise stone earrings, a plain wedding band. Noticing it caused Delaina to touch the band on her hand.

"Mrs. Kendall, I'm Jed McCrae."

"I would've known. You look like...you did when you were young. Thanks for coming." Della looked at her. "I'm glad you came to the service, too."

Why? Delaina simmered. No mention of Fain's respectable first wife or abandoned daughter in the tribute, no acknowledgment that he had a stepson. What a slap, especially to Ms. Cass and Jed.

"The lawyer's agreed to meet us in a room here. He should arrive any minute."

The first part of the will was legal jargon, then the attorney said, "Fain and I were friends and associates for years, but I didn't agree with this final draft. Della doesn't know details, Fain's way of bringing his family together."

Delaina flinched. *Family?* A family should get mentioned in a memorial.

Della massaged her temples, wondering what Fain had done. Jed remained stony. He knew.

"Fain's cash goes to you, Della. The land in Mallard, fifty-five hundred acres, goes to you, too, under certain conditions. It's yours for one year and he's asked that it not be sold or deeded to anyone during that period. The Barlow family has agreed to stay on as hired help. Jed may continue to do as much as he has been, too."

Delaina raised her hand to stop him. "It should all be Jed's."

"Fain hoped you would say that. You have one year to re-establish your relationship with your mother. Fain laid out guidelines. You and your mother are to talk on the phone twice a month. You will also spend time together, minimum 100 hours, including a weekend within the year. The criteria must be met or else Fain has requested for Della to sell the land at public auction, not to include bids by or for Jed McCrae or Delaina Cash, one year from today. Delaina, if something happens to you during this year..." The attorney looked at Jed. "Death or incapacity, I mean, the land is Della's to decide. That's to prevent harm to you in order for Jed to acquire the land. Jed, if something happens to you, the land is Della's, or if she so chooses, Delaina's, from now on."

"This is absurd," Della said. "I can't believe Fain did this."

"It's all voluntary. His death wish with letters defending his decisions for each of you." He presented the letters to the trio. "Della, the deed is legally yours to do what you want."

"What happens if I do meet the criteria?" Delaina asked coldly. Jed stared at the floor. He knew.

"Fain wanted three-quarters of the acreage to become Jed's one year from today, of his choosing. You'll own what's leftover, Delaina. He wanted to leave something to you, his only daughter, you'd appreciate. Land. He thought he earned at least that, because he did grow the farm larger and because of his commitment to Jed and Cass."

"Commitment to *whom*? Jed and Cass? Who are they?" Delaina rolled her eyes. "One would not know, after sitting through Fain's memorial." Her index finger tapped her temple. "Oh, I remember! His wife. The one he cheated on for years. Jed, the stepson who works his ass off on land that his real father already owned." She glared at Della. "You *will* give that land to him. No matter what I have to do to you!" "*Delaina*," from Jed quietly. "In other words," she said, "Fain hoped that I loved Jed enough to form a relationship with her." She pointed at her mother. "So Jed could get the bulk of his father's land."

The attorney said, "And logically, you and Jed might learn to work side by side and get along, which would be an improvement on Cash-McCrae Road, from what I've heard. Plus, Fain said in our last meeting, 'If Jed does anything to hurt Delaina, she can stop meeting the stipulations, and Jed will lose his land.'"

"A good deal for Fain all around," Jed commented. "Not really," Della commented. "His daughter never knew him, and the closest thing he had to a son never wanted to. He sacrificed living a normal life for you two. Neither of you wants to hear that, but I have to say it."

"I won't listen to this." Delaina looked her mother in the face. "Please, don't say anything else about what *he sacrificed.*"

The attorney slipped from the room to give them privacy.

"Let Della finish," Jed said. "She and Fain have been silent all our lives. Her explanation might be helpful." His Adam's apple bobbed. "Somehow."

Della expanded, "Fain held on to the land, not easy for a non-farmer. He stayed married to a woman who never tried to love him, for you, Jed. He had some affection for you as a child, as much as Cass would allow. A child with a legacy, you needed him. He stayed in Mallard and stayed away from his daughter so he could watch you grow from arm's length, Delaina, after he found out. I signed over rights to children, biological or not, the day Tory and I married and vowed to remain silent in our prenuptial agreement."

That easy for her? Delaina was appalled!

Della went on, "You were able to have the life you knew at Cash Way."

"You think I wanted to live in that enormous house alone?" She stood. "Did Fain Kendall think he did me a favor letting me believe Tory was my father? A man who drank day and night, a man so violent *you* couldn't live with him! Don't tell me Fain did me favors." Her breath came in hard. "How many times did you come to Mallard? To see your married lover and not your daughter! It was not easy..." Delaina's childhood crashed in. She gripped her middle. *"Delaina,"* Jed said again.

She breathed in and repeated, "It was not easy to...convince myself that...you stayed away from..." She got the courage to make eye contact with her statue-like mother. *"*You stayed away from *your little girl* because Tory was too mean to you, but...that's what I told myself." Tears streamed. "Convinced myself at age four, five, six, a helpless and sad child, and later, a confused teenager that, maybe, you thought Miss Maydell was more maternal. *How* does a mother leave?" Delaina held her waist, nausea elevating. A baby. A little life designed to be dependent, from the first moment, on its mother. "The truth is, you provided Tory's heir. You and Fain didn't want me, too into each other! Otherwise, nothing could tear apart a mother and child." Both arms circled her waist. Pregnant; she knew it to her bones. Jed's child. The timing. The wills. The revelations. The coincidence, not a coincidence. She released a sob. Jed touched her arm simultaneously. *"Delaina."*

"True? Right, mother? Admit it! You didn't wanna be a mother."

Della still sat, hands folded in her lap. "As you've grown, I've wanted to know more about you." Delaina stared, watery-eyed and clutching. Waiting for years. "Honestly, it never felt like you were ours. I guess Fain felt the need to rectify that once he was dying."

Delaina pulled herself erect, shaking inside, and marched toward the door. "Damn right, I wasn't yours. I am Tory Cash's! Through and through." Tory, gone forever, drunken, enraged, uncontrollable, probably because of *them*. "For years, Tory Cash was handicapped. Practically mute, for God's sake! For a month, Tory's been dead. You remained silent. What pathetic parents. I am *his*." She looked at Jed. "You knew about the will, and you did everything in your power to make me love you."

LAINEY AND JED, BOOK TWO

"I didn't have to do anything, Delaina. Seeing us together at the river is what caused Fain *to write* his will this way."

"Whatever." The door crashed behind her.

Della watched the door. "I never meant to hurt her. I grew up an orphan, turned to prostitution early, left Mallard with little. Fain didn't know she was his for a long time. She had everything at Cash Way."

Jed had no response to that. His mother would've never left him. "I want you to know the fact that I *do* love her has nothing to do with this will. It never did."

"Tell her over and over. I want her to be happy, and you."

~ ~ ~

From her bed, Holland saw sunlight out the window. She had slept past noon.

She got up and undressed to take a shower. Blood ran down the insides of her legs. *No.* She feared for her unborn baby's life, dressed hurriedly, and drove to the gynecologist's office that Maydell recommended in a previous conversation.

She rushed in and told the receptionist, "I'm Holland Sommers Smith. I don't have an appointment. I think I might be losing my baby."

The receptionist looked at the distraught woman standing before her. "Have a seat, please." In seconds, a nurse appeared in the waiting room. "Mrs. Smith? Come on back." Holland followed the nurse to an exam room. "We don't have a record confirming pregnancy. You're not a patient of record. Typically, we send someone to the E.R. under these circumstances."

"I did a home test two weeks ago! I got an appointment here for next month. My mother-in-law is a patient. Please, please, help me."

"We need to do blood work. How late are you?" "About a month. This morning, there was a trickle of blood." "Any cramps?" "No." "Are you bleeding now?" "No, but I'm under tremendous stress. My husband...passed away."

The nurse frowned as she drew Holland's blood. "My sympathy. If you're pregnant, bleeding in the beginning is normal. So is cramping. If bleeding and cramping occur together or either lasts more than twenty-four hours, you should call. We're pushed today." The nurse watched Holland slump. "Everything will be fine. You need to fill out paperwork. Go pee in this cup."

At the front desk, Holland quizzed, "When will you have the results?" A young lady shrugged her shoulders. "I'm not sure. I'm a substitute from next door. Let me ask." She disappeared and returned. "You do have positive urine is what they told me. We'll have blood results this afternoon. Be sure to drink water and get this prescription for vitamins."

~ ~ ~

Jed tried to call Delaina ten minutes after she ran. She answered by text, *Not going with you*.

She paid a driver in New Orleans to take her to Mallard. Meggie called her in the cab. She told Meggie that the will had confused her, and she needed to go home and try to figure out what next. Meggie argued for the safety of Houston and told her that she would be calling Jed. Delaina thanked her for everything and insisted Jed was not her guardian.

At Cash Way, she retreated to her bedroom in an empty house and reclined on her bedspread. Revelations paralyzed her body. She curled into a ball to rest. What could she do? After gathering things, she slipped unnoticed from the house.

~ ~ ~

Holland spent time in the city to get away from gloom and grief. Truthfully, during the night, she had wondered about...an abortion, to fake a miscarriage. To get away from Cabot. Today was her punishment.

She wanted her child. She browsed her way into a children's shop and bought a soft blue blanket.

At Cash Way, she closed herself in her guest room and slept on the bed, holding the blanket until her phone rang. "Hello, this is Katie calling from Dr. Welch's office." "Hi. Do you have my results?" "Your test is positive. You're pregnant."

"There's been no more blood or cramping."

"Okay, good. Take your vitamins. We'll see you at the scheduled appointment. Avoid undue stress." Impossible. "Let friends or family help you. Rest. Refrain from sexual relations and heavy exercise until the next appointment." Holland stayed in bed, gripping the blue blanket, making deals with fate, after they hung up.

~ ~ ~

Delaina sat on a deserted bank of Carr's Creek.

Low thunder echoed. She rubbed her tummy with one hand, Jed's watch clutched in the other. How would it feel to never have a child of your own flesh and blood?

Tory, Fain, and her mother made choices based on passionate emotions, hard to deal with logically. She began to understand people could make anything seem honorable if they wanted it badly enough. To be a grown woman, she had to keep going, regardless. Delaina closed her eyes and forgave her three parents for their faults and mistakes. She thanked them for whatever sacrifices and hardships they endured on her behalf.

~ ~ ~

Jed refused to worry about whatever decision Delaina would make about the will. People were more important than things, more important than land, more important than money.

He would've left her alone, at risk of peril, so she could figure out things, if there had been only her to consider.

She might be pregnant with his child.

She could run. She couldn't hide.

~ ~ ~

Tory owned a one-room cabin isolated in hardwoods on the farthest edge of Cash property. The place stayed unlocked. As far as Delaina knew, no one had been there since his stroke, except Miss Maydell cleaned it periodically. It was the last place anyone would look, and only Meggie (and probably Jed) knew she returned to Mallard. Delaina felt safe.

Dust covered every surface. She went into the kitchen, filled a pail with water and soap, got a sponge and scrubbed, attempting to scrub away a lifetime of deceit. She got bed sheets out of a closet, aired them in the sun, and made the bed in the open main room.

Near dusk, she went for a walk. Fast-approaching summer had spring in its grip. A lone bird cawed. A fish jumped in the water.

She would meet the requests in Fain's will for Jed's sake. If anyone loved the land more than she, he did. He'd also be managing Cash Way. Instead of renewing Jed's management contract at the end of the first year, she would offer to sell to him. In the meantime, she wanted to re-enroll in college. If Jed refused to buy... She'd figure out a new solution.

Perhaps anyone else in her position would consider the family drama and both wills too much. That's how she felt at first. Now, she could see it for what it really was.

Her way out.

~ ~ ~

After dark, not to be seen, Holland drove to the rental house, seeking extrication from Cabot Hartley and a need to be near Rhett.

Her plan, a brilliant way to get both.

Lights were on. She tapped on the door. Rhett answered. "Good evenin', Miss Holland." His eyes scanned her. "What in the world brings you here?"

"Rhett, I can't sleep." She stepped in uninvited. She wore fashionable jeans and her hair was brushed. No bleeding. Progress.

He stepped backward. "I'm havin' Jack and tap." He lifted his glass.

"Tempting, but I can't drink because of the baby."

"How pregnant are you?"

"Uhm...several weeks." She glanced at him. "I had an appointment today due to a minor concern. I must take extra good care of myself."

Rhett wore frayed denim cut-offs and nothing else. "Anything I can do to help?" From the neck down, he was as much Eli as Eli was, and from the neck up, pretty darn close.

"That's why I'm here." She admitted, "You and your brother are nearly twins."

"He was better-looking."

"Not by much, and it doesn't matter. You'll never be side by side again." Holland sat. "I'm here because I think there's more to the accusations about Eli. He didn't do this alone. Jed agrees. I despise the nasty gossip. He was a good person. I have to clear his name and...I believe that will also implicate Cabot Hartley."

Rhett held out his glass and watched ice cubes swirl. "You did bad stuff for Cabot."

"Yes." He drank a hefty swallow. "Kind of like, you sold pot in the past, Rhett." His head whipped to her. "Bad things but...neither of us is capable of anything like the marijuana scheme. Right?"

"Damn straight." He frowned. "I ain't never done nothin' that bad."

"Good." She took a shallow breath. "If it's Cabot, I don't have proof, other than I know he had maps of the land tracts out here."

"How can we prove it?"

"I need your help regarding Eli. We'll need Jed's help, too, when he returns. He and I are old family friends."

"Where's he got off to?"

"He had to settle Fain's will in New Orleans today."

"Lainey went runnin' off with him again."

"She's safe that way. They love each other. Tell me everything you know about Eli and marijuana, Rhett."

"Unbelievable about Lainey and Jed." His tongue clicked. "Eli and pot...whew, how long ya got, ma'am?" "All night."

~ ~ ~

His first baseball glove. His mother's pearls. His father's album collection. Flames ate the house from the inside out.

Raybon Hall settled in his truck and watched. He warned Lainey Cash and Jed McCrae. Raybon got results one way or another. He flung an empty longneck in the passenger seat and opened another. Time to make the call. He dialed 911. "This is Chief Hall. Bad fire out at the old McCrae home on Cash-McCrae Road. Send trucks ASAP."

~ ~ ~

Moll Smith paced the front porch at Cash Way.

If guilt didn't destroy his mind, grief would make sane living unbearable. Death was the blackest of blacks, braided into lighter shades of hopeful words and promises of heaven and eternity and salvation. Moll Smith had been a Christian all his adult life. Those ideals didn't do him a bit of good now. He had a lifetime of what-ifs and should-not-haves to suffer through. Some said, "Give it time." Time would serve him and Maydell with concrete measures of how long it had been since they'd seen their son alive. Time would fill them with questions that had no answers. Only parents who lost a child could understand how they felt. Moll found no comfort in that morbid bond.

Moll halted. Distantly, orange flares rocketed. The McCrae home-place was burning to the ground. He left, sped down the driveway to the house, and screeched on the brakes, coming upon another truck. He raced to the driver's side and looked Raybon Hall in the face.

"Moll."

"Raybon."

Raybon had a beer in his hand and an empty bottle on the passenger's seat. "I've called the fire department. I rode out here to apologize to Jed for the grueling interview and accusations. I saw this first."

"Ain't there somethin' we can do?"

"Too dangerous. Better wait for the firefighters."

Moll swore and shook his head. "What else is gonna go wrong, Raybon?" Before he answered, they heard trucks.

~ ~ ~

Rhett and Holland sat on the sofa in his den. They drank coffee and munched doughnuts. "Never seen a lady drink coffee pure black."

"I won't drink it any other way." She smiled over the rim of her cup.

"Could tell you more things about Eli, but I think we ought to see if he wrote about this."

"I'm sure he didn't leave written evidence."

Rhett cocked his head. "He sure might've. I overheard you tellin' folks what a storyteller Eli was at the funeral visitation..." He clicked eyes with hers. "I figured you knew." "What?"

"Eli, the born writer. He didn't piss without recordin' it somewhere. His funny stories you heard, he keeps 'em in a notebook. Got that ability from our daddy. Daddy used to write in a journal, then somethin' happened when Lainey was little, maybe four or five. Now Daddy won't write about nothin', but Eli did. I imagine somewhere around here, we could find somethin' real important."

Holland was amazed. "Those stories, did Eli try to publish them?"

"No, ma'am, not that I know of. Eli, he did it for hisself, ya know? Didn't worry about impressin' nobody." He struggled to speak. "If you were...lucky enough to hear...his stories, you...were the one better for it." He pointed to a scar on his arm. "My brother did this to me. Stabbed me with a screwdriver 'cause I kissed Paisley Patterson." Rhett's mouth tipped in a sentimental grin. "I had a crush on her. The three of us parked by Carr's Creek one afternoon. Eli was workin' on his old heap of a car, trying to impress her. He went inside the shop to look for somethin', and I dove in and planted a wet, dog-lickin' kiss on Paisley's mouth. She looked like she'd been bit by a rattlesnake. Eli jabbed me with a screwdriver then gave me a January dunkin' in the creek."

Holland had settled beside him and closed her eyes. "There's no one here to stab you tonight, Rhett."

He stood up. "What do you say we look 'round here for Eli's notebooks?" He led them to Eli's bedroom, pulled journals from a shelf

LAINEY AND JED, BOOK TWO

then thumbed through a notebook entitled Country Boy's Cuisine. "This one's about what country boys eat. It's funny."

He handed one to Holland with her name scribbled on front. She flipped pages.

She's more beautiful than river at sunset.
I can touch her, hold her, see in her...a life.
Sun warms my skin; she warms my soul.
She's my lover, my friend, and today, my wife.

~ ~ ~

Mallard's hoard of volunteer county firefighters extinguished flames, no hope of salvaging much. Things that didn't burn were destroyed by smoke or water.

Moll Smith shook his head at the sight. A nice place, especially in its heyday. He felt almost relieved to have something different to concentrate on.

The fire cause hadn't been determined. Some men said electrical. Some speculated arson. Mostly people wondered where Jed McCrae was.

Cabot and Boone Barlow were among those on the scene. "Raybon," Cabot whispered to Boone.

Boone chewed a wad of tobacco. "He's out of control." He jabbed his hands in his pockets. "And looks like Jed and Lainey are gone again."

~ ~ ~

"This bed smells like Eli."

Rhett thought it smelled like a rose-enhanced female. He sat close, notebooks scattered. "Eli's part in the marijuana plan don't seem to be written down nowhere."

"Did he have an office at the Cash workshop?"

"Not by hisself. Me and him spent most of our time on a tractor or in our trucks."

"That's it! Eli's truck." She sprang off the bed. "Where is it?"

"Knight's body shop. Looks like a stomped-on can. You don't wanna see it."

"I can handle it. Maybe Eli kept a notebook in his truck." She tugged Rhett's arm. "Let's go."

~ ~ ~

138

The cabin creaked. Animal noises outside sounded close. Re-fluffing her pillow, Delaina sat up. She dialed her mother on her phone. Her mother answered quickly.

"Hello, it's Delaina." Her own voice sounded loud after hours in the cabin alone.

"Delaina, are you okay?"

"I'm settled. You can tell Fain's lawyer this is my first phone call with you. Only twenty-three more to go." She hung up and put her head under the pillow, blocking night sounds.

~ ~ ~

"Holy God." Holland saw the mangled truck, a metal ball with jagged punctures. "How, Rhett? I don't know how he survived."

"He didn't." Rhett shined his flashlight through the shattered back window. The passenger door wouldn't open. He reached through ragged glass and felt around in the glove compartment. Shards pricked his skin. Steadily, he pulled his arm through and faced Holland. He held out a leather binder for her inspection. "I hope to hell this is what we're lookin' for."

~ ~ ~

So far, Jed McCrae hadn't answered.

Once again, drama on Cash-McCrae Road. Once again, a menacing culprit. Once again, officials couldn't proceed because Jed was gone.

Jed didn't want to be found.

His phone and considerations of Mallard County got left inside his truck parked on a path near Tory Cash's barren cabin hours ago. Jed McCrae was not inside his truck.

THIRTEEN

Us

Initially, it felt like a dream.

She knew the face, the body, the walk. She didn't know where or why.

Flames flickered through darkness as he continued lighting candle after candle. Short, tall, skinny, fat, dingy white and old, pulled out of cabin storage, intended for an emergency or special occasion.

Memory began to register in her fuzzy brain.

She had fallen asleep in an unfamiliar bed. She hadn't fallen asleep naked atop a blanket in a blackened corn field, protected by drooping stalks and curved leaves, seduced by burning candles on bare ground. He set the scene, undressed her, and toted her out here?

Bewildered, she stared at the sky to decipher the time or a reason not to succumb, and got neither.

He blew out the match.

Their hiding place exhibited three colors. Silver from moon, gold from candlelight, black from shadows. Intriguing and mysterious. Rural royalty.

He undressed with his back turned then settled on his side beside her. She lay on her back, upturned face watching his. She could think of nothing to say or do.

He seemed to study every strand of her hair, every feature of her face, every part of her body. Chills playing theatrics on her skin were misleading actors. Inside, she burned. She looked at him, too. The curved muscles of his chest, the length of his arms, the tapering

140

of his waist, his perfect manhood, his full legs, familiar to her sight and memory now. Every inch of him, warm, smooth, hard, strong.

Feelings between them were too poignant, too potent, too personal to be violated by sound. They had said it all before. Everything had changed. Nothing had changed.

He leaned over her. She felt his breath on her skin. She puckered her lips to kiss him.

He did not want the meeting of mouths. He put his lips on her most intimate place, taking his time with a masterful method. She came superbly for him.

He moved up and over her. At first, lips on lips then the polite introduction of tongues, who exchanged names ravenously and touched a dozen times.

A pattern of flames danced on their bodies. Time meant nothing, and reality would be swept into a favorite memory. Tomorrow.

Her face mirrored his in candlelight. No fear. No anger. No judgment. In one motion, he slipped into her. She winced; she took a breath; her legs went up; he went all the way. He gasped from such sweetness, such tightness. They meshed until the synchrony, the meshing, developed into an ageless model of eroticism. Leaves ruffled on the stalks. They smelled damp earth. They rose and fell deftly. For each of them, the experiment bloomed into search and discover, want and need, lust and love.

His arms encircled her as he turned onto his back, maintaining a stronghold. A move so suave, she found herself straddled over him before she realized what happened.

She twirled her hair on her finger, this person who, despite pompous courage, didn't give of herself easily. He tilted within her, an earnest plea. She arched intuitively and slid against him.

He entered a new dimension of thrilled.

He watched her bathed in gold luminescence, rising and falling, honey hair flouncing from one shoulder to another, eyes glittering. Apparently, the point of his life was to be her personal girl-on-top trial. He loved it. He held out for as long as she needed, which turned out to be a long time. She collapsed on his chest, legs trembling against his hips.

His hands slid down her ribs and gripped her waist as he rolled them over, put her on her back, staying fitted together. Earth didn't give beneath them. What gave was him; all he had was hers. His face hung over hers by inches, damp strands of black hair teasing and tickling her forehead. The ending fought him, the impact of their union tugging at him like weighted robes about to break free.

Through sultry, swaying shadows, she opened her mouth and shattered silenced. "Come."

"Come with me," he mumbled through clenched teeth, sweat rolling down his face, his eyes and hair black as tar. He pushed her arms over her head, fingers laced. His chest smothered hers; his mouth covered hers.

He would take them to their fullest potential, the height of human emotion. A place few dared to hope for and still never got.

She sought rest. She sought air. She sought departure, believing it would be easier to give up rather than give in. His eyes pierced hers with unwavering need. He did more to her body.

She became suspended, swinging over anything solid, mindfully begging for feet, secretly hoping for wings. He wouldn't quit sliding lead through silk. Weightlessness jerked her upside down like a bungee cord into heavenly disarray. He struggled to hold on to one last sensation, to string it out eternally, that sweet, tight feeling, then let it happen with her.

They gave then took, opened then closed, walked in the clouds then crawled on the ground, built up then broke down, flew then fell.

With every breath, loving the absolution. Hating the completion.

He dropped onto her. She whispered, "That was indescribable."

"No." Jed shook his head and mumbled breathlessly, "That was Delaina."

Fourteen

Pain

Rain came down in sheets outside. The sky split with a streak of lightning. The room shook with booming thunder.

Jed had carried Delaina to Tory's cabin, to the bed, and lowered her, just in time.

He climbed in with her, traced her jaw with his finger. *They had done it again.* The tense conversation about birth control last night, and now...this.

She uttered, "It's never been like that for you before."

"No." A succinct, humble answer.

She touched his cheek. "I wanna be with you again, and I want it like that again."

Jed looked at her, a raw sort of look. "Later, maybe."

She spoke like she caught on to the rules of a board game halfway in. "I get it. You're like those guys I read about in the sex blog, V-J-J. Let's see, what are they called? Rare Romeos."

"Rare Romeos? *V-J-J?* Dang, why can't you read something like the newspaper or National Geographic?"

"You go for quality over quantity."

"Actually, I like to think I'm good at quality and quantity."

She raised her eyebrows. "I could go for that." Thunder vibrated the windows.

"I could go for it, too, if you weren't a...Hapless Juliet."

"Do I dare ask? What's a Hapless Juliet?"

"You go for pleasure over practicality." He lay on his side, facing her. "*We* do," he corrected.

LAINEY AND JED, BOOK TWO

She huffed a breath and puffed in true Lainey-style. "You, Jed McCrae, would not wanna have sex with me if I were practical about it." Jagged lightning forks brightened the room followed by booms.

"I'm talking about making a baby."

No admission from her. Evidently, no test yet or else no baby. Jed took a breath of disappointment and swallowed a ton of relief. "I intended to talk to you about that first, earlier tonight, but I saw you sleeping and..." The look she gave him made him nervous. "What did I say wrong?"

"Nothing." She got to her feet. Silver droplets of water ran down a blackened window, diamonds on onyx like Jed's eyes. He could see through her.

Jed came up behind her, their naked bodies brushing. She tensed. He turned her in his arms. She looked at him with bashful eyes. "I don't like this. What is it, Delaina?"

"Nothing." She found the nightshirt she fell asleep in. Jed pulled on jeans. He clamped her arm. "Back to running again, are we? If it's Fain's will, listen, I don't care what you decide." He shook her. "I mean it."

"I'm sleepy," she complained

He combed fingers through his hair, frustrated, and gripped her upper arm. "*Delaina.*"

She pulled away. Thunder and lightning continued to entertain with a sideshow. "Jed, you were breathtaking. The field, too. Goodnight." She climbed in bed and hovered under covers.

Jed felt dissatisfied. She dismissed him like a lazy employee. He sat on the opposite edge, backs to one another. Delaina sighed on a little cough. He twisted around. "Talk to me."

"It's my fault. It's not your responsibility. You're not trapped."

Jed peered over her shoulder. "Trapped?"

"I'll take care of it. I love it already."

"It?"

She rolled toward him and nodded. "Our baby." Tears skimmed her face. "You were right. I'm pregnant. According to an over-the-counter test at a pharmacy restroom on the ride home earlier today."

An emotion Jed couldn't pinpoint, maybe relief that she told him, maybe joy that she was, maybe fear that she didn't look happy. Something washed over him with more force than the torrents outside. Pulling her close, he searched for the right words. Damn, he never thought about what to say when his wife told him she was pregnant. Delaina wasn't his wife; she was his... Didn't matter because as soon as possible, they would get married. "I told you we'd handle it if you were pregnant. In fact, I'm excited for myself, not for you. You don't look happy at all."

She sniffed and wiped tears. "I'm not."

He hugged her. "Delaina, I already asked you to marry me before the baby, so don't mention the word trapped. I know this is happening fast, but I'll be there. We'll hire help or whatever you need." He caught her lips for a kiss. "In case you've forgotten, I'm right where I want to be." For someone who never thought about it, he assumed his response was a good one. Until he looked into her eyes. Ruthless gray-green. She leaped from the bed. "You don't get it, do you?"

"I guess I don't. Explain it to me."

His face. Its beauty, the caring, the concern. "Think, Jed."

He closed his eyes. "I'm having trouble following you."

"I don't want to marry you!"

He opened his eyes. Delaina saw the pain. His pain went to anger. Neither reared their ugly heads. Determination knocked them out with an encompassing punch. "I treat you like the goddamn world revolves around you. That's my baby. I'll do whatever it takes." He stood over her, a soldier prepared for battle.

"It's my baby too, Jed, not a piece of property! Marrying you, coincidentally, solves all your McCrae land problems."

"And yours at Cash Way."

The old conditioning, the competition and mistrust, surfaced. "You can't scheme and lie and seduce me into giving our baby to you! I'll win this time. I swear I will." Delaina slumped into a chair. "Don't make this hard."

"Don't make this hard? You yelled that you don't wanna marry me. Delaina, marrying you would have nothing to do with our land." Jed shrugged his shoulders. "God, don't you know that by now?" He peered down on her. "I'm *sorry,* but we can't go back and change Calla. We agreed to no protection." His expression was defeat. "Why are you fighting me? Why do to our baby what was done to you?"

"Because I love you too much to expect you to deal with my insecurities!"

He gripped her arms and dragged her to her feet. "This isn't about me and you now. It's about our innocent baby. Our baby deserves us to try."

"The baby will be fine."

"Like you? You turned out fine, right?" Fury chose Jed's next words. "You are your sorry mother's daughter."

The blow, too fresh and accurate. Delaina pulled on her jeans, grabbed Jed's keys, and bolted out the door into stormy darkness. Jed watched as she cranked his truck and left him standing.

~ ~ ~

It happened again.

Every time they touched, Earth flew across the universe in a starry escapade enviable by any human standards, and a short time later, it catastrophically fell off its axis.

Delaina had nowhere to go. She stopped the truck on the path. Jed's phone rang, an unknown number. She decided to answer. Why hide that they had been together tonight? His child was growing inside her body. "Hello?"

"Uh, yes, this is Fire Chief Mitchum from the Mallard County Fire Department. I need to speak with Jed McCrae."

"I'm sorry. Jed's not available. This is Delaina." Confession, as much freedom as confinement.

"Delaina? Lainey Cash?"

"Yes, Delaina." The fire chief's shock forced Delaina to realize the immense size of the pill that she and Jed were about to jam down Mallard County's throat. Many would choke. Not for long. They'd be too eager to talk. She and Jed would be the gossip, the focus of hawk eyes, for as long as it lasted, which would be for life since they were parents together. It dawned on her. Fire Department! What's wrong? Is there a problem?"

"Jed's parents' home burned to the ground tonight. We don't know much. Little salvaged. Possibly arson." *"Oh my God.* He'll be in touch ASAP. Thanks for calling."

The door to Tory's cabin stood open. Walking by lamplight, she saw a black shadow streaked in silver. Jed sat on the porch steps out back, head bent, skin and hair wet from the drizzle, wearing BC jeans.

She stood behind him, illustrated in shadows. "Tonight, you offered me the very best, and I threw it away because I'm a coward and that's the sorriest excuse." She came forward and faced him. "Jed, someone wants you to suffer." His brows drew together. "I have something to tell you. The McCrae homeplace burned to the ground tonight." Jed ran one hand through his hair, black clumps across a shattered pale face. "I answered your phone. Talked to the Chief. May be intentional."

A man usually so adept made standing look difficult. He walked until grass met water, Carr's Creek. He sat on the rim of silvery liquid shining through blackness. She sat beside him on a damp rock. Delaina wore her thin nightshirt stuffed into moist jeans, hair glued to her neck and face like wet yarn. She was a mess. She was in better shape than Jed. Silence, which had been marvelous an hour ago, became intolerable. "What others have done to us is inconceivable. You don't deserve anything that's happened to you in the last month."

"I'll take the bad with the good."

"You say that, but you, more than anyone, spend your time making up for people's shortcomings."

He kicked his foot in the water. "That's not true. I've always lived for myself."

"You've lived for your father. What do you want? Have you ever allowed yourself to find out?"

"I don't owe you an explanation for my decisions."

"But I owe you an explanation for decisions I'm makin'? That's not fair. Neither of us is accustomed to answering to anyone." Delaina's tears were spent. "I planned to ask if I could help you sort through Fain's belongings to learn more about him. Now..." She shivered. "Nothing left."

"I guess I've lost the tangible things that were my mother, my father."

Delaina shoved her hands in her pockets, not to reach out to him. Her fingers met with the cold metal of Jed's watch. "Not everything." She reached for his hand and closed his fingers around it. "This land isn't that important. I have no real rights to either place. I'm finished fighting others for it or fighting you over it. I quit."

"You're right. You're finished fighting for several months." He pointed. "No argument. As for us, I guess you knew it before I kissed you the first time. There's too much water under the bridge. At any rate, I insist we go see Meggie as soon as she says we should. You're under tremendous stress. This incident alone was enough to make you miscarry." Jed scanned her body. "You're supposed to be takin' vitamins, and I wanna see an ultrasound." Delaina felt a brand-new, scary feeling. He made the pregnancy *and* their apartness real. "You need to stay in Houston at my apartment until things are better here, so find a way to tolerate me. You might as well find a way to get along with me permanently; our child will know me. I'll be spending a lot of time with him or her."

Delaina's heart skipped a beat at the thought of Jed with their child then skipped again when she recalled yelling at him that she didn't want to marry him. He retreated irrevocably.

Jed gripped the watch and looked up grimly. "Thank God for Houston."

~ ~ ~

"It will take time to sort these papers." Holland yawned. "I'm convinced answers are here. I think we should wait for morning. It's late."

"I agree," Rhett answered, eyes halfway shut. "You wanna stay here and sleep in Eli's room?"

"Yes." Holland hugged him "Goodnight, Rhett. Thank you for everything." He looked into her chocolate eyes as he pulled away. She stared back at him. "Actually...I want to sleep in your room."

She took his hand, led the way, and didn't appear to have mixed feelings, probably because of missing Eli, which made it more wrong. Rhett pulled on her arm. "Honey, I'm Rhett, not Eli."

Holland just wanted *to sleep* beside someone, fled the room, and retired to Eli's bed. She indulged in a crying jag. When she had the composure to get up, she went into the den, got the notebook, and sorted pages.

She had to get to the bottom of Mallard's dramas before Cabot showed up again. Before he forced her to be his secret accomplice at Cash Way.

All Eli's other stories were in bound notebooks, dated. These from his truck were loose leaf, often cryptic, as if he scratched things hurriedly and randomly in fear of anyone pinpointing anything. Holland hunted the truth.

~ ~ ~

Jed made phone calls and left, saying he'd return. Delaina showered, dressed in his dry T-shirt, and went to bed.

All her life, she faced problems alone. That's why she fell in love with Jed. He offered only what she needed, although he never had to ask what that might be, and she never felt weak for leaning on him. Delaina could beg or plead or manipulate. She wouldn't. Jed seemed done with her. Her fault.

Behind her, he sank with a thud. Dimly, one candle burned. She glanced over her shoulder and caught a glimpse of his rippled muscles. "What about the house?"

"I met Chief. Not much house left. Can't really see in the dark. The rest can wait till morning."

"I'm so sorry..." Her voice tapered off.

Jed turned over, watched her back rise and fall. Delaina proved to be more than he could imagine, as reckless as she was determined and as brave as any man, yet unforgivably childlike and undeniably female. The final break didn't come because she was pregnant with his child and unwilling to marry him. Another less selfish reason caused Jed to tell her it was over.

She wasn't ready for him.

She needed time to learn, make mistakes, test her wings, take dares, try new ventures.

He curved his arm around her waist, no guilt for touching her there, nothing sexual about it. That part of her body belonged to him the next nine months. He planned to put his hands there as much as he wanted. Stroking her through the thin cotton, he realized something else about Delaina. There was no other woman he wanted to have his child. He imagined a sassy little girl with Delaina's golden hair and shiny eyes. Or a son with their combined strength and innate love for the land. Either way, their kid would take the world by storm! He closed his eyes with that thought in place, clutching his heart.

~ ~ ~

By the time the sun came up, Holland had texted Jed that they needed to talk. He dropped her a phone pin of his whereabouts. She headed to his location, Tory's cabin in the woods.

Jed mumbled, "Hey, D. Holland's on the way with vital info." His Bleu Cotton T-shirt, words *Get Dirty*, bunched at her waist. Her hand curled in the hair on his abdomen. "We gotta get up." Jed untangled in time for the knock on the door.

Delaina stumbled across the room and stood behind him. Jed opened the door. Holland struggled not to gawk. A man's T-shirt skimmed Delaina's thighs. Jed's jeans were pulled on haphazardly, his hair a hand-tossed mess. She stepped in, no mistaking what happened between them. A burned-down candle bedside; the bed itself a crumpled wad. Jed cleared his throat. "You said ASAP."

Delaina stepped about meekly. "We, uh..."

"No need to explain. I'm glad it's both of you here." Holland reached for his arm. "Moll called and told Rhett and me about the house. I'm sorry."

"Thanks." He sat on the bed. It smelled of Delaina, of him, of them. "It's not the most important thing. I'm more concerned about Delaina's safety and nailing everyone responsible for these tragedies." Jed cut his eyes. "Glad to have you on the winning side."

"Me too." Holland sat in a chair. "Let's explain how we know each other and our agreement to Delaina." Jed went first.

Delaina seemed taken aback. "Where did I fit into this neat plan?"

Jed said, "Never any plans regarding you." Holland added, "Not where Jed was concerned. Cabot, on the other hand..." Delaina interrupted, "Cabot was hookin' up with you and God knows who. How does Eli fit in? Isn't that what you came for, Holland?"

"Delaina, I'm sorry about Cabot. I, uh, he's like that with everyone. I mean, uh..."

"Forget it. I'm in no position to judge."

"No comparison! What you and Jed have is much more. Y'all love each other." Delaina snapped, "What?" "Let's talk about what you came here to talk about," Jed suggested.

Holland opened a notebook. "Eli journaled life events. Rhett and I searched until we found this. You were right, Jed. Eli got the plants for Cabot for a premium with no idea how they would be used. He wrote his last passage minutes after he left my apartment the night of his accident. He expressed concern for Delaina, feared I was Cabot's partner, and believed Cabot tried to frame you."

Jed said, "I saw Cabot at a gas station in Hammond the morning after Fain died. He basically admitted it and swore we'd never prove it."

Delaina had forgotten that. "I saw Dacey Boyd in the café. Looked like she'd been caught with her pants down."

Jed turned to Holland. "Do you know anything about Dacey and Cabot?"

"Never thought about how they act. He avoids her... She's the only employee he isn't openly flirtatious with. Maybe he tries to appear like there's nothing between them because there is?"

Jed agreed. "Cabot had Dacey call me from Mill's Pond so someone could put marijuana in the back of my truck." Delaina stated, "Cabot didn't attack me in the woods. A bigger, older man who'd been drinkin' strong liquor."

Holland shrugged. "Cabot's not working alone. He has scores of indebted people to do his dirty work." Jed tapped her arm. "Are there clues about who is involved?" "Eli believed one of your workers because it wasn't him, Rhett, or Moll."

"Boone." Jed frowned. "You and Delaina are in danger. You know too much."

"The Smiths need me."

"I don't want y'all in Mallard until we have answers. Go home to Atlanta and see Garrick. Your father loves spending time with you. Call Rhett and tell him I'll be in touch. I'll get you a flight."

She stood up and gave the notebook to Jed. "I'm trusting you with this. All I ask is that Mallard citizens know how limited Eli's role was in the drug operation." Her palm touched her middle. "Please nail Cabot. *Please.*"

"I'll take care of it."

Delaina stepped in front of Holland. "Eli was like a brother. What he did with Cabot, I realize, was about money. I hope your pregnancy is smooth."

"I'm sure you can't understand wishing to be pregnant with a man's child when you have no hopes of being with the man, but I'm glad I am."

"I understand. A permanent link and unmistakable reminder of what you shared." Eyes glistening, they understood each other in a way that surpassed time and culture.

After Holland left, Delaina uttered, "Excuse me," and went into the bathroom. Jed had noticed she looked scary pale during the discussion. He heard commotion, gagging. "Delaina?" He went in. She had a wet cloth on her head. "What's wrong?"

LAINEY AND JED, BOOK TWO

"I feel odd. Tingly." She got to the main room, to a chair, weakly. She turned to the window, curtains parted. She held her bottom lip between her teeth.

"What do you mean?" Jed took her pulse, med school kicking in. "Talk to me." She started to say something, and he interrupted with, "Your heart's racing." He bent to her. "Are you anxious?

"I don't think so."

"Is it...our baby, maybe morning sickness?" *Now? Already?* He felt his own heart racing.

She started trembling. "Something's wrong. Bad wrong." She started crying. Like totally un-Delaina.

Jed grabbed his phone to call Meggie, walked to the kitchen instead and got her a glass of water. "Here, drink this." He had medical and emergency training. It went to hell fast. He took the cloth and wiped her face. "Delaina, has this happened before?" She shook her head violently. "Please calm down, sweetheart." If being pregnant made her this scared... "Breathe." He felt helpless, hopeless.

"Jed, what's wrong?" She felt like she might pass out. He picked her up, put her in bed, told her to curl in a fetal position while he called Meggie. He went to the bathroom and shut the door.

~ ~ ~

In a little while, there was a tap on the front door at Cash Way.

Rhett answered. Looking awfully humble, Jed stood before him. He told Rhett everything he knew about Eli, Cabot, and Holland plus details of Delaina's life-threatening attack. He asked for Rhett's help, telling him he had no idea who to trust. He used Holland's pregnancy and his farm management contract to encourage Rhett to cooperate. Rhett obliged and swore Jed and Delaina could trust him. They swapped cell numbers. Jed sent Maydell up to Delaina's bedroom to get items she needed. He assured her that Delaina would be safest with him and to talk to Rhett for details.

Then Jed McCrae crossed the road he crossed thousands of times, drove down the tree-lined driveway, and parked in front of a black skeleton frame, his childhood home. He stared at it for a minute before hitting the road to Houston.

Delaina rode with him, going to his apartment indefinitely. She would've been going anyway, before this health incident, until Jed could get things better handled in Mallard. Now, she was going primarily to see Meggie and figure out if she was pregnant, miscarrying,

152

had an anxiety attack, or what. They were driving in Delaina's car. Meggie restricted airplanes, sex, alcohol, and exercise until she could ascertain Delaina's condition.

FIFTEEN

On the road

The ride to Houston would take six hours and forty-four minutes according to GPS.

Delaina seemed better. They agreed on ground rules for the ride. No mention of Mallard, farming, family, wills, their relationship, or pregnancy resulted in quietness. What else was there?

Jed didn't feel like small talk- What's your favorite movie?—They didn't need casual bonds. As soon as things halfway calmed down, he would be cutting the rope with Delaina, apart from taking care of their baby, if there was a baby. For her own good. The thought wasn't comfortable or comforting.

Delaina slept. They had one brief conversation. Enveloped in late afternoon sun, past the Texas state line with music playing low, she reached for his hand. "You know something I just thought about? I've never really slept with anybody, you know, sleeping in the same bed. I sleep peacefully with you. Like I don't notice you're there, yet we're all cuddled up."

He squeezed her hand. His heart allowed, "I love sleeping with you."

She nodded, satisfied, and looked out her window. "I like the Lone Star signs."

~ ~ ~

As close as Meggie and Jed had been, he had never been *so* glad to see her. She invited Jed and Delaina into her den. "Okay, you two. Jed told me details on the phone. Delaina, you're super pale. Do you have anything to add?"

ON THE ROAD

Her eyes blinked several times. Jed felt like he should sit closer to her on the sofa or, hell, something. "Uhm, could I have miscarried this morning because of what we did the past two nights?" Jed's guts ripped. She thought she miscarried? Did more happen in the bathroom than she told him?

Last night, not twenty-four hours ago. The sparkling field. Such hotness. Such synchrony. She gulped a sob.

Meggie said, "Jed thinks maybe you had a panic attack. We don't know for certain you're pregnant. Unreal what you've been through the last six weeks, the last few years, actually, honey." Her voice pampered. "Unless there is *already* an underlying problem, sex causing miscarriage is a myth."

Jed twisted toward Delaina. "Do you want me here? In here right now?"

Delaina shrugged. "I..." She didn't think Jed wanted *her* after last night's argument. "I can do it." Her mind felt putty-ish. "But I want you here if you're comfortable with it."

He cut in too quickly, "Of course. I was close to being an ob/gyn." "This isn't a random patient," Meggie inserted.

"I know." Jed looked at Delaina intimately with clear blue eyes. "She's the most important thing." Delaina cut in too quickly, "I am?" He took her hand. "What's next, Meg?"

"You're welcome to stay here tonight. To monitor how you feel, Delaina. We don't normally see a patient until your period's late."

"But the pharmacy test..."

"Home tests are accurate." Meggie validated her. "You took it as soon as possible, though. Early pregnancy, or the possibility of it, is a gray area. Given what you've been through, this morning's episode could be unrelated to pregnancy." Jed nodded. Meggie went on, " We're going to change pace, distract, rest."

"An ultrasound wouldn't show anything yet, either," Jed said and sounded like Meggie was absolutely right. "I want to know!" Delaina exclaimed. She let go of his hand. "See, you're getting worked up, D." "Of course, I am!" "Delaina, I'm not tryin' to control this. It's just time for you to rest, with all you've been through."

Meggie agreed, "Your body knows what it's doing, baby or not."

Delaina felt frustrated. "This is an intervention. Like I'm unstable or something. I'm *strong*."

LAINEY AND JED, BOOK TWO

"Strongest person I know." Jed took both hands. "But you should be taking time to be twenty." Twenty said aloud in front of Meggie, in this situation. *Jesus.*

"You're going through the same things I am," Delaina tried.

He disagreed. "I'm thirty, a lot bigger, and definitely not pregnant." Somehow, they laughed. "I'm gonna get a shower. Give y'all time to talk." He glanced at Meggie. "I might stay here tonight." Delaina looked at him. He had a cute dark stubble. "I gotta fly to Mallard first thing tomorrow if everything goes okay tonight. Want me to stay here, D?"

"I..." Fatigue loomed. A thought surfaced. "I want you to sleep with me." Familiarity doubled in rawness, spoken in front of a witness. Jed's heart, and other parts, tugged. "She means sleep," he said to Meggie.

Meggie nodded. "I know." He hugged Delaina. "Okay, I will."

He did and left at dawn.

~ ~ ~

Holland Sommers Smith's pregnancy along with Eli's death and involvement in the marijuana scheme would have been enough gossip to satisfy Mallard County's flapping tongues for months.

Holland's pregnancy had been topped by a greater one.

Lainey Cash. So the story went, a receptionist at a doctor's office in Vicksburg, the girlfriend of a Mallard country boy, told him that Delaina Cash scheduled an appointment for a pregnancy test. It took a few passages from mouth to mouth that Lainey was pregnant, coupled with her broken engagement to Cabot Hartley. Older folks remembered another time Mallard, Mississippi, had a beautiful blonde and nice young man planning a big wedding, a big wedding that never took place. The beautiful young blonde named Cassie Jane Darrah didn't marry Raybon Hall. She got pregnant with James Ed McCrae's baby.

Supposedly, Jed McCrae and Lainey Cash disappeared more than once at the same time and Lainey was missing again.

The lunch crowd at MacHenry's buzzed with speculation. Dacey Boyd overheard one such conversation as she emerged from the restroom into the dining room. They were right. If Lainey Cash got pregnant, Jed McCrae fathered her child.

156

ON THE ROAD

Hmpf, Dacey could tell folks something better. Walking out, she used her phone to text Cabot at work. *Meet me at Moon Dog Creek. Now!*

She drove there and waited. Cabot arrived, aggravated. Dacey wore a slouchy sweater, a strand of pearls, and dark blue jeans with new red cowboy boots. She smiled an I've-got-a-secret smile. He didn't notice, too busy worrying about the phone call that came before Dacey's, from Investigator Cardin Morris. He claimed that they discovered journals kept by Eli Smith implicating him in the marijuana investigation and asked Cabot to come to the Sheriff's office immediately.

Cabot was lucky, damn lucky, they hadn't come to get him in a patrol car. He had called his father and confessed. Other arrangements had been made. He squeezed this impromptu meeting into his plans.

"Hey, Butterscotch," she said in a flirtatious voice.

"What do you want, Dacey? Hurry."

She twirled a wiry red curl through her fingers. "I know something real important." He frowned. "Cheer up, honey. Ain't every day you learn you're gonna be a daddy."

Cabot shrugged. "It's not my baby, Dacey. You know that. Lainey screwed around with Jed McCrae one too many times. You see, she's Fain Kendall's daughter." Cabot cut his eyes. "McCrae Farms wasn't willed to Jed. He lured Lainey into his bed. One way or another, he meant he would get the land." Cabot laughed ironically "I thought about getting her pregnant to get married fast, but I guess I don't have what she's looking for. The dumb whore."

Dacey listened to the incredible story, searching Cabot's cold brown eyes. His face looked rigid, not a scrap of kindness evident.

"Sweetie, I wasn't talking about Lainey."

"If you're accusing me of getting Holland pregnant, her baby is probably Eli's."

Dacey gasped. "You've had sex with Holland?" She stepped back. "In the last few weeks?"

"Business. Now hurry up."

"That's always your excuse. Business! My daddy's the sheriff. Do you use me for protection, in case your crimes come out? Do you think that I'd beg him to let you off the hook?"

LAINEY AND JED, BOOK TWO

"You listen to me, bitch. Don't ever say I'm a criminal." He grabbed her wrist. "If you're stupid enough to think I get sex from you exclusively, you're more stupid than I thought." Cabot glared. "If you're here to accuse me of knocking up sluts, I'm leaving."

"I'm pregnant with your baby, Cabot. Don't worry. I won't tell nobody it's yours. After you started gettin' serious with Lainey, I got scared you was gonna avoid me, so I stopped taking my pills. We've done it a lot since then."

Cabot dropped F-bombs and paced. "You're going to a clinic."

"No!" She dashed.

He grabbed her. "*Dacey*, there will be no bastard baby!" He put his hands around her throat and squeezed. "I'll see to it that you are escorted to the clinic properly."

"No!" She kneed him in the crotch to break free. "I'm not having an abortion!"

"You don't have a choice, you stubborn whore!" He slammed her into a tree. She cried out and fell to the ground. Cabot stood over her, ready to grab hold again. Dacey crawled to her feet and made an escape toward her car parked beyond the creek. "I'll tell everybody everything I know about you!"

"The hell you will!" He grabbed thick curls. Dacey's footsteps faltered as the slick soles on her new boots met dirt and pebbles. Her head came back. Cabot tried to pull free, fingers ensnared in her locks. Her feet slid. He heard a snap. The strand of pearls flew in all directions. Her body fell to the ground in a lifeless heap. Shaggy red hair partly covered her death-grimace face. "Dacey, get up!"

Shock gave way to motivation. Cabot didn't have time to grieve or cover tracks. He had to disappear.

~ ~ ~

The regular lunch crowd thinned by the time Jed McCrae came in to grab a bite to eat at MacHenry's. He had taken a swallow of his drink when Joe Mac slid in the booth across from him. "How ya been, Jed? We ain't seen much of you 'round here lately."

"Hey, Joe Mac. I've been caught up with other things."

"I heard, and I'm gonna be honest with ya, since you and me, we go way back. Your name's been comin' up in this place more than Budweiser's."

ON THE ROAD

"Doesn't surprise me." Jed bit into his sandwich. He didn't act like it bothered him. Joe Mac found that hard to believe, considering the extent of it.

"I stuck up for ya during those first round of rumors about the marijuana bust. But, this latest..."

"Thanks, man. Appreciate you for defending me, but I really don't care. What's the latest? I burned my parents' home to the ground for insurance money, something like that?"

Joe Mac chuckled. "No, nothin' like that. I guess you ain't heard." Jed motioned for him to continue. Joe Mac shuffled in his seat then blew his nose into a handkerchief. "About Lainey." Normally, had they been discussing a rumor about Jed's latest fling, they would've cracked jokes. Joe Mac didn't smile when he saw Jed's face. "Joe Mac, how 'bout we go chat in your office a minute?"

In privacy, Joe Mac told him the rumors around town.

Jed listened solemnly. "About Delaina being pregnant..." He stood. "Damn, why can't they leave her alone?" He wanted to bulldoze houses and hot glue lips. His hands went to his hips. His breath huffed. "It's nobody's business."

Joe Mac rubbed his forehead, watching a different clone of the Jed McCrae he used to know.

"Aw, man. Oh brother."

"What?" Jed sat.

"You love her. You love Lainey."

"Oh hell yeah I love her." Jed leaned in. "Look...Delaina hasn't had sex with anybody." Nobody would say his baby belonged to Cabot Hartley. "Except me, a time or two."

"Well...Lord have mercy."

Startling news they were, as a pair. Jed thought he saw Joe Mac's ears turn pink. "Maybe you could twist it up around here, Joe Mac. Say the appointment was probably Holland's. She's been staying at Cash Way, you know. Delaina doesn't deserve this."

"Jed, ain't she, like, nineteen?"

"She'll be twenty-one on May twenty-second." He felt like a piece of trash.

"*Mercy.* Folks are sayin' that's why she broke her engagement. She went runnin' off with you. You know, she's pregnant, and y'all eloped. Uh, where is Lainey?"

159

LAINEY AND JED, BOOK TWO

"Out of town for her safety during this investigation. I assure you, she's decided she's not ready to marry me or anyone yet. I've proposed more times than I care to count. In fact, tell everybody. Tell 'em...I'm down on one knee daily, straight from the horse's mouth. Let the sons of bitches chew on that."

Joe Mac made a clucking sound. "Lainey Cash, she's...the sweet spot in this town." He glanced at Jed. "I've always liked ya both. I'm gonna help out." He rubbed his chin, pondering. "Shoot, I'm liable to tell 'em that our little Lainey wants to wait till she's married and she's turned you into a sap." Joe Mac got plumb tickled at himself. "Yeah, I'm gonna tell 'em that."

"Good, you tell 'em that." Jed walked to the door. "I will marry her one day, Joe Mac." He grinned. "You can bet on that as sure as you can bet on sellin' beer tonight."

Joe Mac sat in awe for several seconds then returned to the bar. The story of a lifetime in Mallard County. Gossip, so good for business.

~ ~ ~

Sheriff Daniel Boyd chewed on the end of his cigarette and made eyes with Chief Raybon Hall while they waited in his office for Cabot Hartley. Investigator Cardin Morris and Attorney Warren Gage were also present. Two hours passed since they contacted Cabot. He wasn't answering his phone at work or his cell.

Sheriff Boyd and Raybon Hall were in no hurry to find him. For all they knew, Cabot would implicate them to take the heat off himself. "I'm going to see his father," Warren Gage said and slid on his blazer as Raybon Hall's phone rang. He answered, and listened with concern.

He hung up. "Men..." He looked at Sheriff Boyd. "Cabot will have to wait. Dan, your daughter's been found dead."

~ ~ ~

"I want the killer who did this in my custody in the next twenty-four hours, or so help me God, I'll tear up this town!" Sheriff Boyd turned from the crew of men to his patrol car. "I'm going home. I have to tell Sally Ann."

A spring afternoon, its beauty felt grossly inappropriate. Someone murdered his baby girl in daylight. The only blessing he found was that she was dressed, motive not sexual.

Then why?

His car felt stuffy. He let down the window. Jed McCrae passed, traveling toward his farm. Words from Jed's mouth, at the courthouse, reverberated in Dan Boyd's head.

'Under my belt would be an appropriate phrase. I was at the party on Mill's Pond because Sheriff Boyd's daughter Dacey called me, seriously inebriated, and asked me to pick her up and take her home, to my house, to my bed, two weeks before she was supposed to marry someone else. I planned to take her straight to the Sheriff's house as sloppy drunk as she was. Cops came right after I got there. Someone may have been trying to make a quick escape and dumped bags in my truck, but I believe it was planned and deliberate.'

Daughter Dacey never went to redneck parties, a born actress who sat home crying, who sneaked out of the house each Saturday morning at four a.m., who worked at the bank. Sheriff Boyd and his wife realized she secretly saw someone with enough money to give her nice presents. They said nothing; she was grown. For months, they assumed Jed McCrae. Now it seemed an absurd joke that Cabot Hartley had the pleasure of playing. Something went wrong between them related to Cabot and the marijuana scheme, and he killed her.

No one would suspicion Cabot. If the Sheriff told what he knew, he'd lose everything. His house, his wife, his job. He could keep quiet and pay the ultimate price. Guilt.

Sheriff Daniel Wayne Boyd might as well have broken his own daughter's neck.

He climbed out of the car, stumbled down the ditch, and vomited until there was nothing left.

~ ~ ~

Chief of Police Raybon Hall sat on granite and stared into space. Intake of gin and bittersweet nostalgia made for cold companions tonight. All his adult life, he wanted one thing.

Cassie Jane Darrah. She had been beautiful. She had been vivacious, flirtatious, and compassionate. Soft as rose petals and sweet as rain. Raybon's hand stroked the gravesite. *Cassandra Jane Darrah McCrae* it read, followed by *Loving Wife*. Her memorial stone left no hint she knew Raybon Hall or married Fain Kendall. Letters at the foot of the marker, *Devoted Mother to Jed*.

Raybon had waited and waited for anything to ease the pain or rekindle hope. He remembered the last time he saw Cass McCrae Kendall, written on his brain as accurately as a journal entry. Less than an hour before she died, December twentieth of last year, Raybon Hall sneaked into her house. Her nurse was in the kitchen. Cass slept in her bed, in snowy sheets, skin deathly white. When he looked down on her, he didn't see a fifty-year-old woman with ashen hair and dark circles under her eyes, body riddled with cancer that made ugly cavities where her breasts should've been. He saw his pretty Cassie Jane. He clutched her dainty hand, as he'd done when she rode the pony so long ago, and muttered identical words, "I've got you. Honey, it's Raybon at your deathbed. Raybon, not James Ed."

Her body had jumped so suddenly, Raybon jumped. Her eyes flew open. "*James,*" she pled. He remembered hearing footsteps against the wooden floor, signaling her nurse's return. Raybon dropped her hand, his heart anguished. He hid and waited for a clean escape. Cass's head turned toward the doorway. "James" she pled again. Raybon ran to the woods.

The memory hurt worse than the incident, Raybon realized, returning to the present. On bended knee, he slammed his fist into the cool earth. "I'm coming," he said in a sinister voice. On the flat granite marker beside hers, *James Ed McCrae, Loving Husband.* On the bottom, *Jed's daddy.* A weathered ceramic airplane propped on one corner. "I'm coming, Cassie honey." Raybon Hall pulled the pistol up to his temple. He squeezed the trigger and shot himself.

Red spurted into the air and splattered the center headstone, engraved *McCrae,* rising over the two flat markers of Jed's parents. Raybon Hall hit unforgiving stone with a thump, sprawled over James Ed's tomb, his bloody body covering words meant to memorialize a life.

~ ~ ~

Dacey Priscilla Boyd's autopsy revealed two things. One was surprising, one not so surprising. Nine weeks pregnant, died from a broken neck. The pregnancy, a crucial factor in her murder investigation, if it could be called an investigation with the sheriff grieving and Mallard's Chief Raybon Hall missing.

Cardin Morris from the state office took over. Currently at the Boyd residence, he questioned Dacey's mother Sally Ann, a woman soft from age and babies, a face wrinkled from poor living and three buck-wild sons. She sobbed each time her daughter's name was spoken. Not anything classy about her, other than her Southern hospitality, which was gracious, even now. "Drink, Mister Morris. Awful

ON THE ROAD

hot out," she said with typical Mississippi slowness. They sat on her back porch.

"I'm tellin' you, I don't have no clue whose baby she was carryin'. My Dacey was not no slut." Sally Ann Boyd blew her nose. "She was a dreamer, going places, didn't want babies. I named her Dacey Priscilla after Priscilla Presley."

Cardin Morris swallowed syrupy tea. The Mallard criminal investigation was a riot. Public servants as crooked as hell mixed with town folks as backwards as a tribe. "She'd been with two men, far as I know. A high school boyfriend and Coby Pollock, the boy she was engaged to."

"Does her ex, Coby Pollock, presently reside here?"

Sally Ann Boyd's face scrunched. "Does he do what?"

Cardin Morris sighed. "Does he live in Mallard?"

"Nope, and Dacey ain't laid eyes nor nothin' else on him since it ended. She lived with us. I can't explain this baby. There've been times when her daddy and me was thinkin' she might've slipped out and met a man..." She blushed. "I can't swear to it, and I feel like I'm betrayin' my daughter for talkin' such privacy with a stranger."

Cardin Morris jotted notes. "Coby Pollock. Why did their engagement end?" Sally Ann Boyd proceeded to tell him the story about Dacey's broken engagement after the Mill's Pond incident. At the mention of Jed McCrae's name, Cardin Morris raised his hand. "She called Jed McCrae to come get her that night." He had forgotten that fact from the courthouse interview with Jed McCrae and Delaina Cash.

"That's what folks claimed, but it didn't sound nothin' like my Dacey."

"You admitted that you don't have a clue whose baby she carried. There are things about your daughter you didn't know."

Sally Ann Boyd got to her feet in a huff. "I beg your pardon, Mister High-n-Mighty, come strollin' in here from Jackson. Me and my Dacey talked every night."

Cardin Morris wrapped up the interview. Time to nail someone and get out of this redneck riverside dump called Mallard.

~ ~ ~

Holland Sommers Smith partially obeyed Jed McCrae's orders. She went to Atlanta. She stayed only one night. So much going on in

LAINEY AND JED, BOOK TWO

Mallard that she couldn't separate herself. The next afternoon, she tapped on the door at Cash Way and tested the knob.

"Miss Holland, is that you?" Rhett appeared. He smelled like plowed earth and breezy cologne, like Eli. Holland banished that, glad to see him. "Jed thinks Mallard is dangerous for me."

"Yeah, me and Jed had a long talk. Looks like Cabot's tucked his tail feathers and ran, though. Gosh, Holland, I hope these tragedies are over."

"Yes, for everyone's sake. How are your parents?" Their eyes landed soft on each other.

"Going through the motions."

"Rhett, I want to go to Eli's grave at the Cash cemetery. I never saw it after the burial portion got canceled due to rain. Tell me how to get there."

"Darlin', his grave is a mound of dirt. Nothin' there to pay your respects to." "I want to go."

Rhett touched her arm. "Then let me drive you. I'll wait in the truck."

Perched on a hill on one side of Cash-McCrae Road, the cemetery featured a huge oak tree in the plot center. Black iron fences encased the area, gates on one side engraved *Cash*, the other *McCrae*.

"They share the cemetery?" Holland inquired.

Rhett pointed. "That big ole oak tree is the property marker. When Jed's father died, Jed's mama wanted him buried on the land. This area is no good for farmin'. Tory Cash did one of the only nice things he ever did and offered for James Ed to be buried here, so she wouldn't have to go through county procedures to get another plot approved." Holland nodded, thinking Jed McCrae and Delaina Cash's lives were braided as tightly as Indian hair. Rhett parked the truck. "Gates stay unlocked."

"I'm going to talk to Eli. To say goodbye. I must get on with my life."

Rhett gripped her hand. "My family couldn't have made it without you." "We're going to be okay, Rhett." He watched her elegant body as she followed a trail up the hill. He was not okay.

Holland opened the gates. Far corner of the cemetery, a newly covered grave stood out like an ugly brown mole on china skin. Wilted flowers encircled the mound. She knelt and scooped dirt in her hands. "We could've been happy. So much I never learned about you. Goodbye, Mollfred Elijah Smith."

ON THE ROAD

She glanced over the horizon, storing Eli's surroundings. Her heart collapsed. She tried to scream. Her mewling grew louder and louder. She stumbled in high grass. She tried to call Rhett's name.

He had been staring into space. Holland's image came into his peripheral, ghostly white and screaming. Rhett dashed out of the truck. "Holland honey, are you okay?" Viciously, she pushed him and crouched to the ground. "Blood," she managed. "So much blood." She fainted.

~ ~ ~

Sheriff Dan Boyd had a gut feeling Cabot Hartley wouldn't be showing his preppy face in Mallard soon. Their secrets were safe. The trade, his daughter's murderer ran scot-free.

No one in Dan's house knew the truth. His wife couldn't handle it right now. The longer he waited, the less likely she'd forgive him. Neighbors, friends, and fellow church members crowded nearby. Their tiny kitchen, packed with fried chicken, potato salad, chocolate cake, pies. Nothing seemed real.

A voice inside encouraged him to forget it. Truth wouldn't bring Dacey back. The sheriff closed his eyes and leaned into his recliner. What was done was done and best forgotten.

~ ~ ~

Mallard County had more gossip than it could hold. Dead Chief Raybon Hall had been found sprawled over the tomb of Jed McCrae's father with a letter in his pocket.

To whom it may concern:

I have been involved in a criminal plot with Cabot Hartley. Our goal was to incriminate Jed McCrae in a planned marijuana bust which took place in April. Cabot Hartley purchased the plants later discovered on McCrae Farms and Cash Way from Eli Smith. Eli did not know how the plants would be used; he sold them to Cabot because he was blackmailed about selling pot to college kids. I take full responsibility for my inappropriate actions. I believe eternity in hell is sufficient punishment.

Respectfully submitted,

Raybon Hall

Sheriff Dan Boyd was the best friend Raybon Hall had. The sheriff found a second letter tucked in his desk drawer.

Dan,

LAINEY AND JED, BOOK TWO

The loss of a child is a worse loss than any I've known. Sorry it's come to this. I appreciate the fishing trips, many times you could've been at home with the wife and kids. Live your life; I'll take the blame.
  Ray

~ ~ ~

"Where you headed first?" Dale Barlow did his best to take his youngest son's leaving like a man.

Boone Barlow spit tobacco juice. "Tournament over in Eufaula this weekend. Had an offer last week to move up to Branson. Hell, I got cash and nothin' but time."

"Son, I know you've got to make your own way, but call your mama often or else she'll worry herself to death and hound me more than she does now. That's enough to send me packin'. Last thing you want is your daddy showin' up at your doorstep."

Or the police, Boone thought, as he cranked the engine. His mama ran down the steps with a picnic basket on one arm. "Boone! Gotta keep the meat on your bones. Plenty snacks in here." She shoved the basket at him. "Call me quick as you can. I'll be worried sick till I know you've found a place."

"Come on, Mama, don't cry."

"Don't pay me no mind." She began walking toward the house. "Dale, looks as though you got extra time on your hands this afternoon. Grass needs to be cut."

Mallard County out of sight, Boone relaxed, thanking his lucky stars that Chief Raybon Hall came to see him before he killed himself. 'I've been in the business of investigating crimes long enough to know you ain't a criminal,' Raybon had said. 'Guilty of greed and jealousy. Common weakness among men. Leave here quick as you can. There ain't nothin' for a young man to aspire to around these parts."

Boone Barlow dug out a fried chicken leg from the basket and drove away.

~ ~ ~

"Honey, you need to rest." Rhett stood in Holland's room. Tucked in the sheets of a guest bed at Cash Way now, she had spent last night in the hospital, treated for exhaustion.

Maydell sat close by, watching. She accepted Holland as Eli's wife because of the baby. But this. With Rhett. She could see it in his eyes, the way he felt. Eli had loved Holland, and perhaps lost his life because of it. Maydell didn't want dramatic Holland involved with

166

ON THE ROAD

her only living son. Too fresh. Too complicated. "Rhett." "Ma'am?" "Let her rest." "If I leave, she won't rest."

"I will, if you promise me a walk in the garden after my nap." Holland smiled and melted him.

"All right, then." He walked out following his mother.

When the door closed, Maydell said, "Rhett, she ain't your responsibility."

"I'm doing what Eli would do for me."

"By fallin' in love with his wife?"

"I'm not in love with her. We're friends." First time Rhett remembered lying to his mama.

~ ~ ~

Several things demanded Jed's attention.

He had multiple conversations with authorities in the last few days. With Cabot considered a fugitive, the case had been turned over to agents. Jed stayed in close contact with Rhett regarding Cash Way. When he checked in with his Uncle Dale Barlow about McCrae Farms, he found out Boone left town the day after Cabot Hartley did. Good riddance to both. Raybon Hall's suicide at his parents' grave came as a low blow, leaving things to handle at the cemetery. He had discussed the fire with his insurance adjusters, ruled arson. Police assumed Raybon Hall the culprit based on his place of death and a testimony by Moll Smith. From Delaina's account of her attacker, Jed assumed it was Raybon and wondered if he also killed his dog Lucy.

Locking his office at day's end, Jed had enough time to ride around before sundown. He checked fields and went to his cabin at nightfall. It didn't feel good to come home. He cooled off from a shower. TV aired a game in the den while he sat on the couch. His phone went off. *Delaina Cash* blinked. He read, *I'm a few days late. Appointment tomorrow afternoon.* Jed called her.

"Hey, you didn't have to call."

Yes, he did. "You want me to fly out there?"

She made a startled noise. "For a pregnancy test? I think we know the results."

"Any more symptoms?"

"I'm unusually tired, and I've never been late."

Which could mean, or not mean, anything given her circumstances. "How's it going at my apartment, you okay there?"

167

"Yeah. JJ ate with me last night. I'm fine. Trying to stay calm. Thank you."

"Are you sure about me not comin'?"

"Stay there." Delaina sounded unreadable.

He started to say, *You know I love you*. Instead, "Soon, I'll update you on everything here. There've been major changes and breaks."

"Soon." She didn't sound like she cared. "I'll text you tomorrow."

He'd rather her *call him* about their pregnancy test. "Okay, tomorrow."

Silence, then, "Well, bye, Jed."

Sixteen

On the road again

Turned out, Jed flew there anyway.

If Delaina got mad, she'd just get mad.

Turned out to be a good thing he did. He landed about 11 a.m. to a message, *I'm bleeding. Going to Meggie's office during lunch* (with yellow crying face emoji). He didn't answer, unwilling to discuss it over text, and showed up at his apartment to stop her from driving. She argued with him about coming, asking to drive, basically existing, then threw the keys at his chest. That was his girl.

Meggie's office was situated in a modern complex of medical facilities. Jed spent significant time in those types of buildings during med school. That didn't settle him down today. Meggie's waiting room had emptied for lunch, other than posters of healthy babies on the walls along with mom bellies, vaginas, and breastfeeding ads. Jed or Delaina would've felt more at home inside a monkey zoo.

Delaina wore a polo-style dress, tiny underneath, and her red sneakers, hair in a bouncy ponytail. "We're not ready for this," she declared. She looked like the coolest version of a mom, or un-mom, Jed had seen. Meggie came out. Jed hugged her.

"I didn't expect to see you."

Delaina piped up, "I told him not to come."

Meggie tried to de-wrinkle. "I see dire situations every day. You're lucky he did. Come on back. It's the blood test that matters. Results take longer. Looking for the presence of the pregnancy hormone. If positive, we'll take your blood again tomorrow to determine whether it's increasing or decreasing."

LAINEY AND JED. BOOK TWO

About to go ape, Jed found a chair apart from the testing area. How did men do this? He happened to glance at a live birth video on a wall TV. "Ouch," he overheard from Delaina. She thought a needle hurt? While staring at a wholesome baby in a diaper on another poster, he heard Meggie say, "Urine's actually negative." "What does that mean?" Delaina asked in the shrillest voice. Jed headed to her. She looked scared and young. He had to get a handle on himself, for her. "Hey, it's okay, D."

"You may not be pregnant," Meggie commented, labeling a blood tube.

"That test in the pharmacy was positive. Jed, it was a double test, twice positive, and this bleeding isn't like my periods. It *hurts*."

She crushed him. "I believe you." He crouched beside her. "We believe you," Meggie soothed. "You two should grab lunch. Try to relax. I'll let you know as soon as I have blood results."

They got lunch in a cafe across the street, threw away uneaten sandwiches, and said little. Stepping into blinding sunlight on the sidewalk, Jed asked, "Do you wanna sit on that bench over there?" He pointed to a shade park.

Way too quiet for way too long, they sat. Hot day. Birds sang. People passed. "Delaina, whatever happens in there, we have to be okay with it."

She shook her head back and forth. "This isn't helping, Jed, please."

"It is." He looked outward. "Talk to me."

"I don't know how I want the test to turn out. The last few days, our baby felt real." He touched her arm. "I can honestly say there is a purpose for this. A sense of parental love and fierceness allowed me to see into the hearts of my parents. To begin to understand."

Their phones beeped. Meggie sent, *Come to my office.*

The front room, full of pregnant women and some fathers, welcomed less than the empty one had.

Delaina was taken in; Jed wanted to go with her. No one said he could. He sat and waited, scrolling nothing on his phone, until Meggie called him into her personal office. He passed by a nurse mumbling to Delaina. She had been crying. That could mean pregnant *or not*. Meggie closed the door and seemed somber. He sat, stood, sat. "*What?*"

"Negative." She shrugged. "I'm guessing here. I think fertilized egg, hence the positive home tests, then she experienced improper uterine implant from back-to-back highly stressful episodes."

"Chemical pregnancy."

She nodded. "Talking with her, I focused on stress and changes in her life, maybe a late period now, blah, blah, instead of a definite miscarriage because..."

"There's no point in her being overly emotional this early on without proof. She's too young anyway."

"Exactly." Meggie smiled sympathetically. "She needs rest while her body, emotions, and mind absorb these changes. May be tough for days, weeks, months. She's been through hell." Meggie had tears in her eyes, out of character, a born professional. "She's welcome to stay with me. Or get counseling."

"I'll let her decide. I'd like to take her home with me."

Delaina had walked in. "I'll go to Mallard." She felt shattered and confused, like they weren't ready for pregnancy or a miscarriage. Jed didn't know what he felt, other than in love with her and holding back.

Meggie directed, "Any major changes overnight, I want her/y'all here tomorrow morning for a follow-up." Jed suggested, "What about my apartment tonight? To give us time and to rest. If you're okay in the morn, we'll drive your car home." He got up and put an arm around her.

They had a simple afternoon, sitting on lounge chairs in the shade at the apartment complex ultra-posh pool. People straggled in and out buying a sandwich at the cabana or swimming laps. A musical playlist bellowed from the sound system; a midday British invasion of things like Jude and yesterday fit the mood. Jed told her everything going on in Mallard. They ate light fare from the cabana, watched clouds take shape, and drifted into naps more than once. Jed said he figured Cabot was somewhere like the Maldives by now, and he thought she'd be safe. That Cabot wasn't sharp enough to pull off anything too complex.

They never mentioned a baby.

They went to Jed's apartment and took separate showers, climbed into his bed after sunset, lying on their backs, bone-deep tired.

LAINEY AND JED, BOOK TWO

Jed didn't know what she felt or what it felt like. "Delaina, uh…" He sensed her face turn. He turned into her. Their bodies warmed each other; he felt her breath. He didn't mean to kiss her. Their mouths warmed each other; he felt her need. "I know we're not together anymore, but I…"

She kissed him more intimately. Her hands were in his hair. He stopped because he had to, for a multitude of reasons. "Are you still bleeding?"

"Jed," she muttered, "we can't anyway."

For a week minimum, he knew that. Meggie was clear. Not that Delaina would want to have sex again anyway, thanks to him. Especially with him. "That's not why I asked. I asked because I care." "It's not much now." "Still in pain?" "Cramping from the waist down, front and back."

Those words sent knives into him. He didn't know what to do for her. He didn't mean to kiss her again. She didn't respond. She wore a loose nightgown. Pale pink and flirty with cotton bikini underwear; of course, he noticed after her shower. He tugged the hem. "I like this. I wanna take it off." He lifted the hem.

"We're over," she said with bite. He was the one who said they weren't together anymore.

"I wanna give you a massage." Her nightgown melted away. "Turn over." She did. He kneaded her lower back, skimmed fingers, squeezed muscles, rubbed bones, scratched skin. She cried tears into her pillow until she felt nothing but his hands.

He lifted her hair, his head close to her neck. Darkness and proximity encouraged intimacy and honesty. "You need time, sweetheart. Space. That doesn't change the fact that I love you."

Delaina wanted to curl up in a ball. She wanted to flip over and reject doctor's orders. She wanted to cry her eyes out. She wanted Jed near her, so she could bite his head off, or kiss him senseless, she wasn't sure. She flipped. "I don't know what I need." She reached her arms around him, bringing his upper body down over hers. They kissed deeply.

"I swear I only wanna make you feel better." Jed returned to his side, lying on his back, stroking her arm.

"I know. We're…craving…closeness. Today was tough."

Jed stored that. He didn't know what to do for her. She craved closeness.

172

On the Road Again

"Do you like your back scratched?"

"Uh." Jed couldn't remember any woman's touch pre-her, at that moment.

"Turn over. I'll scratch your back."

"Give me a sec. Gotta practice multiplication tables before I turn over."

She did her trademark "Huh?" She laughed gently. "*Oh*."

"Cupcake, I have something to tell you." Closeness. Here goes.

Cupcake. Tears sprang into her eyes.

"When I'm on the farm now, either farm anywhere, it feels like it's not mine or yours. It's ours."

Delaina couldn't describe the relief. *Exactly how she felt.*

He curved his face to her and went on, "Maybe we should put it all together. For ease and efficiency. Not ownership, but you know..."

She interrupted, "Labor, equipment, decisions, orders, storage. I do know. I agree."

Jed had to kiss her. Had to. He did briefly. "Good. I'll start on it as soon as we're back, but not without runnin' everything by you. You're gonna be home resting, I hope."

"Doctor's orders. Okay. *Thank you*." Their collaboration fostered more closeness. "I have something to tell you, big guy."

Big guy. Uh-oh. "Hmm. All right." His hand held hers.

She took an audible breath and offered him an olive branch. "That night when you surprised me in the field. Uhm, when you pulled me on top of you, it was really, really, mmm, amazing."

Whoa. Closeness. She still loved sex. With him. "I noticed."

"At one point, I put my head on your chest and started movin' slowly with my legs between yours. You held my hips and it was... I don't know the word, Jed McCrae."

"That was you, Delaina Tory, makin' love to me."

She felt like a flowy night princess regarded most highly. "Turn over. I'll scratch your back."

He chuckled. "Just a sec. Gotta do long division in my head."

Turned out, he got addicted to having his back scratched *by her*.

~ ~ ~

GPS said six hours and forty-four minutes to Mallard.

Inside the Mississippi state line, they talked about whether she should stay with Jed for safety or go to Cash Way. Her eventual decision, "I wanna go home and get my act together."

LAINEY AND JED, BOOK TWO

Jed helped her unload when they got there and gave her a hug on the front steps.

~ ~ ~

Long, hot, empty days passed. Jed managed Delaina's farm via Moll and Rhett and texted to check on her daily.

Cabot Hartley's parents offered a grand reward for information on his whereabouts. Jed figured they knew where he was. In a faraway land.

Tire tracks at the creek where Dacey Boyd got killed matched a loaner car from the only car lot in Mallard. Jed confirmed that he saw Cabot in that same car in Hammond, Louisiana. Since Raybon's death and Cabot's disappearance, there'd been no threats or crime. Jed had visited Holland, temporarily staying at Cash Way, regaining strength. She told him that she planned to leave for Atlanta soon.

Town gossiped about him, Delaina, Cabot, Holland, Eli, and Dacey-horrendous combinations involving drugs, sex, murder, marriage, and illegitimate babies.

Currently at the Denton Place, Jed checked a rain gauge. The vibrant field, the post-shower sunshine, the damp air, made him think of her. He had postponed talking in person long enough. He drove to her house. Maydell Smith answered the door. "I need to see Delaina," he said.

"I'll tell her." Maydell turned toward the staircase.

"No, let me, please."

Maydell shook her head. "I'm not sure she wants to see you." She twisted her hands in her apron. "Mr. McCrae, she's havin' a heck of a time."

"Call me Jed. What do you mean?"

She frowned. "I don't have no idea about facts. All I know is Lainey don't hardly leave this house. Bless her heart." Maydell had an accusing look. "She don't even go to ride on the farm with Rhett or Moll. I don't know what you done to her. I wish you'd undo it."

"Where is she?" "Her bedroom. Upstairs on the left." Jed walked through the foyer. He felt Maydell's censure, caught her watching him like a mother bird watches its nest.

"Maydell, I love Delaina. I don't know if that makes it better or worse."

ON THE ROAD AGAIN

Maydell didn't respond. All her life, she, as a Cash employee, had automatically disliked McCraes. There Jed McCrae stood, admitting feelings for Lainey Cash, humility spread across his face.

"She's got a lot to figure out with her family situation and the farm and being so young to have all of it, including me, thrown at her. I just wanna see her, check on her."

Maydell didn't stop him.

Throughout the morning, Delaina stayed poolside swimming and reading. Afternoon got too hot. Then it rained. She had gone to her room and called Della. Their second and third phone calls had been more than a stipulation in Fain's will. Delaina needed to know her biological mother. Fain had been right about that.

Eccentric Della Kendall spent time in her garden greenhouse growing herbs or in her home studio sculpting. She had seen the world, not from elegant hotel windows but from rented RVs, discount motels, and men's bank accounts. She went to college, using alimony money from Tory, and became a nurse. She admitted to Delaina that Tory paid her well to stay out of their lives, and she wasn't a good mother. She sensed her mother's anxiousness for a visit. Delaina was not ready.

She stripped off her swimsuit in her walk-in closet. Her wedding gown hung on the door. She hadn't taken it out of the bag since final alterations. Today, she did. Her hands ran over the silk fabric. The dress in person, more outstanding than her dreams. She held it up. A mirror hung on the far wall of her closet. Backing into her bedroom, she could see herself in the closet mirror.

She had an urge to wear her dress.

She slid it over her nude body like a cool caress. A row of buttons Delaina fastened with effort trailed down the back. Her image startled her. The woman in her dream, the bride. Jed's bride. She made her hair into a twist and stood.

Jed eased down the hall. Delaina's door stood open. Sunrays flowed onto sage green painted walls, antique furniture, and a brown teddy bear on a white chenille bedspread. Beneath the window, acres of land stretched. Jed took a step, captured by the intimacy of being there, where Delaina slept since she was born.

A rustling of fabric interrupted his thoughts. She stood in the doorway of her closet. Her beauty slammed into him. Dressed in her wedding gown, she looked at herself in a mirror. A spectacular dress, silk of utmost quality, glowed white as angel wings and fit her elegantly. A thin strap on each shoulder held it to her body. The neckline scooped low on her soft curves. A delicate row of clear crystals, the only adornment, ran under the cup of her breasts, encircling the back, giving the dress an A-line fit. The pure material clung to her waist and opened into a semi-full skirt.

Delaina began to undo buttons, exposing golden skin on her back. Jed shoved his hands in his pockets. Images, swift and powerful. Delaina, his bride. Delaina, his wife. Sliding her dress down, easing her body onto their bed. Sliding over her, sliding into her. Fifteen thousand times for fifty years. He walked out and went downstairs.

Mother Hen Maydell stood at the foot of the staircase. Jed didn't blame her. "Maydell, what will she do with her wedding dress?"

"Well, she, uh, told me I could remake it for my niece in Alabama who's getting married."

"I want it. Her dress was for me, Maydell. You understand?"

"Lainey would never forgive me."

"She won't know." Jed weighed words. "I'll pay you for the dress. Enough to give your niece her dream wedding." He bent several inches to her face. "Miss Maydell, you raised a real lady."

She fumbled with her apron, trying to think of a reason to refuse. She looked at the handsome face fixed on hers. "Oh, all right. I'll get it for you."

"Our secret." Jed smiled. "She was...in her closet. I didn't interrupt. Please go tell her I'm here."

When Delaina came downstairs, she looked nothing like the blissful vision who ripped the heart from Jed's chest. She motioned to Tory's study.

Jed pivoted, taking in framed aerial photos of the farm, identical to those in his office. One hand cupped the nape of his neck. "A little intimidating...to stand in Tory Cash's study with his daughter."

"I'm not his daughter."

"Mallard's slingin' plenty of mud..."

"I'm fine."

"I've been out checkin' rain gauges." That got her attention. One of the best parts of a farmer's job, riding around to check gauges after a good rain.

"How much?" she asked. "It didn't rain long. We could use a soaker."

God, she looked sexy, becoming instant farmer. "About an inch."

"Everywhere?"

"I don't know yet. Wanna ride around, listen to music, and help me check? It's why I'm here." Jed smiled. "Rainy Day Lainey."

Delaina's breath caught. "I'll get my boots."

The first ride led to another the next day and so on. During lunch hour, they would discuss business and ride out to look at areas. He'd show her how he did things. Sometimes she'd show him.

Anyone who knew her before and after the deaths of Fain Kendall and Tory Cash could see the change. She hadn't re-enrolled in college. She didn't leave the house other than to ride with Jed or piddle. He looked for topics to spark her interest like Meggie's wedding and baseball scores. He avoided silence because when they were silent, he nearly had to tie his hands to keep from touching her and tape his mouth shut not to ask how she was, regarding their pregnancy scare.

Jed couldn't shake the feeling. If it weren't for the wills, she wouldn't stay in Mallard, Mississippi, another day.

~ ~ ~

Holland Sommers Smith stood in the driveway of Rhett Smith's rental house. She already said goodbye to Maydell, Moll, and Delaina. A gold rope chain with an eagle pendant hung around her neck, Eli's, the only object of his that she kept. She spotted a beat-up truck coming toward the house.

Rhett stepped out. Grimy shirt, greasy hands, hair curling from sweat and need for a trim. Trees shaded the lot. She couldn't see Rhett's dark eyes under his hat.

"Thanks for coming to say goodbye, Rhett. Time to go."

They stood between the driver door and the interior. He scooped his hat off and held the top with one hand. His eyes squinted. "Not much on goodbyes." Eli's golden eagle gleamed like fire into Rhett's eyes. "Ain't got the gift of words my brother did." He ran the back of his hand down her arm. "Take care and keep in touch, Miss Holland. Drive safe."

Holland got in the car and slid on sunglasses. She hoped for an intervention, any protest, that didn't come. The best thing she could do for herself would be to hightail it out of Mississippi, having emailed her notice at the bank to Joe Cabot Hartley, minutes ago. "I'll be in touch soon." She shut the door and cranked the engine.

Rhett backed onto the porch, shoved his hands in his pockets, and watched her go. All the way to the gates and beyond, until he could no longer see the blur of her yellow car.

He walked inside and retrieved a bottle of whiskey, last of Eli's. He sloshed amber liquid into a glass with ice. "That was for you, brother."

SEVENTEEN

Hometown

D elaina made her first venture into town to get her hair trimmed at *Salon Doreen*.

From the sidewalk, she could see the place crowded with women. Ironically, she thought, she wore a scarlet red tank sweater. Might as well have the "A" sewn on it. She walked in.

Owner Doreen Rosemund spoke. "Come on in, Lainey. Mary Jo will shampoo you in a sec." No one else said anything. Mary Jo came to take her to sink stations in a cubicle near the back. "How are Maydell and Moll?" she asked as she positioned Delaina at the sink.

"Takin' it pretty hard." Mary Jo sprayed her hair. Delaina closed her eyes. Warm water ran over her scalp. Mary Jo stopped spraying to get shampoo.

The conversation in the next room, broken by the interruption of salon services, went something like, "...weekend in Houston together...engaged to Cabot." Delaina's eyes flew open. Mary Jo sprayed more water to drown it. Delaina could tell that she strained to hear what they said, sorry to be missing juicy gossip. She stopped the water to lather conditioner. "tacky...planning a showy wedding...cheating with Jed....slutty, if you ask me...well, I heard she's a virgin..." Water sluiced across Delaina's hair. Mary Jo scrubbed her scalp, tension in her fingers evident. Delaina squeezed her eyes shut to hold back tears. "not a Cash...somebody told me Fain...Fain with Lainey's mother?...heard she was a prostitute, way back...Cass didn't deserve..." "Okay," Mary Jo interrupted, toweling her hair. "Doreen will cut your hair."

LAINEY AND JED, BOOK TWO

The words, "Jed used Lainey...started these tragedies...her fault," escorted Delaina out of the cubicle. She entered the room to women congregated receiving services. Everyone quieted and smiled. She felt young, stupid, and cheap. She reached in her pocket. "Here, Doreen, this is for the shampoo." She laid cash on the desk and walked out.

~ ~ ~

Mallard was home. All he had known. Where Hartleys reigned supreme. With every creature comfort at his disposal. Where people bowed to him and kowtowed to him.

Remote islands, fruity drinks, and women in bikinis on the beach. Things to enjoy for a few days, then go home.

Mallard, Cabot Hartley's town.

If he couldn't live there peacefully, powerfully, perpetually, no one else would.

It felt good to be home.

~ ~ ~

Too much for one person, that's all Jed knew.

Irrigation units needed checking, insect reports needed monitoring, two fields needed nitrogen applications, someone needed to meet the vet at a pasture, a well unit at an orchard was problematic, and he hadn't touched paperwork for either farm in days. He leaned against a tractor, talking to Rhett. "I'm doing what I can," Rhett said for the second time.

"I know, Rhett, but I'm givin' you more responsibility. You're the best we've got."

Rhett puffed at the unexpected compliment. "I tryin' to make up for sellin' pot and for Eli getting in with Cabot Hartley." Jed instructed, "Meet the vet to take care of cattle vacs. Let me know." "Gotcha."

Jed felt vaguely satisfied. Cash Way came first; whatever McCrae Farms needed would have to wait. He dragged his arm across his face to wipe sweat.

Workers did all they could. Jed discerned that Eli, being the elder son, had originally been given more responsibility. Rhett was considered second best, second in line. Only now was he beginning to shine.

Jed needed someone to do paperwork so he could get out and oversee labor. Plus, he had research projects with the university, ag committees, and other investment opportunities tabled lately. He ate, slept, and breathed farming, up before dawn and never home before nine.

Delaina worked more each day but preferred field work. He wouldn't insult her by asking her to stay indoors. She, as capable as any man.

He took a swig of lemonade, wishing for something stronger, and ambled toward the truck. ...She seemed uncomfortable with him when they were around each other, and she should be. All he could think about when he was with her was touching her. An exercise in self-restraint, self-flagellation, and self-indulgence, if there was such a combo, every time he saw her. He texted, *Hey. We need to meet. I'm at my shop.* She answered, *Driving from town. Ok.*

He drove closer to the entrance at the road, the spot where they shared their first kiss, got out, let the tailgate down, and sat. His head itched from heat and sweat. He adjusted his hat, turning it backward.

Her SUV came down Cash-McCrae road as he reached in his cooler for another lemonade. Delaina stepped out. She wore a cap over damp hair, sunglasses, a sweater tank top, and tight jeans. An electric reminder blasted through Jed's loins.

She sat on the tailgate. He handed her the lemonade. "Thanks, it's pretty warm out."

"Hot as horse piss."

Delaina frowned. "I'll get irrigation checked before dark."

"Delaina, we gotta hire someone for desk work. I'm a good farmer. I'm not a fuckin' magician."

She flinched. "Whatever you think." No attempt to elaborate, contribute, converse. A tear dripped off her jaw. Jed's stomach balled. What now? His fingers clamped her sunglasses and removed them. Her eyes were red.

He motioned. "This'll have to wait." Pushing his sunglasses onto his head, he said, "Tell me, whatever it is." Eyes as soft as chambray focused on her.

"Compared to this, it's unimportant. I went to Doreen Rosemund's salon. Took me God knows how many pep talks..." She told him the story.

When she got done, Jed said, "Be right back," and walked to his office. In a minute, he came out, cleaned up, hatless with a fresh T-shirt, Bleu Cotton's *Plant Good Seed.* "You drive." He slid into her passenger's side. He smelled like cool water, like mouthwash, like outdoors, like Jed. Leaning over, he tipped her hat. "Take it off."

"What, the cap?"

"The cap and anything else you're willin' to shed." She shook her hair out. He eyed her skeptically. "You got any lipstick or eye makeup?"

"Do I look that bad?"

"I want you lookin' extra good. I need a ride to town."

She dug lip gloss and mascara from her purse, put it on, and cranked the engine. Halfway down Cash-McCrae Road, Delaina said, "I don't wanna make a scene."

"You can go with me, or I can do this myself. It'll be prettier if you're with me."

She gripped the steering wheel. "I've told you I don't need you to..."

"It's obvious how little you need me." Quiet over a stretch of road, Jed eventually tapped her arm. "I graduated high school with Dori June Salinger. Yep. Dori June come-too-soon Salinger had a gap between her front teeth and mousy-brown hair. She went down on any boy who'd drop his pants at Mallard High." Delaina made a puzzled expression. Jed revealed, "She's now the Honorable Judge Paul Rosemund's wife, owns a salon."

"Doreen Rosemund?"

Jed winked. "Everybody knows everything about everybody." Delaina said, "Tell me again what she was like." Jed told her more juicy info. "Since we graduated, Dori June had her fat sucked, her boobs tucked, her hair bleached, her freckles bleached, braces. Heck, I bet she had her teeth bleached; that was a lot of semen for one mouth."

Delaina laughed loudly. "Stop it. Did you ever..."

"Hell no." Jed chuckled. "Well..."

Delaina rolled her eyes.

"Seriously, no. You wanna hear about her best friend Mary Jo good-for-a-blow Duffner?"

"*Stop.*" Then on a straighter face, "Truthfully, Jed, you're talkin' about Mary Jo who does shampoo?" He nodded. She snickered ungracefully, tried to chastise him for being rude, but every time she looked, he mouthed, "Dori June and Mary Jo."

They reached downtown Mallard. "Park in front of her salon." He walked around and opened Delaina's door. She stepped out and gave him a tentative look. He pinched her on the butt. "Come on, this might be the most fun we've had in Mallard." He ducked and kissed her cheek. "Inside the city limits, anyway." Delaina noticed downtown sidewalk shoppers stare, women peer out shop windows. He wrapped his arm around her. "*Jed*," she warned.

"Hey, I have a reputation to uphold. Look interested in me, or I'll have to force a kiss on you in broad daylight." Her shiny hair swished in the afternoon breeze. "I'm gonna lay one on you anyway."

He reeled her in. A rough stab of lust streaked through Delaina. She leaned into him and opened her mouth. Tongues touched, then his mouth left hers. "Never have put up much of a fight…" He patted her back, moving them along. "Want an ice cream?" *No, you fool, I want another kiss.* "Don't worry. I'm planning on kissin' you again. Vanilla or chocolate?" He led her into the drugstore. "Hey, Miss Millie."

Miss Millie, wife of local pharmacist Mister Harold, also his drugstore clerk. A seventy-year-old, churchy, plump, known-to-everyone lady. Conversations ceased, heads turned, eyes scampered. Miss Millie stuffed a prescription in a customer's bag. "Hi there, Jed," she replied nimbly. "Lainey."

"She's liable to go cardiac on us," he whispered.

He had that look. Oh God, Delaina thought, *that* look like he had at the baseball game in Houston, when he enjoyed pretending that they were married. "Oh no, please no. Don't."

He sat on a stool at the counter. "I want Cherry Coke, Miss Lucille," he said to a familiar clerk. His deep voice floated over the room. "Can't beat that cherry taste." He winked and smiled, all blameless blue eyes and pearl teeth, at Delaina. "What do you want, doll?"

Heavenly God… "Uh, single scoop of vanilla on a waffle cone." She tried to sound casual.

His hand landed on her shoulder and traced circles. "A sweet treat for my sweet treat."

Giggles bubbled out; she couldn't help it.

Miss Millie and a customer paused mid-sentence, staring. They weren't the only ones. The mundane motions of customers in a drugstore, picking up pills, paying for toiletries, were on hold.

Delaina whispered, "They're ridiculous." Jed nodded imperceptibly. She took an indulgent lick of her ice cream. Jed choked on his drink. She patted his back. "You okay?"

LAINEY AND JED, BOOK TWO

"Yeah," he answered, coughing. Delaina propped one arm on the counter to face him. She raked her tongue up the mountain of ice cream and slurped. "Very good," she said, voice as liquid sweet as the drop of ivory cream caught on her top lip. Impulsively, Jed kissed it off. They finished flirtatiously while ordinary drugstore proceedings resumed in slow motion.

"Let's go, cupcake." She took a last bite. Jed's eyes raked over her. "Makes me wish I was made of sugar and cream." "You are." Smiling sweetly, she pranced in front of him. Neither gave the drugstore the satisfaction of a glance.

Jed had a mission today, regardless of their future.

He would publicly adore her so thoroughly that no one would ever doubt she was on a short list in Mallard County, Mississippi. In fact, a single name.

Love of Jed McCrae's life, Lainey Cash.

It would be one of *those* days, small-town scale, where everyone remembers where they were and what they were doing when it happened, like Kennedy, like Challenger, like the day the towers fell, where the story got repeated over and over as time moved on. 'You remember when,' and details and eyewitness claims increase infinitely. So valid he would be, it wouldn't make a difference what news, or who else, either of them brought to Mallard from now on. For the rest of their lives, all the way till old and gray, all the way to the grave, fifteen thousand times for fifty years, the concluding statement for any McCrae or Cash gossip, any happening, any mention of their names would be, '...and you *know*, Jed McCrae loves Lainey Cash.'

"On we go." Jed slipped a finger in her back pocket.

"You're taking unnecessary liberties."

"Like this..." He pulled her head to his with his free hand and kissed her. Delaina wrapped her arms around him for more. Jed looked over Delaina's shoulder. "Preacher Ward, Ms. Sue, how are you?" She angled around, spinning from the kiss, mortified that her pastor and his wife stood in front of them. "Jed," the preacher replied. They shook hands. "Lainey, we've missed you on Sundays. I know you've had a lot going on. We're prayin' for everyone at Cash Way. Hope to see you in worship service soon."

"Yes, thank you." She fanned her fingers through her hair.

"I know he's Methodist, but perhaps Jed could join you on a Sunday," her preacher invited. Delaina risked a look. Jed stood erect. "I'd come with her anytime. She's such a lady." "Perhaps he will," she squeaked, going past them on the sidewalk.

"Oh God," she muttered when they were out of earshot. Chuckles rumbled in Jed's chest, edging outward, reaching her. She giggled and stopped beneath a towering tree. "Jed...we can't do this. I can't have my entire hometown thinkin' I'm your latest thing."

He rocked on his feet, looking amused. "Based on what I've heard, they're already thinkin' you're my...thing, sweetheart. Over two weeks of abstinence on my part proves you are the latest." He pushed her toward the sidewalk casually. They strolled for a stretch of concrete, holding hands, arriving in local enchantment- Historic Mallard Town Park, amidst young families, couples from the college, and singles.

Everyone noticed.

Jed walked, stopped, kissed her. Told her she was the most beautiful thing there, standing by the largest magnolia tree, blooming majestic and white. Oldest in the plot, according to the dedication plaque, that certainly God and the mayor and The Anderson Family intended to be the most beautiful thing there.

Time turned supernatural, a definitive interruption, an energetic buzz that propagated itself because of a rare occurrence, like the President passing through, like whether the groundhog saw its shadow, like fireworks on Independence Day, like a snowfall in May. People came out of the woodwork, onto the streets, up to the windows, using any excuse or no excuse. To watch, to find out if it was true. Too see just how much snow might fall in May.

Jed walked, stopped, kissed her. Instigated selfies of her with his phone, for everyone to see the way he beamed, how he focused on getting her just-right picture in front of their hometown's famous soldier statue.

Was he going to post pictures? He wasn't on social media, was he? No one had ever seen him downtown in daylight with a female. They pondered that and more and said it aloud from cars, benches, and shops. Much less had they seen Jed McCrae head over heels like a fool!

Standing at *the* koi pond, rippling water darkened teal by lily pads and inhabited by the sweethearts of Mallard, a pair of swirling fish. No one really knew if they were male or female or if it had always been the same two fish, but they were forever there swimming together, so Jed, like hundreds of Mallard males before him, draped his arm around Delaina, pointed while she watched delightfully, and said, "Look, there's Lainey and Jed," like he was supposed to. Delaina burst into laughter and love like she was the first to have the fish named after her, like she was supposed to.

He walked, stopped, kissed her. Under the big loudspeaker that played always too loud, always cracked and popped, always aired songs from the guy with sideburns and blue suede shoes, Mississippi's biggest claim to fame born several towns over. Then Jed did something far fewer Mallard men had done. He twirled her around to the music like a daylight ballerina and dipped her in front of the roped-off gazebo covered in vines. Her laughter echoed through the streets.

He walked a dozen steps, stopped, kissed her. And put himself in a class of his own. With the grace and giddiness of the "Just Married," he lifted her hand and led her as he stepped over the rope. "Jed." Delaina laughed uneasily. "*What* are you doing?" He kept going forward, tugging her. "We can't."

He leaned back. "Where's my Sunflower riverbank girl?"

"She learned her lesson."

He would not have it; she would not turn bitter. "Bullshit." He offered her the best smile he had, deadly fine and shining. "Come on, Lainey Cash. This is our town."

How Hollywood they must look there, in the middle of Mallard, Jed holding her hand up, daring her. A big laugh popped out of her mouth. She offered the best smile she had, deadly fine and shining, and stepped over the rope. Once in a lifetime now, like Christmas in July. They went into the gazebo, he bent into her, and they swayed sweetly. While The King of Rock and Roll pondered whether Lainey would be lonesome this evening, into the second verse, Jed said, "You know, I never believed Elvis actually did this."

The gazebo truly was unusually magnificent, older than The War, towering above the park with giant columns and what seemed like millions of flowers surrounding it. The tale went, the music star, traveling through Mallard to somewhere else, had seen the town's alluring gazebo from his car window and stopped time to get out and dance beneath it with his own princess while he serenaded her.

Delaina had a popping laugh again. She never thought to question it. She got a feeling, then and there. "You're right. It didn't happen." Jed shook his head no. They giggled about their secret while their world looked on in wonder.

With more lovely emotion flowing through her than she had felt in days, Delaina flirted. "Maybe it was meant for us." Jed pulled her tight. "Positive." Deep into their feelings, painting a non-erasable image of beautiful love and perfect dancing for curiosity seekers, Jed wanted to say, *I can't do this, Delaina, now that I've had you in my arms, in bed, in my life. I can't go back to the way things used to be, while you're sleeping three hundred yards away from me night after night. I can't be un- in love with you.*

How long could he hold back? Until she got older, finished with school, till she felt ready. With an upbringing like hers, would she ever be ready?

May had been exponentially harder than April for Jed. She had not sent him one text, unrelated to the farm, or initiated one conversation, one meeting, anything. He didn't point out any of that. Instead, he tossed her over his shoulder and threatened to haul her to the sparkling fountain, with her laughing and squealing, "Jed, stop!" Town folk through the whole block heard and saw. He set her down, lifted his phone into the air, and caught the most shameless, lust-faced, iridescent-fountain-sunlit backdrop, startling picture of them inside the gazebo, cheeks together, in the middle of downtown. Totally in love. Totally convincing. Totally real.

Arm around her, Jed walked until they reached Delaina's car. He went to her side to open her door. He slid off his sunglasses and waved at someone across the street. "Hey, Dori June." He inched forward, maneuvering Delaina against her car door. "The Honorable Mrs. Doreen Rosemund is frozen in the salon, gaping at us with her clients." His eyes incinerated Delaina like blue blazes. "Your call."

Broiling sun beat through her clothes, mixed with the nonchalant scent of spring flowers, flirty ruffles hemming a conservative breeze. A rainfall in Kentucky crackled across music airwaves. All of it rolled inside Delaina, pushing her. She motioned to him with the tilt of her head. He closed in, breathing on her.

For an hour, they had been *Jed and Delaina* again. How glittering.

"Kiss me like you love me," she uttered. "I'll never forget today."

Rays of sunlight intensified longing on Jed's face. He lowered his mouth to hers, his eyes slit, and the kiss flourished. Both of them, the angle of their heads, where their arms, hands, torsos, legs, and feet were positioned, made a picture of movie-poster perfection. Cozy, timeless, impeccable. She nipped his lower lip with her teeth. Jed owned her mouth. "Too much," she moaned. "Not enough," he grumbled, sliding his fingers through her hair, pushing her harder against the car as he arched his pelvis into hers. His lips pulled away; the rest of him pressed into her while he gave her the most extended, adoring look in county history, model of picture perfection solidifying to infinity. He breathed words into her hair, "Come see me tonight, D. I want you in my bed." Delaina's fingers clawed into his arm. Car engines whizzed. Shoes clapped against the sidewalk. A little girl squealed.

For Delaina, the town scandals and stipulations in both family wills had been nothing compared to trying to come to terms with their pregnancy incident. Something she shared with no one, not even Jed. Christmas in July was one of those things, like catching the King with Priscilla, like Houston in the gold dress, like a wonder-filled love story in the park. So uncommon, it couldn't be verified, too risky to believe in, particularly in this distracted millennium.

Awkwardly, she moved out of his arms and got in the car. Jed stood a moment longer then got in. Riding to the farm, each watching outside, there could've been a thousand miles between them. On the driveway at his shop, Jed slid out. "I'm headed to Houston after irrigation finishes a round. Haven't seen a game in four weeks." He shut the door.

Eighteen

Happy Birthday

Something catastrophic was bound to happen.

Delaina and Jed knew to expect the unexpected, managing thousands of acres of land. Delaina had been doing what she could to prevent further destruction for fifteen minutes. The expansive irrigation unit that she and Jed shared on Farm 130 got stuck, a fact of life in farming. Little plants drowned in their sustenance. She estimated hours of damage. She sank to her ankles in mud, looked no different than a pig in a mud bath. She felt like a hornet whose nest had been poked one too many times. By the wrong little boy. Her nerves jumped like they had been flayed open with a dressing knife, eyes gummy from exhaustion, clothes plastered against her skin like drenched blankets.

Thursday afternoon in the park with Jed left her unsettled.

Two nights of sleeplessness left her stirring for a fight.

Just six o'clock on Saturday morning, she had the rest of the day to trudge through. The rest of the year. Whatever restraint on her temper she had managed broke. No excuse Jed could muster would explain why he had not checked the irrigation during the night or answered her text. It was his job!

She agreed to do afternoon checks. He, middle-of-the-night/early mornings. How easy; they had monitors on their phones. She stomped to her SUV, water squishing out of her boots. She gunned the accelerator. Her vehicle fishtailed into a bog. She bore down to make traction in the muck and gained headway. She turned the wheel and accelerated, accidentally biting her lip, catapulting to the beaten path. Delaina wiped blood from her mouth, paying attention

LAINEY AND JED, BOOK TWO

to herself in the rearview mirror. She plowed the brakes and almost jackknifed another car. A yellow convertible parked front and center of Jed's cabin. She dragged herself out and subconsciously grabbed at her shirt, pulling it from her breasts. She was saved the inconceivable motion of knocking.

Holland strolled onto the porch, blinking heavy lids and wearing a man's T-shirt worn to the point that the word Astros was barely detectable. Barely but detectable. "Hi." She squinted. "What on earth..." She perused Delaina's disheveled appearance. Delaina was thinking the same thing and asked, "Where's Jed?" with comical superiority given her state of dress and distress.

Holland spoke on a yawn. "I was half asleep when he said something about checking irrigation." She jerked herself erect when she saw the look on Delaina's face. "Oh God, Delaina. Oh my goodness, I..."

"Spare me the details." Delaina offered a deliberate smile and sailed off the porch. "I'll find him." She had the urge to yell at Holland that she had been Jed's first choice in bed. Emotions swelled to a boiling point as she drove down the path. Shock, hurt, anger, and disappointment rolled into one tangible feeling. Confusion. She told herself that she had no business worrying who Jed had sex with; she admitted she'd never survive the year if she knew. She scanned field rows, saw no sign of him, rammed her foot into the accelerator, and sent dirt flying. At the main road, she reached for her phone. He had answered, *Otw,* two minutes ago. She called him. "Where the hell are you?"

"Lookin' for you."

"That makes two of us...both of us," she stammered. "Irrigation's been stuck for hours!"

Delaina saw his truck coming toward her. She parked at a precarious angle on the ditch and jumped out. She reminded Jed of a mad mud wrestler. She opened the passenger door, climbed in, and slammed it, shaking the interior. "Go! East corner." He gained speed, uncertain how to handle such a slippery female this early in the morning. He navigated the truck on the field row like a captain at rocky sea. "You okay?"

Delaina laughed, a sarcastic, about-to-go-over-the-edge laugh. "Am I okay?" Her hair would give Medusa's a run for the money. "The damn roosters hadn't even crowed when I discovered this mess,

HAPPY BIRTHDAY

traipsed in the muck..." She looked down at her boots. "I bit a gash out of my lip, almost ran my car into Holland's. I'm running on no sleep. If you would've checked the phone app or the field during the night like you were supposed to..."

She saw Holland. They reached the field. "You already turned off the water. That's good."

"Hell yeah! I'm not an idiot."

Jed's eyes widened. "I'll get on the tractor. You..."

"Hand motions. I know this shit!" She ran across muddy rows. House-high sprinklers, connected by horizontal beams that jutted downward into tires, rolled the unit, propelled by a motor, across the field. They would need to hook the tractor to the unit to pull it out of the bog. Jed backed up the tractor, jumped off. She was there, hitching. He leaned over to help her. "Okay," she yelled, not realizing his proximity. "Ready to go." He hurried to the tractor, raised one boot to the ladder, looked out. Delaina plowed through muck backwards, her hands batting stringy hair out of her eyes while she squinted at him.

He had never loved her more.

It took an hour to straighten out the mess and ensure the unit ran again, minimal compared to what it would've been if Delaina hadn't shown up when she did and held out like an expert. They worked amicably. Now they sat on the back of Jed's truck, eyeing the unit from afar to be sure it continued. They were wet, somewhat edgy, and mostly relieved.

"I'm sorry for the outburst, Jed." He claimed he checked the unit and his phone overnight. "Must've happened right after you checked."

He scanned rows. "We need rain."

Out of nowhere, tears filled her eyes. She turned her head farther away. The motor hummed. "Holland told us goodbye before she left. I guess she needed longer to tell you goodbye properly. That's, uh, gonna happen sometimes, I know. Other women. Working together is necessary this year. Don't want it to be awkward. I'm a big girl."

Jed brushed her shoulder. "Yeah, a big girl. Twenty-one today."

...When Jed propositioned Delaina at the park after such an enjoyable afternoon, he had hoped in his heart and thought, probably due to his sex drive, that they could have a relationship.

They *could* make it work; he knew that, and he wanted it more than anything.

LAINEY AND JED, BOOK TWO

But, no. His proposition, another giant red flag. It took her by surprise for a lot of reasons. One reason had nothing to do with their families, the land, or leftover feelings from the pregnancy scare.

She was too young. To be enticed, loved, controlled, or seduced into staying in Mallard.

Jed had been thinking A LOT lately, about what was best for her, for them. Because it was his obligation as her farm manager and because he loved her.

What was best for her was all he thought about after she turned him down.

He wanted her to go to school, to *experience* college, to get out of Mallard, so if she came back, she'd appreciate it. He wanted her to *choose* him, not because he was available and the obvious choice, but because she had lived enough to know what he already knew: It didn't *matter* if they never left Mallard till the day they died or moved to Australia and lived in a tent and sold surfboards. They were fifteen thousand times for fifty years.

Delaina felt the same in her heart, he knew. Yet with her vibrancy and tenacity, he also knew she'd wake up at 25 or 35 and wonder, resent, regret, rebel, or worse, force. The reason would be that she *stayed in Mallard*. The reason would *not* be him. He would get blamed, though, and that would be a shame.

He wanted their full potential. Lasting love, at the right time, when she was ready.

He wasn't so blinded by what was best for her that he didn't realize a major problem with her leaving: She was Lainey Cash; he was Jed McCrae.

She would not leave and leave him behind.

That would make him the winner. A grand discovery he made last night, a truth he'd been standing on top of. That she would go, if she knew he was leaving.

She also needed to think that she decided. The one who chose to go, and hopefully later, chose to come back to him, not that he figured it out and maneuvered the outcome.

They would get to all of that tomorrow. Late tomorrow. Someway. He counted on God or the universe or fate to show him how, like a deal he made with the future for being this selfless now.

Today, he would take her to the game if she wanted to go. They needed a break, a birthday. Good baseball and good times with good friends. To show her again what it felt like to get out, to *live*. Then maybe it wouldn't be so hard for her to leave or understand his leaving. Such a good plan.

Jed knew better. The whole thing, the transition, would devastate them. It would damn-near kill him. The Plan would happen, though. He had made up his mind.

He pushed off the truck and stood. He cleared his throat. "I'm sorry about the park, what I said to you about spending the night with me, Delaina." He assumed she felt emotions that a man couldn't begin to comprehend from their pregnancy episode.

"No, I'm sorry." She took in a breath. "I wanted to spend the night with you." Her face changed. "I wish I could be like, you know, Holland."

Jed frowned. She needn't be like Holland. She wanted to be grown. That's what she meant, and that's why his strategy needed to happen. "I guess you don't have birthday plans with all we have going on here." She shook her head no. He started to reach for her but didn't. He wanted a wall up, so it didn't totally shatter them when he told her tomorrow about leaving Mallard- and simultaneously he wanted to enjoy the next twenty-four hours as much as possible.

Nothing came easy with Delaina. Yet everything did.

He looked at her. Their history flooded him. Borrowing the wrench when she pranced in Bleu Cotton jeans. Their first snake kiss. Their river date, oysters and dancing. Houston, her gold dress. Playing cards, stripping her clothes on his balcony. Her, on top of him in a corn field. The...miscarriage. Could he leave her? Could he trust that, if he were so sacrificial, then *one day*... Did he have that much faith? In fate. Or God. Or them.

"Jed." She took his hand. Sunlight angled on their faces. "You seem awfully quiet, deep. If this is about what happened between you and Holland, I know you won't be abstinent this year while we're workin' together."

He certainly would. He didn't *want* anyone else. "Holland came by yesterday to tell me that she spent the night before in a hotel, unable to make herself leave Mississippi. I got an idea and offered her the job of financial assistant to both farms. She was so happy, and I was so relieved, we stayed up half the night going over what she'll be doing. That's all."

Jed did take Delaina's hands then. Holding her hands gave him the courage to say it, the stepping stones to giving her up. "It's your twenty-first birthday. You gotta have a little fun. Guess what I did on mine?" He grinned genuinely. The clouds of Mallard and years of living and learning dissolved.

Delaina grinned, too. "Dare I ask?" He chuckled. "Other than being an undergrad at Baylor, and it started in a bar with guys, I can't remember."

"Of course, you can't remember." Delaina jabbed his ribs. "Just like you never counted."

Briefly stumped, then Jed got it and started to defend himself. Nah. He smiled. "Right. That's my point, Delaina thirteen. Live in the moment and move on." He kissed her, legal Lainey Cash sitting on his tailgate in the hot sun. *Happy Birthday to me*, he thought. "I leave for the game in about two hours," he said to stop the kissing. "Meggie and Pate are going. We were friends in grad school. Pate, at Georgia Tech while we were at Emory. My best memories, even if I can't really remember." He winked. "Come if you want. It's *your twenty-first* birthday. Do whatever the hell you wanna..."

Her mouth plastered his. Delaina, so glad about Holland, and she so liked Pate and Meggie; she so loved baseball; she so loved Jed; she so wished, after she turned him down, for one more chance to say yes. Her twenty-first birthday *was* like Christmas in July. Jed took their steamy kiss as confirmation and planted another seed. "Plan whatever you want for after the game, Little Miss 21."

~ ~ ~

The door stood open at the Cash Way office. Rhett didn't see Delaina's SUV parked out front but assumed she was inside. "Hey, Delaina, I'm headed to the..." Looking up, he paused. He stared into the prettiest pair of chocolate brown eyes. "Miss Holland."

"Rhett," she said cheerfully, standing up. "There've been changes literally overnight. Jed invited me to stay in Mallard to manage farm finances. I'm more than glad to help. He's done business with my father for years."

Rhett looked over her professional attire from beneath his cap, looked at her gorgeous straight hair trailing over her full breasts. He tried to imagine walking into this every morning. He didn't know how long he could keep his feelings hidden. "I see." He took backward steps, ramming against the open door, ducked, and cursed under his breath. "Work to do. Good to have you here, Miss Holland."

"Jed said you usually drink coffee with him to set the daily itinerary. I made it like you like it, Rhett. Steaming and jet black."

"It's how you like it, too." Holland handed him a Styrofoam cup and smiled. "Are you feeling okay?" he asked, taking a sip.

"Yes, fine. Are you okay? You're pale."

Rhett cleared his throat. "Who, me? I'm...fine."

~ ~ ~

The game was never-ending clapping, cussing, chatting, cheering.

Pate Hendricks, an all-American super guy like Jed, made the two of them the best entertainment with their back-and-forth joking. Delaina sat between Jed and Meggie. During lulls, she and Meggie giggled and girl-talked. Delaina and Jed bumped arms and brushed knees. Seventh inning stretch came; everyone stood. Jed and Delaina went to their feet, singing together, singing to each other, moving like fluid. Like someone dropped a live screen of the most romantic movie in the middle of an afternoon game. People adored it. Pate and Meggie gaped. They did not *know* that Jed.

The Astros got their first homerun in the ninth. Pate reeled Meggie and Delaina into a bear hug.

Jed kissed Delaina. His eyes burned like a blue-flame sea. "I really shouldn't call you little girl anymore, huh?" He smelled like beer and fun. "Did you decide plans for later?"

She loved the way he looked at her, in his element, casual and fine. She stated without shame, "I wanna take tequila shots and dirty dance and call a cab in the city at night because I'm tipsy."

Ah, she had taken the bait. Without much persuasion. "Perfect," he lied. He clapped in rhythm to a riling game chant. "You're invited," she flirted.

He stopped. "Good." That wasn't a lie. "Want me to take care of you, so you can let loose?" He suppressed a deep sigh.

Her face scrunched. "No."

"What then?" He tried to be unbiased.

That stumped Delaina. She wanted him to be *Jed*. "My boyfriend?" Why not go for it? He had said plan *whatever*.

Jed had an unusual look, like someone closed the shutters on a stellar day. She rushed, "I mean, this is pretend. I don't get to be twenty-one for long. You can be my..." She made it up as she blabbed, "Really cute, on and off, drunk college frat boy. Like your own twenty-first." She tried to laugh. "Back to real life for me and you tomorrow."

"I wasn't in a fraternity, but yeah, sounds like a plan." The Plan. He started clapping to the chant. Delaina did too, when she couldn't catch his gaze.

After the game, they went to Meggie's. She had baked a German chocolate cake, Jed's favorite. Everyone gathered around the table while Meggie lit candles and sang "Happy Birthday" to them. Pate poured wine. "We gotta toast," Jed said with shiny eyes, hair falling across his forehead, relaxed smile for Delaina. Her throat went dry.

"I'll do the honors since it's your birthday." Pate held up his drink. "To *Jed and Delaina*, to old friends and new friends. May we all four live long enough for you two to discover what we..." He looked toward Meggie. "...already know. You won't find anybody else to love you like you two already do. Happy Birthday." Meggie lifted her glass heartily to Pate's.

Jed and Delaina left near ten. Night was young for twenty-one-year-olds. They went to his apartment to change clothes. Delaina took time getting ready, for her, Jed noticed while he watched sports in his den. He heard the unmistakable sound of high heels in the hall.

"Okay, let's go."

Lord help him. She wore a strapless hot pink silk top, dark Bleu Cotton jeans, sleek heels, sloppy hair, cat-eye makeup, her cross ear-rings, and carried a metallic clutch. He knew this style- the chic, classy drinker. She would be *that girl*, the one who didn't show everything, who didn't quite do everything. Congratulations to himself, right? That this was his aim, that she would willingly enter real college life soon. "I'm gonna need a pregame," he said.

She made a perplexed face, then "Oh." Delaina wanted to go out for their birthdays, seeing Jed in a stylish printed shirt, good-fitting BC's with kind of spiky hair. If he'd rather stay in, she wouldn't deny him. He looked about 25 and unattached. Her heart did high kicks. She glanced toward the bedroom.

Lord help him. "Pregame, you know, drinks before you go out drinking." He walked to the kitchen and reached into a cabinet for whatever alcohol came out.

"*Oh.*" She giggled.

He poured an overdose of dark liquid. "You want ice?"

Happy Birthday

"I don't need pregame." She felt intoxicated by a night of unmodified abandon with really-hot him.

"Did you call a cab?" He drank until it was gone.

"Oops. No." She got her phone. "There. Done." She smiled broadly. "I downloaded a cab app today!"

Great. At least she wouldn't be one of those girls who tried to drive home drunk *or* got driven home by a guy because she was drunk. That should make him feel better. He drank another half glass.

His liquor buzz started in time. Delaina, what a beauty. Her twenty-first birthday belonged to him. What a privilege. He loved her definition of a pregame. He led her out the door, not to tote her to his bedroom instead. She grabbed his hand. "This is gonna be fun and funny." They went down steps into night. He pulled her behind an ornamental shrub and kissed her lips messily. Good buzz now.

She laughed then tried a serious face. "You, Jed McCrae, had too much to drink already."

"Obviously, not enough. I'm standing. You're fully clothed." Very nice. Alcohol and freedom. "Ever done it behind a bush?" he asked, then, "No, you haven't. I know the answer. Me either." He nipped her earlobe. "Want to?" He set fire to Delaina inside. "You didn't give me a birthday present yet, cupcake."

"We're in Houston together, big guy. That's our present."

Wind lifted her hair from her naked shoulders. It shone like gold satin in the security lights. He sifted it through his fingers. Why not go all the way? He felt close to drunk. "You know that pool?" She glanced. The fancy apartment pool with Beverly Hills quality fountains, palms, and lights was closed. The cab arrived. She said yeah.

"We're gonna strip each other and break the pool rules about 3 a.m." He would play his role flawlessly.

They burned for one another on the ride, making out blatantly in the backseat. Right on cue, Delaina reapplied lip gloss before they stepped out at the bar.

Yep, she would world-class her future scene. How perfect.

Taking his hand as they made their way toward the glitzy entrance, she said over booming music, "I tried this once that week at Ole Miss. Guys were rowdy." She had a wide smile. "Glad you're here!"

Rowdy bars, guys in their young 20s, a backward flash to his college days- to how guys were. A forward flash to hers- to how they would try to be with her. Jed couldn't think about it.

LAINEY AND JED, BOOK TWO

The music was rap, uncensored and loud. The crowd, pretty much the same. Jed took her first tequila shot with her and about ten people, including another gal, Gracie, in slutty black attire with a tinseled 21 headband and colored party beads around her neck.

Delaina went to the dance floor after her second shot. Jed sat at the bar with men. They paid attention to a game on a screen and drank longnecks. He glanced at Delaina periodically, images of her laughing, talking, refusing men, dancing, tossing her head back, wiggling, bouncing, world-classing her ass. Her patient college frat boyfriend had stood about all he could stand, watching her outshine the dozen women on the dance floor, whom Jed was certain showed up nightly to do what the rap songs suggested. Lainey Cash was gonna get carted to his apartment for a *post-game* in an hour, tops. She appeared, breathless and beautiful, and asked in a tipsy-loud way, "What should I order, Big Mister 31?" Her fingers climbed up the back of his hair.

He flirted, when he got a voice, letting his eyes roam. "Lookin' like a martini drinker to me."

She looked down, as if she saw herself for the first time and hadn't a clue what she did to men around the room. "You would know." In a streak of independence, she slid across the bar toward a good-looking bartender, definitely about 25 and unattached. Delaina sounded sophisticated when she said, "I want a Tom Collins," which she, that very second, noticed on a chalkboard list. She got the mixed drink from the drooling guy who took his sweet time sizing her up, and paid cash from her crossbody clutch. Back on Jed, moving herself between his legs, she sampled her drink. "Yum."

He judged her. "Tequila before gin makes you sin." She made her perplexed face. "You know," he elaborated, "beer before wine, feelin' fine. Wine before beer, no fear, and so on." No, she didn't know. "Look it up sometime." He ribbed her.

She squealed, "Listen, Jed!" She got his hands. "They do a birthday song five minutes before midnight, only for birthday people; Gracie told me. Oh, and she thinks you're so freakin' hot." Jed thought Gracie 21 was so freakin' not. "DJ announced it! Come on." She finished her glass.

Next, he hardcore danced to a hardcore song about birthday girls in their birthday suits with Delaina backed up and bent into his crotch, arms over her head. She knew every nasty word. They were gonna go home and sin a lot sooner than he thought.

A lot of people forgot about birthdays, including glitzy Gracie, and watched them. Delaina and Jed, they had this thing. A magnetism everyone felt, anytime they stepped out in public together. A trance of more stylish, more attractive, more in love. Tonight, they looked like sex with clothes on. They could not be denied.

"When do you wanna leave?" she asked urgently.

"Your birthday, you say," he could hardly get out.

"Your birthday too, Big Mister 31." She pulled him, moving through the crowd with a mission, toward the exit. She reached into her bag and booked a cab without reminder. They were quiet on the sidewalk, quiet on the ride, not touching, too overcome with desire for a mere demonstration in the backseat.

They stepped out at the complex into a muggy night under a starless sky. The black universe permitted them anything, after midnight and under the influence. At once, kissing and tearing at clothes, Jed pushed Delaina away from the metal staircase to his apartment in the direction of the pool gates. He let her go long enough to lift her up. She giggled and started climbing. He came overtop behind her. Clothes scattered. "Break the rules, Jed," she dared before he shoved her into the water. Delaina came up for air as he landed in the pool. He pushed her to the wall, with his hands grabbing at the same fleshy bra she'd worn in Houston, their first time.

This was it. For certain. For how long, Jed did not know. A year minimum, for her to finish at a university, if she came back to him at all, and he would not touch her again until she got done.

She deserved it. The freedom to just be. They deserved it, if they were ever going to be more. She would be rock-star good at living it up, too, this next year or more.

Great. Perfect. Swell. Jed kissed her harshly.

Stacked fountains poured water over rocks into the pool, crashing around them. Lights and shadows bent and changed. All of it compounded, right then, into a bonus night of recklessness in which she remained his. Jed had never felt anything close to the need that overtook him. He could not stop himself, hands on top of her bra and panties, using the fabric to remind her that she wasn't naked yet.

He would let her go. Tomorrow. She could go anywhere with anyone, and he wouldn't intervene, wouldn't know. He wasn't selfless enough to let her go, without making her remember this from now on.

No life experience of any kind would compare. That would bring her back. That's what drove him.

Delaina had wanted Jed in the rawest sexual way since their first encounter on his porch that rainy day in March. He had touched her and loved her and taken care of her in multiple ways, yet absolutely nothing compared to this. He was out of control. Gloriously sinful. Soaking wet, they craved each other in the lavish pool. He had her up and on the edge. He pushed himself out beside her and led her toward a luxurious lounge chair in grayish landscape. A plush cabana towel magically appeared in his hand then on the chair. He stripped her underwear while he kissed her; his clothes were off. Black eye makeup streaked Delaina's face. She could feel it rolling off her jaw. He watched it run. It made her more unbolted, more his.

He laid her down, seducing her with no restraint. She had begun to recognize Jed's way, his moves, his map to her destination. How intimate. Had begun to know his sequence, his preferences, the feel of different parts of him on different parts of her. How personal. Tidbits from both nights in Houston and mounds of memories from the field in Mallard manifested into Delaina's own mouth and hands and body doing exactly what Jed liked. They acted without pause, knew without thought. This is *how it should be* between two people became glaringly obvious. Love and sex in one, to give as two, to receive immeasurably. Bodies so slick, he almost slid into her more than once, he asked, "You want more or now?" in the thickest voice from him she'd never heard. Jed didn't care about her answer. They had all night. She lifted for reply, and he went into her for the fourth time. Her legs lifted to her chest instinctively until shifting became smooth, and they would be working on that fit fifteen thousand times for fifty years, and it was perfect and total because it was their favorite part of them. Towel spread soft underneath her, she felt cool and Jed felt warm. They couldn't take their eyes off each other, watching in faces what they felt everywhere else. Their first time as equals. How erotic. Each made moves and initiated changes and held on methodically. The sliding lounge chair, the shaking and scraping, made better love than any bed or music. Everything was just so total, so perfect.

Swept up in erotica, Delaina got a premonition- that this was too good for their real lives- and whispered in the sweetest voice, "I love you, Jed." Her words were too much for him. Too true. He had barely let her come when Jed jerked out of Delaina, their fantasy above fantasies over. His semen splattered her stomach, their bodies touching everywhere like glue. Delaina was struck by that purest form of dirty, the essence of him, outside his body on her, and between her legs, the essence of her, outside her body on him. She slid her hand over her torso. "I love us," she whispered. Jed had no reply, seeing her, his soul mate, uninhibited.

A speeding freight train hit them, carrying a thousand tons, years of mistakes and connections on Cash-McCrae Road, rolled into a word stronger than love, a word un-invented. The feeling, theirs alone, immobilized them. Spent, stunned, silent, sleepy, it was out of the question to get up. They were instantly freezing cold everywhere their skin was exposed and soothingly warm everywhere their skin touched. A second plush towel magically appeared in Jed's hand. He fumbled to pull it over them while he slid to her side, positioned himself lightly, holding her around her back, and put his head close to her face. They fell asleep within seconds.

Nineteen

My Boyfriend's Back

Out since dawn, Rhett had worked nonstop while Jed and Lainey were gone. Moments ago, news came that stopped his work cold.

Cabot Hartley had been spotted.

With Lainey safely tucked away with Jed, all Rhett thought about was Holland. He blew into Jed's office at the shop like a storm.

She sat behind Jed's desk, typing on a laptop. "Hi, Rhett."

"Holland, you okay?!"

"Yes. I'm fine." She stood and stretched. "The question is, are *you* okay?"

His breathing had not returned to normal. "If you're...okay, I'm...okay."

Her face appeared surprised. "Uh, okay." She situated her hips on the desk. "Is there something I should know?"

He hated to scare her. She'd been through enough. "Miss Holland, there's a rumor flyin' this mornin'." Such scandalous things had been said about her and others, Holland could only imagine. "What now?"

"A woman is claimin' she's positive she saw...Cabot." She gasped. He trudged on, "Supposedly downtown around midnight last night." He reached out and brushed her arm. "Accordin' to Daddy, it's caused quite the ruckus 'round Mallard this mornin'. Patrol cars, state and federal agents." Holland smelled good, like something rosy and sweet. His face stayed serious. "I don't want you out of my sight. We ain't safe."

My Boyfriend's Back

She stood, walked around, thought. "I'll be okay at Cash Way." Sounded like she tried to convince herself. "Gates and the security system, plus your parents are nearby."

"Cash Way'll be his first stop."

She looked ready to cry. Rhett decided what the hell. They'd been playing a waiting game too long. "Come here." She let him hug her. "Stay close, I mean it."

"Now? Or in general?" Her voice shook.

"Both." Heartbeats thumped, thumped, thumped. Rhett couldn't hold back. "About Cabot, you, uh...don't have nothin' to hide, do you?" Rhett knew she'd come to the farmhouse to buy marijuana for Cabot and his cronies, more than once, but other than that... Her eyes darted. She stepped away. Rhett winced. "How bad?"

Tears presented. "I did... questionable things for Cabot. Business transactions, acquiring maps and photos, setting up meetings, secretive in nature. I eluded to that when you and I were sifting through Eli's notebooks." Swift guilt knifed her conscience. She did questionable things *with* Cabot. Atop the bank. Their steamy penthouse overnighters there, months ago. That's what started her loyalty switch from Jed to Cabot. Even worse, when she visited Cash Way after Tory Cash died, to offer condolences to Delaina and the Smiths. Following Cabot into town. Their quickie in her apartment before Eli showed up unexpectedly. Being intimate with both men that night.

"Uh, I've heard he's...kind of a womanizer."

She could only nod. Yes.

Yes meant *yes.* Rhett knew what it meant. He made a strange face. "Okay. Well." Well, what? He didn't like it a damn bit. A game-changer maybe. But he loved her. "Did Eli know?"

"It's part of what we fought about the night he left me and had his accident. His suspicions, but I never told him." Rhett stood on the other side of the room. He looked disgusted. The truth pummeled Holland again. The baby she carried *could be* Cabot Hartley's.

No one would ever know!

Too devastating for the Smiths. Too detestable to face. Too shattering for her...and Rhett. "After I met Eli, though, I never. Cabot and I, uh, didn't..." The tiniest lie with the biggest potential consequence.

Rhett put up his hand. Nodded yes. Yes meant I've heard all I wanna hear.

203

LAINEY AND JED, BOOK TWO

Her compulsion to make the baby belong to Eli prompted, "Had my doctor's appointment yesterday."

Rhett's eyes dropped to her waist. Perfect figure still. "Everything good so far?"

"I guess. They' re doing genetic testing next appointment. Acted like it's routine." She shrugged. "Heard the heartbeat. 151. Probably a boy. I had complications early, so still no sex or heavy exercise until I'm out of the first trimester. As if I'm in the state of mind or have a partner for either. Uhm, sorry. You're tired and riled up about Cabot. Last thing you want to hear is a woman's pregnancy problems."

"I'm here for ya." He hadn't come closer. "A boy, huh?" A nephew, Eli's son. "Miss Holland, when you need to get some fresh air, a walk or something, just holler. I especially wanna hear about the baby."

She twisted the hem of her shirt between her fingers. He caught sight of her belly button, her flat tummy. "I might take you up on a walk soon."

"Good. 'Cause I don't want you walkin' alone out here till we know more about Cabot. Lock the door when I leave and go straight to Cash Way when you leave." He glimpsed her fearful expression. "Scratch that. I'm going home...gotta get me a shower. Good chance it's gonna start stormin' the next hour or so. You're comin' with me."

~ ~ ~

Delaina and Jed slept until seven a.m. in his bed. Deep in the night, they had come alive shivering and uncomfortable, wrapped in the towels, gathered clothes, walked to Jed's apartment, showered, and gone to bed. A delicious crosswire of slightly hung over and fully content made each aware the other woke up this morning, without the need to say anything or rise.

Delaina awakened as Jed's girlfriend.

Such a passionate night yielded sweet resignation that they belonged together and temporary amnesia to anything back home. Neither had to say it, that she was his girlfriend. A new and glistening thing, it presented itself in how they behaved with each passing moment. On their sides, he spooned her, his bent leg over her legs. She slid her top leg from under his, and laid it atop, pulling his leg between hers. She began to rub his calf with her toes. His hand grazed her middle. He moved his face over hers. She twisted hers to his and said, "Mornin', Jed." in the happiest voice.

204

He kissed her cheek. "Mornin'." Deliciousness overflowed. Jed wanted to do this. He wanted to wake up to her and do this every day of his life. Closeness and the knowing. That she'd be there. That they were in love. That everything felt right in the world. "I'm askin' you on a morning date, Delaina."

"Mmm, really," she murmured, grin on her face. "Where?"

"Mmm," he countered, sated. "Sweetheart Square. Couple blocks from here." His voice vibrated on her skin. "Lots of couples around doing the easy mornin' thing. Cool place." He kissed her neck. "Never been the right time to stop. Today is." He patted her hip. "Let's get dressed if the answer's yes."

"Mmm." Delaina caught his hand and squeezed. "The answer's heck yeah."

Jed told her to go ahead and pack. They'd leave from breakfast-n-browsing to go to the private airport. He sat in his den watching sports highlights and downed bottled water, hydrating before he piloted. Delaina came out in minus ten minutes- messy pigtails, short flimsy gray dress, pink lip gloss, black rubber flip flops, overnight bag slung over her shoulder. He almost hauled her back to bed. He wanted to do this. Have her as his girlfriend, his wife, taking less than ten minutes to appear amazing, like no big deal she knocked him breathless. "You're so pretty," he commented. His mouth made a crooked smile. "No bra." He stood.

Her shoulder hitched. "All I brought was my nude pushup. Sticks out too much with this dress." Jed wanted to do that, too. Know unimportant details about her, his girlfriend, his wife. Delaina took a sideways glance of him. He wore a used-up, green Bleu Cotton T-shirt from their crazy-popular, tractor-sponsored line, with cargo shorts, leather flip flops, unfixed hair, no shave, his father's watch. Oh yeah, Sweetheart Square with him. Mmm. Her shoulder hitched again. "Forgot to pack clean underwear, too. Gonna have to rectify that when we get to the shops." No big deal, she started walking to the door.

Jed's good intentions went south as his arm went around her back. An elegant 180 straight to his bedroom, to rectify no panties his way. Delaina realized, as they reached the bedroom, what she said produced this reaction. The fact that she did that to him so quickly, so effortlessly, made her want him immediately. The room was air-conditioned cold and midmorning light, curtain closed. They had left the bed unmade since a cleaning service would be coming in behind them. She stepped out of her shoes, sat on the edge, pulled up her skirt, and spread her legs while she watched Jed drop his shorts and boxers. He looked at her face as he pulled the strap of her dress down on one side. His mouth blistered her breast. His tongue swirled up her collarbone, her neck, into her mouth, kissing her with lips and teeth. They wanted sex with each other, no frills. He knelt. She wrapped her legs around his waist and yanked him forward. Jed just about choked. He laid her down, towering over her, with the words *Ride the Green Ones* over her face. Her feet went to his shoulders; they moved how they liked it with each other. In a minute or so, he folded her up to the edge, her sitting, his kneeling.

The change, the angle, the edge, the motion, like he knew it would, produced Oh and God and Jed from her, *way* louder than their past four times, along with bad words she must've picked up in the club last night. He chuckled, kind of arrogantly, and put his fingers to her mouth to shush. They watched each other, her face upturned and legs hooked, his face down-turned, arms bracing her back. She made a face like she tried to be quiet but, "Oh God…" His apartment was in a complex with hundreds of other people; Delaina informed them that his name was "JED McCRAE." Quick learner was she that she tried, with her wrapped legs, to trap him. He, stronger and bigger, won the struggle and finished outside her body.

Quick learner was she that she didn't complicate something so basic with sap. "Thanks. I'm starving." She cleaned herself up, dropped her dress, got her bag, put on her flip flops, and walked out. Jed wanted to do this, to be constantly knocked out by how fitting she was, and to put on his pants and follow her like he was whipped, because well, he was.

~ ~ ~

Sweetheart Square proved to be, in a word, lovely. May flowers unabashed in their giddiness dappled cobblestone pathways, which crisscrossed the four sides of the shape. A park, fountains, and benches made the center, and hip eateries and shops dotted the outside lines. Music drifting over the lot misled, speaking of a different era, when guys and gals felt nervous about holding hands on the first date and wouldn't wake for breakfast together until they shared the same last name. It was absolute romance to be reminded when a man loves a woman, what a wonderful world, at last, always. Unforgettable.

At least here, decades later, modern people made time for lazy lattes on a weekday. An overcast and breezy morn, Delaina and Jed sat outside at a corner-of-the-square, all-day breakfast café on a patio full of couples. Couples who smiled intimately, conversed easily, laughed often. All-American couples, mixed race couples, gay couples. Couples with dogs, couples with tattoos, couples with babies, couples with phones- showing the wireless world their love and almond flour waffle stacks. Delaina ordered a mimosa, repeatedly said, "Yummy," while Jed downed more water, chilled, glass-bottled supposedly from the springs of Tuscany. They took off their sunglasses to eat, to see each other. He ate free-range eggs and grass-fed meat; she ate whole wheat French toast and organic strawberries. Unlike most around them, they didn't mark the event with a social media check-in or discuss who would pick up the dry cleaning, who would run by the market and get tonight's dinner, who would pay for breakfast.

Novelty was potent. These two wanted to smile, hold hands, date, let a man love a woman.

Finishing food bliss, Delaina did tell Jed, with a shy smile, that she needed to go somewhere around there and buy panties ASAP, that she felt uncomfortable sitting, going commando in her short dress. Jed wholeheartedly agreed, with an un-shy wink, that he needed to go with her somewhere around there to buy her panties ASAP because he too felt uncomfortable with her sitting, going commando in a dress. That if she didn't put on panties, they would join the mile-high club sooner than planned, in a plane with him as the only pilot.

"So..." Delaina drew out the word. "I see a place over your left shoulder. Texas Two's."

Jed glanced back to couples going in and out of a swanky clothing store with peppy faces. "I get to pick them out."

"Sure." Delighted, Delaina smiled. "Where else should we browse?" She did a happy clap.

She acted lusciously female since dawn. Jed surprised himself with how much he liked it. They held hands across the table and stroked each other's fingers. He commented, checking store signs, "I can bypass *Soap Dope* and *Hair Flair*, or we'll go if you want to. Next,

Couples' Cave. Massages, bath soaks in who knows what. Wood chips, oils, waxes, the whole nine yards. Hmm."

Delaina had shaved herself into a nice shape before she left Mallard yesterday. She might've been born a decade behind Jed, but she read romance novels, the V-J-J blog, did girl talk with Meggie, and listened to crazy tales from college friends Mary Beth and Waverly when they came home from college. She knew what guys liked. "You want me to get a bikini wax."

"I did not say that." His guilty face looked boyish and pardonable.

"It's okay. I wanna hear what you like." She did a sultry thing with her face and mouth and looked about five years older.

"You, Lainey Cash. I like findin' out what you are and what you aren't. I wanna do it all, from fancy nighttime dates to waking you up with quick mornin' sex." His blue eyes, a laser of authenticity. "I wanna know that your bra doesn't fit your dress; you forgot your panties. Who kissed you first, the name of every guy who put his hands on you." More of his eyes, drowning her eyes. "What toppings you order on pizza. Your favorite color, your favorite flower, your favorite joke. The books you read. What makes you mad, sad, and what put that gorgeous smile on your face that you've been wearing since we woke up. You're what I like."

"Mimosas, romantic music, and mainly you."

"Huh?"

"That's what put the smile on my face this mornin'." If possible, her face revealed more wonder than his. Jed picked up her hand and kissed the top. "It's pretty now but a landin' strip. That'd be...even prettier on you, D."

"Huh?"

"Please don't launch into a tirade over the *Dirty Dozen*. If you get a wax, you'd be pretty with a strip."

She seemed overly pleased. "As long as you promise to continue landing your plane there."

"Cupcake, I'm afraid you're the owner of my permanent hangar." Delaina's laughter jingled like bells as she crossed the table and sat on his lap.

"That's..." He bounced the leg she sat on. "...brutal of you." Giggles from her while the server brought her a "quick mimosa on the house," perhaps a hint that they basked in bliss longer than the normal stay at a table.

My Boyfriend's Back

"Kemp Rainwater was my first kiss then Brice Buffy." Delaina smiled in his face. "Josiah Ward aka PK, Boone, Cabot, you. Uhm, that's it." She pondered. "Nope, the one guy at Ole Miss." She snapped her fingers like she couldn't remember while Jed asked, "What?" One pigtail brushed his cheek when she sipped. "The guys who put their hands on me. And usually cheese and pepperoni. Thick crust. But I'll eat veggies. *Little Women* is the best book ever. I read books every day, a chapter per night."

"Repeat that. The part about the damn guys, not little women." At the next table, a couple with matching tattoos on their left arms sat.

Delaina watched them gaze at each other. "Jed, geez. You wanted to know."

He baffled himself, that he wanted to know. He forced a smile. "Right, so repeat it."

"Kemp Rainwater, seventh grade, first kiss. Dr. Stan Rainwater at Mallard Medical, his son."

"I know who he is." Did Jed really have the urge to fistfight the memory of a seventh grader?

"A dare, last day of school." She smiled candidly. "By Homecoming, ninth grade, he tried to do more than kiss. Had hooked up with looser girls." Her tongue clicked. "I dropped him in my driveway."

Yep, Jed wanted to punch a ninth grader from seven years ago. Laughter around them and a song about a pretty woman didn't flip his mood. His jealousy felt petty, yet he couldn't prevent, "Did I hear you right that Brice Buffy, Mallard's baseball star who's playin' in the minors, had his hands on you?"

Her pigtail smacked him when she looked in his eyes. "He's majors now! Cubs, that's what his last text said. Yeah, tenth grade. Dugout Diamond Girl, you know, team helpers."

"I know who they are." Jed had intimate knowledge of Mallard County High School's Dugout Diamond Girls.

"More like, my hands on him…Jed, I gave him a hand job. He taught me in the *dugout*."

So, that's how she knew what to do with her hand. "Let me guess." His eyes narrowed. "To save your virginity." Her mouth went -O with, "Yes!"

"Buffy's a…giant. Clarify. You text him? Currently?"

Delaina finished her mimosa. Her bare bottom and future landing strip taunted Jed's leg, not on purpose. "He *is huge,* Jed." Seeing his

209

expression, she edited, "*Oh*, he's not you, big guy! Yeah, he texts me, usually bare butts in the locker room. I rarely answer." Ha, ha, hee, hee, from her.

Jed wanted to blow up the bleachers, burn the grass, bust out lights on the new scoreboard, *Home of Brice Buffy*, at Mallard's field. He pushed Delaina's back. "I'm ready to put on your panties."

"Yay. Fun." She jiggled. God Bless his leg. She stood, snapped her fingers. "Tanner Mooring. T-Mo. Ole Miss." She pulled Jed through stone paths and daffodils. "'Get it, T-Mo!' That's what his frat bros were saying when we were at the bar that night." Her entertained smile took aim at Jed, who trailed behind, wanting to de-petal daffodils. "Good thing I came home early from college, huh?"

Get it, T-Mo? "Yep, glad you did." Jed had been thinking red lace boy shorts or pink bunny-printed thongs, something sexy-cute. His girl might get white, waist-high granny panties. Delaina turned abruptly and smashed into him. "See *Doggone,* the pet place? Where cutesy couples are gettin' their pooches primped. Makes me think of our precious Lucy. I wanna share a little dog with you." She put her hand to her mouth. "An itty-bitty fuzzball with a snazzy rhinestone collar named..."

Jed kissed her mouth shut and forgot about Kemp Rainwater and maybe Brice Buffy. She acted plumb adorable being his girlfriend. Dang, if he didn't wanna do that, get a pup with her. "Only dog we're gettin' is a big ole brown lab named..." "Astro," she chose with a basket of geraniums blooming from her pigtails. "Perfect with prissy little Bleu Cotton!"

God help him, if she didn't know him better than he knew himself. They were getting Astro *and* Bleu Cotton. He smiled like the whipped soul he was with a melody about being happy together carrying them closer to Texas Two's. "We'll start shoppin' for each other's dogs and give 'em for Christmas this year."

She cheerleader-clapped. "Love it. Can't wait to pick out Astro!" She kissed him in front of a beagle-and-boxer couple. Jed erased Brice and who was next? He couldn't remember, with her panty-less and wanting to be his puppy mama. "Sweetheart Square's awesome, cupcake. We can get the doggy and pussy primped at the same time."

"You. Are. Terrible. I'm up for it, though!" Hee, hee. "Ooh, and tattoos! I considered options, in my head, at the table." They had walked beyond *Doggone* pet shop to *Think Ink* tat shop. "What about

MY BOYFRIEND'S BACK

small matching Farm 130 outlines right there?" Her palm swiped among his naval, hipbone, and Big Guy. "And here." She patted herself in the same spot. "For our eyes only. Except in my bikini!" Her eyes made starbursts. "Have you noticed Farm 130 is shaped almost identically to the state of Mississippi? Ooh, how fun!"

They were getting matching tattoos? "It *is* shaped like Mississippi, darlin'. Tory and James Ed cleared the land that way on purpose. My cabin's in the bottom of the boot heel."

Delaina never knew that... Cool. She did that thing with her face and mouth where she looked older. "My, uh, cabin's gonna be in the bottom of the boot heel, know what I mean?" She patted herself on the future tattoo spot. Jed stared at that area. How naughty. It'd hurt like five surgeries getting tattoos there. Dang, if he didn't want to, with her. He officially lost his mind with, "How about birthday 22 and 32, we go to Calla, spend the weekend around here, and get tats?"

"Woohoo!" They made it to the posh, beachy, summery window displays of Texas Two's. "We're gettin' matching swimsuits," she sang.

They were? *When* were they going swimming? *If* they did go swimming, *somewhere*, Jed had to match her in front of people? The mannequins matched. Ah, screw it, they'd load up Astro and Bleu Cotton in his jeep with Delaina's tattoo peeking from her teeny-weeny bikini and drive to South Padre Island someday. "That one," Jed chose, pointing to a black strapless bikini with turquoise sharks on it. The guy wore turquoise board shorts with black sharks, only option with hope of being manly. "No, Jed." Delaina turned sour. "You should *know* better." She oozed XX chromosomes this morn. She pouted and pulled him toward the next display.

"What's wrong?" Around them, couples walked inside un-matching and happy, came out matching and sappy. "I don't do strapless," she whispered. "On me, in the water, it's topless."

Stupid him. "Uh, okay." He scanned. The only top with straps... Good Lord, *he'd* be oozing XX chromosomes. Navy blue tiny triangle tie bikini with Barbie-pink surfboards, and lucky him, navy board shorts with Barbie-pink surfboards. "That's gonna be so hot on you, D." *And I'm not matching*.

Delaina did her cheerleader clap with, "Oh Lord, you in pink surfboards. I'm gonna eat you up! Here we come, California."

They were going to California? Wearing pink surfboards?

LAINEY AND JED, BOOK TWO

She dragged him in and went on a shopping spree, the likes of which he'd seen only with his mama. Her microscopic bikini cost $$$. Delaina grabbed a headband and shell rings and rope anklets and leather bracelets, egged on by matching salespeople, Ethan and Eric. She spotted a T-shirt on the wall and told them, "That has my boyfriend's name on it! Get a big one down, please." Navy with Barbie-pink words *Wet Wood*, apparently the surf clothing company name from which they were purchasing their gear.

Jed joined Delaina in the fitting room, clearly the norm. She changed into her bikini and modeled in the tight confines, headband, jewelry, and all. She morphed into a saucy hippy surfer. Looking in the mirror, she backed into matching surfer Jed, were it not for his black hair. "How hot!" She drooled over their twin swimsuits, farmer tans on fit bodies.

"Baby girl, where are we headed lookin' like beach bums?" If Jed sounded skeptical, he forgave himself that they were landlocked in Houston and flying east to Mississippi farmland.

"Jed!" She twisted. Her boobs felt squishy. "These would be *the cutest* Halloween costumes! I *really* wanted to go to Mallard's first annual Dark in the Park last year. It was over-21 only, and Cabot and I *just* started moving in the couple direction. He invited me, but..." She had firecracker eyes. "I'd love to go with you! Second annual Dark in the Park could be *our* first." Jed, smart enough not to experiment with his XX-oozing angel, figured this moment was not the proper time to admit that he attended the first Dark in the Park. Or that Cabot had no problem going without her, as Hugh with a gaggle of bunnies. Delaina, scrolling on her phone, paused. "You've got that look."

"What look?" Aw, hell.

"You know, your Dirty Dozen look. You went, didn't you?" She punched his chest. "Those days I was...recuperating at Cash Way. To pass time and get my mind off, uh, stuff, I pinned ideas on my virtual board. Us. Camping, traveling the world, ideas like dressing as a pirate and mermaid for Dark in the Park. You're the perfect pirate. But you went already." She held out her phone. He saw where she saved example costumes, sort-of-slutty mermaid and black-haired, patch-eyed pirate, on a board titled Me&BigGuy.

"Jed, are you on social media?" She appeared to be doing calendar math in her head.

Uh-oh.

...Since late March with Jed, Delaina felt like Alice in Wonderland. Often, she thought of nothing but him. Fell into a stupor of unfathomable swept-away love. Out of nowhere, she would get bounced back into reality. Reminders like she lived in a small-town fish bowl, the wills and family drama, she hadn't finished college, she could get pregnant if she didn't use birth control, and *Jed had a life*...a broad, interesting adult life, pre-her. Never crossed her mind to scope him out on social media.

"Uh, yeah." He tried to hug her. "It's the way to communicate, seems like these days. I don't post; I don't like to be tagged; I'm not very active."

Too late. She connected Point A to Point B, synonymous with her techno generation. "Oh God! There I was, moping in my bedroom, dreamin' of possibilities. Me the mermaid, you the pirate. In reality..."

Uhm, not only had he gone to Dark in the Park last October, he dressed as a pirate with, yep, Sam Hensley as a substantially qualified mermaid. Delaina saw his life, pre-her, in a technology-friendly flash and reminded him with the jolt of her phone. Photo on Samantha's wall, Jed untagged, he always specified, but scorching hot. Delaina the saucy hippy surfer looked crushed. "*Fine*." She studied the photo. "Not to be mean, but she looks trampy. You *are* the perfect pirate."

Big guy felt the need to make everything good in her world. He pulled on a pigtail. "Hey, surfer girl, I haven't been there *with you*."

"Oh, you can bet your bottom dollar, you're going." She had her hot-mama, little-boy-finish-your-peas voice going. "And you're gonna let me tag you on social media, buddy. Nobody has tagged Jed McCrae, but I will."

"Okay, okay." He had begun nibbling her neck while she ignored him, glued to her phone.

"We'll be so much better than trashy mermaid. We're gonna be..." She searched couple costumes as a 1970s mega hit dropped into the fitting room like greased lightning. You're the one that I want, Delaina sang along. Wham, bam. "Sandy and Danny!" She showed him an image. Jed pulled out his own phone. "They look like Mama and Daddy." He showed her a screenshot of an old photo. Jed's parents on a motorcycle, black leather beautiful.

"Oh, Jed." Delaina's heart ached. "I wish we had known your gorgeous parents; I wish they had known *us*. We'd hang out, go on dates.

I'm positive they were fabulous together." She felt his stiffness and hugged him. "I love you."

"Yeah, that would've been fun. I love you too, surfer girl. If we're gonna buy this stuff, let's get movin'."

Delaina wore her little gray dress like a swimsuit cover-up and insisted that they go to the checkout in their new duds. Jed caught sight of a man in a turquoise shirt and lemon-print tie, girl toddler in a lemon-print dress crawling on his shoulder, baby boy lemon in a carrier. Lemon Guy looked overwhelmed until a lemony queen appeared twirling in a sundress and exclaimed, "Perfect for our beach pics! Love you, honey!" Jed glimpsed his future life. Lemon Guy smirked at Jed. Man to man, *Some girls are worth it*.

TWENTY

Wild, Wild West

Delaina felt a new emotion, melancholy.

She and Jed soared along the interstate in his jeep. She didn't want it to end. Jed held her hand. He, too, seemed quiet. The song coming from his phone shuffle surprised her. Jed could be such a softie sometimes. Come away with me, Norah chirped, incompatible with their destiny. They looked the part, at least. Delaina laughed.

"What?"

"Us. This swimwear. I get kooky sometimes."

Jed the black-haired surfer pulled on his T-shirt, grimacing at pink words *Wet Wood.* His phone rang through his Bluetooth screen. *Rhett Smith.* "Hey Rhett. Going crazy yet?"

"Nah, man. I got it under control. You and Lainey shacked up celebratin'?" Rhett snickered. "Christ, that never gets easier. You gettin' the goods from Lainey." Delaina had moon eyes. From Jed, "Dude, you're on speakerphone. Your boss is right here." "Hey, Rhett," Delaina interjected.

"Aw hell, *I'm fired.* Unless this good news saves me… It's pourin' rain. I called to catch y'all before you take off, in case you wanna stay. Three inches out of a 50/50 chance. Won't get in a field before midweek."

Jed looked at Delaina. Delaina looked at Jed. Delaina spoke up, "You're not fired! You're too good on the farm. But I would appreciate it if you wouldn't say I'm doing the F-word with Jed. To us or anybody."

Jed sniffed.

"Yes, ma'am. Sorry. Uh, y'all, there's something else I called about." Rhett's tone had changed. "A local woman, who's anonymous, is claimin' she saw Cabot Hartley last night around midnight behind a building. Town's gone nuts. Law men and agent cars. More folks claim seeing Cabot since sunrise. The next county over and in Jackson. Hell knows if it's true, or if it's just one of those things, you know, that's blown out of control."

"Especially with reward money involved." Jed had a jutted jaw and aggravated face.

Delaina didn't want to think about it. "What will you do at work if we don't come home yet, Rhett? You get paid regardless of weather."

"The truth? I'm on the porch of the farmhouse, watchin' rain with Holland." Jed looked at Delaina. Delaina looked at Jed. No judgment, after what they'd been through. "*Oh*, I get it," she joked. "You want me shacked up, so you can shack up. Fair enough."

"There's that," Rhett said. "More important, I don't think you or Holland should get out of our sight." Jed nodded, like two men in charge of their women. Delaina didn't want to think about more chaos in Mallard, being unsafe, or Cabot. She didn't want to think about it! She instructed, "Everything we used for spring plantin' needs to be cleaned and put away whether I'm there or not this week." "Yes, ma'am." Jed added, "We hear you loud and clear about Cabot and we'll let you know. Thanks, Rhett." "You're welcome. Bye, lovebirds."

Jed made up his mind easily that Delaina would not return under those conditions. She looked troubled. "Dang, you're a hot boss." Jed chucked her chin. "You missed our exit," she observed.

"Not so, Miss Cash." He had that look, that Do-you-like-Japanese-food look. "We won't see our exit for fifteen hundred miles."

Her surfer attire didn't match her we're-not-going-to-California face. "*Jed*, we don't have clothes." He clucked his tongue. "Best part." She cracked a smile. "*Jed,* I've never done anything like that." "Ah, now, *that* might be the best part." She watched Texas whizzing by.

He pushed his sunglasses onto his head. "I've never been west, except Colorado ski trips. You have about five minutes to choose I-10 through the desert or north through Vegas, that is, if you wanna go with me."

Cheerleader claps from a surfer girl. "We're going!"

He handed her his phone. "I gotta be in Mississippi, Jackson Capitol, Wednesday at three. Ag Committee. Tory's seat, actually. To be truthful, we'll see if you get to go home then, under these conditions. This is your farm manager talkin', in charge of your best interest."

She couldn't disagree. Her heart pounded, from Jed's road trip idea *and* the possibility of Cabot in Mallard. "My farm manager AKA my boyfriend." She smiled.

"Plan our route. Get return plane tickets, L.A. to Jackson. You should go to the Capitol with me, too, if you get to go home."

Thus far this morning, Jed had ignored THE original plan, to be deserting Delaina for her own good when they got back to Mallard. They had made a phenomenal transformation into perfect soulmates today, all the more reason for her to come back to him *one day*.

The time to tell her that he was leaving Mallard, and to finagle her into leaving, would arrive soon enough. Cabot Hartley sealed his motivation. But this vacation experience first would be good for her, orientation for her future-planning. He would be all in till Wednesday. God made exceptions.

"Your jeep?" "Find somebody in L.A. to transport it." Delaina, singing, smiling, scrolling, said, "Okay, poor little rich boy!"

"Oh, and baby, we don't need a hotel in California. I, uh, invested with Pate. Calla Hotel has sisters. Layla Hotel in Malibu opened in March. I missed it, but..." He shrugged. "Willa's Grand Opening in Atlanta over Memorial Day, I'll be going to."

Delaina had moon eyes again. His broad, interesting adult life, pre-her. Good Lord!

~ ~ ~

West Texas flew by in a maelstrom of phone scrolling, mapping, deciding. Jed didn't know when Delaina had ever been cuter, declaring things like: "Jed, New Mexico is wine country?" "Oh my gosh, you can't legally dance there while wearing a sombrero, ha!" "*Jed*, three-fourths of New Mexico's roads are dirt."

"Sounds like back home," he commented, patting her leg.

"How true... Dirt roads are the best part of Mallard. Or fish fries. Or creek fishing. Or..." She looked over at him with the prettiest face. "Duck hunting! Do you hunt ducks?"

"We live in *Mallard*." He grinned a hot-country-boy-Jed grin in his surfer garb. "I hunt the hell outta some ducks, D."

LAINEY AND JED, BOOK TWO

"Ooh, I'd love to wake up on a cool misty morning, traipse through a pond with you, and hunt the hell outta some ducks." She bit her lip. "Gosh, I kind of miss home. I mean, not whatever's going on with Cabot. It's...horrible." She shivered. "But, you were right. Being away...makes me appreciate where I come from. There's the Christmas parade with the big red fire trucks leading the way, the Elvis gazebo, Preacher Ward and Ms. Sue and my church family, Miss Maydell. Big, hearty meals and good values. I learned good values, growing up there. You know? Taking care of the land, hard work, being kind to people, respecting my elders." She looked outside. Flat ground, no trees for miles. "Our state is gorgeous. Giant hardwoods, the river...our Mighty Mississippi *and* Big Sunflower."

Uh-oh. They were driving west; Jed's Plan appeared to be headed east. "Hey, surfer girl. You almost forgot. You're West Coast bound with Mr. Wet Wood." He tugged a pigtail.

She clapped. "You're right! Enough of that. I have the rest of my life in Mississippi."

Maybe, maybe not, Jed's Plan bullied.

She looked outward again. "I hope we see a wild mustang!" She scrolled the phone. "Oh my, we'll be within five minutes of the Mexican border? My passport's in my purse. Got yours?"

"Always. Never know when you might get the urge to..."

"Do it in a hut in Jamaica." She rolled her eyes and laughed.

He gave her a point for humor *and* maturity. "I was gonna say, the urge to have dinner across the border, but whatever."

"Oh gosh, yeah! Dinner with your girlfriend." She started planning their evening in Mexico.

~ ~ ~

Cabot had become unreachable to his parents, in society, and in reality.

Unreachable but not invisible. The sightings were mostly fabrication. Here and there, though, he did pop up.

He didn't worry about getting caught. He had nothing left to lose. Good thing he knew Mallard County like the back of his hand. Small and safe for someone who had seen the big, bad world. He could show up in a lady's backyard garden or stand near a stop sign on an unpaved country road or pass by the storefront window of a coffee shop in the next town. Then be gone and home in a flash.

218

He had money at his disposal, but his house was not a home. As large as he loomed, his hiding place, or places- because there were two of them so he had options for a clean escape- were the biggest evidence of his fall from grace. None of the creature comforts, no making a phone call or two to have whatever he demanded at his fingertips.

The simplicity, the solitude, of his makeshift homes merely served to make him bolder when he did go out for a stint. Riskier. Deranged and determined.

~ ~ ~

Delaina's exclamations perpetuated, walking under Avenida 16 de Septiembre's night lights, bellies stuffed with homemade tortillas, shopping bag stuffed with a rainbow of sundresses. "We won't ever forget this, will we?" Jed kissed her. "No, ma'am." "Ooh, Heart of Juarez sculpture!" She squeezed his hand. "Pic, please!" A Mexican guy nearby charged $$ to take one snap on Jed's phone. Delaina and Jed climbed steps, bent together, and kissed between -r and -z with the city's historic cathedral atop their heads.

~ ~ ~

Jed felt like Fred Flintstone pumping his foot into a pretend brake on the floorboard. Delaina asked to drive across New Mexico. She blared old rock music, sped, and sang. He said prayers, wished for cigarettes, repeated, "Slow down." "You're passin' on a double." "Hands on the wheel." He'd be a liar if he denied that he also grinned a lot, relished it, and fell deeper in love.

Later, she chose hymns and contemporary Christian songs. Nearer to Thee, 10,000 Reasons, I Can Only Imagine. She knew the words and made a "no sex till the coast" rule. She hooked him tighter.

"Look! Arizona, The Grand Canyon State Welcomes You." She pointed to the sign.

"In record time." Thanks to her NASCAR skills. "Hey, I'm supposed to drive when we cross the state line."

"But I love drivin' your jeep..." Her hair flew in the wind.

"I haven't smoked since May fifth, and I'm about to."

She eyed him.

"*D, eyes on the road*. You're doing 85."

"I've never smoked," she admitted as she took the next exit and pulled over, headlights on long earth. "This is how you're supposed to do Arizona. Get lost in the middle of nowhere! Your turn." She

LAINEY AND JED, BOOK TWO

hopped out. They swapped seats. "I wanna try a cigarette. My first can be your last." Her smile, like a lantern in the desert.

"It's a deal." His eyes were on her cupcake. Jed opened his console, retrieved an unopened pack.

"You're naughty. That was sweet." She kissed him for the fiftieth time today, first time in Arizona.

Jed slapped the box upside down on his palm. "This is how you pack tobacco. You do it." Eager, his cigarette virgin, she slapped and packed. He white-teeth smiled. "We're gonna do this?"

She giggled. "If it's your last, *yeah*." Jed unwrapped cellophane. "Okay, my last." He gave her a nicotine stick; she put it between her lips with excited laughter. "Easy now, sweetheart. Don't inhale too hard or fast." The lowness in his voice made her eyebrows raise. He flicked his lighter. She took a breath. The end glowed orange.

"Ha!" she exclaimed. A gentle intake, strange tingles. Jed bent toward her mouth, cigarette in his. His eyes squinted. He smelled like earth and fire.

Delaina swirled into. weird, wonderful suspension. Night and dares. Smoke and promises. Jed lit off her light; his stick glowed orange. They grinned at each other, the originality of their moment encircling them. He settled into his seat, pulled onto the road, drove, and enjoyed. Her Marlboro Man, one last time.

~ ~ ~

"Okay, *this* is the middle of nowhere," Delaina observed when they pulled into their slot.

"Wilderness campin' was your idea." Far away, a truck camper and one tiny RV, nobody else anywhere.

"It's romantic," she suggested. They stepped out. "Get our beach blanket from Texas Two's. I'll get our, uh, there's not much to get." They laughed. "Jed, that cactus is huge." He spread the blanket on their designated patch of ground, got naked, and sat. She looked down at him. "It's *cold*."

"Take off your clothes. We'll be warmer if we sleep like Eskimos."

"There aren't Eskimos in the desert." She discarded her gray dress, her sweet bikini. "I already told you, we're not doing it till California." She knelt on the blanket.

"You sure?" His fingers unwound her braids. "Things are gettin' damn good between us, Delaina."

220

WILD, WILD WEST

Damn good, from Jed McCrae. Heck yeah. She stayed her course. "We're building anticipation for Cali. You think there'll be snakes or... prowlers here?"

"Probably." Lying, they faced each other. Jed doubled the blanket over them. "I think Arizona has the most venomous reptiles of any state. Get closer to me." They were cocooned and cool in West Hell.

"Any closer, we won't be waiting." She giggled; they French-kissed. "I have a little something for you, big guy."

"I know you do, and I want it. We could tear each other up, D."

Wow, wow, wow. She held off, certain his Dirty Dozen had been ready and willing every time. -How to Be His Best Sex Ever 101. Not an easy course. "Tomorrow, Jed, it's gonna be unreal." Delaina cupped his face. "Tonight, I thought I might...play with a snake." Her tongue started at his sternum and licked to his navel. "Talk me through it. I wanna know exactly how you like it."

How he liked it was between her legs. Jed folded his arms behind his head and contemplated a starry western sky. "If you insist." He said something explicit. Delaina's mouth went south.

~ ~ ~

A lot of people in Mallard County lay wide awake too, worried about their little world, that night. Many of them had never been past the Mississippi state line. Some had never been as far as Jackson. Everything they knew and loved could be measured in 934 square miles, guarded with guns and gumption.

One of life's ironies: The smaller the place, the bigger the fear.

Screeches, bumps, creaks, and shadows were Cabot. He had grown larger than living.

He reveled in it.

~ ~ ~

"Rise and shine, baby girl." Jed woke Delaina with a predawn kiss. "You wanted to see sunrise." Her eyes popped open. Jed, half dressed, smelled like her coconut body wash. "I showered." He wrapped her in the blanket and lifted her, carried her through wilderness. Life had no sound other than his footsteps. Was she dreaming? "I found the perfect spot." He sat on a bench, held her swaddled in his arms.

"Sweetest morning ever."

"I love you, Delaina."

"I know." Gray horizon had a golden line across the bottom carved by cactus-rock figures. Jed sniffed her hair. "You smell like cigarettes."

"I'm tossing that pack in the trash. I liked smokin' more than I thought." They watched sky. She turned into his face. "I didn't realize it'd be so blue and pink." Mother Nature, or God, spun cotton candy in liquid gold.

"Speakin' of blue and pink, it could be that time of the month for you, I think."

Both were riveted by their never-seen picture. Top of the universe, solid blue, then a band of hot pink etched in eternal light. Bottom of the universe came to life. Cacti of every shape and size jutted from the ground to salute May 24.

Delaina flashed back to their appointment in Houston with Meggie. It came on her like electrocution. She burrowed into Jed. He didn't sense it, her automatic pain from remembering. She miscarried, or started her period, two weeks ago. "Maybe so."

"Hey, D, over there. Our first critter." A jackrabbit with gigantic ears leapt and took off.

No response caused Jed to check her face. Time thumped. He muttered under his breath, "Jack has a friend." He pointed. Two big-eared bunnies gallivanted.

"They're precious." She felt sadness dissolving, replaced by bunnies playing and her own need to carry on. "I have a mental list. Things I wanna do with you. Like my virtual board. I've wanted to try a condom since you told me the whole box was mine."

"You'll get your wish in California."

"Anything you wanna do with me, Jeddy?" Her voice became childlike of its own accord.

"Jeddy?"

"Sorry, it's the rabbits. They're so cute and happy."

"Not enough time in the day to tell you everything I wanna do with you, Lainey-lainey."

Lainey-lainey. Jed, complying with her foolishness. Be still, her heart. "Give me an example. Non-sexual. And what should we call our list?" His warm lap, her comfy blanket, Planet Cacti, and scampering critters. They didn't need a list. Every moment supplied wonder.

He kissed her lips. "Easy. I wanna take you to Baton Rouge. To meet my Gran Jane. God, she'd love you."

She touched the wedding band on her middle finger. To have a family... "Ms. Cass's mother." A holiday with Jed, a homecoming with his grandmother. Was it possible to swoon when she was already on her back and wrapped up? Delaina swooned. "I'd love that more than you can imagine." She looked into his blue eyes and narrowed hers. "Okay, tell me one thing sexual."

"Sexual. Hmm, Lainey-lainey." He glanced, grinned. This casual, foolish, bare-chested-in-shorts Jed McCrae. Delaina wished sunrise could last forever. "Easy again. I wanna make love to you fifteen thousand times for fifty years."

Her neck stiffened. Her eyebrows scrunched. Jed watched per-plexed Delaina. He laughed, opened his mouth to explain, and... "Oh god, *Jed*. I get it." She had tears in her eyes. "15,000X, that's our list. To go everywhere and do everything. I want all your days and nights."

A stab of what was best for her future almost reminded him. The Plan. Jed ignored it and motioned to a concrete pad with a single pole and showerhead beside a creek. "Want a shower?" Delaina looked skeptical. "I'll hold your blanket up like a curtain. Scrub-a-dub, Lainey-lainey. Roughing it was your idea."

She giggled. "Okay, Jeddy." She stood under the stream and soaped, hidden and viewed by him, then jiggled off water droplets.

Morning in Arizona beamed hot and bright. Jed chalked it up, watching her soapy shower, one for their 15,000X list. Done, ahead of schedule.

~ ~ ~

First up, Saguaro National Park, per Delaina, because, "Jed, it takes 100 years for the saguaro cactus to grow an arm, and they bloom in May!"

They were farmers with natural, profound appreciation for a fif-teen-minute stop, that it took sixty years for the cactus to sprout. Saguaros for acres, sprouts to grandpas in size. Dirt, rock mountains, selfies taken at a green spiky monster plant with daisy-like blooms.

On the road again, fry cakes. a regional must, for breakfast. Next, Gila River Indian Preservation. Tribal lands, breathtaking scenery, art, reptiles, baskets. Their journey twinkled at every turn. The Eagles Essentials, full volume, per Delaina, transported them across Phoenix. They sang together, and to each other, along with more of Delaina's, "Arizona is the sixth biggest state, bigger than all of New England." "Roadrunners are real?" "The original London Bridge was shipped, stone by stone, and reconstructed not far from here. We're going!"

They stretched their legs and ate lunch in Lake Havasu City. Sonoran hot dogs- wrapped in bacon stuffed with pinto beans, onions,

LAINEY AND JED, BOOK TWO

tomatoes, mayo, and mustard- washed down with a bottle apiece of local craft beer. Delaina, no makeup, in ankle-length, purple, South-of-the-border sundress and rubber flip flops, blazed. "Jed, if you told me two days ago that I'd be standing with you at London Bridge in Arizona, I would've accused you of smokin' dope!"

He took her in his arms. "Wouldn't be the first time you accused me."

They chuckled. "True." She wondered at the ancient bridge. "This is neat. Probably not better than the real thing in England, huh?"

He held up his phone, snapped a pic, kissing her in Somewhere, Wild West. "You're here. Way better."

"I'm going to London with you, Jed McCrae. Paris, Rome..."

One day maybe, the bully in Jed's mind taunted. Kiss-kiss replaced it.

She held hands and prissy-tailed toward their parking space. "I have a feelin' you've never done this picture-taking thing you're doing *a lot of* with me..."

"Never. Want me to tag you on social media?"

Oh God, would he? "I'm female, aren't I? I dare you." She shimmied. "Surprise me. Okay... next stop, Joshua Tree. *California*, I cannot wait." She tugged him to the jeep.

U2 Essentials hauled them over the state line with more singing and handholding.

~ ~ ~

They played a color game the last ten miles. "Texas?" "Blue," Jed said.

"Yes! How'd you know?" She squeezed his hand. Bono serenaded in the background, still hadn't found what he's looking for. "Mexico, me first. Red!"

Jed agreed, "Right again. New Mexico, we may disagree. I say orange."

"Hmm. If we give orange to New Mexico, what's Arizona? We said one color per place."

His girl took their color game and road trip seriously in the most amusing way. Jed, never more satisfied. "Pink? Who knew Arizona is pink?"

She giggled. "Pink, yeah! Love it. Okay, veering off, but Mississippi?"

"Green. Cotton and cash." He winked.

"God, you're cute. I caught that. California, so far?" Delaina looked out her window.

"Tan?"

"Sort of golden tan. Like me, from sunshine on this trip. Here we are! Web says we need four hours at JT, that's what you call it if you're legit, and we have..." Delaina checked the time. "About four minutes. Oh well. We'll come back."

"Give me the Joshua Tree, excuse me, JT rundown, Miss Tour Guide."

"Almost 800,000 acres. We're small fries, Farmer Jed." She patted his head. "Trails, stones, wildflowers, and stargazing."

"Shoot, JT's got our names all over it. We'll come back. Vegas and Grand Canyon, too."

"Yes, before I'm twenty-five!"

A guy could hope, wish, sacrifice, and make a sketchy deal with fate. Jed prayed to God, before twenty-five, she'd be back in his arms.

"Okay, Jeddy. Let's hop out, snap a sexy pic, and..."

"Get to Malibu before sunset, Lainey-lainey." Jed scorched her with a look hotter than the Mojave Desert.

~ ~ ~

They were stuck in workday traffic on sunny Pomona Freeway.

Jed paid attention to the road. Delaina gabbed, a plethora of things she wanted to know about James Evan Darrah McCrae. Today, he'd been wholly compliant. What a treasure. "I'm surprised you haven't been west."

"Mama tended to take me east, growin' up. East Coast, and east as in Europe. Recent years, I chose new countries, rather than states."

"How many states and countries have you been to?"

The jeep inched forward. "Uh." Jed calculated. "Twelve states and...twelve countries, not counting this trip."

Delaina swatted him. "Ridiculous. You definitely needed a new number." Jed made a face, then, ding. The Dirty Dozen. He chuckled.

"Your favorite?" She swatted him again. "And I'm not talkin' about Mallory."

"Texas and Greece so far. Update: Mallory's not my favorite, Delaina thirteen."

"Ooh, Greece! I'm adding that to our 15,000X list." She kissed his cheek. "Love the update. Your new favorite should reward you."

LAINEY AND JED, BOOK TWO

"Soon, she will." His smile for her, better than seeing Southern California.

~ ~ ~

In legitimate small-town fashion, Cabot Hartley sightings multiplied hourly. Locals locked their doors in the daytime, many for the first time, and stayed in. A temporary camp, a team of investigative agents, set up in Mallard County's sheriff department. A hotline was established. No one, including officials up to the federal level, knew real from fake. For now, they had to chase every wild goose.

~ ~ ~

Jed called Rhett and got exactly that report about Cabot. Next, he called Pate to get details about their California hotel property before he and Delaina arrived.

"Patrick Calhoun Hendricks," Jed stated. "You'll never guess where I am, buddy."

"Don't have a damn clue, but you sound like you got laid for your birthday. About freakin' time." Pate snorted; Jed sniffed. "I sure as hell hope you're somewhere with that pretty young thing."

"She's right here, man. You're on speaker. I'm drivin'."

"Aw, well...hell." Pate cleared his throat. "Hey, pretty young thing. Sorry for the jabs."

"Hey, Pate! You're always forgiven." She did a cute laugh. "Your cousin who's-not-your-cousin-but-is-your-best-friend is on a California road trip with me, honey." Delaina, as flirty as Jed had seen her. She adored Pate Hendricks. Jed didn't know whether to be mad or glad.

Pate whistled. On a curious snort, he told them they were getting bumped to Layla Rock, whatever that meant, and said Delaina was the best thing to happen to Jed.

~ ~ ~

"Do guys always do that?" Delaina had a funny smile when they were off the phone.

"Do what?"

"Rhett and Pate talk so raunchy and openly to you about me and sex."

"Oh yeah, way worse."

"Huh." Delaina watched a yellow Ferrari zoom by, pretty boy and pretty girl enjoying SoCal's wind and rays.

226

WILD, WILD WEST

"What does 'Huh.' mean? Am I in trouble?" His thumb grazed her lip.

"It's just…you don't really talk dirty to me." She jiggled. "I might like it."

"Dang, be patient. You've been with -quote- JED f-u-c-k-i-n' McCRAE just five times." He grinned.

She should slap him. "I did *not* say that."

"Right, you didn't say it. You yelled it. For everyone in my apartment building to hear."

Okay, maybe she did, in the heat of the moment, but did he have to point it out with a ridiculous grin now? "You loved it," she boasted and watched a milk-white Range Rover on her side.

His finger traced the V- of her dress. "I…love all of it. All of this."

His light touch made her yearn. "Say something seductive." She raised her sunglasses.

Jed couldn't tell if her eyes or the sun seared him. "I've stood all I can stand of your waitin' game, Miss Cash. You're about to get your sixth go-around."

Forget jeep rides. Hurry, Layla Rock. "Speed up, big guy."

~ ~ ~

L.A. showed out, hectic and multicultural, laidback and glitzy. Delaina reminded Jed that tomorrow they would shop, on Rodeo Drive for kicks and giggles, for clothes to wear to the Jackson Capitol. He said he was mighty glad he brought his Amex.

Closer to the coast, she pointed at everything from inside the jeep. Loved the bikes and skaters, the spontaneous carnival rides and ice cream shops. "Hey, Jed, I had a crazy thought…these guys and gals are probably my age." She watched scores of young adults on the sidewalks. "Isn't it crazy that I could conceivably be at…USC or UCLA right now?"

The Plan alerted Jed to plant a seed. His Adam's apple bobbed. "Not crazy at all. If you want to, you should."

She enjoyed a sarcastic laugh. "Yeah, right. Who's gonna take care of the farm?"

"Me."

Her head jerked.

"Until you're done with as much education as you desire." He saw her mouth open to protest. "Wait. I read the letter from Tory. Have you? That's what *your daddy* wanted."

How could sad tears pool in her eyes when she viewed Santa Monica for the first time? "Tory *was* my daddy." "Agree." "I didn't read the letter yet." "He loved you, D, the only way he knew how. Through Cash Way. You should read it when you get back to Mallard."

Those words, back to Mallard, caused instant dread.

Jed went on, "Tory dropped out of Mississippi State when his own father died an untimely death. He wanted you to get educated, to live a little, and..." He took a breath, contemplated.

Her heart ached. "And what?"

Incredible coastline cruised by. "I think Tory felt ill, wondered if he would live much longer. You know he came to see me twice before you graduated high school. Made small talk, touched on the future of farmin'. I think...he was leadin' up to telling me every-thing. Maybe hoped you'd choose me to manage while you finished Ole Miss."

Delaina watched happy-go-lucky Californians out her window. ...Tory's last words to her. Flip sides of the same coin. 'Watch out who you love, Lainey. Or hate."

Jed was probably right.

TWENTY-ONE

Hotel California

L ayla Hotel was Calla's rebellious little sister. Windswept, adventurous, tanned.

Instantly sensational was the realization that they were staying on a ranch, on a cliff, on the ocean. A swaying palm tree, here or there, blended with jutting rock-things, scraggly herby-looking flowers, citrus scents, and crashing water. An open-air, drive-thru lobby, made of beige stone columns, corridors, and mellow sunshine, greeted.

Delaina would've been speechless, were Jed not astonished. "Uh, Jed." She gawked. "I think I had California mixed up with Hawaii. This is how I picture Spain...or Greece?"

"Me too." He drove under a creamy sail cover. "Greece is blue and white. More like Spain or Portugal."

Her jaw had come unhinged. "I'm stunned. We're in the mountains on the beach and..."

"Driving inside the hotel, I think."

"Now you know how I felt, arriving at Calla."

"D, I don't think you felt what I'm feeling." He pulled into a parking space betwixt two rocky things.

"What are you feeling?"

"Like I should tote you, in front of God and everybody, across the threshold."

My, how dreamy. She leaned toward him and kissed. "Precisely how I felt at Calla. Blown away and seduced. Are you gonna come to my side and sweep me into ecstasy?"

229

Delaina thought he looked nervous. "Uhm, no." He pushed sunglasses on his head, and she saw how much sun had baked his face during their expedition. Never a finer man to share two nights at a ranch-mountain-beach-rock place. "That's reserved for my wife."

She blinked, blinked, blinked, then stepped out and reached for her bag. "Your absent wife sure is high on a pretend pedestal. Her special wedding song, a sacred bedroom loft, a spectacular hotel arrival." Her shoulder raised. "You carried me across the desert this morn. Guess I'm lucky."

"Certain things belong to her."

Delaina stumbled. An immunization of something real but foreign needled her. It was Jed. He looked...ready to be a husband.

A toast-tinted surfer type with buttery tresses appeared on a stretch golf cart. "What's up? I'm Luca. Welcome to Layla." He took their bags.

Jed shook hands, introduced Delaina, and said something about himself and Pate. Luca nodded, invited them aboard, and veered in a direction. They sat on the back bench to watch the views. Layla Hotel, designed so fluidly, so mystically, so effectively, Delaina and Jed couldn't tell when they were inside or out.

Delaina picked up where they left off. "Maybe I've decided to save some things for my husband, then." "Maybe you should," Jed countered.

Were they on the verge of a fight after fifty hours of god-and-goddess bliss?

Luca bypassed a courtyard check-in via willowy, skirt-wrapped swimsuit bodies. This stay, seemingly "on the house" for James *Darrah* McCrae.

~ ~ ~

If Calla's suites mimicked bird nests, Layla's were aquariums.

Secluded, square, stucco-and-glass villas with noun names, separated by tile paths through fruit trees. Layla Beach, Layla Tree, Layla Hill, depending on the lay of the land.

Layla Rock required a ride and a trek; it hovered a mammoth boulder on Pacific waves. They had to climb steps to enter. The ocean-facing wall, totally glass, the crux of their aquarium, echoed dull splashing. Delaina wondered if the vast blue surge might swallow them overnight. Around them, cliffs and steep paths opened to sand peppered with pebbles and geologic statues.

HOTEL CALIFORNIA

She rotated. The back wall/bed wall, also glass, revealed the lengthy return to Layla Hotel's activity center through scrub grass and red earthen terraces. Inside their villa, a boxy room, one tan hue. Indistinguishable where the floor, wall, bed, or doors began and ended.

"The beachside window wall lifts." Luca demonstrated on a panel. Ocean broke on a slick deck not far from where they stood. "Tide's rolling back. Hella-sweet hidden crannies on your front." Delaina stepped outdoors. Luca turned. "I'll let you two marinate. Need me, text me. Cart's yours."

For a ponderous span, neither spoke after he left. Jed walked onto the deck, sat, took out his phone, scrolled and texted, or something, caught up on real life, Delaina supposed. She went to shower and change. When she returned, freshened in navy-and-pink surfboard bikini with wet hair, Jed stood. "Hungry?" He glanced. "You're so pretty."

"I'm hungry, and kind of peeved, honestly." She got her purse, hunted her phone.

"I'm sorry." Jed was sorry. He probably got her pregnant, definitely scandalized her in Mallard, and stupidly, had the gall to tell her that he wouldn't carry her over the threshold. He didn't mean it how it came out, a fact he planned to correct in multiplicity.

Delaina inched onto a glossy lounge chair and studied their coastal bluff. Felt that Calla feeling, out of her league. How much had Layla cost him? "Two missed calls from Miss Maydell and one from...Della?" She called home to Miss Maydell.

Jed meant to go somewhere to give her privacy. There was none. He left the villa.

"Lainey, *thank goodness*! My lord, sweetie, Holland showed me pictures. For heaven's sake, what in the world have you got yourself into?"

"No worries! I told Rhett we were stayin' longer, but I should've called you. I'm great; it's great. Thanks for checkin' on me. The West is unbelievable. Miss you." Delaina did miss her. It hit her; wait a minute. "*Pictures?*"

"I miss you, too! Yes, honey, those pictures. Goodness, that fella loves you. That thing on your phones, what's it called? Facechat? I panicked when Holland showed me." Miss Maydell laughed. "Hard

LAINEY AND JED, BOOK TWO

to believe, you and Jed McCrae. Lots older, you know. Be smart, Lainey. He's lots more experienced."

"I'm having the time of my life." Not at the moment, but... "He makes me happy, Miss Maydell."

"I know he does. Just remember your roots, your raisin', and, uh, your raincoats for the rain, dear." She quieted. "Truth is, I'm awfully glad you're away from here. All these folks spottin' Cabot Hartley. It's enough to raise the arm hairs on the devil. Rhett and Moll call it a bunch of hoopla, but I tell ya, I've been lockin' the doors with my shotgun loaded."

That raised the hair on Delaina's arms. "Rhett is keepin' us posted. Doesn't sound good. I can't imagine."

"Love you, Lainey. Stay there long as you can."

"Supposed to be home Wednesday. Love you, Miss Maydell. Be safe. Bye."

When the uneasiness from hearing about the Cabot Hartley saga faded, which happened rapidly since Delaina sat in a human aquarium on a boulder in California, she couldn't check social media fast enough!

What the heck had Jed done? ...A phone notification twenty minutes ago. *Jed McCrae tagged you in a post.*

Her heart...completely stopped.

She saw on his profile page: *Jed McCrae* is with *Lainey Cash. May 24, 6:34 p.m.*

Oh God. Oh dear God.

Six magnificent photos, an adventure collage of them. Impossible to decipher where they were, other than somewhere gorgeous and western.

Jed's caption: *Happy Birthday every day to us.*

Their pictures were dreamlike, a trailer to a blockbuster. The sunlight, their smiles, the scenery, his splendidness. She felt her blood pounding, tears on her cheeks. She started to type. Out of nowhere, maturity whispered, *Hold off, Delaina. Give it time.*

208 likes? 64 comments? In mere minutes. It was official. They were official. Jed had officially lost his mind. Over her.

~ ~ ~

Delaina knew straightaway that's why her mother had called.

232

HOTEL CALIFORNIA

Her phone rang before she could decide whether to return her call. *Waverly Wallace,* one of her two best friends from high school. Uh-oh, here goes. "Hey, Wave."

"Girl, OMG! Why didn't you tell us? We are *dying*."

Delaina laughed, not a shy giggle, more like quasi-hysterical. "Well, I..."

"Mary Beth said we shouldn't bother you two, but I was, like, oh heck yeah, I'm callin'. Lainey, those pics!"

"I don't know what to say. I'm...in a dream." Her hand touched Jed's mama's ring, habitual these days.

Waverly sang the words, "I bet somebody's not a virgin anymore." Ha, ha! "We're home for summer, and you promise me, we get all the details ASAP when you get back. Pool day at Cash Way. You look, oh gosh, in love. I'm staring at 'em now while I'm talkin' to you, and this is crazy! You and Jed McCrae? God! He is so freakin' good-lookin'!"

"He's gorgeous and good to me. Gotta go. Thanks. Luv y'all. Bye." Off the phone, in a haze, and feeling sort of... thrilled.

The door shut. Delaina glanced backward. There he stood.

Framed in glass and sun, holding a picnic basket and a bottle of bubbly. "Hey," from Jed.

"Hey." "I got food." "I see that." Her phone flopped in her hand. He watched her face. "I'm sorry, Delaina."

"Are you trying to make up?" So, she smiled.

So, he smiled at her. "Yeah, tryin'. I think I'm bad at it." He stepped closer.

She waited on purpose, to let him worry a little. Dimly, she heard ocean waves. "You haven't had much practice at begging."

"Never tried."

He never had to. They stood inches apart. "Question for you. Is it always like this?" She looked around, let her eyes land on the bed.

Jed made a face. "Always like what?"

"Sudden. Anytime we arrive anywhere, any place we're alone, I immediately...think of sex with you. Is it always like that for two adults involved with each other?"

"I'm too wise to answer." His grin, subdued. She waited, which demanded an answer. "Fine, D, yeah. Yeah, it is." He set down the basket and bottle. "It's different with you, and that sounds like a line. I was hopin' you'd wanna... find a cove with me."

233

"Maybe." Good Lord above, he smelled and looked like the best kind of temptation. Oh, to heck with his apologizing or begging. "Positively, let's find a cove."

"Dang, I forgot the golf cart keys. Will you get them while I change into my suit?" Some morsel in Jed's tone...something seemed... suspicious.

"Uh, okay." She walked out.

Jed changed into his matching swimsuit in record time, dashed out the door. She climbed steps, keys in hand, to their rocky-top house. He swept her into his arms. "Let's try this again." She gulped, faces close together. He carried her through the door, tossed her on the bed, crawled over her, smiling, and kissed her. "Best tour guide ever. Best trip. Thank you." Then he got on his feet, basket and bubbly in hand. "Come on. I'll keep makin' up to ya."

"You're forgiven." Nothing would steal her joy or their time. "Something I gotta do, Jed. You find a rock. I'll find you... I need your phone." She held out her hand; he complied. "Go on. I'm comin'."

Jed stepped onto the deck and vanished. She found the photo on his phone that she wanted: Their afternoon at Mallard's park. The most shameless, lust-faced, iridescent-fountain-sunlit backdrop, startling picture of them inside the gazebo, cheeks together, middle of downtown. Totally in love. Totally convincing. Totally real.

She sent it to herself, uploaded it to her profile page, and typed. *Twenty and thirty weren't half bad, **Jed McCrae**. Thank you.*

If they were going to be notorious on social media, they were going big. On a whim, she added #LaineyandJed #nofilter.

They'd read their deluge of comments another time. Delaina texted her biological mother. *In Cali, extended birthday celebration w/ Jed. Call you when I get to MS unless it's urgent...*

Her mother answered: *Wanted to say Belated Happy Birthday to you both and enjoy CA.*

She'd respond to that later, too.

For now, Jed McCrae and the Golden State belonged to her.

~ ~ ~

Hunger addressed by their picnic, they floated chest high in sluggish, gray-blue, chilly current.

Sun drooped behind diamond reflections. Their bodies bobbed like corks.

HOTEL CALIFORNIA

The meal on the sand had been quiet. Delaina didn't mention social media. Buying time. Growing up.

Their ocean-bobbing, a muted love scene, emotions and beauty without words. Unexpected swell shoved her against him; she wrapped her legs around his waist and gripped his shoulders. It startled him. Jed's erection startled her.

"Jed, I want you."

"Let's go to shore. You're not gettin' a UTI on my watch."

UTI? Delaina frowned. Under The...Water? No. Under The...I-word. Huh, she had no clue.

They crept into a cave-cove discovered earlier, beneath their villa's rock bed. A plank had been constructed within, a landing place for lovers. Soaked sand and a thin tide pool made the ground. The water felt freezing to her feet. Shadows and light crafted a yellow and black world. They could see cliffs and coast. Nothing could see them. It was seventh heaven.

Jed sat on the plank and pulled her onto his lap, straddling and facing. Her legs circled his waist; she leaned into his warmth. He nibbled her neck. His fingers pulled her bottom ties loose on one side. "We're okay now?"

"Mm, hm," was her consent. He slid her bottoms away. It made her want to get closer to him. Delaina untied her neck straps, let her top fall. "Jed, what's UTI?"

Fingers on her back tie, he looked like he wanted to laugh. "Uh." She adored that face, amused by her. "Stands for urinary tract infection." He pulled the string and disposed of her top.

She got it, like taking too many baths and getting a kidney infection. "People do it in the water," she challenged. He attempted to get his swim trunks off. She shifted and helped slide them down his legs.

He shrugged. "You're, you know, unaccustomed is all. We'll get there."

They stared, absorbed each other nude, on the verge of copulation.

"*Jed.*" Her green eyes implored. "Am I okay for you so far?"

The bluest eyes and blackest hair, skin glistening. "Let me see. How to answer. Delaina...am I okay for you?"

Her involuntary laugh was a shrill bell. "You know you're perfect." She felt salty and sexy.

LAINEY AND JED, BOOK TWO

His satisfied smile, a pearl at the ocean. "You answered your own question." He fumbled around behind him for his suit and took a wrapper from the Velcro pocket. "About to check one off the list, D. Afraid you're gonna be disappointed, though."

"Try me," she enticed.

"Open. Carefully." Those eyes of his, puncturing. "We're gonna start from the start." The demonstration that followed drew them in, drew them closer.

He cupped her shoulders. "If you ever, for any reason...have sex with anybody else..."

"What?" Delaina made an awful face.

He looked at a dimming Pacific, reorganized his words. "Remember Pearl Harbor. Rafe and Danny?" She nodded, still bewildered. "If something happens to me, you use a condom with anybody else. Guys are jerks, so I don't care who, when, why. You understand?"

She positioned herself over him, on him, like a pro. "Jed, *nothing's* gonna happen to you." She dragged herself up and down unhurriedly, gripping his shoulders. She looked between their bodies. "I don't like it."

His stare into her eyes. Oh how he regarded her. "Baby, focus on us...alone...together."

She tried to focus. She giggled. "We're doing it Indian-style."

He pulled her face to his with hands on her skull and kissed her deeply. "What do you know about how Indians do it?"

Her nails dug into his skin. "What do you know about how Eskimos sleep?" He chuckled, nipped her shoulder. "Please take it off."

His teeth sank deep. "Don't do that to me. All that matters, we're in Cali...naked in a cave."

Lotus, this position was lotus, Delaina recalled that from her self-education, days and nights spent alone and recuperating at Cash Way after...after the baby.

Protection was a must.

He slid off the hard plank, bodies sealed. She intended to get underneath him, to lay, but he went first. His jaw clenched when his back hit the shallow puddle. "Ah god, cold." Delaina whispered, "I'll get you heated up." "You're dirty-minded, cupcake." "You like me." "I love you."

"Jed, I like how we're talkin' while we do it."

236

His long stare lacerated her. "Chalk that up to the condom. When it's just you on me...I can't speak."

The way he held her, the way he let her move, the way body parts illuminated. They saw everything for the first time. "Talk to me," she begged.

"Whatcha want me to say, angel?"

"Sweet. Dirty. Anything."

He commented on scenery, the significance of their moment, what he wanted to do to her. She replicated. They were open, every meaning of the word.

Act complete, sun absent, he held her over him. No two humans loved each other more.

~ ~ ~

Mound Bayou, Mississippi. Holland didn't know it existed until today.

Cabot's bold message should've been shocking. An unknown number, but she knew who. *You and me. Mound Bayou. 11 p.m.* It wasn't shocking. He knew she wouldn't disclose his location. He had her.

She searched the destination online before she left Cash Way. Population, 1500, 98% African American. A town settled by former slaves. Astonishing.

A long, dark trip northwest with no address. She trembled and drove.

The radio played. She recognized an iconic song about a California hotel. It made her think of Lainey and Jed's beautiful pictures. Then, of Rhett, of her deception. Lies she told, more lies today, to get out of town after dark. Listening to music did nothing to diminish her fear. She crossed the county line into her next nightmare. A car slipped in behind her, bumped her bumper. She screamed. She tapped the brake. The car pulled over and parked.

A male walked to the passenger window. A teenager. Dark and small. She would've punched the gas to squeal away and escape. He got in faster. "Nobody's in here?" His round head poked between the seats, checked the back.

"No," she muttered.

"Somebody a-wantin' to see you, missus. Drive."

Holland's eyes couldn't focus on the lines of the road. Her hands had trouble holding the wheel. Somehow, she drove. She expected groups or a congregation when they got into town. Men wearing chains and shades at night, shiny cars, shiny wheels. A stereotype, for sure, it would've been the most welcome relief. Proof of life. People just living.

She got a ghost town. Dilapidation. She might've felt fascination, a respect for history, if it had been daylight or a different circumstance. Music, art, a painted town, she might've seen Mound Bayou's culture, had she known what to expect.

Instead, they drove beyond street lights into more barrenness. He pointed. "Right here, ma'am." A low-lying, ghosted shack. "Go on in."

In there? Holland got out. *Take steps. Walk.* She dug into the pit of her being to make herself go. The door stood open. Porch planks bent and whined beneath her feet. A lightbulb hung from the ceiling. Inside smelled dead.

Human motion pushed a scream from her gut. Hands over her mouth blocked it. "Hush."

Her ribs bucked up and down. Her nostrils sucked the scent of a man incongruent with the place. "Relax." She twisted. A homeless Cabot. "You should feel welcome here." He watched her, circled her. His eyes glared at her waist. "Right?" He snickered. "With black men." His eyes, at her waist again. "What are you going to do, *Ms. Smith*, if that kid is blond and fair? Like I am."

"Kill me, Cabot, because if I escape here, I will tell them everything." She stepped away. "They're good people. They're my family. I won't live like this."

His hands went up. Surrender. "Drive away, Holland. Go tell them. You're free."

She gripped onto anything for support. A wobbly table bumped the floor. The bulb swayed. The room mourned in the shadows. Old, deserted, broken. She thought of Moll. Of Maydell. The way they pushed forward daily. Hanging on. Rhett's kindness. The purity of her child. A child *never* to be Cabot's. "What do you want from me?"

"That's good judgment, Holland. This won't take long." Cabot patted her arm. "Now then. Let's talk."

~ ~ ~

To bury themselves in beach bungalow blessedness was their plan, when Jed carried Delaina out of the cove, up the rocks, across the villa, into the shower.

HOTEL CALIFORNIA

The power of social media trapped them, though, and put them to bed, moonlight and screen glow, wall window open, ocean splashing. Naked, clean, side by side, each with a phone up.

A public frenzy neither could've predicted, they were flabbergasted, sparsely conversing. Hundreds of interactions, they viewed. Likes, comments, shares.

Mallard and Mississippi had fallen in love with #LaineyandJed.

She elbowed him. "This is your fault, big guy."

"You want the truth? Half the reason I did it was Cabot. To give our town something new to think about and to lure him out of Mallard. He has no hope of finding us there. Or here."

He sniffed her coconut hair. "The other reason I did it is *your* fault, D, not mine. You wanted pics and tags, pouted at Texas Two's, dared me in Arizona." He put his phone away and whispered in her ear, "I like a good dare. I don't like for my Lainey-lainey to pout."

She shivered. *My* Lainey-lainey. The glory of it, a first. "Jed, you said my." He was slobbery-kissing behind her ear. They were gonna do it again. All night, he had vowed in the cove.

"Uh, what do you mean?"

She turned into him. "In romance novels, the guys…" She felt juvenile.

"Uh-oh, I warned you about fairy tales."

She stroked his arm muscle. Waves resounded and moon sparkled in their private aquarium. "Yeah, 'cause this *isn't* a fairy tale?"

"Point made." His breath smelled good, like toothpaste. "So, storybook guys do what?"

"The men are always, I don't know, flattered and possessive. Say things like, 'You're mine.' 'You belong to me.' Jed, you don't do that. You cut a wide path around me and let me do my thing. You've never said anything like that, until now. One time. *My* Lainey-lainey."

"Your independence drew me in. It's a constant lure." He scooped her close. "Besides, the *you're mine* kind of talk, that's, uh…" He clicked his tongue. "For my wife."

His beloved wife again. Geez. "Let's talk about this wife."

"Let's make love and forget about my wife."

She had to laugh. "So, what makes you think of her like that?'

"Because…" He squeezed Delaina. "I'm ready. I want her."

"How long have you been ready?" Childish parts of Delaina hoped he answered two months, since he met her, even though she had *never* given a thought to what marriage with him would be like.

"Two or three years, maybe?"

Oh Lord. Wow. Jed McCrae, a husband. Over-ready.

Like he read her mind, "That's to be determined, though, and may be a long way off." His words rang so true neither heard the ocean or felt anything.

A void.

He picked up the pace. "Surprises, love notes, church, nicknames, flowers, sex- a lot of it, minimum fifteen thousand times, devotion. She'll be my world, not possession or overprotectiveness, more like respect, reverence, being personal. A lifetime of awe because the right one is gonna be there. *Mine and ours.*" He touched his nude soulmate on the cheek and wished.

He was the greatest man God ever made. "We're gonna do it again," she flirted, to ignore long-term, meaningful questions of How, When, What if, that had no answers yet.

"If you say so, ma'am." He had a lower voice. "I thought you might wanna...do that thing they were doing on the porn channel in the cheesy Hammond honeymoon suite. Try it out."

Heaven help her. Reverse cowgirl on Jed McCrae. His worshipful words about his wife lingered. "I wanna save something for my husband." Delaina longed to be as ready as Jed, as able to comprehend their future. She wasn't.

"Hurry up and decide, cupcake, for that hubby of yours because you and I are steadily knockin' out the best of the best." He tickled her ribs.

Delaina laughed loudly. "What do you wanna do more than anything with me? One big thing."

"Easy again." He reached backwards for his phone and typed. Her phone beeped on her nightstand. She got it and read. Emojis. Two puppy dog faces and a red heart.

Her phone screen lit up her stumped expression. Then, "Oh! Bleu Cotton and Astro. Gosh, how sweet." She texted: *I meant sex ha, ha* and watched him read.

"Hey Jed, I've noticed that I'm *Delaina Cash* in your phone. That's too formal."

I meant sex too, came from him onto her phone with the doggy faces and red heart again. She made a face. He handed his phone to her. "Let's see what kind of name you come up with, Delaina Cash."

Hmm. She grinned and scrolled to edit her name. The smile flipped. She got a giant reminder of his broad, interesting adult life.

My God, how many were there, the past two months alone? Three, four, more. Flirty texts from women. Sent to him, none deleted, but none answered by him either.

It hit her, what he wanted to do with her. Doggies. Oh, goodness gracious. "There are a lot of Jed's wife wannabes in your phone." ~How to Be His Best Sex Ever 101, such a challenging course.

"I kept their texts, in case you wanted to see. Haven't answered anybody since you asked for my wrench, Day One. They don't wanna be wives. Wouldn't be mine regardless, Delaina thirteen."

Delaina thirteen got her every time. No fighting about silly women with the greatest guy alive, when he chose two days and nights with her at Layla Rock. *Delaina13*, she changed her name to in his phone. She twisted it to show him.

Jed read. "Okay." He chuckled. "Heck, I like it." He took his phone from her. Texted to her phone, *Do I get to be Jed1 in your phone?* with the doggies and red heart.

She laughed, changed his name in her phone: *Jed1*. She showed him. He chuckled. She typed two puppies, a red heart, and a text to him. *This is reserved for my hubby.*

Ooh, he made a bad face when he received that. "Lucky dang hubby."

"You're okay with it?"

He scooped her body into his arms. "I can wait."

She grinned into night air. "Oh, so you're my hubby?" "If I am, it'll be the best damn wedding night, beyond anything we can imagine."

Sweet Lord, whispered in her mind.

Plant a seed, whispered in his. "And the best marriage. When you're ready." Jed squeezed her tighter. "If I don't get to be your hubby, I hope you give the bastard hell, waiting."

Their laughter combined. "It's a deal, then."

"Deal. Good deal. Actually, I think it's awesome, Delaina."

God, his sweetness. "But Jed, reverse cowgirl is kind of..."

"Nope. Just a night at the rodeo. Not even close to the same thing."

They snuggled to an ocean lullaby. "I'm sleepy."

"I was afraid it was me, gettin' old."

"Not just you, Big Mister 31. It's been a giant fifty-five hours or so. Wake me up when you're ready for the rodeo."

"Okay, Lainey-lainey. Night."

Twenty-two

Awake

The ocean galloped away. Window wall up, Jed woke to the sound of soft-breaking waves. Delaina, nowhere to be seen, her phone on the nightstand.

Jed woke up tired. He and Delaina shared a passionate night.

He had today left, to spend adoring her. Tomorrow after the Jackson Capitol meeting, he could not put off The Plan any longer.

He rose, found cargo shorts. He had a hunch that Delaina took a beach walk, maybe trying to sop up what they'd seen, and been to each other, this week. He stepped onto the deck with his phone to sit and wait.

Nothing could have prepared him for what came next.

Their relationship was a circus act on social media.

Anybody from Mallard's park, the day they went downtown, had shared whatever they captured. Every angle or slice of #LaineyandJed depicted. Mallard salon owner Doreen Rosemund posted a striking photo of them bent over the koi pond and started a campaign to #namethefishLainey&Jed #onceandforall. More than a thousand likes and over seven hundred people commented positively, not a single dissent.

Among hundreds on Jed's original trip-photos post, Pate Hendricks: *About time.* Meggie Henderson: *What a birthday gift! Xoxo to you both.* Holland Sommers: *Same birthdays?! Destined.* Rhett Smith: *Crazy. Y'all have fun.* Della Kendall: *Beautiful.* A half dozen of the Dirty Dozen heard from. Sophie in Houston: *Tell Lainey Cash, what a catch!* Jenna Lee Lester: *Love this match.* Nealy Daniel: *Now I know why you never answered me! LOL.* Mallory Rich: *You deserve this, Jed.* Keely in Ireland: *Best wishes from The Orchard County.* High school girlfriend Shay: *Perfect pair!*

On Lainey's wall, the same overwhelm. Mary Beth Bell: *Our bff in love...Finally!* with **Waverly Wallace**, who commented, *Shocking. Thrilling! Congrats, #LaineyandJed.* Brice Buffy: *WTF? Jed McCrae? Seriously (thumbs up emoji).* Josiah Ward: **Hears heart breaking* Looking great, Lainey+.* Maydell Smith: *Rhett bought me a smart-phone just for this! God Bless You both.*

Random adulations went on and on. Jed's mother's first cousin in Baton Rouge: *Yes, yes, yes! Cass predicted this.* Another relative: *She certainly did! She's singing with the angels (praying hands emoji)*

What? His mama saw this coming?

Bits and pieces, conversations and occurrences with his mama, merged in Jed's memory...

His mama knew. She saw it coming. That rocked Jed to the core.

~ ~ ~

Still no Delaina, he put together a rudimentary breakfast in the kitchenette. They needed to eat fast, dress quickly, and make a stop at a pharmacy on the way to Rodeo Drive shopping. The morning-after pill, a vow they made to each other during the night, to be *extra* careful.

Coffee made, bagels browned, he was scrambling eggs when he heard, "Jed?" Wearing gray knit dress and nothing else, sand-caked, drenched, traumatized Delaina.

"What the hell?"

Her left hand gripped the middle finger on her right. Jed saw a whitened circle on tan skin. "It's lost." She crumpled at the waist. "I never took it off since the minute you gave it to me. I'm so sorry." She sniveled. "It's gone." Oh god, Jed's face... Unable to bear it, Delaina stepped onto the deck, tiptoed on the rocks, bent, felt around. He came up behind her. "Delaina..." Then, "Aw, for Christ's sake!"

She watched him dash into Layla Rock, saw scratch marks on his back (She did *that?*), saw smoke scamper. She darted in. Jed beat flames with a towel. She grabbed the pan and tossed it into the sink, into gushing water, as he yelled, "No!"

Too late, a puff of smoke jumped from the sink to the ceiling and blackened. "Aw, no! Damn, Delaina!" The backsplash stained gray while more smoke mushroomed. Air smelled like scorched rubber. Both started gasping and coughing. He pulled her with him out of the villa, pushed her into vehement sunlight facing Layla Hotel. They struggled to clean their lungs. Tears streamed from her eyes, from fire or circumstances or both.

Jed rushed inside. A piercing siren vibrated the villa. Sprinklers sprayed every direction. He yelled, "Jesus Christ!" Before Delaina could do anything or think at all, surfer Luca appeared with a throng of employees who stampeded the interior. An emergency vehicle sped onto the scene. Two uniformed men climbed rocks. One asked, "Are you okay?" while the other shoved past her. She heard Jed say, "Fire's out. Not much damage."

Fogged, she approached the doorway. She looked to Jed, duplicate expressions. Stupefied.

"Come on. Get your stuff and get out of here," Luca stated. "We'll take care of this. No worries."

~ ~ ~

They were deposited into a miniscule room, three stories high in Layla's main hotel. "Pods" were the only availability left, midweek going into Memorial Day weekend.

Definition of the pod: A sliver of floor, bed for two built into narrow wall space, glass shower, tiny toilet, and upscale sink. Sleek and contemporary, one beige hue, one huge view. Faraway ocean, cliff-ranch coves, astounding villas, and tops of fruit trees teased from oversized glass.

Jed seemed like he wanted to avoid her, but where? She took a shower in her dress to rinse the sand then stripped in the stream. Like his back, her breasts were marked. She touched a whitened circle on her middle digit frequently.

Dressed, they wound up shoulder to shoulder, lodged on the skinny strip of floor between the bed and the door. "I'm *sorry*, Jed. What now?"

His serious blue eyes darted on her face. "Pharmacy, food, and clothes, I guess."

~ ~ ~

Delaina wanted to go inside alone, she said in the drugstore parking lot, and wanted to pay. They argued. Jed gave her cash.

She scurried to the tampon, condom, family-planning aisle. Her eyes stung from smoke. She scanned boxes, couldn't find what she needed. She darted to a pharmacist's niche and asked. He gave her a box from behind the counter and instructed, "Take with food. You need the second dose if you vomit within three hours of taking the first. Any questions?"

Is this wrong? Do I have to do this? She couldn't look at him. "No, thank you."

She went up front to pay. Short by 68 cents. No purse or wallet. *For real?* She stepped into vehement sunlight; it stung her sunburned shoulders. Ready to cry, she walked to Jed's side. "I need a dollar." He fished out his wallet, viewed a stack of bills, and motioned for her to step aside. He walked in, returned holding the pill box.

They sat at a brunch place and picked at food. Jed checked in with Rhett and got the latest on Cabot.

The old saying, It only takes a spark... Cabot Hartley sightings were a wildfire burning out of control, to the point that, according to Rhett, stories became silly, maybe even un-worrisome. Desensitizing, Jed replied.

...Delaina's sundress had no pockets, morning-after pill in Jed's shorts. She held out her hand when their plates were cleared and excused herself. Staring in the restroom mirror... She shoved it in her mouth, cupped water from the sink in her palm, and swallowed.

~ ~ ~

Extrication from Cabot Hartley would come with a high price.

Holland did what she had to do. She could not live under the tyranny of a fugitive-murderer.

Health professionals in the office where she went were kinder and less judgmental than she would've imagined. She had a lot of questions before she decided to go forward.

She cried before the appointment, during the appointment, and all the way to Cash Way.

She would work, stay busy, try not to think about it, and pray. How to handle the Smith family did not have to be decided today.

~ ~ ~

Delaina and Jed walked into the most opulent boutique that Delaina ever saw, a men-women's place, and separated.

A stunningly dressed ethnic guy, Oliver, greeted her with a mojito and lime and brought urbane suits on glossy wooden hangers. He had an amusing personality and babbled over her, even though she had funky tan lines and wore a cheap sundress.

246

She undressed, no bra with cream, silky panties that Jed bought at Texas Two's. She turned her back on -Never mind me, I'm gay- Oliver. She downed her tasty drink, selected the first suit she tried- petite, faultless, black- and thanked Oliver.

Dressed, she caught sight of Jed across the way, standing before a bank of mirrors, barraged by two column-esque women with pearl teeth, breast implants, suave clothes, hair extensions, and long nails. They tugged and tucked and touched a dashing charcoal gray suit and white shirt on his mouth-watering body. Jed McCrae turned her belly over and caused Beverly Hills ideal beauties to gush.

She asked Oliver to bring black heels in her size to the counter. Thousands of dollars in apparel at the desk, she realized she'd have to call Mallard First Financial to transfer money. Her phone, in Jed's pocket. She saw one Beverly Hills beauty packaging his suit. He must be in the fitting room undressed, with the other one? She stepped toward the area to get her phone.

"I'll pay," Jed breathed down her neck. She twisted, their eyes meeting. Her spine rolled. "Oh hell, no," she didn't mean to say loudly. "I need my phone to call Jenna Lee."

"Lainey, that's not smart. The bank'll know where you are if you make a purchase." He muttered, "*Cabot*."

"Oh please. He'd never find our tee-tiny pod in Malibu and we're leaving tomorrow before sunrise. Give me my phone." He did. She went to dial the number and...

For God's sake, cyberspace torpedoed overnight. 3239 notifica- tions? Any slice of #LaineyandJed shared, by EVERYONE ELSE.

Mallard Town Park, the huge magnolia tree, holding hands, laughing, in love. Dancing beneath the gazebo. His arm around her at the koi pond #namethefishLainey&Jed #onceandforall. What the hell? A fish-naming campaign?

Among hundreds of comments on Jed's original post, Pate, Meggie, Holland, Rhett, her biological mother?

...*Tell Lainey Cash, what a catch!* from Sophie LeBlanc. Who? She touched the name. Oh my, his ex, Sophie from Houston, former Miss Louisiana, hut-in-Jamaica sex, a sumptuous brunette.

Jenna Lee Lester: *Love this match.*

Really?

Nealy Daniel: *Now I know why you never answered me! LOL.*

Ha, ha, not funny.

LAINEY AND JED, BOOK TWO

Mallory Rich... Her last name was Rich? She touched the name to see a picture of Jed's former favorite lover. *No,* she didn't want to see.

Her own social media, the same overwhelm. Mary Beth, Waverly, Brice Buffy? Josiah's heart breaking...ouch. Miss Maydell got a smartphone?!

Random adulations. Lorraine Calhoun Johnson: *Yes, yes, yes! Cass predicted this.* Michelle Landry Calhoun: *She certainly did! She's singing with the angels (praying hands emoji)*

Jed's mama saw this coming? Delaina touched her naked finger. That rocked her to the core.

~ ~ ~

After 3 PM in Mallard, Delaina calculated. "Hey, Jenna Lee. Yes, a glorious trip! Uhm, out West, yeah. No itinerary. Yep, he's right here with me. For sure, I'm lucky." She was clearly lucky, according to Jenna Lee *and* Sophie LeBlanc. Delaina produced a smile worthy of Beverly Hills and rolled her eyes in Jed's direction.

He held his credit card, *Let me please.*

Hell no, she communicated and stepped away where no one could hear. She felt queasy.

They were breaking up.

She knew it when she searched the shoreline for his mama's ring. She had put the puzzle pieces together. Jed telling her that she could go to USC or anywhere to finish her education, telling her marriage was a long way off, the saga with Cabot in Mallard and taking her to the West Coast on a whim, the validation that he gave her on social media like she meant more than any other Jed-McCrae-has-been.

She stated a ludicrous amount to Jenna Lee and glanced as Jed went into the fitting room with Beverly Hills beauty #1. Maybe the beauty would see, or had seen, Delaina's claw marks on his back.

"How's the weather, by the way? Oh? Sorry you're cooped up in the bank on a pretty day, Jenna Lee. Thanks again."

~ ~ ~

Tab and Rory, the Beverly Hills beauties, brought a stack of clothing to the desk. Tab spoke to Delaina. "Your boyfriend said you have reservations at fabulous Layla Chow. Lucky you, huh?" Delaina was the lucky one, according to ladies everywhere. "Yeah, lucky me."

Dang, they did make reservations at sought-after Layla Chow yesterday, for tonight.

248

"Your little accent is *adorable*," Tab said, like it was *deplorable*. "Where do you live?"

Delaina felt like a lobster-red country bumpkin in a Mexican-bright gunny sack. "We're farmers from Mississippi."

"Mississippi?" Tab laughed. "Ooh, cute. So, he's, like, genuine farm to fork?" Delaina was a real farmer, too. She didn't bother correcting Tab. "How trendy! Named Jed to boot." Tab shimmied. "Super guy. Lucky you. Want me to help you select something for tonight? Jed will be dressed to the nines. We selected fabulous stuff for him." Her eyebrows wiggled.

"Sure, why not?" Jenna Lee just moved twenty thousand dollars into her account, after all.

"Hey, Rory? Grab that gauzy white midriff and long black skirt that came in this morning." Tab's eyes measured Delaina. "It'll be fab on you. Grab the Tit Tape too!" She winked. "Gotta push those puppies up." Oliver dropped into the conversation. "She has a beautiful shape. No tape, in my opinion."

Jed appeared and gave Tab his card. "My treat." His eyes conveyed to Delaina, *You won't risk our lives to make a point to pay.* "If I get a vote, no tape. She is beautiful."

No, he didn't get a vote. She wasn't his pretend girlfriend, his peaches, his ho, anymore. She hunched her shoulders at Fab Tab. "Oh, okay, I'll let him pay. He likes to spoil me. But get the tape."

~ ~ ~

Jed said, "It's not your fault," once they were out of traffic and put a dent in the one-hour drive back to Layla.

"Which part? The lost ring, the hotel fire, that Cabot is destroying Mallard, or our breakup?"

"When we get to the hotel, I'm going to the manager's office, gonna see if there's anything I need to do about Layla Rock. Don't worry about the ring or fire. Accidents happen. As for Cabot, it's for authorities to handle now." Jed shrugged.

They were breaking up. She might vomit before they got to the hotel. "I may need the second pill." She scanned her phone while he drove. Holy hell. Just holy hell. Glittery Gracie21 had joined #LaineyandJed #nofilter, posting: *I've got the prize!* Wearing classy club clothes, Delaina and Jed gyrated on a dance floor. Cyberspace devoured it.

~ ~ ~

Delaina went to swanky spa Layla Zen while Jed went to management. She got waxed into a landing strip. It felt like yanking a bandage off a blister for thirty minutes but made her cupcake look...provocative, along with an all-over tan accelerator to even her sun streaks.

She vomited moments after leaving the spa.

In their pod, she swallowed the second pill. Never again. She would take care of birth control like a grown woman when she got home. Her phone vibrated. Text from *Jed1*: *Meet me at pool bar @ 6 for pre-dinner drink?*

I'll be there, answered *Delaina13.*

~ ~ ~

Delaina made an entrance at 5:55.

At the boutique, Fab Tab had encouraged, 'Knot your shirt under your new cleavage, no bra. Why not entice him...' So, Delaina did that, along with mermaid waves and seashell-adorned sandals, and found Jed under a ship-sail umbrella at a bar made of rocks, served bourbon from a beauty. Sweet Lord above, he looked like Miami Vice met Maroon 5.

She didn't want to go through a breakup with Perfect Jed. She wanted to give his swimmers a chance to sink or swim, 15,000 times.

Ocean crashed, breeze dashed, sun clashed. A man who looked nearly as good as Jed, dressed nearly as well, stood first. "The other half of hashtag Lainey and Jed! Hot damn."

This guy was Southern?

"I'm Rob Banks." He took her hand briefly. Delaina could feel her squished cleavage and hardened nipples on display in her thin white shirt. Below, under her flowy black skirt, Jed's runway. She felt nude and lush. And light years out of her league. Nope! She could do this.

Jed stood. "Yeah, this is the other half of the frenzy. Delaina Cash."

"The better half," Rob Banks assessed.

"So much better." Jed wasn't looking at her. "Lucky me. ...Hey D, Rob will be managing Willa Hotel. Got here today from Georgia to check out Layla's format before the Grand Opening in Atlanta. We're business partners."

"That's cool." Wind blew her hair. To Rob, "Social media's crazy. We were havin' a... friendly spontaneous road trip, fun with pics, and...poof." She gave her best try at sexy-casual. "I'd like a mojito, please." Jed informed a server before Rob could.

Rob pulled out a stool. "A seat, Miss Cash. Jed bragged on you, said you might get in on the next venture, might be interested in future hotel investments."

"Did he?" Her mojito tasted scrumptious. "I might have a bag of money to burn."

"Up next, DC. Set tentatively for spring during cherry blossoms. We could use another 500K...and a good girl name." Rob Banks treated her like an adult.

She sipped and contemplated the investment. 500K. She might have to *rob banks*. "I trust Jed, but I'd like to visit the property, take part in plans, if possible. As for a name, Calla, Layla, Willa, very hip, but..." A sudden Abracadabra thought. "Wait, are there other existing hotels?" More getaways with Jed. What a magical prospect that would've been.

"Ella, the first. In New York," Jed commented.

Delaina glanced at him, got jabbed in her crotch by his eyes staring at her peaches. Couldn't tell if he liked it, or not, that she was on display. Swiveling her stool gently between the men, "Me personally, I think it's time to drop the -la sound. Lovely girl names, but it could start to run together." She felt intelligent, the way they listened. She hunched a shoulder. "I like Jackie Hotel for DC. Not Jacqueline, not Jackie O. Just Jackie. Finish the interior reminiscent of 1960s White House. Demure, prestigious. Presidential."

"Jackie Hotel. Wow, she's good. Is she for hire?" Rob asked Jed.

Jed lifted his shoulder. "Ask her."

Delaina tensed. They were definitely breaking up.

"Next meeting in DC, August. I could put you down." Rob Banks looked like he wanted to put her down. And steal her booty.

Delaina felt her sumptuousness multiply under his stare. "Count me in."

Jed finished his drink. "Hey, interesting story, D. Rob's engaged to Mallory Rich. *You know*, from Atlanta. He originally introduced *us*, then I talked *them* into going out last fall." His smile, so casual. Broad, interesting, adult life, pre-her.

Rob held up a hand. "Wait a minute. Not engaged. We moved in together." Their empty drinks were cleared, full ones provided without asking. They, the most important trio on the property. "*Big difference.*"

She gave Jed the subtlest, no-you-didn't-say-her glance. "Wonderful. Mallory's a fan of the whole Jed-Lainey debacle. Posted *several* comments."

...Was there a 'big difference' in this world between engaged and moving in together? Married, making a baby, sharing a bed. It all meant the same to Delaina: The right person to share her life. Would she grow up to the point that it didn't? Sipping her second mojito on a West Coast terrace in daring clothes with influential men, she hoped not with all her heart.

~ ~ ~

Layla Chow, an outdoor rock cave adorned with lanterns and fruit trees. Jed and Delaina sat at a table for two, sipping delicious Cabernet. Eventually, he wondered, "Should we talk about Mallard? Hell's gonna break loose when we return."

"I don't think it will. I think they're genuinely happy about us."

"I meant the farm." Growing season, always a bitch.

"Oh. What then?"

"Seven o'clock Thursday morn, assuming you go home, I think we should meet in my office, set an itinerary, and explain our new arrangement to the employees when they arrive at eight. Whatcha think?"

Delaina tried to act grown up, angling her body, drinking red wine. But it felt like she wasn't wearing a shirt, white gauze in lantern blaze. To his credit, Jed didn't stare too long at a time. "What *is* our new arrangement, Jed?"

"Putting it all together, right? Mainly, what either of us says to employees, goes. We support each other's on-the-spot decisions. We need to discuss our own wills, too."

They did? They did. She would leave everything she owned to him. "Sure."

Entrees arrived. Between bites, Delaina said, "Jed?" That made him look at her, but fleetingly. Her insides, like breaking glass. Their last night in Cali, she couldn't imagine they wouldn't kiss, make love, sleep naked. "Why did you encourage Mallory and Rob to date? He seems like a man-whore. I thought you liked her."

"A lot of men are." He studied her thoughtfully. "Rob's brilliant in business. They have, uh, similar outlooks on relationships."

"She cheated on you."

"No." He finished his glass. "But she, uh, toward the end, she made a bold suggestion and…"

Delaina gasped and leaned in. His aquamarine eyes glimpsed the tops of pushed-up peaches. "They swing?"

"They're open."

"She wanted to be open *with you*?" Delaina's eyes and mouth made matching O's. "Why? Your looks are perfect, *you're* perfect, and you make love perfectly. I cannot imagine."

Ending it with Delaina would be infinitely harder than Jed envisioned.

She, of magnificent beauty, intellect, and possibility. How much she'd evolved into the Delaina of his dreams, while staying true to Lainey Cash, just on this road trip. A fascinating female, love of his life, currently declaring he made love perfectly. He ate bites on his plate. "Mallory offered a threesome. Extra woman of my choice."

Jed had a threesome? Delaina didn't eat anything else. She wanted to believe what she said next, "It's not you, to do that." Jed was sappy movies with his mama. Jed was chocolate chip cookies, afternoon baseball games, and candles in a corn field. Jed was fifteen thousand times for fifty years.

"Right. That was around the time I decided to go home to Mississippi." He smiled and looked somehow old-fashioned, wearing suave clothes in SoCal.

She released her held breath and instantly re-sucked it. "Oh God, Jed, I told Rob I'd go to DC with him."

"I'll be there."

The crux of their bad day climaxed. "Will it matter, Jed, in August?"

He stood. "A walk?" No dinner tab for James *Darrah* McCrae. She stood. Delaina felt every part of herself shatter. It was happening. They walked a tile path in fruit trees toward water away from people and light. Jed stopped at a boulder, took off his loafers. Delaina took off her sandals.

"Here." He bent and knotted her skirt above her knees. His hands, close to her cupcake, her landing strip, that he knew nothing about. She wanted to show him her surprise wax job and laugh at their private joke. She wanted *them* back. He climbed the rock and sat. She followed. He faced the ocean. "On this trip, Delaina, you've been the woman of my dreams. You're…incredibly smart and beautiful."

LAINEY AND JED, BOOK TWO

He risked a look. Her hair and shirt blowing in the wind. "Jaw-dropping, tonight."

"Please don't make it sweeter." She blinked tears, hoped he couldn't see them. "That's what you've been doing on this trip."

"You're the best thing I've ever known." He touched her hand. "I like being sweet to you."

"You're trying to make The End sweeter."

She knew him too well. Where was the universe, God, fate? Jed counted on help from some-damn-where to get through this.

"I look like a whore on social media." "You do not look like a whore." "Have you seen Gracie's pic on the dance floor?" He pulled out his phone. His eyebrows went up. He swallowed. "Uh, you, we... look like we're in love. Livin' a fantasy."

They certainly did. She wouldn't change a thing. "Why are we... breakin' up?" Amazingly, she got the words out.

"Don't say that." He would never break up with her. That's why he never asked her to be his girlfriend. When he did ask her, one day, it would be the beginning of till the end of time.

"What's going on here?"

Fate, God, The Plan, the universe didn't show up. Jed stared at the Pacific and grabbed syllables from thin air. "You're unhappy in Mallard." "So are you," she retorted.

Delaina, of all things, helped him know what to say.

"You're right; I don't wanna be there." That was not a complete lie. On her deathbed, Jed's mama asked if he would stay in Mallard, and he told her that he did not know.

"Be there, as in Mallard or managing Cash Way or with me?"

The quickest answer, "All of the above."

He saw Delaina stiffen. "That's breakin' up, Jed."

"You don't need to stay in Mallard, either. You should be at a real university. Tory's will was drawn in your best interest. He intended for you to finish a prestigious degree."

"What exactly are you saying?"

"I'm about to interpret my management contract with Cash Way most leniently. I can hire whatever help I need and decide what position you fill." Her head whipped towards him. "You're the owner, but as long as I'm the manager, you'll have no real work at Cash Way until you get a degree."

254

"Oh God," she mumbled. Waves tumbled, moon glowed. They sat still and dull.

"I'll...continue until the first year's contract runs out, grooming Rhett, giving him...more responsibility. He's not school-smart, Delaina, but he knows farming like the back of his hand. By next year, he should be your manager, especially with Holland on finances. She's a career girl. She and Rhett will probably marry. Maydell can help with the baby."

"Where will you be? What will you be doing?" Delaina's life went out to sea with the next set of waves.

"I'm leaving Mallard. I'll travel back and forth until Rhett's ready."

Whatever Delaina felt, she hid it well. "What about McCrae Farms? I'm meeting the stipulations in Fain's will. That land will truly be yours in eleven months."

"I'll lease most of it, along with shops and equipment, to Uncle Dale and his two decent sons. They worked hard for my father, for me. They've earned it. Mama and I talked about that possibility before she died. Both farms will need a few more hired hands, of course, but...it's a good plan."

Delaina's mouth fell open. "Jed, can you do that? It's yours. All you wanted."

It took him half a minute. "I'll probably buy more land somewhere. Land is land. It's ownership that makes it irreplaceable. Delaina, Cabot may not be done with us. I'd like for you to essentially disappear, as long as Maydell and Moll can reach you. You have money. Choose a university. Keep it under wraps."

Delaina crumbled. "Does Rhett want this responsibility?"

"Rhett doesn't realize his capabilities. I have a year to prove it. If Rhett saves his salary as farm manager, I've calculated on paper that he could afford to finance a portion of Cash Way, by the time you're twenty-five. You'll have a better idea of whether you want to live and work there. If you do, it'll be yours, and Rhett will be exemplary support. If you're ready to sell, Rhett and Moll will have the working capital and good financial standing to buy parcels. You could keep the timber plots because it's easy to manage. Plus, you could lease as much farmland as you want, to any number of farmers."

"Are you moving to Houston?"

LAINEY AND JED, BOOK TWO

"I don't know." His tone implied end of discussion. Delaina stared at the panorama before her. Endless possibility. A whole new world. Mallard was all she'd known. "I...can't."

"Regardless, I'm leaving soon." Was it enough to make her go? "We have to be up at four a.m. We better get some sleep."

"We'll continue this my way." She bunched her skirt around her waist and tilted her hips to the moonlight. His look; there were no words for it. "I did this. For you." She crept toward his body. "What about 15,000 times for fifty years? Was that a lie?"

He couldn't deny her that. "Hell no, but..."

"No buts." She climbed onto him. He staggered backwards, grabbing onto nothing, reclining on the rock. She kissed him like her life depended on it. A thousand tiny kisses rolled into one hot mating of mouths. She jerked her lips away. "Why didn't it cross your mind to fight for us? To put us above anything? We would make it work."

It did cross his mind, every hour. He wanted exactly that, so very badly. Naïve of her to believe it and selfish of him to want it. Yet. He didn't know what to say.

"I guess owning land that's undeniably yours will always mean more to Jed McCrae." She climbed down rocks alone.

~ ~ ~

Night was misery. Jed, too big for the bitty bed, bumped and touched her, whether they wanted him to or not. He wore boxers; she wore pajamas. They stared at the ceiling and desired the night before.

Twenty-three

Welcome

S he stood over his bed in predawn light.

What Holland was about to do was unforgivable. Worse than doing Cabot's dirty work, worse than smokescreen nuptials with Eli, worse than carrying one baby with two fathers.

Rhett loved her. She...cared deeply for him. That's why this would work.

She shook him. He made a funny face and sound.

He had been staying at Cash Way. Rhett didn't want her out of his sight, especially after dark. Staying together at the farmhouse, too strange for her; too blatant for his parents. They dilly-dallied around in the evenings. He slept in another room. Nothing had happened; she had been on sexual restriction.

"Good morning, Rhett."

One eye cracked open. "Mm, mornin'." He dragged himself upward, against the headboard. "Something wrong, Miss Holland?"

"Yes." She slid her hip onto the edge of the bed. She shouldn't feel nervous. She had two decades of practice maneuvering males, and this man loved her. She did feel nervous. "I'm worried about many things." She batted her eyelashes. "Do you have feelings for me?" Demure, not her strong suit. She reached out and patted his chest. "I think you do."

Like she knew he would, he took a jumpy breath and watched her hand. "I do."

Dawn grew deeper and wider, glimmering in gray light. She stood, gave him a nice view of her in a lightweight gown. "I'm so scared, Rhett." With the swish of sheets, Rhett came up behind her, like she

LAINEY AND JED. BOOK TWO

knew he would. She almost turned. No, years of practice reminded her. *Make him wait.* She kept her back turned.

"I don't want you scared, honey." His hand touched her shoulder. "I'm startin' to think there ain't nothin' to this Cabot-craziness."

She frowned. How wrong he was.

"Holland, what can I do to help your feelings?"

She turned. Her swollen breasts stood at attention under his stare. "I *am* afraid...about Cabot. But I am hiding a greater fear. I might have miscalculated when I got pregnant, Rhett."

He made a confused face.

"What I mean is..." Holland made sure her breasts bumped his ribs. He made a sound. Her fingers touched his cheek. "There were men, Rhett, before...your brother. I..." She felt tears burn her eyes, something she did not expect. "Uhm." Rhett held her now. "I've been with, uhm, many men in the past, Rhett." She stared at him with a vulnerable face. "Trips back and forth to Atlanta. Business deals." She caressed his flawless light brown skin. "You're so good. Living out here on the farm. Hard worker." She swallowed. "You would probably never understand business men." She smiled. "That's a compliment. Me, a woman attempting to climb the professional ladder. Sex...happens for all kinds of reasons."

He put space between them. Squeezed the back of his neck with one palm, looking at the floor. Nothing for Holland to do but trudge on. "I know deep in my heart this baby is Eli's but..." She reached for his arm. He let her hand stay. Their eyes searched each other's face in the dawn light. "I will find out the paternity of my child. To be practical. For health records. I went to a doctor's appointment, Rhett, and had an honest and very humiliating conversation about paternity testing, conception dates and, ehm, the men."

He put space between them. Put his hand up. *Enough.*

She changed course. "I know in my heart this baby is Eli's. I want that, especially for your parents. It's changed me, being pregnant. I want family and...a lifelong partner." She couldn't make herself finish but surely her expression conveyed, *I need you, Rhett.*

His troubled face didn't match, "Enough of this." He hugged her. His face, so serious, and his nod. A decision made. "Truth is, I guess it don't matter who the father turns out to be, Miss Holland. It ain't me." He hugged her again, breathed in roses on her skin. "I told ya a long time ago, I'm here for ya."

Yes, yes, yes.

"I don't know if I wanna know, though, about the baby. My parents…good God, it'd kill 'em." She could feel his distress, torso to torso. "I'm tired of stayin' up here at Cash Way, don't want you away from me. Will you come with me? Stay with me." He nodded that decisive nod. "We're in this together, ain't that what you're tryin' for?"

"Yes, yes, yes." Her head tilted back. The ends of her hair brushed his arms around her back. "What will we tell your parents if I move in with you?"

Rhett kissed her. Did that nod again. "You're movin' in with me for your safety, for now. I'll handle them. In degrees."

Holland put her arms around his neck. "You're so handsome." She looked away. "God, they will hate me for wanting you."

~ ~ ~

Delaina took the window seat. Jed, the aisle.

On the plane ride home, a lady wearing earbuds sat between them, watching a famous love story on her seatback screen. Allie, Noah, and a Ferris wheel. Jed saw, and tried not to see. Falling in love, the time of their lives. Allie left Noah. To be whatever she was supposed to be. She came back, saved and lost her virginity for him. They built a life because life could not tear them apart, and when they died, they were old and together. Torment. Jed nudged the woman. "Excuse me." She lifted her earbud. "May I?" He motioned to switch seats. "We're…"

"Business partners," Delaina supplied on a smile. He changed places. The woman restarted her movie. Jed stared at Delaina. "Baby, I…" "Don't. You broke up with me."

"Stop sayin' that." She wore a low ponytail, the dignified black suit, and cross earrings. She watched out the window.

"Please look at me." Less than twelve hours in, Jed didn't think he could go through with The Plan. "This is torture, D."

"Us, or the sweet movie where they never give up on each other?"

"Same thing."

"Jed, you gave up on us without a fight." There were tears in her eyes.

Everything in Jed clenched. "I need to hear you say that you know I love you, Delaina."

LAINEY AND JED, BOOK TWO

"You don't love me enough." She turned. "Love bears all things, believes all things, hopes all things, endures all things. You're the one who helped me finally believe that. I know I've been up and down, all over the place sometimes, and I'm sorry. But can't you see? I want once in a lifetime. To hell with the world we live in. Real love never ends, Jed." Felt like her cross earrings whispered, *Yeah, you dummy.*

Delaina clasped her hands in her lap, wishing for a shield, of any kind, to hide conflicting emotions. "I'm leaving," she whispered. She let quiet tears fall as she memorized the sight below her. A swath of Mississippi, shades of green, ran under them, so intricately laced Delaina had no idea where one farm ended and another began.

~ ~ ~

Jackson Capitol turned out nice.

Board members left an empty seat with a sign, *In memory of Tory Cash.* They sang praises of his countless agricultural contributions. They didn't want Jed to relinquish his seat to Delaina; they wanted to add her. Both agreed and participated in the meeting.

On the steps out front, she asked, "We're going home now?" They had to. Growing season couldn't wait. But, Cabot... Her big, lonesome Cash Way. And now, evidently, no Jed.

Jed made a bad face. Separated from her, Cabot would top his list of worries. "I have to go home, D."

"Don't call me D." She glared, the face of a spoiled little girl who gets what she wants. "I wanna go home, too, and I will."

Jed let her win, didn't really know how else to handle Cabot's elusiveness. "Delaina, I think..." His face, incredibly sullen, standing on the Capitol steps in hot sunlight. "Cabot isn't there. Scared people, letting their minds get away from them. If I'm wrong..." He shuddered. "I'm dead wrong, but life, and more specifically the farms, must keep going."

"Believe me, I know all about getting up and getting on with it." She'd take care of herself, gun loaded. "How are we getting home?"

Jed squeezed his eyes shut with his fingers. "Reb Doxie, associate of mine. You may know him. He knew Tory." Jed checked his watch. "In a subcommittee right now. Meeting us at five."

"Oh my gosh! Reb?" Jed received a sliver of Lainey Cash in the suited-up working woman beside him. "Haven't seen him in...ages. Married Bonnie Faye Buchanan. Of course, I know him!" What a rainbow on a cloudy day. She elbowed Jed while they walked.

260

"Bonnie Faye's mom Faye and Tory, don't you remember? They dated for years. Gosh, if Bonnie Faye wasn't wild. Brought Reb home her freshman year at Ole Miss. Daddy and John Rebel Senior, Reb's daddy, were already close friends, two of Mississippi's biggest farmers."

Sure, they were close, Jed thought. Crooked in business, womanizers. The apple hadn't fallen far from the tree with son Reb. "Ha, I'm excited!" She picked up pace and went to a fancy red truck with an Ole Miss tag. "That's gotta be his!"

~ ~ ~

"John Rebel Doxie Junior!" Delaina hugged him. "It's been too long."

"I think we know how long it's been." He chuckled; she giggled on, "True."

What? Jed reached to shake hands.

"Hashtag Lainey and Jed?" Reb gripped hands with him perfunctorily. "Lucky you."

"You better believe it." Jed sensed darts between two men putting down stakes. "I can hardly believe my luck." He smiled at Delaina.

"Oh please," she inserted. "Tell the truth, Jed! A whimsical birthday getaway after dealing with Tory and Fain's back-to-back deaths. Social media blew it *way* out of proportion."

Reb unlocked his truck. "Well, Bonn has fallen for it along with most of Mississippi. She's *dying* because I'm ridin' with you celebrities. Cash with a *McCrae*? Unbelievable. She says, Hi, Lainey, by the way."

Delaina felt a stab. Cash and McCrae. Yes, it turned out to be unbelievable. "Tell her hey! Oh Lord, if we didn't fight like cats and dogs when Daddy dated her mama. Two spoiled little girls." Delaina became a beatific Southern belle interacting with Reb Doxie. He pulled out his phone, looked awkward. "Bonn asked if I'd snap a pic on the Capitol lawn of y'all. Wants to play hashtag Lainey and Jed." He grinned. "Serves me well to try to keep my wife happy. I generally fail."

Suddenly, Delaina remembered kissing Reb's lips. How did she forget that one night with Reb Doxie, when she listed everyone she had kissed for Jed at Sweetheart Square? He was a dang good kisser, and Bonnie Faye was a witch. "Sure! We'll pose." She cackled. "Why not? Jed?"

Oh yeah, they were gonna pose for her leering friend. He gripped her back, angled them in front of the Capitol. What about a kiss? Hell yeah. He grabbed her under the ponytail and kidnapped her mouth while he dipped her body. Beautiful kissing, as biological as being alive for them. His tongue touched her chewed-up gum. She laughed when she stood, a fake laugh, and Jed knew, she was angry that he stole such liberty.

"Well, damn." Reb studied the terrific shot on his phone. "You two..." "Need a ride," Delaina exclaimed, climbing in front. "Jed, you mind riding in back? So much catching up to do with Reb!"

"Of course not, baby doll. Whatever your little heart desires." They headed toward Mallard.

So, Lainey and Reb made out, middle of the night, behind Bonnie Faye's back on a family camping trip. Tory caught them, yanked junior-at-Ole-Miss Reb up by his Bleu Cotton jeans, trying to get into fifteen-year-old Lainey's pants. Lainey recalled exactly what Tory said, too. 'Wouldn't mind this match a bit in three or four years. Do Bonnie Faye till then.'

What a dad.

Hilarious, those two found that memory to be. Reb enjoyed contributing, "I did what Tory suggested with Bonn, but it got me Emma Bleu instead of you."

"Oh gosh, Miss Maydell did say something about y'all getting pregnant, I mean, married... What, last year?"

"Yeah, September. Shotgun wedding and baby girl. Life's over. Two rotten females in the house." He handed Lainey his phone. Then she showed Jed their brand-new baby girl named for the Bleu Cotton empire that Bonnie Faye Buchanan Doxie had ties to.

"Cute," Jed said. Poor baby girl. What a dad.

"Sorry I didn't get to Tory's funeral, Lainey. Same week Emma Bleu was born."

"Oh, I understand, Reb. Hey Jed, you know, Bonnie Faye's mama and Sam Hensley's mama are sisters. Faye and Kaye. Bonnie Faye and Sam are first cousins."

Samantha Kaye Hensley, Dirty #11. Jed did know that, indeed.

Delaina twirled around and shot him a smile. "Jed was with Samantha last year."

"Yeah, your ole Jed here spread it around, I think, before you came on the scene." Reb snorted.

"By the dozen," Lainey agreed with sugar sweetness.

Reb enjoyed another snort. "I think the, uhm, hookin' up with Samantha started at our wedding." He clearly liked slinging mud at Lainey's spontaneous road trip guy. The dickhead. "You and Sam didn't stay together too long, what a month, after you met that night, Jed."

Jed enjoyed snorting, also. "Stay too long, you get a baby, right, Reb?"

Delaina turned again. *You did not say that.*

Hell yeah, I did. It's on now, Lainey Cash. He watched as she pulled out her own phone. To check Reb's wedding, for certain.

Delaina scrolled. ...So, Jed met Samantha at the wedding and hooked up with her that night. Broad, interesting adult life. He could have it back now! She saw that Bonn Doxie already loaded the dramatic Capitol kissing picture #LaineyandJed #nofilter with, *They're home, y'all!*

She scrolled to Samantha's wall. Jed (in his Calla suit) untagged with sensuous Sam at Reb's wedding. "How good y'all look, Jed! Small world, huh?"

Home sweet home.

~ ~ ~

Reb let them out on the Cash Way driveway, at Jed's insistence. He pulled away after a ridiculously drawn out, you-must-keep-in-touch goodbye to Delaina.

Overnight bags and Rodeo Drive garments in hand, she and Jed stared each other down. "Oh, for God's sake," she said. "You can't walk to your cabin with that garb. I'll drive you."

"Rhett's on the way. I texted him. We have a lot to discuss."

She set her bags on the asphalt. "I can't let you go without using my manners." She touched his sleeve. "Thank you for the best twenty-first birthday. An awfully generous trip."

"Of course." They stared again. Sun bore down, no breeze. Growing season's arrival upon them, a total bitch. "Please stay safe. Use your head. I contacted the professional security team. They're callin' you in the next hour or so."

She gave him her most disgusted look. "Oh please. Stay out of my personal business."

LAINEY AND JED, BOOK TWO

The Plan, a bigger bitch than growing season. Jed felt parts of him start to crack. He shrugged to communicate okay, whatever she wanted, but could not help, "Carry your gun. You know you can call me."

"Are you gonna tell Rhett that we broke up?"

Jed's jaw jutted. "I did not break up with you."

"I won't be callin' you, if I need anything." A full-blown argument brewed because of frustration, sleeplessness, fear, disillusionment, jet lag, jealousy, and desire. "Because you did break up with me."

His eyes made slits. The two of them in high-status suits stood on the border of Cash and McCrae, the only thing she'd known. Delaina needed to go conquer the world. *Say it and leave* descended on Jed from nowhere. "I didn't break up with you, Delaina, because...I never asked you to be my girlfriend."

Jed thought he saw her actually sway.

She bent for her baggage. Rhett drove toward them. "Seven in the morn?" asked by the woman of his dreams.

"Yeah, lotta work to do."

She turned her back and walked into her Mallard County palace.

~ ~ ~

Mound Bayou, Mississippi. Holland knew the way, knew the routine, now. Darkness, trailing car, ride with the teenage boy to the house on the other side of the county.

The boy claimed his name was Nate. He called her ma'am, used manners, appeared nervous.

Cabot proved smart. He had her escorted to a different house, which looked the same. Holland stepped in, dressed to the nines, spreading her rosy smell among the dust and shadows. She recovered marginally better when homeless Cabot appeared behind her on this visit. "What do you want?" he snarled.

Holland realized she might die. Her usefulness to him, about to be terminated. Worth the risk, she wanted to see his face when she told him her lies and her truths. "My baby is Eli's," she lied and smiled. She did not know that for certain, but she had Rhett now, no matter who the father was. She patted her tummy. "I've been to the doctor for extensive testing." Her heart tapped anxiously. "Rhett and I are together. I confided in him about my paternity concerns. I have his support. But, thankfully, Eli is..."

Her head snapped backwards from the jerk of Cabot's hand in her hair. Holland cried out. "You're using bad judgment, Holland." His hot breath touched her neck. Her eyes rolled back. "So, the bastard is Eli's. I'll expect proof...if I decide to care." He let her go with such force, she toppled forward. Her hands gripped a chair. It teetered and slammed to the ground. She landed atop it, bruised. Tears wet her cheeks. Cabot shoved her back. "You're good at double duty, aren't you? Eli and me, same night. Now, brothers back to back. Moll and Maydell do know, right? " He shoved her again. "Doubt it." He yanked her arm. "Get up."

She stood, shaking visibly, which put a grin on Cabot's face. "You're out of your league, *Ms. Smith*." He folded his arms. "Lainey and Jed are home. Your incompetence bores me." He laughed when she reached to hold on to the wall for support. "I'm about to tear that place down."

"Cabot, *please*. Go away. You have the means." She sounded helpless.

His arms stayed folded. "Tell Lainey, I'm coming to see her next." His mouth made a careless sound. "Or Moll and Maydell. Better tell them about your past. Before I do. Get out." He smiled. "If I change my mind and decide you are useful, I will let you know."

~ ~ ~

Delaina arrived at seven in the morn to a locked office and no Jed.

She had slept like a baby, since she was a baby, by herself inside Cash Way's walls.

Last night she couldn't sleep, wondering about Cabot. Couldn't sleep without Jed.

He drove up in a puff of gravel and sand and got out. "Sorry. Overslept."

...He slept and she couldn't. Their time together, feelings and experiences, were beginning to feel like a lie to Delaina.

Jed glanced at her. Delaina wore a Bleu Cotton tank top, words *Farmer Charmer*, with shorts and boots, nothing underneath except sucked peaches and a waxed runway, he knew. Her workers were used to it.

His workers would have a field day, working beside that.

Jed jingled keys and pushed open the door. He had no right to set a dress code, no rights to her, other than those Tory laid out in his contract.

They sat. He slid keys and a piece of paper across the desk. "Labeled keys to everything I own." He gestured at a separate set. "Rhett made me copies of everything you own. Okay?"

Delaina's heart pounded. Her face burned. "Okay." She touched the paper.

"My thoughts, scribbled last night, when I couldn't sleep." Ah. That made her feel marginally better. "Amend it however you want."

She skimmed his handwriting. *Us: Discuss schedules. Agree on security. Talk about wills. Combine for growing season. (What is combined? Decide.) No fighting. No kissing. No crying.*

Employees: Tell them what's combined. Address #LaineyandJed and our relationship status.

Pounding. The room, her heart, and her eyeballs. "Looks good."

He leaned forward. He smelled like woodsy soap, like fresh water, her Jed. He asked about a specific employee. They talked about workers' schedules and made notes. Moving along, he glanced up, "You know I started combining some stuff while you were..."

Stashed away in my room, dissected by locals, recuperating from our miscarriage, dreaming about Me&BigGuy? "Out of commission," she remarked and jotted. "Let's make a new account. J&D? You bank in Georgia, right? Holland can do it." He nodded okay. "We can estimate what it'll take. Each deposit 50/50 money. Combine our disposable expenses like chemicals, fuel, seed, power." She looked up. He was watching her. Pounding became a slow roll. In her chest, down to her belly, into the vee between her thighs. "We'll know what makes sense as it goes along. Moving on to wills, I don't have one."

"You need one. Everything of mine was willed to Mama. Pate's my executor. I haven't...changed it." He looked her up and down again. "I wanna leave everything in Mallard to you, but..." His voice had softened.

"But what?"

"I don't want it to be too much, to burden you, D."

"Don't call me D, since you've set a stipulation of no kissing or crying."

He stood up. No windows in his office, he looked at a wall, squeezed his neck.

"I can handle it, Jed. I'd have Rhett, Holland, Maydell, Moll, and like you said, your Barlow family is deserving. Putting it together makes the difference, makes it manageable. I'd be okay." She would certainly not be okay if Jed *died*. The pounding returned. Did he think one of them *might* die?

Wait, didn't *he* die *yesterday*, as far as her future went?

"Then everything I own out here is yours in my will, Delaina." Time lapsed. "From now on, regardless of...what else. Cash-McCrae Road should be yours, mine, or ours." They studied each other's expressions. "Same to you," she vowed. "No matter the future. Yours, mine, or ours." It felt like a wedding, humble and acquiescent.

She forged on. "Our relationship status and employees. When we gather this morning to explain farms, I think we use a blanket statement like, We know y'all have probably seen or heard stuff about us. As long as we don't make the working environment difficult, we expect the same."

"Agree."

"Security..." Jed stood over her, black hair, crystal eyes, good jeans, in control.

"I told you, stay out of it, Jed."

Jed rubbed his chin. Arrogance, at its best. "Turns out, I don't need your consent. I manage Cash Way. This is in the farm's best interest. Your guard is here, somewhere, all the time, just so you know." Hands on his hips, his shoulders jerked up. Towering, as basic and powerful as earth and sky. "You're welcome to meet him, if you decide to put on your big girl panties and accept that security is an absolute must."

She stood, put them chest to breast. She glared. "True, I would actually have to *put them on* since I'm not wearing any." Lungs moved up and down, both sets. Green eyes left blue eyes. She stepped toward the door. They got on with the day.

~ ~ ~

They learned things, working beside each other. Jed acted stricter than she would've guessed toward employees and about organization, equipment, or applications. Delaina used the closest tool for whatever task, right tool or not, and tossed it when done. He sweated under his arms. She sweated above her brow. He wiped his hands on his jeans and made streaks when he got dirty. She pulled her tank top up to wipe her face. He said damn before nearly every noun, talking to employees and while working. Damn tractor, damn pliers, damn heat, damn cotton. She said shit a lot, talking to herself

LAINEY AND JED, BOOK TWO

and while working. Shit, that won't work. Shit, I forgot. Shit, that's perfect! Shit, it's hot.

Delaina brought lunch from town to workers convened under Jed's shelter. She stood beside him at a wooden work horse, turned away from others, while they gulped sandwiches. She heard someone chuckle and looked backward. One of Jed's guys, the decent-looking, country-boy type, which her days at Mallard High School and Mallard Community College were full of. She caught him on his phone. No rule against it during lunch. He grinned at her, a grin she'd seen from his type, *I'd like to get in your pants*. Another of Jed's guys said something under his breath. Both grinned. She got it wrong, the meaning of the looks, because they looked at her *and* Jed with his back turned, still eating.

Their phones had been vibrating all morning. They answered when necessary, no social media. A possibility shook her. Delaina excused herself to the half bath in his office, pulled out her phone, and almost died. **Brad Cummings** *tagged* **Jed McCrae** *in a post at* **Houston Life Apartments**. One hour ago. A photo of Jed making out with her. Submerged in the off-limits fancy pool after midnight, ripples and lights and skin and blurs. From Brad-whoever. #LaineyandJed #nofilter #getaroom #livelaughlove 194 likes and 43 comments she didn't read.

Delaina took her time coming out. Jed sat at his desk, reading on his laptop. The face he gave her, she recognized. In Meggie's office after the blood test. When Tory died, at the funeral home. *I'm sorry*.

"Delaina, Brad lives beside JJ at the apartments. Wild and single. We know *of* each other. He just deleted the photo."

"What are you reading?" She leaned in. An email.

Announcement to tenants:

Reminder that the pool area is closed between the hours of 10 PM-7 AM, not to be used for personal recreation. Beware the entire complex is under 24/7 video surveillance. Security will strictly enforce this ordinance. On a lighter note, we wish you a fun and safe Memorial Day weekend.

Thank you,
Management, Houston Life Apartments ~Live, Laugh, Love~

She would *not* cry. "Jed, you're smirking."

He was. "Attached to my eviction notice." "*What?*" "Yeah, I'm kicked out. Furnished apartment, so Joey and Jessie are boxing the few things I kept there. Thousand-dollar fine, too." He shrugged.

Her chin dropped. "Good gracious." At his office door, she thought it, twisted, and said it. "I hope I was worth it." She put her hand on her hip.

"I'd do it all again in a heartbeat."

~ ~ ~

Times like Saturday night, Sunday morning, and Memorial Day didn't matter in agriculture. Farming depended on one variable: what needed doing. Forty-eight-plus hours past the start of working together, Delaina and Jed toiled after nine p.m. on Saturday night. He finished working on a pipe, middle of a field, and stood. "We never discussed our personal schedules."

Delaina lifted her shirt and polished her face. "How 'bout after church tomorrow? Your office."

His tongue clicked. "It'll have to wait. Willa, the Atlanta hotel, Grand Opening is on Memorial Day. I fly out nine a.m. tomorrow, return Tuesday." He glanced at her. "Rhett knows. He'll need all the help you can give him, too."

"Sure. We know the drill." A noise came from the pipes. She reached for a tool and slammed it on the pipe fitting. "There's a trick. Bang the shit out of it."

Jed grimaced. "Maybe your damn bangin' is why I can't get it right."

She rolled her eyes. "I tell myself many times a day, I'm not gonna argue with you about technique."

"Been tellin' myself the same." He bent and tightened the fitting. "Supposed to rain Monday. That's your chance to start plannin' your future." He straightened and saw her frown. "This is Tory's farm manager talkin'. I want you to decide where you're enrolling in the fall by the time I get back."

"Yes, sir, Mr. McCrae."

They left in separate vehicles.

~ ~ ~

Tireless work helped two things. One, Delaina slept, despite rumors at an all-time high about Cabot showing up all over West Mississippi. Two, she couldn't worry about Jed, wearing Beverly

Hills clothes to gala festivities in Atlanta at Willa Hotel with Rob and Mallory the Swingers.

The crops got a good shower on Monday after lunch, which forced her inside. Her mind took off like a jet; her heart walked around outside her body in another city, a glamorous world away. That feeling of helplessness compelled her. She planned her future for the remainder of the day.

~ ~ ~

Late Monday night, restless in bed, Delaina checked Mallory Rich's social media and found a photo of Willa Hotel's Grand Opening dinner and dance.

Mallory- impeccable, best lover Mallory- stood with Rob Banks in a ritzy, barnlike venue. She wore a fire engine red cocktail dress. In the background, Delaina distinguished Jed sitting at a bar with a dazzling redhead wearing baby blue. She cried herself to sleep, after promising that she'd never social-media stalk him again.

~ ~ ~

Delaina rewarded herself for skipping Memorial Day and getting work done with a girls-only pool party and friends Waverly and Mary Beth on Tuesday afternoon. Woohoo! Wine coolers, loud rap, teeny-weeny bikinis on the back side of Cash Way.

Man, had those two grilled her about Jed! She didn't say much. A grownup decision had formulated for Delaina, partly from her upbringing, partly from their rival history, partly from #LaineyandJed.

She wanted what she and Jed were, or weren't, to be theirs alone. Private and special. Her tight lips produced an unintentional result. Mary Beth and Waverly weren't crazy about him.

Delaina lay on her front, top untied, sunning. No communication since Jed left for Atlanta, her main thought. That, and wondering who the redhead was, or if they...

Waverly went on and on about a break, not breakup, that she and her current boyfriend were in the middle of, because she caught him and another girl at college swapping phone nudies. Delaina thought, but did not say, Waverly and Mary Beth's sagas seemed... petty. What she and Jed had been together cemented in her heart at a time when they had actually fallen apart. The music lowered, so she raised her head.

WELCOME

He stood there in the sunset, Cash Way cotton at his back. His hair a mess, wrinkled clothes, he looked tired, hot, and *hot*. She reached to loop her back ties.

"Lainey, looks like you have company," Mary Beth said.

"Hey, Jed." Delaina secured her top and flipped.

"Sorry to interrupt. I texted you." Jed did not admit that seventy hours was as much as he could stand apart.

She put on a happy smile and sat up. "Oh okay. Is there a problem on the farm?"

He shrugged. "Haven't talked to…anybody else yet." He glanced at Mary Beth and Waverly facedown, tops untied, as if to convey *You aren't gonna introduce us?*

"Y'all know who Jed is," she said. "Hey, Jed," they answered in unison. Mary Beth began putting on her top. Jed moved about picking up stray bottles. "Don't clean up, Jed." "I don't mind, cupcake." Oops, the word fell out. "We're not done drinkin'." He paused, empty bottle in midair.

"Sorry we're half naked," Mary Beth called from her position.

"That's all right. I've seen y'all naked before."

Waverly laughed. "True!"

Delaina walked over to him. "Why are you here?" she whispered.

Waverly joked, "Lainey was the only one wearin' clothes, back then." The trio were young teenagers skinny-dipping in Carr's Creek and Jed appeared out of nowhere. "Wow, the tables have turned!" Her friends giggled and made their way to the showy pool bar.

He and Delaina stood close to each other. "I, uh…"

"What are you gonna do when she's far away at University of Texas?" Mary Beth pondered. She popped the top on a cold drink, slid a Koozie onto it. FSU gold and garnet. "Bet you're gonna miss your Lainey-lainey, huh?"

Jed received a punch in the guts. Perhaps it showed. Perhaps it didn't. He looked only at her. "Can't imagine it. Sorry to bother y'all, ladies. Checkin' on the farm. Have fun." To Delaina, he stared and didn't move. Wanting. He could not help it. "Seven in the morn?"

"Seven in the morn." She returned his stare, conveying *I love you.* She could not help it.

University of Texas? he seemed to reply. "Okay, seven." Then he was gone.

LAINEY AND JED, BOOK TWO

"God, he is freakin' sexy. I mean grown, big guy sexy. Whether I like him or not," Mary Beth declared.

Big guy? Did that term come instinctually to females around Jed? Delaina watched his back.

From Waverly, "I like him. It's the way he looks at you! Whoa, Lainey." She made a sound. "If he called me cupcake, I'd show him something he could *eat*." She fanned herself.

Well, Waverly got that right... Delaina continued to watch him walk around the side yard toward the driveway.

"You have to tell us more! We *know* you've done the dirty with him, Little Miss Cross Earrings."

"That's *why* she's not tellin' us anything. It's too good between them to reveal."

How did they know this stuff? He disappeared around the front of Cash Way. Delaina rejoined them at the pool bar. Mary Beth sighed. "Lainey, he's too hot to be...realistic. Women will constantly throw themselves at him."

Redhead, blue dress came to mind. Delaina played defense. "What if he's taken and makes that clear?"

"Will only make females more determined," Waverly said matter-of-factly. Mary Beth added, "He's gonna break your heart."

Delaina got a chilled bottle from the cooler and popped the top. "Remember, y'all, only the Smiths know about college in Texas. Because of Cabot." "Of course!" they chimed and tapped bottles with her.

~ ~ ~

Jed clanged on an irrigation unit in the field. Monday's shower, not enough to curtail more irrigating. He did not know HOW he and Delaina were going to live through His Plan for them.

He knew what he did not want.

An angry, uncertain, therefore rebellious Lainey running away to Texas. Surely not what fate, God, the universe, or Tory Cash intended.

"Good mornin'."

He twirled around. There she stood, short shorts, tan legs, prettier than sunrise. "Mornin'."

"I skipped the office. Figured you were here already."

"You're not hungover?"

"Of course not. Want me to flip the power switch?" "Please."

WELCOME

She walked to a large electrical box, needed no instruction on how not to electrocute herself.

He loved her too damn much. She shot 480 volts of juice to the unit without flinching. Water ticked from overhead guns, one of his favorite sights, gushing over verdant fields, creating rainbow arcs. Jed sat atop a pipe to watch. Delaina closed in so near, Jed thought she might kiss him. "Are you mad, Jed?" She looked at his raveled BC T-shirt, words *Stack It & Pack It*, then his face. If his eyes got any bluer, the sky should give up trying to compete.

"I'm not mad. You?"

She hunched her shoulders. "I don't think so."

Liar. "What are you mad about, Delaina?"

Her ankles twisted in her boots. "I'm not." Her boobs were level with his face. He couldn't stand it. He took hold of her wrist.

She looked down at his hand, didn't pull away. "So, are we gonna do the Hashtag Name the Fish Lainey and Jed event in the park on July Fourth? And will it be safe?"

He let go and scrubbed his hands over his face. "Who knows? Downtown, broad daylight, security everywhere, ought to be okay. It'll be easier to give in and make an appearance than to come up with an excuse, don't you think?"

"Everybody likes us together. They mean well." She shrugged, which bobbed her boobs. Jed was about to relieve her of her top. "Town needs something positive. It'll be fun, maybe. The annual patriotic stuff. I guess you figured out that I settled on University of Texas."

He stuck to The Plan. "Yeah. Good. When do you leave?"

"July. For the second summer semester." *Take that, ex-lover.* "That should please my farm manager Mr. McCrae."

Jed's heart disintegrated. "I guess we'll do the fish-in-the-park thing and..."

"Do another fake breakup, in front of the world this time. For real."

Jed scowled. They would not break up in the park, fake or real. The sooner she could put distance between herself and whatever Cabot might try was best for her. She had to leave Mallard.

Irrigation had begun walking, causing mist to spray in their direction. "I love to feel the spray." She smiled at the field. "Almost as much as I love the rainbows."

273

He jerked her to him. His hands went under her shirt. He had to feel her, feel her there. Fingers slid upward. Ah, God. Perfection in his hands. He kissed her urgently. They were about to do it, hot and fast, in the field. Forget The Plan.

She pulled back, out of breath. Her tears stunned both. "*Why have you done this to us?* Why does owning your own damn land somewhere mean so much to you?! *How* can you leave me? I can't do it." She swiped her face. "Who's the redhead?"

"Huh?" *Redhead?* "You can't do what, Delaina? Do *it*? Here and now?" Big Guy stood up in disagreement.

"Not that. I'm...dying to do that. *Thanks to you*. This." She motioned around her. "Us, in shambles."

He pulled her in and held on. "I'm sorry, D."

She jerked away. "Don't D me. Give me answers!" A truck engine had them searching the dirt road. Rhett closed in. Jed walked into the spray, to cool his pants. She did, to hide her tears.

Rhett got out. "Aw, man, sorry. Looks like y'all got this one going."

Delaina went first. "No, it's fine. Gotta move to the next one. Thanks, Rhett."

Jed stepped out of the spray. "I'll get the Denton Place. You and D...uh, Lainey get the triangle field."

Rhett went toward his truck. "Sure thing."

Delaina and Jed stared at each other, like they'd been doing for days. His Plan was a good one, he reminded himself, and carried on. "You're really leavin'? Going to Texas." Jed couldn't look at her face when he asked her.

"I..." Damn him. "Yeah, I think I am."

"You're positive?" He sounded relieved.

Double damn him. "Are you really leavin', Jed?"

"Eventually." He still couldn't look at her. "Yeah, as soon as I can, Delaina."

"Hell yes, I'm leavin'."

Jed had five weeks to figure out how she'd go, and live her life, un-rebelliously.

~ ~ ~

"We live together, but no one knows."

"We sleep together but don't have sex."

"You're pregnant, but it's not mine."

How they laughed with each new line, only Holland and Rhett could understand. Tonight, they prepared supper on the back deck of the farmhouse. Southern nights stuck to them, literally and physically. Heat and bugs, meat smoke and tree shadows, ribbits and starlight. After ten p.m., Rhett hadn't showered yet. Straight off the farm, straight into her arms. Their routine. Work late, meet fast, grill, talk, laugh, kiss, sleep.

"Here." He fed her a hunk of deer sausage off the grill rack.

"Mmm, yummy. You know I'm never gonna leave here, right?"

Rhett's hazel eyes beamed. "Probably ain't. You've started sayin' gonna, shoulda, coulda, and y'all."

They laughed again. Holland gazed at the night sky and let crickets sing her toward courage. "Have you heard anything about, uh, Cabot that you *do* believe lately?"

Rhett, mouth full of sausage, swallowed and sipped his whiskey drink. "Matter of fact, somebody said lights were on at the top floor of the bank last night, and they ain't been on, nights prior. Police wound up checkin' it out, but nothin'." He sipped again causing him to miss Holland's startled face. "Always heard the asshole's got a special place for his women up there. Hard to believe, but, heck, he grew up rich and wild." He looked at Holland. "I reckon if he were gonna show up for anything, it'd probably be a damn woman. Whatcha think?"

"Mmm, I don't know. Let's eat."

~ ~ ~

Wednesday, Thursday, and Friday disappeared into starting, checking, and stopping irrigation. Ninety-five-plus degree days.

Delaina came into the house near dark and nibbled leftovers in the kitchen. Maydell conversed with her and loaded the dishwasher. Delaina excused herself upstairs, showered, climbed into her comfy sheets, and turned on an animated movie. Ariel *always* cheered her up. ...Cartoon fish and kid songs. Sigh, nope. She muted the volume. She heard Maydell coming upstairs. Strange, she usually locked up and left without notice.

"Uhm, hey."

"Oh God, hey." Delaina pulled the covers around her. "What the heck are you doing here?"

Jed took barefoot steps toward her bed. Her chest caved. "We need to talk."

LAINEY AND JED, BOOK TWO

"Now?"

"Delaina, we've needed to talk since Tuesday. Farm took precedence."

He, too, had showered, wore distressed BC jeans, hands behind his back. "May I?"

Her head swiveled on her pillow. "Get in my *bed*?" "Uh, huh." He grinned. "I have chocolate." A bag and a water bottle appeared. "Doughnuts. Fresh."

How yummy. Better than Disney. "The closest place you can buy fresh doughnuts is..." "Yep, drove there to stop me from comin' here. Didn't work." He set the doughnuts on her bedside table, pulled his shirt over his head.

"Oh God." She scooted to the far edge. "Miss Maydell..."

"Knows I'm up here."

She blushed. "You told Miss Maydell you wanna sleep with me?"

He reached for a doughnut, started chewing. "I never said I wanna sleep with you." He grinned. Heaven help her, if he weren't the best-looking creature alive when he ate treats. "Told her we need to talk."

"I'm naked."

She got to him.

Finally.

His eyebrows went up. He stopped chewing. He stared. He looked like he forgot how to breathe. "Do you always sleep naked?"

"No." Jed seemed to get breath into his lungs. "Not until the river. You know, after I stripped for you. Every night since then, I've slept naked." She got to him again. His breath caught.

He took his time drinking water, undid his pants, dropped them. Same boxers he wore when she returned his wrench that night, their first day ever. Heaven, just help her.

"So, do you..." Jed did a funny motion toward the Big Guy. Delaina's eyebrows raised. "You know, get off to the fish?"

"Oh God." She closed her eyes. His knee sank on her bed. "Not to the fish. Geez. That's Ariel. She's innocent."

"Mmm." He watched frogs, fireflies, and flamingos serenade a cartoon guy and girl twirling in a moonlit boat, watched them capsize into the water. "I don't know, looks like he's about to get some tail." He crawled into her bed.

"You're horrible."

276

"They're your favorite." "You remember?" "You named my dog Ariel." On their backs, he slid closer. She slid away. His hand found hers. "So, do you? You know..." He hand-motioned again. His head turned in. He smelled better than warm doughnuts.

"No. Not once." Jed nodded and didn't appear surprised. "Not until Calla, Jed. You know, after our first time." Delaina shrugged. "When you never showed up here, almost every night in May, forced to take matters into my own hands, know what I mean? Doesn't look like June will be much better."

He got a doughnut and fed it to her. "Delaina, June is gonna be better. Know why?"

She chewed a bite and watched the screen. "I should tell you to get the heck out of my bed."

"We could be dating." Before she could reply, "A summer...thing before you go."

His body, close and warm. She finished her doughnut, drank water when he handed it to her, and focused on Ariel's love story for an extended span. "I can't break up again." She gestured to herself, the movie. "I'm not good at it."

"We won't."

"Because I won't be your girlfriend? No thanks."

He got out of her bed. "Your decision." He put on his jeans, stood watching a fairy tale. "Ariel's pretty. Those innocent gals get to us."

"Plus, she's a redhead."

He pulled his shirt on. "Took me hours to figure out what you meant. Natasha in Atlanta. The dinner party at Willa Hotel. She's an investor/acquaintance who asked me a couple questions about the new DC project and about seeing *you* on my social media. Lasted all of two minutes."

"I social-media stalked," Delaina confessed. "Never again. I believe you."

"You should."

A summer thing... A month to persuade Jed to be her long-distance boyfriend while she went to college. Boyfriend, what a lowly word for him. He was a man, one who cared more about buying his own land somewhere. "I should tell you to get the hell out of my life, Jed."

"Every day, you have that choice."

"This summer thing. Why?"

"Why not?"

"Define dating."

He crossed his arms. "Huh. Okay. Two people are attracted to each other, so they spend time together."

Lainey Cash, ever considering Jed McCrae's challenge. "Sex?"

He offered her an honest look. "I wanna be around you, more than at work." His palms flipped. "In a summer...romance, there's probably sex. I wanna take you on a date. I miss you."

He hurt her tremendously in California. "We wouldn't be in this situation, Jed, if owning stupid land that's yours alone weren't more important to you than us!" He looked at the floor. He said nothing. God, she had it all wrong. But it was working. "Where would we go on a hypothetical first date, this time around?" Her sarcasm dripped.

"Easy. Sunday. A dedication to Mama at church, a new prayer garden." He leaned over her bed, found her hand, and kissed the top. "I need you. I want you there."

Ariel married her prince. The screen blurred for Delaina.

"Do you always cry at the end of a movie, D?"

She shook her head fiercely. "No, never. Not until California." She sniffed. "When you told me how you'll treat your wife. Good movies make me cry now."

"Uh, Lainey?"

"Hey, Maydell." Jed turned to her and smiled. "On my way out."

Maydell was a fish out of water. "I didn't know what to do about lockin' up."

"He watched Disney with me!" Delaina, convincingly joyful, used her sheet to dab tears.

Maydell patted her own heart. "Jed's a keeper."

Delaina hunched her shoulders. "We're just...dating. Night, y'all."

Twenty-four

Summer Romance

Yellow roses, she thought to herself, should be for lovers, a vase in the bedroom or a romantic dinner table set for two.

Delaina had never been one to talk to granite. Shortly after dawn, she walked to Tory's grave, put one stem on his stone, and sent a silent thank you to heaven for her daddy. She had read the farm manager's letter from Tory, included with his will, after Jed left her bedroom. It explained the manager's obligation to Tory. To do what was best for her. It illustrated something true of both men: Jed and Tory's shared inflexibility about land they owned. It's what she most liked and disliked about each of them. She moved down rows of headstones, scanning names, none her kin.

Land did not mean more than love.

Jed's parents knew what it meant to love above all else, didn't they?

She sought the cemetery because of them.

She spotted their graves across the opposite iron fence. She ran her hand along the barrier as she walked its length. She unlatched the gate and tiptoed in, as if someone might detect her presence on the wrong turf. A plot bordered in gray marble, manicured and covered in gravel, one center headstone and a tombstone over each grave.

"Ms. Cass." Delaina cleared her throat. "I'm going to your church tomorrow to honor you. I'm…scared to death." She laughed quietly. "You're a lot to live up to." She touched her headstone. "I love your Jed. I guess that's what matters." To his father, "So, James Ed, did you love the land more than she, like your son?"

LAINEY AND JED, BOOK TWO

Jed's mother certainly sacrificed living a happy life so Jed could grow up on the land.

"I don't know what's gonna happen to us, y'all." She bent to her knees, infinitely grateful James Ed McCrae and Cassie Jane Darrah once fell in love, and left roses between their bodies. "Be with me. Please be with Jed."

~ ~ ~

"Miss Maydell, help me!"

Delaina darted into the kitchen on Sunday morn, where Maydell prepared lunch before leaving for church. She turned from the oven. "Lainey honey, what...*Oh my*." Her palms went to her cheeks. "Delaina Tory Cash, you're a vision. A grown woman."

Delaina's face, doubtful and perfectly made up, paired with her cross earrings, a low knot, loose tendrils, and a fleshy-pink dupioni silk suit, which she scurried to Memphis to select yesterday. Modernly tailored, almost too tight, almost too short, just right. Her new shoes, *high* heels and leather, hurt her feet and cost more than her suit. She rambled, "I should've done black! I got to the boutique and thought about Ms. Cass in her pretty colors, classy and serene. She wouldn't want Jed to be sad. And she wanted us together! She *never* wore black to church." Delaina clutched her hands. She stepped toward Miss Maydell. "You admired her on Sundays, going into church. *Help me*. Should I wear black or...am I right?"

"You're right." Jed, in his Rodeo Drive suit, heard it all from the doorway and gleamed.

"Oh God."

"I told her she's a vision." Miss Maydell beamed. "Ms. Cass Kendall is shinin' down today! Jed, you're welcome to eat Sunday dinner here."

"He is?" Delaina looked at him. "I look okay?" She twirled slowly. "I'm nervous!"

"You're blushin'. You match your outfit."

She twirled again. "You're the best-looking thing in Mississippi this mornin', Jed McCrae."

"Thanks, ma'am." He grinned. "Miss Maydell, I do appreciate the invite to lunch but thought I might take Delaina to the levee after church. Do you mind packin' us a picnic? We'll plan on lunch with y'all next Sunday, after we go to your church." Surprise on Delaina's face brought a twinkling to his. "Cupcake, you are a vision, Maydell's right. But can you walk in those shoes?" He extended his arm. "Half of Mallard will be watchin' us. Wanna practice?"

"A picnic ready after church for you two." Maydell giggled. "To go to the levee, what fun! Jed's right, sweetie. Go on out to the foyer and walk around a bit. Scuff your heels up on the concrete, too. Grace has never been, ehm, your strong suit, and with the, uhm, graphic pictures floatin' around, you gotta walk straight and hold your head high, Lainey."

"She hasn't done anything that I haven't done with her." Jed walked beside her to the foyer.

Jed's acknowledgment of sinful equality felt incredibly liberating. "I can walk in these shoes." Delaina pictured Ms. Cass in front of the First Methodist Church every Sunday of her life with good-looking Jed and floated like the vision she was. She took her Sunday date's hand. "We've got this. Let's go."

~ ~ ~

They finished picnic food, climbed high on concrete, and found a dab of shade. "Can't stay long. I should be farmin'." Jed wore shorts and a smile.

Delaina wore her gauzy L.A. shirt over a bikini top with shaggy shorts. He sat higher, pulled her to sit between his legs and watch the river. "Take the day off, D. Work on details of your move."

They gazed out at the Mighty Mississippi. The church service glimmered in their minds. Jed had held her hand, held her hymnal, held her heart. They prayed, commemorated, mingled, and charmed.

He wrapped her loosely.

Jed felt good, smelled good, like always. Delaina said, "The Cabot saga appears to be fading. I'm glad downtown is starting to look more normal and feds aren't camping out anymore."

He nodded close to her jaw. "Agents can't operate like that for long. Too costly, too demanding. I hope the case doesn't grow cold before they find him. The sooner you go, the better."

Jed tightened his hold on her, savoring. "Delaina, were you Homecoming Queen?"

"Oh, this is a real date."

He shrugged against her. "What else are we gonna do?"

Passion teased them with memories of other times, other places. Heat, rocks, and water. Things they could be doing.

LAINEY AND JED, BOOK TWO

Her neck twisted. She grinned. "No. I didn't put out in high school. I was maid of honor." He picked up her hand and brought it to his lips. "Oh, Jed, that reminds me. Don't know if it matters, but Josiah visited. Last Sunday while you were in Atlanta, he came to church, home for the holiday weekend. Maydell and I invited him to lunch at Cash Way because... that's what we've always done."

Redhead in the blue dress, Jed got a taste of what that felt like for Delaina. "How was it?"

"Fine, I guess. He's about to start a job as a youth pastor in Vicksburg. He came to..."

"Check in on his virgin bride?"

She sucked air through her teeth. "More like, 'Lainey, are you okay?' You know, he's seen #LaineyandJed. Like the rest of the world."

Her old boyfriend, pastor-and-wannabe-husband, protecting her from big, bad Jed. Jed could've busted up Mississippi River concrete. "Did you tell PK what you *are* savin' for marriage, sweetheart?"

She really did laugh. "Lord, no! Josiah probably wouldn't do *that* with his wife."

Oh yeah, PK definitely would, if his wife were dazzling Delaina.

"I told him I love you, Jed, but I'm going away to school. He's the only one who knows besides the Smiths, Mary Beth, and Waverly. I didn't tell him where."

Sitting together in sunlight, dating, four more weeks, thanks to God, fate, the universe. Jed squeezed her. "Does he usually kiss you goodbye after Sunday dinner?" He kissed her cheek. He didn't want to waste another minute, talking about PK or anyone else.

"He hugged me before he left and wished me the best with school."

"Next time, shut the door, please, ma'am."

She turned her upper body in his arms and made Ol' Man River look uninteresting to Jed. "How? I'm not mean."

Jed planted a seed in her mind that might take longer to sprout than a saguaro cactus. "Tell him I said thanks for stopping by and caring about you, but he should probably start shopping for his own wife."

Delaina got instantly hopeful. They would be *something* before she left. "I'll keep it in mind, *Jed1*." A wave of wanting ran through them. Obvious and palpable. Hastily, she picked up where he left off on good first date questions. "So, do you prefer beer or wine?"

"Depends on what I'm eating and where." He kissed her fingertips.

SUMMER ROMANCE

Her pulse kicked. "Beach or mountains?"

"Depends on who I'm with." He kissed the inside of her wrist. "Or what we're doing." He rested his head on her shoulder, looked between her legs. He wanted to lick up and down the insides of her thighs, like he did that night in bed at Layla Rock, while she arched and begged. "Delaina, ask me another question. Hurry."

"Fridays or Saturdays?" "Sundays," he mumbled, "with you." He loosened her and stood. "Will you go out with me for pizza at Mac's... maybe later Tuesday night?"

"Why not?"

~ ~ ~

Holland spared the evening in Tory's study to help Delaina figure out funds and set a budget for University of Texas. "All set," she said. "I'll arrange everything during business hours tomorrow."

Delaina got bottled waters for them. "Thanks so much, Holland." They sipped.

"Delaina...I'm worried about you."

"Oh?" Holland's baby bump showed. No father for her child, involved in a hush-hush tryst with the baby's uncle, and Miss Maydell didn't support them. Maybe Delaina should be worried about *her*.

Holland went on, "Those pics, hashtag Lainey and Jed...I mean, people posting at church? For real?"

Delaina hadn't looked at social media since the redhead. People posted their pics *at church?* "We're the big fat elephant in the room right now is all. Everybody noticing and wondering." She shrugged. "It'll blow over."

Holland offered a sympathetic look. "I feel like the big fat elephant in the room, actually." Both women laughed.

"Holland, you know, it's kind of like Moll being black and Miss Maydell being white. It was there, obvious to others, I guess. Tough for them in the beginning, I know. Moll told me, after he found out about Jed and me, how hard it was, the public scrutiny. People said mean things and they almost didn't stay together. He still doesn't attend First Baptist with her. People probably wonder and talk sometimes, but we never made it a thing here at Cash Way." Delaina looked contemplative. "That might've been my favorite aspect of my daddy. Not once in my life did Tory mention that they were a mixed-race couple even though we live in rural Mississippi. Look at Moll and Miss Maydell. The best example of happiness I've had. Private,

LAINEY AND JED, BOOK TWO

committed, doing their own thing, all these years." Delaina smiled.
"I hope that's me, through all this drama. Learnin' as I go, no matter
what people think."

Holland sipped water. "I've never given much thought to Eli, or
Rhett, being mixed. Such sturdy men. You're right." She squeezed
Delaina's leg. "No need to worry about those silly pics." Her smile
broadened. "You're an amazing person. I admire you."

Delaina didn't feel nearly as confident as she let on. "Well, thank
you. I'm trying."

"Y'all are super together, you and Jed. The real deal." Holland
nodded. "These years you're away in Texas will be a cinch for you
two. You're right to get that master's degree."

~ ~ ~

Delaina and Jed cruised into Mac's late on Tuesday evening. The
place had emptied except two young guys from a local farm, sitting at
the bar. Nealy Daniel, Jed's last lover- Delaina immediately recalled-
and a friend of hers, who Delaina knew as Amber-somebody, sat in
a secluded corner booth. The farmhands acknowledged Jed. "Hey
Jed, hot as hell, huh?" said one.

Jed closed in and shook hands with both. "Sure is." The other
one commented, "At least the price of cotton is up." Jed agreed,
"There's that."

Both, who knew Delaina, and any other time would've made the
same talk with her, hardly acknowledged her. "Lainey," one mumbled. The other nodded.

"Hey, y'all," she said brightly and walked toward an empty booth.
Evidently, on the arm of Jed McCrae, a woman got banned from
normal conversation with other men.

Joe Mac Henry approached, dish rag in hand. "Evenin', Jed,
Lainey." They spoke. Jed slid in on the same side of the booth as
Delaina, a nice surprise. Their legs bumped. Her tummy dipped.
Delaina wore one of her Mexican sundresses, pigtails, and flipflops.
Joe Mac and Jed shook hands. Delaina felt Nealy and Amber's stares.
Jed's arm went around her.

"What are y'all havin'?" Joe Mac asked.

"Whatever's quickest for you to fix," Jed answered, then, "Nothing
new on Cabot in here?"

Joe Mac sniffed and frowned. "Nothin' worth repeatin'. Same
old, same old. The wondering. Haven't been no claims the past few

SUMMER ROMANCE

days of people spottin' him, which is good. I'm sick to death of it. I just hope this isn't when Cabot chooses to strike, you know, now that the hype is settling down."

"Maybe law will haul his pretty-boy butt in soon." Jed looked the part of the new boyfriend who had enough of Delaina's old flame. "Cardin Morris tells me that they're pumpin' big-time resources into the case." He turned to her. "Enough of that." He smiled. "Want a beer or anything, D?"

"That'd be great." "Two beers then," from Jed. "How 'bout pepperoni pizza, thick crust?" Joe Mac suggested. "Her favorite," Jed commented, glancing at her.

"Sure is her favorite, Jed, since she was a little girl." Joe Mac sniffed. "First time I've served you a beer, Lainey. You grew up too quick. Tory would be proud of ya." He went to the kitchen.

"Tory would be proud." Jed leaned over and smacked her lips. "I'm dang glad you grew up quick. You look beautiful tonight."

"Thanks, but your ex is watchin' us, you know..." Delaina arched an eyebrow.

Jed looked around slyly. "Hmm, never saw her."

Delaina rolled her eyes. "My plane takes off Thursday at six a.m., okay?"

"Yes, ma'am. Your farm manager's got this while you're in Austin. Take your time figuring out the details."

"I'll be back Saturday night at the latest. My summer...fling mentioned taking me to *my* church this Sunday." Her hand rested on his thigh.

He looked down at her hand. The booth heated up. "Your summer fling will be there, then." He put another smack on her lips. The guys left, calling out, "Bye, Jed." and "See ya, man." Joe Mac arrived with beer bottles as Delaina and Jed's phones beeped identically. Jed said, "Thanks," and tapped bottles with her. "To your trip to Texas."

He said it with such ease, Delaina wondered if it would matter to him if she moved to Mars.

They sipped, checked their phones, and made aggravated faces. A unit had quit. "Hey, Joe Mac?" Jed called. "Box up the pizza, will ya? Irrigation's actin' up."

Joe Mac brought their to-go box and grinned as he set it down. "Too bad y'all can't stay. The two of you feedin' each other pizza, hashtag Lainey and Jed. That would be awfully good for business."

Lainey and Jed, Book Two

Delaina and Jed were nice enough to laugh. "Aw, come on, Joe Mac, not you, too," Jed said. Delaina agreed, "We're ready for that frenzy to die."

"Nah, I wouldn't post a pic, wouldn't do that to y'all. Besides..." He snickered and whispered, "Those gals are gonna take care of it for me."

~ ~ ~

Jed and Delaina sat holding hands in his truck on a McCrae farm. They watched the irrigation after a quick repair to be sure it walked properly. "Here's a tidbit for you, Miss Cash." Striking sunset enhanced their summer romance.

"Can't imagine. What?"

"I was conceived right here." He glanced at her. "For their second date, my dad asked Mama to ride the tractor with him. They had a picnic in that orchard, rode the tractor..." He winked. "Or vice versa, and thankfully, I don't know the rest of the details."

She giggled loudly. "Remind me not to *get it on* with you here, then. That's quite the precedent they set." Old pecan trees with mangled trunks, green-leafed for summer, saluted the conception of her James Evan Darrah McCrae. She felt his parents' blessings. Delaina hunted a different subject, their reliable date talk. "I'm not impressed with that organic corn trial, are you?"

"Not really." Jed looked more stellar than twilight in a field, wearing shredded BCs and T-shirt with words, *Farm: The real F- word.* "A secret between us," he whispered.

"What now?"

His mouth clicked. "We can't feed the world on organics."

"Agree." She patted his leg. "Don't tell the rest of society! They'd run us out of America."

"Hmm, maybe I *should* post something controversial about farmin'." He took her hand. "We could run off to..."

"Anywhere but here." Delaina kissed him. His tongue went into her mouth. Jed pulled back fast. "Society buys into a lot of farm myths."

Great. Date conversation again. Delaina played along. "Okay, farm myths...like farmers are filthy rich."

"Or farmers are dirt poor."

She grinned. "Right. Or food is cheap to grow."

"Or groceries are expensive to buy. Get real. Americans spend less on groceries than most of the modern world."

SUMMER ROMANCE

Delaina loved this Jed. Compatible in a lot of areas, their outlook on farming might be their best. She had learned a lot from him, and she believed he had, maybe, learned from her since they combined resources. She chose, "How 'bout farmers are dumb and low tech?"

His finger ran up her arm and under her shoulder strap. "Yeah, that one pisses me off, for sure. We're scientists, engineers, bankers, gardeners, accountants, teachers, marketers, machinists, mechanics, human resource managers, legislators, computer specialists, researchers, and God knows what else, all in one body."

"So true." She nodded. "What about gluten-free? Ha! They print those words on stuff..."

"That never had gluten to begin with," Jed finished for her and smirked.

They laughed quietly. She joked, "Hashtag Lainey and Jed, I guess that's the latest farm myth."

His fingers rubbed her collarbone. "Actually, it'd be the truth tonight."

Whew, this June night and Jed. "Know what makes me mad?" she rushed. If his hand wanted to explore her collarbone, hers wanted to caress his ribs.

"What makes you mad, Lainey Cash?" His breath swished when her fingers touched skin under his shirt.

"The whole non-GMO thing. Yeah, whatever. All these moms worried about altered genetics in their kiddos' food, but they have no trouble swallowing the birth control pill."

"Brilliant analogy."

Irrigation had long been mobile. Darkness had fallen. Things got quiet. They wanted each other.

"I'm gonna miss the hell out of you, D, these next few days, but I'm proud of you about Texas."

Shoot, why did she have to get tears in her eyes? "You know what's on my 15,000X list, Jeddy?"

"What, Lainey-lainey?"

"Parkin' in your truck on the farm. Makin' out like teenagers. Like there's not ten years between us. Like we were together from the start."

"Crawl to my back seat, please, ma'am."

LAINEY AND JED, BOOK TWO

She squeezed through the middle. He got out of the truck, pulled his shirt over his head, and climbed into the back. "Makin' out only, Jed McCrae. Bet you've never heard that before."

"Yeah, I have." He untied her shoulder straps. "From you in Arizona."

Their kissing got ridiculous, wrapped them up in each other's arms, had them toppling, him on top of her, on the seat. "I'm takin' you home in fifteen minutes, I swear." They lived Delaina's teenage fantasy, in reality. He walked her to the front door of Cash Way before ten p.m.

~ ~ ~

The atmosphere inside the walls of Cash Way intensified day by day, making Delaina glad for an escape to Texas.

Maydell wanted to be good to Holland because she carried Eli's child but didn't want her with Rhett, and it showed.

Then Wednesday evening during supper, Holland and Rhett lowered a bomb to Miss Maydell, Moll, and Delaina. They were officially moving in together at the farmhouse, not just for her safety. Because they cared about each other. Moll left the room without a word. Maydell protested about how soon they were moving on after Eli's death.

Delaina didn't know what to say after Moll and Miss Maydell left the table, so she said what she would want someone to say to her, if she and Jed took a big step, if they started a life together. "You have my best wishes. Always choose happiness."

~ ~ ~

Delaina had settled on University of Texas, three hours from Houston, as an attempt to make a future connection with Jed. Secondarily, she liked what she read about Austin.

In less than two days, she crammed all she could. As if someone took her and Jed's Wild West road trip itinerary and morphed it into her *future life*, she could hardly comprehend the possibilities.

Austin: Slow-paced enough to break in a Mississippi girl yet contemporary enough to be interesting. Trendy neighborhoods were walkable. She explored abundant entertainment, vibrant culture, a variety of food, and fabulous outdoor settings. Succulents and barbecue smoke. Cacti and wind chimes. Guitarists on street corners and leather in the shops. She got to be in the city. She got parks, patios, and rooftops. She got the Colorado River. She got to be Southern but not overly Southern; Austin proved edgy, artsy, and political. And the music! Fantastic live music in clubs every night until the wee hours of morning. What a treat.

She considered dorms, apartments, duplexes, and sororities, and decided to lease a small house in an old neighborhood near the college. Too grown to act too girlish. She would call Austin home in July.

~ ~ ~

Jed bought a ranch ninety minutes northwest of Houston, a deal in the works before Delaina chose Austin. He had considered the place many times, even discussed it with his mama. It belonged to his Houston accountant, a man named Royce Upton. Royce had no interest in the estate, inherited from his father, and one son, at age twenty, not ready or interested.

The ranch had deteriorated in Royce's father's last years. Jed aimed to lose himself in the project while Delaina got her degree.

~ ~ ~

This evening, cause for celebration! Delaina prissed around hunting what she needed in Jed's marvelous cabin kitchen.

7:32 p.m. *Hurry up, big guy.*

She dipped her head in the oven to peek at barbecue chicken. Hopefully, Miss Maydell's step-by-step instructions would pay off.

"What's this?" Jed leaned into her.

She turned and laughed. "Hey."

He backed up and scratched his head, filthy from farming. He glimpsed a wine bottle on his counter, heard a mysterious guy singing on his music system.

She pointed to a speaker. "That's George Ezra. Didn't know he existed till Friday night in Austin. It's like he wrote every song for us, big guy."

Oh hell. "Is that so?"

"*Yeah*," she dragged out and smiled. "What do you think of me in your kitchen?" She twirled.

I think we belong like this, he did not say. "You're happy."

Nothing seemed complicated to Delaina. "We've made mistakes, Jed. That's love." She lifted a shoulder, no big deal. "Thank you for coming to my church this morning." Her smile, right then, maybe the sweetest Jed had seen on her face. "This summer romance thing, I like it. Let's keep it going after I leave." She did a quick shimmy. ""It'll be easy."

LAINEY AND JED, BOOK TWO

Double, triple hell. "Uh, I need a shower. I'm filthy." The Plan was working, sort of. Uh, not exactly. She got a year ahead of herself. "I wanna hear more about your trip when I'm clean."

Delaina met him at the bottom of the staircase with wine. Jed, clean and damp, wearing BC's *Moisture matters* T-shirt and shorts. She had that same easy smile. "God, you're perfect for me." She toasted. "To Austin. To the future. It's all gonna be fine. You can come see me while I'm getting my master's whenever you want, and, of course, I'll come here. I love you, Jed."

Master's? Two years? Two-plus? Jed bumped glasses.

She led him to dinner-on-the-patio utopia facing Big Sunflower River.

Twenty-five

Cash Way

The shit burned up.

Farm lingo for consecutive hundred-degree days. They were in a dry spell. It hadn't rained since Memorial Day. Jed and Rhett interacted like parts of a well-greased machine, two executive farmers with a common mission: Do whatever has to be done to keep the crops alive.

But shit did burn up, no matter how good the farmer was.

Today, neither could've stated the actual day of the week or date. They slaved beside a pond, struggling with an irrigation system that sustained a ninety-acre Cash Way cotton field. Heat raged. Plants wilted.

"Christ!" Rhett yelled. He had gashed open his hand.

Jed went to his truck, got a shop towel. "Go to the house, Rhett. I'll...call Delaina to come help. Thirty percent chance of rain tonight."

"I don't wanna go to the house. I can work with a bad hand. Anything to avoid Holland." The nightly kissing and cuddling, and nothing more, became challenging quickly, not to mention his parents' unending disapproval.

Jed knew the feeling. Delaina flirting and trying, on him like white on rice.

He had stooped to the lowest low of his life after they finished eating dinner on the patio.

He faked sick.

Yep, he did.

Worse, Delaina fretted and carried on, wondering if her barbecue chicken did it to him.

Her barbecue chicken tasted better than her damn-near-perfect chocolate chip cookies.

Her barbecue chicken tasted almost as good as her cupcake.

But he couldn't tell her that because *she had to go* in less than three weeks.

So, not only did he fake sick, he insisted that she return home right away in case he was contagious. They couldn't risk both being bed-ridden during a drought.

It was the lowest low of any low he ever stooped to with anyone. Lower still, he used work for an excuse the rest of the week while he made up his mind. Tonight, he had decided, he'd tell her everything. That he had tried to trick her into leaving. That he bought land. That he thought she deserved time for herself. That he would wait on her, if that's what she wanted. Or they could keep the summer romance going for as long as it lasted, if that's what she wanted.

She was a grown woman. She could decide. She should decide.

Tonight, he counted on rain. Tonight, she could come over. Tonight, she could decide.

His phone beeped. *Text message from Delaina13.*

Hey J. Got the Denton Place going. Maydell's niece's wedding in Mobile this weekend, remember. Maybe it'll rain before they have to leave. What next?

From *Jed1*: *Come to the triangle field. I need your help.*

~ ~ ~

Delaina breezed onto the scene. "Bless you, you're exhausted." She handed Jed a chilled sports drink. He guzzled it to empty and said nothing. She walked around, studied the units, flipped switches. Nothing happened. "Shit, it's hot." She glanced at him sitting atop a pipe. "So are you, big guy. Forget trying to fix this. We'll roll the dice on rain."

"Too damn risky." Jed resumed working and barked orders at her. Nothing worked.

"We need Lowndes, the specialist." Delaina typed on her phone.

"He's probably strung out, can't get here for days." Jed looked around. "*Screw it.*"

Delaina walked closer to him. "Sounds like a fun idea. Right here, in the wide-open field. You and me. That's on my 15,000X list." She had taken care of birth control, got the shot at Meggie's office while she was in Texas. She had been more than happy to announce that to Jed at dinner on the patio.

She lifted a shoulder. "Lowndes will show up in a half-hour or so. It's Cash Way. He'll come." She kissed Jed.

Delaina looked like a billion bucks, shiny, upbeat, and desiring only him. Jed did that to her, turned her into this grownup lady who loved him, wanted him, wanted them in a cotton field. What perfection. To say forget it and fall together to the ground. "Sorry, baby, I can't think like that right now. Too hot and stressed."

~ ~ ~

Everything blurred after Lowndes showed up. They got the unit going, and Jed told Delaina to come over later. They could cook dinner together, after he got a shower and chilled for an hour or so.

All at once, a truck roared down the path out front of his cabin. Jed jumped up. Rhett blasted in. "It's Cabot! I saw him." He paced Jed's den. "Lainey, Mama, and Holland are locked in, up at Cash Way, guns loaded with Daddy." He stopped and stared at Jed. "What the hell are we gonna do?"

"Jesus, where? When? You're sure?" Jed went to a side table, pulled out his pistol. "Holy hell."

"I'm goddamn positive, Jed." Rhett could hardly catch his breath. "I tried to call you."

Jed had put away his phone, not to deal with *anything* for a little while before he confided The Plan to Delaina, truth be told.

"I called Sheriff Boyd. Don't know if that was a good idea, but..." Rhett continued to pace and fret. "Cabot was in that ole beat-up Ford truck that Boone used to drive around your farm. The one he left here, you know, parked at his place when he skipped town."

"Okay." Jed had retrieved his phone, scanning for a number. "Keep talkin'. You sure you're not hallucinating from heat and work?"

"No, hell no. He had a full beard, longer hair, and wore a cap. Looked nothin' like Cabot, but it was him. Almost sundown, so I don't think he saw me. He turned off Cash-McCrae Road in the direction of Jackson. I was way behind and by the time I realized it and tried to chase him, I couldn't catch up, so I called Sheriff. Went to Boone's trailer on a hunch. Fresh tire tracks everywhere. Truck gone."

"It wasn't Boone? You're sure?"

Rhett frowned. "No. Smaller build, lighter hair, but if you wanna check with Dale..."

LAINEY AND JED, BOOK TWO

"Oh, don't worry. I'm gonna check with my uncle." Jed typed in numbers. "First things first. I'm callin' Cardin Morris from state. Get ready, Rhett. Cash Way's about to be a riot."

~ ~ ~

Jed and Rhett drove to the trailer. Jed had a key. Evidence aplenty that someone had been staying there, right under their noses. Two grown capable men experienced anger, shock, and terror.

Jed's Uncle Dale Barlow claimed Boone went to a place called Lake Seminole, Georgia, verifiable, and hadn't returned to Mallard since the day he left.

Sheriff Boyd called, informed them that every officer in Mallard was stationed around the farm or patrolling town. Agents were on the way, according to Cardin Morris, and he warned them not to touch anything at Boone's.

Sheriff Boyd called again. He wanted to meet them at Cash Way.

~ ~ ~

Blue lights flashed, cars lined the long driveway, and Sheriff Boyd arrived before they did.

Rhett and Jed busted on the scene, praying nothing had happened inside. The sheriff sat in the den with the ladies and Moll, so quiet they could hear a pin drop. Lamps were on. The house loomed large and dark and smelled like lemon furniture polish. Jed and Delaina's eyes met briefly. He blurted, "What is it, Sheriff? You got info for us?"

All eyes on Sheriff Dan Boyd, he sighed aloud. "Y'all...I don't know how to say this, so I'll just say it. I was part of Cabot's scheme. So was Boone. He paid us a lot, had some kind of offer from a buddy in Vegas. A riverbank casino, to save Mallard from dryin' up. Boone planted the sprouts. Eli got us the plants 'cause he was scared Cabot would have him arrested for selling pot to college kids if he didn't go along. I think y'all done figured out most of this." The sheriff blew his nose in a handkerchief. "Told my wife everything tonight. I can't take it no more. She kicked me out. I turned myself in and resigned... asked to come out here and tell ya myself first before they haul me to the pen." He looked around at everything and nobody. "I'm so damn sorry, Jed, Lainey, Maydell, Moll, y'all." He started to cry. "I'm headed to jail, for the first time in my life on the wrong side of the bars." He motioned to a uniformed officer standing by the front door. "I'm ready, man." He glanced to the group, Cash and McCrae united.

294

CASH WAY

"Do what y'all can to help'em catch the bastard. He snatched my Dacey's neck. He's gonna burn in hell with the rest of us."

~ ~ ~

No one moved until Maydell began to cry. Moll consoled her. Holland cried, too. Jed and Rhett made eyes, thinking the same thing. Jed asked first, "Ladies, are y'all packed for the wedding weekend?"

"We are," Holland said quietly. "We're leaving at sunrise for the drive."

Jed and Rhett looked at each other again in silent agreement. "You're leaving earlier than planned."

"I'll stay here," Rhett offered.

"No, go with the ladies." Jed moved closer to Delaina. "You and Moll go like you planned." "But the farms, the drought," Moll argued.

"It's all ours," Delaina stated, looking up to Jed from her seat on the sofa. "Our land and our problem. We'll handle it. Y'all have done enough for now."

"We will handle it," Jed agreed. He twisted to yet another officer by the door. "Can the Smiths leave?"

"I don't see why not. We need a statement from Rhett, then yeah. That's probably best."

"Good." Jed seethed inside. He wanted to bomb something, fire machine guns at concrete walls. "Moll, go with Maydell and Holland. Get whatever else you need to pack before you leave. Rhett can make his statement. Delaina, don't move off that sofa till I get back. You're with me for now." He pointed at the officer. "Get somebody to stay here with her till I get back."

"Jed, you're scarin' me," she mumbled.

"Good 'cause it's time to be..." He grinned softly at her. "A little bit scared."

"Where are you going?" Her pretty green eyes, wider and more apprehensive than ever.

"I'm going to see my Uncle Dale. We're gonna get some things straight." He knelt and hugged her. "I'll be back."

~ ~ ~

Delaina and Jed lay in her bed but didn't sleep. Together in profound darkness at Cash Way, they tossed, turned, and stared at the ceiling.

There were noises below them and outside, the commotion of trained professionals setting up and planning. The significance had stakeout written all over it. Somewhere in the bottomless night, he grabbed hold of her hand. She whispered, "This is a nightmare." She turned into his body. "But you, me, my bed at Cash Way, that's on my list. I hope one day we get to make love here. Peacefully."

If only. Jed squeezed her hand. "Me too." They resumed silent sleeplessness.

~ ~ ~

Freaky Friday, it could have been entitled. Vileness lurked.

Delaina and Jed had work to do on another hundred-degree day. They did it among agents and guards. Special unit cars rode sporadically, uniformed people appearing and disappearing across their land. Mallard's most curious folks tried to get a glimpse of what went on out at Cash-McCrae Road. The turnoff, barricaded. Delaina and Jed, quarantined. They carried on the best they could in their fields, doing what had to be done.

~ ~ ~

A violent thunderstorm jolted them from sleep after four a.m. Bewilderment had put them to bed early. Exhaustion had put them to sleep. Delaina jumped to her feet first and exclaimed, "Irrigation, Jed!" Rain pounded her bedroom window. Wind howled.

He rose. "I'll do it." Any running units needed to be shut off in fields that received enough rain. He pulled on clothes.

"I'm going too." She pulled on clothes.

They went downstairs, obtained an officer, and rode chaperoned from field to field.

They came in, soaked and worn out, after the sun rose. They took showers and crawled into bed. In their slumber, Jed held her. They slept like babies until noon.

~ ~ ~

Saturday softened.

Ground wet, plants satisfied, and a security plan in place, Cash-McCrae Road remained barricaded. No farm work pressed.

The sun came out. Temperature crept upward on the thermometer. Temperature crept upward between a restless, stir-crazy Jed and Delaina inside the confines of Cash Way home base. An officer guarded the front door.

Late-day sandwiches finished in the kitchen, Delaina clasped his hand. "Wanna swim?" Jed looked at stunning, sweet her, dragged through another unnecessary hell and not let out of his sight in almost forty-eight hours. "Yeah, I do, but I don't have a suit."

"I know," she flirted. "Come on."

"Delaina, security…"

She marched to the palatial front door, opened it, and said, "Hi," to a guy named Wade in uniform. "We're about to go crazy, not used to this bedlam or boredom. We'd like a private swim out back. Do you need to check anything first?" Jed had to chuckle. A woman on a mission.

"No ma'am. All is well."

"Great! Give us a couple hours, okay?" She pranced inside and closed the door.

~ ~ ~

Those two swam naked in broad daylight. Blue-water wading refreshed them.

Jed never let Delaina go, kissing her constantly. She wanted to make love to him in the pool. She would not be refused, and he didn't try to refuse her. A mild sense of danger loitered. A mild form of exhibitionism joined in.

Jed really didn't care if someone, somehow, caught a glance. Social media had blasted similar images for weeks.

He situated her on a built-in tiled seat in the deep end. An in-your-face salute to deranged Cabot Hartley drove them higher. They did a grand and open and sultry deed on the backside of Cash Way, with tall cotton stalks in the wide field beyond as protection. Splashing, coolness, and smiles composed their love scene. Jed starved for her. She gave every piece of herself to his hunger.

~ ~ ~

She got her 15,000X wish about her bed, too.

First, they grilled fresh corn on the back porch and ate then checked in with the agent at nightfall. He said he planned to drive to the end of the driveway and spend his shift in his car. They assumed he knew what they were doing. They did not care.

They shared a beautiful night. Peaceful, perhaps not exactly the correct term for what they did. They basically replicated what happened in bed at Layla Rock. Delaina really, really liked going to the rodeo, and she loved that number between 1 and 100, too. With Jed's head worshipping her below her waist, she, in a flash of carnal instinct, turned on her tummy. In a flash of carnal instinct, Jed covered her back, gripped her breasts underneath, and...

"Hold on," he muttered. He chuckled. "I almost forgot." "Go ahead," she urged.

"No. We're caught up in the moment. That's for your hubby."

She flipped in his arms onto her back, laughing. "Okay, Jeddy. Like this, then."

He made love passionately to his perfect Delaina. Her cross earrings sparkled in the night.

~ ~ ~

Jed rose and dressed at daylight. Delaina stirred in bed. "What're you doing?"

"Leavin'. You're safe. Guarded. Sleep, angel. There's work to be done."

"Jed, you're *leaving*-leaving!"

He halted in her doorway. "You're safe. Guarded."

"Why?" Tears streamed her face. "I just want you to be my boyfriend. We love each other. Please try."

He didn't turn around. "I'll talk to the guard about safety measures. Cash-McCrae Road will stay barricaded and you're guarded 24-7 until you're gone to Texas or Cabot's in cuffs, whichever comes first, if I have to pay for security my-damn-self and catch the lowlife bastard on my own."

Without thought of her nakedness, she rushed to him and reached her arms around his back. "Don't make me beg. I feel like I've been beggin' since I got back from Austin. *You know*, that's not me to beg. Let us be what we are."

He sighed. He turned. "Delaina, you need to get away from here. You know it. You loved Austin."

She clung. "I can't move into my house before July, and I have a lot to do before then."

"Then get it done. I..." He turned his back again. Two more weeks like the past three days, and he would drop to one knee with a ring and a lifetime proposal.

Delaina would live to regret it. He *knew* it. He knew her better than she knew herself.

The debacle with Cabot made it clear. He wanted Delaina to go. Forget telling her anything about The Plan. Forget letting her decide.

Fate, God, the universe, and Cabot Hartley decided. Everything set up, for her to *go*.

Get out of here. Get a master's degree. *Live.*

"I'm breaking up with you, if that's how you want to look at it."

Maybe the world stopped turning.

He couldn't look. She couldn't move.

"I'll come back as soon as I graduate, okay? Next May. I don't have to do a master's in Texas. You don't wanna be apart from me forever, right?" She touched his shoulder. "Okay, you wanna buy land, put your own stamp on it. You don't want your new place to have anything to do with the whole Cash-McCrae saga? That's fine. I *understand*. Do your thing while I'm studying. *Jed...*" She stopped. "Oh God, I'm naked and pleading. I," she sniffled out, "hate you for that." She swiped the sheet from her bed. Tucked it around herself. "Jed, look at me. You owe me an explanation if you're going."

She could not have tormented him more with whips and chains.

He thought, tried to think.

Moments ticked, ticked, ticked.

She stood in her white sheet, random tears toppling.

He blinked tears. Her separation from this nightmare didn't mean that he didn't love her more than life itself or that they wouldn't be together. Maybe even, soon.

He said, "I've taken on a new project away from here. I'm looking forward to it. Vanish on July fifth like you planned, Delaina, if not before. You know you can always call me." His voice cracked. "I have meetings in DC this week. Ag legislation. It rained right on time. While I'm gone, do everything the officers tell you to. Please, baby."

Then he was gone.

Twenty-six

Independence Day

On pins and needles. Two weeks of guards, farms, and nothingness, Delaina and Jed spent.

Farming took all Jed's time and whatever time that Delaina's Austin arrangements did not. Agents requested she get a new phone number and not to interact on social media until further notice. A moving company transported her possessions from Cash Way. She went through every drawer, cabinet, and closet and left most of the belongings as they were inside her childhood home.

~ ~ ~

There was a place in the world where almost every acre of Cash and McCrae soil was visible. On a hilltop in the middle of a vacant pasture behind the McCrae home, Delaina went to watch the sunset on July first. An officer waited in a car nearby.

The wind lifted her hair off her shoulders and her shirt away from her body. In the center of the landscape, an ashen black area blotted out where the McCrae home once stood, the only unsightly object in view. As far as the eye could see, trees trembled, cows ambled, and cotton reigned.

Jed had known she'd be there. Authorities wanted to meet with them at 9 p.m., they informed him, to discuss strategy going forward.

He showed up and sat beside her, for what seemed like eternity, on their soil. Both took in as much as the human body can with its five senses. The sun hung low and pink in the westward sky when Delaina spoke. "I could sit here all night, and it wouldn't rid me of this sense of loss."

300

INDEPENDENCE DAY

"You can always come back, but there's life beyond Mallard, Mississippi. When you're away, things will be different." No clue of affection from him. "Delaina, authorities want to meet with us at nine p.m. It's..." He checked his father's watch. "Eight-forty. He'll bring you." Jed motioned to the patrol car and left her sitting.

The sun exhaled golden gray breath, bid farewell to their heritage for an evening, and took with it the only view they coveted and the only future she knew.

~ ~ ~

The lack of agents startled Delaina. The location did, too. The officer drove her to Jed's cabin. His truck, the only vehicle, parked around back.

Her heart swelled. Jed set this up!

An outstanding trick, a night alone. When she stepped through the door, he would whisk her up the stairs into his treasured hideaway meant for someone special. Meant for her. She had never spent a night in his bed. He would tell her that he couldn't live without her! They could sort out the rest later.

She stepped from the car with a smile and walked the path to his front door. Memories nearly knocked her down. Stampeding his porch to demand a wrench in March seemed like yesterday, or a lifetime ago. The way he stomped around and sniffed. She laughed in the present.

The patrol car pulled away as she reached the railings. She lingered there, in case Jed meant to come outside and get her. She lacked the patience to wait very long. She opened the door. "Hey, Jed? Surprise?" She stepped in, ready to be carried into paradise and begin their lives together, Cabot be damned.

Jed sat in a chair. Investigator Cardin Morris sat on the sofa. Delaina stopped. She looked around. No one else. Her hands found her back pockets. "Uhm, what's this?"

Cardin patted the sofa. "Sit." The air seemed tight. "Please."

"Jed?" she asked worriedly. Jed motioned for Cardin to start.

"Do you know what a sting operation is, Delaina?"

"Uhm. Yeah, kind of... Like where you set up somebody who committed a crime or something like that?"

"Close enough," Cardin said. "We have a plan, a handful of us special agents. To catch Cabot. No one else is here tonight because this is classified. Okay?"

301

LAINEY AND JED, BOOK TWO

"Okay." Delaina felt like her blood might beat through her skin.

"Hashtag Name the Fish Lainey and Jed..."

"Canceled," Delaina inserted. "Because of security concerns."

Cardin corrected, "No, the event is going to happen and so will the traditional patriotic park activities, if you agree to what we want to do."

She tried to catch Jed's eyes. Nothing. She nodded hastily. "Go on."

"We'll make it look like life goes on, promote that Mallard is safe, that people need a positive day of community spirit. You, Jed, and a security team will be aware of the actual details. It's a sting operation, Delaina. A setup meant to lure Cabot." He shrugged. "We're basing this sting on loads of experience about this type of thing. Typically, an event like this, especially with so much attention focused on you and Jed, is too tempting for a guy in Cabot's situation. We're hoping he'll show up and try something stupid. Then, bam, we'll get him. Mallard can't rock on like this. Neither can we. Funds don't allow. We need a big break."

Jed spoke up. "Plus, it'd be a Godsend to get him behind bars before you're off in another state alone." Finally, they looked at each other.

"So, you're in, Jed?" Her voice shook. She needed him now more than ever. Didn't he see that?

"Oh yeah." His eyes scanned her. "I'm all the way in." Nothing affectionate about his declaration. A man, maddened, pushed to his limit, ready to act.

Goosebumps popped on her skin. "Okay, let's do it."

Cardin Morris shook his head expectantly. "We'll go over the details."

~ ~ ~

Two hours later, Cardin Morris called an officer to come get Delaina.

Shyly, she asked Jed to follow her onto his porch. They stood there, everything about it reminiscent of the first night they stood there. Attracted, uncertain, Cabot hanging over them.

Jed was going to kiss her even as he told himself he shouldn't. He leaned in, his breath on her cheek. Her scent assaulted him. Their lips sealed together until he pulled away, his face disappearing into her hair. "Delaina."

INDEPENDENCE DAY

She trembled all over. She opened her eyes. The bones of Jed's face were as precise as cut glass, his skin as brown as copper, his eyes liquid slate. He smelled like her Jed, finished off in adrenaline and desire. "I am leaving, Jed. I'm going to Texas on July fifth, so..."

"You can stay tonight. I want you to stay."

He held her hand as they walked inside. "Cardin, we're, uh, hyped up from all this sting operation talk. She wants to stay here tonight. Can you get an officer stationed at the end of this dirt path?" Cardin looked from one to the other. "Hashtag Lainey and Jed, we're out of practice." Chagrin and a grin from Jed. "The stress of the investigation and farming. You want us to be convincing, right?"

Cardin nodded, pulling out his phone. "I want you completely convincing. I'll work it out, tonight's security." He went toward the door, paused, glanced. "I like you two. Best of luck the next few days. Have a good night."

~ ~ ~

They sipped wine and danced with the doors open. It wasn't carefree or joyful.

It was kindness. Respect. Dark and gentle. Ballads, barely audible.

Quiet words. "That's good wine." "Thirteenth Wish Red." "Mmm, California." "Mm, hm. More?" "No, I wanna dance with you." "I wanna dance with you."

Swaying. Holding loosely. A ballerina twirl. Holding closer. Head on a shoulder. One full song. Silence. Still holding on. Whispers. "Sticky night." "Pretty stars, though." "You're pretty. Want another glass?" New song. "No, let's keep dancin'..." Holding on. "Let's do."

Green eye to blue eye. "I don't know if I ever told you...how much I appreciate you."

Holding tighter. "You told me."

"Good." Head back on a shoulder. "Couldn't remember saying it... in so many words."

"Your smile. Every time you smiled..." Throat-clearing. "I knew."

A tear. A kiss.

Kissing.

"Upstairs?" "Please."

The rest, too sacred to be tarnished by portrayal.

Kindness. Respect. Dark and gentle.

~ ~ ~

They sat on his porch steps and watched the sunrise.

LAINEY AND JED, BOOK TWO

Then parted hands and pathways, so she could pack and he could farm.

~ ~ ~

July Fourth.

#NamethefishLainey&Jed

Publicity planned to perfection. People of Mallard flocked to the park, eager to have fun and forget trouble for an afternoon. American flags dotted the streets and lawn. Children played and The King sang.

Delaina and Jed rode together in his truck into downtown. They had not seen each other since their night in his cabin. Delaina, strung so tight, she couldn't say anything. Jed patted her leg twice.

She wore a color-block sundress, red, white, and blue, with straps and wavy hair touching her shoulders. She'd never been prettier. Jed held her hand as they approached the park. People they knew, and didn't know, cheered.

"Do I look nervous?" Both wore fleshy microphones tucked in their underwear.

"They'll chalk it up to excitement." He grinned at her and kissed her cheek. People clapped. Someone whistled. Happy folks crowded them. Anxiously, Delaina squeezed his hand. "No worries, baby girl," he muttered. "Trained professionals everywhere. Trust me, we've got this."

Delaina plucked the words "Lainey and Jed" over and over from randomness around them.

~ ~ ~

They named the fish. God, it was fun! Delaina and Jed had never been more convincing, because in the most fake scenario, they were real.

They danced in the gazebo. Others couples danced in the gazebo. They drank lemonade.

They bewitched their hometown with their splendid togetherness.

Midafternoon, Delaina slipped from Jed's grasp. She needed to pee.

Planted professionals lurked. Jed recognized them because he didn't recognize them. So, he watched her walk away, across the grass, through the trees, out of the park, into the alley.

Smile on her face, Delaina skipped into the restroom, humming "Glory, Glory Hallelujah." She peed, flushed, washed her hands. She

INDEPENDENCE DAY

skipped out, through late-day sun and shadows, on a broken concrete path.

"Lainey?"

She knew before she saw him.

Then she did see him. A scraggly, shabby, harrowing version of the man she almost married.

Delaina dropped her chin toward the microphone and tried to say, "Cabot," voice so weak she didn't know if anything came out. She ran for her life.

Downtown Mallard blurred. Flags, lemonade, and Elvis. She stumbled out of the alley, into the park, through the trees, across the grass.

Jed talking, laughing, mingling. She ran into his arms. "It's Cabot," she huffed under her breath. "*Please let's go.*" He took her arm and began to walk calmly across the park. "He's coming, I know it," she muttered. She heard awful commotion behind her. "Run, Jed!" They made it into the truck among muffled voices and movements of anticipation everywhere. He cranked and backed out with locals crowding his truck. "Go, go, go!" Delaina yelled.

Shots rang out. A storefront window shattered feet from his truck.

Jed gunned the accelerator, squalled tires, yelled expletives. In his rearview mirror, in her side mirror, they watched panic unfold. Horrified people scattered, huddled, or fell to the ground.

Tears poured out of Delaina's eyes. Her hometown, desecrated. None of that planned.

Speeding at 100-plus, Jed made it to Cash-McCrae Road before Cardin Morris called. On Bluetooth, they heard, "Get Delaina out of here! Stick to the plan. Cabot was armed. Agents shot at him. People got hurt in the stampede. I'll update you two ASAP."

Cash-McCrae Road whizzed by with, "What plan, Jed?! What plan?"

He said nothing until the gates of Cash Way came into view. Agents in black surrounded her vehicle. "Get in your car, baby." She didn't know Jed's voice. Huffing with terror. "I'm gonna follow you all the way to Houston. Drive to Calla, D. You can do it. Don't stop. Don't call anybody. Just go. Every law enforcement agency between here and there knows we're coming."

Now she knew why they told her to have everything packed and ready to go in her car today, instead of tomorrow, just in case...

305

LAINEY AND JED, BOOK TWO

Delaina got out of Jed's truck without a word, with one sad-mad glance at him and home, and followed orders.

~ ~ ~

They drove to Houston without stopping, except for fuel, no words spoken.

They pulled up to Calla's elaborate entrance after ten p.m. Jed stepped out of his truck, left it running. Two armed guards stood by the door, not Calla employees. Jed motioned for a bellboy. The guy took over Delaina's car, mumbling about delivering her bags up to the condo.

She demanded, "What's going on?" standing on the curb. She wore her patriotic wrinkled sundress, one strap fallen carelessly. Her anxious green eyes begged Jed to explain. He glimpsed the glass doors, checked the street. Nothing out of place. He checked his phone. Nothing from Cardin Morris. "What's going on, I said!" Delaina screamed and grabbed his arm.

Then she almost collapsed, seeing a dimpled, dirty-blond-haired, firmly muscled, cowboy-hatted demigod step from Calla's palatial doors. "Hey, sweetheart." Pate had a dim smile.

Jed looked at him. "It's a good thing you're my best friend." Then to her, "And that I trust you both." He wore no expression. "Delaina, Pate's gonna spend the night with you in Calla. He'll follow you the rest of the way. You're under full security at your place in Austin until further notice."

Delaina gasped, staring only at him. Downtown Houston at night, traffic and tragedy, people and celebrations, framed by corporate buildings and luxury hideaways, surrounded them. Their eyes locked, in love and hate and regret and spite and awe. The same feelings that held them back urged them to give in. There was no world beyond Jed McCrae. Only him, his image drawn against a pale background.

Tears watered his eyes.

"Jed..."

"If anything happens to her, I'll never forgive you, Pate."

His eyes caught hers for a moment. "Delaina."

Jed walked toward his idling truck. Delaina swiveled in his direction on the sidewalk. Pate touched her shoulder. "Don't. Everything's gonna be okay."

Jed became one with the view, a graying shadow in a blackened city. At the door of his truck, he faced her and nodded, his features violet-silver.

306

Delaina lifted a heavy arm, curled her hand, and waved a slow goodbye.

Jed disappeared into the truck's interior.

Delaina waved until Houston swallowed him whole.

ABOUT THE AUTHOR:

Clare Cinnamon is from a small town in Georgia. She holds dual degrees in business and psychology and likes to read or write about almost anything. Married to her high school sweetheart, they have two wonderful grown kids. She considers among her life's best: their large, award-winning family farm. When she's not nestled in a book, she enjoys yoga, world travel, and outdoors.